Praise for *Perfect Circle*:

"If ever there was a voice destined for greatness, it is the literary styling of Alvin Horn. Combining emotional storytelling, powerful prose, and rhythmic poetry, A *Perfect Circle* captures your soul and never lets it go. A well-written masterpiece!!!"

—WILLIAM FREDRICK COOPER,
Award-winning *Essence* Bestselling Author of
There's Always a Reason

"Alvin L.A. Horn is a rare literary gem whose talent surpasses what is commonplace in many literary offerings. His ability to create art; paint a vivid narrative with his skill in incredible story-telling ranks him amongst my favorite authors. Heart-wrenching, poignant, engrossing and hard to put down, *Perfect Circle* will take you on a literary ride of pleasure."

—ELISSA GABRIELLE,
Award-winning Author of *A Whisper to a Scream*

Dear Reader:

It is always a pleasure to introduce new authors in the Strebor Books family. With few of our authors based on the West Coast, I am pleased that Seattle-based Alvin L.A. Horn has joined our team.

Perfect Circle is set against the Northwest backdrop and Alvin vividly paints an image of the metropolitan area known for coffee and rainy days. The journey centers around Ayman Sparks, the basketball coach at East Seattle City University. Ayman, along with his assistant coach, Sterlin, are in constant search of the ideal mate. Add the churchgoing single mom, Vanita, who suffers from depression; and Lois Mae, who has a history of marital mishaps, and you have an interesting mix of characters, all in search of true love.

Travel along with each character as they experience life-changing moments in the novel's clever twists and turns.

Alvin, a spoken word artist who travels to recite poetry and play stand-up bass, shares his knack for verse that flows throughout the novel.

As always, thanks for supporting the efforts of Strebor Books. We strive to bring you fresh, talented and ground-breaking authors that will help you escape reality when the daily stressors of life seem overwhelming. We appreciate the love and dedication of our readers. For more information on our titles, please visit Zanestore.com. My personal web site is Eroticanoir.com and my online social network is PlanetZane.org.

Blessings,

Zane

Zane
Publisher
Strebor Books International
www.simonandschuster.com/streborbooks

ZANE PRESENTS

Perfect
CIRCLE

A NOVEL

Perfect CIRCLE

A NOVEL

ALVIN L.A. HORN

SBI

STREBOR BOOKS

NEW YORK LONDON TORONTO SYDNEY

SB|

Strebor Books
P.O. Box 6505
Largo, MD 20792
http://www.streborbooks.com

ISBN 978-1-59309-445-4
ISBN 978-1-4516-8375-2 (e-book)
LCCN 2012933940

First Strebor Books trade paperback edition October 2012

Cover design: www.mariondesigns.com
Cover photograph: © Keith Saunders/Marion Designs

10 9 8 7 6 5 4 3 2 1

Manufactured in the United States of America

For information regarding special discounts for bulk purchases,
please contact Simon & Schuster Special Sales at 1-866-506-1949
or business@simonandschuster.com

The Simon & Schuster Speakers Bureau can bring authors to your live event.
For more information or to book an event, contact the Simon & Schuster Speakers
Bureau at 1-866-248-3049 or visit our website at www.simonspeakers.com.

ACKNOWLEDGMENTS

God, thank you, for giving me the opportunity to write and to be read by many. You have blessed me since my first breath to have done many things in life. Many don't believe you laugh, but I assume you do as the foolishness of men makes no sense. I hope I made you laugh at the some of the unwise things I have done acting as if I was in control. Through your grace my abilities have been given a chance to shine.

I give thanks to Bigmama and to all the elders of women who have all taught me the value of the love of a woman all in their own way. From a switch off a tree to lending an ear to hear my joys and pains, I'm blessed to have had all of you touch me in all your own way. I write about women like you—the textured fabric of life I have been wrapped in.

To the men who helped shape me in the mode of whom I am without ever knowing the impact you have had on me. Whether you were my bloodline or a mentor, I have watched you for what is right or wrong—allowing me to choose which is best for me as a man. I love the old soul I am, in how I dress, talk, and enjoy the music I do because of my elders creating the Renaissance man I am, so I pen you in layers of storylines.

To the women who have loved me when it was easy and when it wasn't, you have taught me I'm a good man but not a perfect man. You have made me feel like a king, but made me aware I must walk humbly in order to be loved. All my writings are to glorify you for being God's love to me. I write to bring awareness to the struggles this world burdens you with and the burdens you bring to the world. Every woman handles the weight of mankind differently and that creates narratives, and I'm going to write them.

Thank you, Charmaine Parker, the lady who clones herself, and adds hours to a twenty-four-hour day. I expect to walk into your office and see a forty-foot-long desk and eight of you all wearing different hats. I'm also very thankful for the people around you who support you.

Zane, *thank you* is an effortless expression that people say all too often out of simple courtesy, but then there are those times when someone looks you in the eye and you truly know they mean it…I'm looking you in the eye.

William Fredrick Cooper, one day you told me, "Alvin—dude, I loved the fact that you don't write to any stereotypical formula. You simply write honest emotions that most writers are scared to let people know they have those feelings and thoughts. You are that writer that others want to be, and so few will be." After talking to you, I sat on the back deck of my houseboat. It was a sunny day and the glare off the water made my eyes water, or was it what you said? I'll never admit you made me cry, and if you tell anybody, expect a double left jab, left hook. Now get back to writing; people love reading you, too.

The friends and family very dear to me, the song says, "We go a long ways back." Even if it's not true dealing with me, I'm sure it can feel like it. Thank you, Toni J, Omar T, Susan M, Ron B,

Vicki P, Monique F, Ms. Jackson, David E, Diedra A, Dwight M, Sandra B, Dana T, Paul B, Kari F, Robert A, Sarah W, Tam B, Keysha B, Benita T, Lady Flava, Taffee T, Wyneice H, Jackie P, Kevin H, Yvette L, and my son, Ivan, and daughter, Danielle. Each one of you somewhere along the way have loved me in your own special way, helping me to stay on course or to get back to where I needed to be and I thank you.

I lost Ivory, Melba, Jay, Sonny, and Henry along the way of writing *Perfect Circle*, and it hurts like hell they are not here to see this book come to print, but I'm sure to write those feelings I felt and feel for them in each and every novel to come.

Mr. Editor, Dennis Billuni, you are a real pro. Besides editing, you teach along the way.

My Seattle family of friends *"Perfect Circle"* is you and me in the 206 and 425, and 253. We are living and loving in the Northwest style of life. I'm writing for the rest of the world to know just how we do it. We are multiethnic often in our bloodlines, and diverse in our friendships. We are rain, and the bluest skies, the fresh ocean air, and snow-topped mountains that can and do blow up, and we are rivers and streams in the middle of our neighborhoods, and fresh fish and crab, and shrimp. We are coffee stands on almost every corner and some have half-naked baristas; who else does silly mess like that? We are the posse on Broadway Beacon Hill, Rainier Valley, and in the CD Renton, Skyway. We are the posse living in Mountlake, Capitol Hill, Mount Baker, Leschi, Madrona, West Seattle, and South Park. We are the posse strolling around Seward Park, Alki, Coulon Beach, Lake Washington, Green Lake, and the University District Ave, Lake City, and the Fremont District, and Queen Anne Hill. We are the posse rolling across floating bridges to the Eastside. We are the posse living in or near Rainier Beach, Duwamish-

Tukwila, Burien, Kent, and Federal Way. We are the posse rolling down to T-town-the 253.

We are Jimi Hendrix, Bruce Lee, and Quincy Jones, Bill Russell, and Lenny Wilkens.

We are Vikings, Quakers, and Bulldogs, and Eagles, and Seahawks and Huskies.

We are the Seattle Super Sonic forever!

We are Ezell's Chicken, Silver Fork, Kingfish Café, Catfish Corner, Anthony's Home Port, Ivars, Dicks and Southern Kitchen in T-town.

We are Mount Zion Baptist, Ebenezer AME Zion, First African Methodist Episcopal, Holgate and Southside Church of Christ, and New Beginnings Christian Fellowship.

We are novelists Charles Johnson and Octavia Estelle Butler, Colleen McElroy, Edwina Martin-Arnold, Debrena Jackson Gandy and playwright August Wilson, and me, author-poet Alvin L.A. Horn.

Playing the Blues

"Coach Sparks," one of the trainers called out, "you have a phone call in your office."

Ayman Sparks walked through the locker room, his top lip curled up in front of his nose. The funk and noise in the locker room was thick and loud. Locker doors slammed and reverberated. The young men were all talking loud, and cracking jokes. Someone called out, "Your mama smells like doo-doo."

"Knock it off! I've told you guys that I won't have that kind of shit on this team!" Ayman stood still, piercing his glare at any eyes that dared to look his way. "Look at what you guys just made me say."

The young men laughed. They understood that the coach's sternness came with humor.

"Coach, the phone is for you," said a large, dumpy white male with a whiny voice.

"Okay, Meredith, do some extra footwork drills. Silly fouls are cutting into your playing time. I'll be checking your weight. Do you hear me?"

"I understand, Coach. I'll work harder."

Coach Sparks did not understand why anybody would recruit Meredith; he didn't. The former coach had made a commitment that Ayman had to keep.

Ayman headed to his office and kept thinking. *Two hundred and eighty pounds of no defense and can't guard his own shadow. No wonder Bucket was a loser.* Ayman chuckled to himself.

Coach Sparks made his way through the weight room while giving instructions to some and praise to others. His attention bounced between evaluating practice and replaying the nasty attitude his wife had displayed earlier that morning. *What's her trip? Last night she was a freak in bed, then this morning she's the queen of the ice-asses.* He reached his office and punched the flashing line on the phone.

"Coach Sparks here."

"Ayman." He heard Vanessa's voice come through with sub-zero coldness. He knew right then he would stay at the gym and watch more game film.

"What?" His voice let her know he was annoyed.

"I'm going to the bank, and I'm going to take all the money out of the second account!"

"What?" Ayman's voice slowly slid through his teeth. He repeated, "What?"

"I'm moving back to Oakland. The second account is mostly mine anyway!"

"Why, and how many times have you threatened to leave? As much as I love you, I really hate…" Ayman took a big breath.

Ayman Sparks and his wife, Vanessa, had been acting out a deteriorating marriage for years. Threatening each other was almost foreplay. Sometimes, it was foreplay.

Ayman felt the anger heating his bald head. He turned the air conditioner on in his office. "I'm really tired of this," he said.

"You're tired?" Vanessa screamed through the phone. "You don't have time for me, and you know it! We've had this black cloud hanging over our heads, and you don't even know it."

"Black cloud? What the f—"

Vanessa quickly cut him off. "Don't dare curse at me! I'm not one of them referees."

"Then tell me what you're talking about. Stop talking in code. If you have something to say, say it! Maybe we can work out whatever your problem is."

"My problem, huh?" Vanessa made a sound that let him know she was disgusted.

Ayman spoke as if his nose was inches from hers. "Whatever it takes for you to stop all your trippin' over yourself; you need to reevaluate what you're doing."

Sarcastic laughter filtered back through the phone. "You feel better now? That was like a halftime speech when you're losing, right?"

Ayman grimaced. He was always out for the win. He didn't know how to respond now. Vanessa had him off balance. "It sounds like the problem is money. Now, we both know I make plenty, but I have to work for it. If it's about time, my coaching career is about being successful. That means I have to put in the long hours. That's what a coach does. You'd rather I work in a straitjacket job. You know what? Most likely, I would come home and still hear you bitch.

"I never hear you bitching about the nice house you live in. I don't hear you complaining about the gardener or the woman who cleans your house twice a week. Oh, you fly home to Oakland and everywhere else you want. You're right, maybe it's time for you to step. If you're talking about my job and the money it puts into the bank for you to take out, I—"

"You egotistical son-of-a-bitch! Why do you think it's all about you and your money? I carried your ass when you went back to school to be a teacher. I've moved around the world for your dreams." She cursed. Ayman's eyes blinked. The F-word was something she'd only said during sex. "You never spend any time with me." Her voice lost strength.

Ayman was sitting on the edge of his desk, twisting and turning in one spot.

"We don't spend time alone unless it's alone in the bed, and I need more—more than sex."

Ayman's jaw clamped tight, as if something with long fangs had bit into his flesh. The pain of what she'd said dripped like venom, killing his ego. Silence over the phone let the emotional poison churn his stomach; he reached in his desk for some Tums.

"I'm sorry if it hurt, Ayman. Look, I need it as bad as you do, but having sex every night as our only connection has become hard on my soul. You got things going on that I didn't sign up for, and now that I know you about—"

"About what? You think there's another woman? Whatever. I'm not jumping off the Aurora Bridge for your insecurities." His tone had no humor in it, but he snickered.

"Laugh, go ahead. You might be one of these fools here in Seattle who would jump if—" A minute-long silence ensued. "Ayman," her voice cracked. He heard weeping. "Maybe you've forgotten all that I've done and been through with you."

Ayman's defense was loud. "No! You can't let me forget it, not even for a week. You know, I don't need this shit today! I'm on my job!" he shouted. "The same job that keeps your ass in Nordstrom and Macy's."

Ayman turned the air up higher. "Enough is enough! File for divorce. I'll sign anything to stop the madness. I'm getting ready for the season, and I don't need your bullsh—"

Ayman's assistant coach and best friend, Sterlin, walked into the office. "Ayman!" Sterlin called out in a hushed voice, trying to stop Ayman from raising his voice any louder. "Man, chill!" Sterlin put his hand up to signal for him to calm down.

A long wavering note of a saxophone solo flowed into Ayman's ears just as Sterlin reached across a table and tapped him. It was two years later. A lounge full of people came into view. They were not in a locker room and not in his office. Ayman had been daydreaming/nightmaring about the last episode of the breakup of his marriage.

The two coaches were in a jazz club in Lexington, Kentucky. They were drinking a little and listening to live entertainment. A sax player's solo had charmed him into his past.

It was Wednesday night. The players from East Seattle City University were back at the hotel, on lockdown, resting for tomorrow's game. The two coaches were taking a break trying to relax. Ayman needed to unwind before the game tomorrow against the University of Kentucky.

A vocalist started singing Stevie Wonder's "Superwoman."

Through the bitter winds love could not be found
Where were you when I needed you, last winter, my love?

The groove of the music was climbing up Ayman's past and present mental walls. The club was alive with people swaying, and fingers popping. Tall, red brick walls lined with staircases led to different levels for seating. There was no room for dancing other than standing at your table. A few ladies were standing and grooving in place. The two coaches were on the main floor. Two tables away stood a caramel-colored, shapely sister. Her red-apple lips and close-set eyes had helped to put Ayman into his hypnotic state. Her long, raven-black hair to the flowing tightness of her black silk dress and her feet, clad in thin leather-strapped heels, locked him into tunnel vision. Ayman was lost in her display of sexiness.

The red stage lights silhouetted her groove. She was joyriding his attention; she knew he was watching. She reminded him of a body he used to know, and her image helped burn a hole into his past. He rode a bumpy ride into a sad rhythmic pulse. Angry noises from days gone by had drowned out the jazz blowing in his ears.

There were other noises going on in his life. As the head coach at East Seattle City University, he was facing losing a third consecutive game. The team was having pre-season difficulties. They had played two games against Top Ten teams and lost both. Their wins had not been impressive. Uneasiness grew like mold when people started asking questions of why, and how come, and when.

ESPN-TV had done a segment on East Seattle City University and its slow start. ESPN wondered if Coach Sparks' last three Sweet Sixteen finishes in the NCAA tournament would be overstating. "Coach Sparks, a preacher of defense, might have lost the attention of his congregation. The players might not be buying into his intense coaching style anymore." In response, Coach Sparks told a local newspaper that he thought the article hinted of racism.

"How many white coaches are compared to preachers? In America, we seem to associate the Black men in different forms of leadership as some type of preacher. As a coach, unless I am a preacher, there should be no comparison. I am a man who believes in God, but there is no connection to me being a preacher.

Coach Sparks was quoted in the local newspaper: "Dean Smith, who coaches North Carolina, is a deeply religious man. Was he ever compared to or called a preacher? Why am I? We know the

Bobby Knight types and other white coaches, are intense coaches, and no one calls them preachers. Could it be white men are just called leaders? Can Black men of leadership only be related to being some type of minister? This is the subtle type of racism that Black Americans are tired of."

Ayman felt strong about what he'd stated, and he would not back down. He told friends, colleagues, and other news media, "If I don't speak up, I'm part of the problem."

Shortly after arriving at the team hotel, he got a call from Coach Nolan Richardson, the former basketball coach at the University of Arkansas.

"Coach, you're a winner in my book for telling it like it is. The work you're doing is thankless," Richardson commented.

"Thanks, Coach Richardson."

"Call me Nolan. You know critics are snakes. They will build you up and tear you down. You must stand your ground as the man; let their crap roll off your back. Stay Black. You said what I wish others would say." Coach Richardson continued, "Coach, at one time the white media hated Muhammad Ali and everything he stood for. Now they honor him for fighting against them. Life is a circle. Stay the course, my brother."

"You're right. Float like a butterfly, sting like a bee!" Both men laughed.

"I had a lot of success at Arkansas, but I knew sooner or later they'd come after me." Coach Richardson laughed. "Now you're playing the U. of Kentucky, and they aren't going to let you come in there and get a win on their home floor. Remember you're coach, first and last. Stay focused on your team and the game."

Ayman reflected on the conversation while the crowd's conversation mingled with cocktail glasses clinging. Sterlin was perplexed that Ayman was so despondent.

"What is going on with you? Wake your dead ass up."

"The boys practiced as if they know they're going to lose."

"Oh yeah, right, as if that's what's going on with you. Look, we have the toughest schedule in the nation, but the schedule will pay off at conference time. You said so yourself before the pre-season started. You got another bug up your butt. What is it?"

Sterlin, tall and wide at the shoulders with a big baby face, was not looking at Ayman as he spoke. He was flirting with every woman in the club that he could engage with glances and grins. His physical stature and good looks received plenty of submissive expressions. Changing colored lights reflected the whiteness from Sterlin's smile.

Ayman leaned forward so he could be heard. "I'm all right, man. It's just that sister standing over there reminds me of Vanessa. I was just thinking—"

Sterlin cut Ayman off, "Don't even go there again! You've been divorced for two years. You should be over it, man."

Ayman jerked his head back.

"You need to move on. What's it going to take? Everywhere we go, you got honeys checking your ass out, but you act blind. You may be known for 'preaching defense,' but damn!" Sterlin smiled at his mocking statement, and Ayman chuckled a bit as his friend continued to talk. "Nigga, you need to go on the offense in the women's department."

Ayman's stare became hard; he was upset. He leaned forward so the flickering candles highlighted the tightness of the lines on his forehead. "First of all, Negro, you need to quit saying 'nigga' before you let it slip at the wrong time. These kids all ready think it's okay. I had to correct a white kid from saying 'wigger' and 'poor white trash,' even though their mommas and daddies got MO-money, MO-money."

"You're right. It's an old habit."

"Well, it's an old habit that sometimes I think of Vanessa."

"Cool, but don't bite my head off. I'm not the one you were married to. How about you freezing all that past misery. You need to be over there talking to that fine female; she's dancing to get your attention. That's what you need—a woman. If I was you, I'd be all over her."

Ayman laughed. "Excuse me, but unless my eyes are going bad, that is a Black woman over there, and you don't do sisters…right?" Ayman knew Sterlin's lifestyle when it came to the type of women he pursued.

"Man, hold up! It's not that I don't do sisters. I like all women, and I mean all women, of every color and nationality." Sterlin's voice was full of ego.He looked around the club, his eyes stopped, and he nodded at a not-so-thin, blonde woman. Ayman rolled his eyes in non-amazement.

A comedian had taken the stage and cracked a joke that had everyone laughing, but Ayman and Sterlin didn't pay attention.

Ayman leaned forward and said, "Just like I said, you don't do sisters. All the women I see you with seem to have blonde, brunette, or red hair. I find that a little strange, but whatever right now, watch your ass, man. We are down South."

"Please! I ain't worried about nobody's South. Don't they call it the New South?" Sterlin smiled.

"Okay, Mr. New South, I'm sure the club is a safe zone, but I bet you still can't walk the back streets with a big booty Blonde Peach."

"Yeah, well, toast to the booty, my man! At least, I pick the ones with a sista booty. You ever watch a blondie with a big booty dance? That's some sweet funky stuff. Ahhhh, I like that shit."

"You freak! Is it all about the tail end?"

"I like me some thighs and booty."

"Okay, Dr. Booty Freak, you're a trip!"

Sterlin's next comment stopped Ayman dead in his tracks from laughing. "It's all about the booty, so I don't end up like you— sad, blue, and alone!" Sterlin tilted his head to the side and lifted his eyebrows up.

Ayman turned away and did not speak until the comedian left the stage. His eyes passed by the caramel sister, and then he turned back toward Sterlin and watched him accept a small piece of paper from a fair-skinned hand. The wide-bottomed woman walked away. Her behind was not really all that round, but it was big. Sterlin turned around with a smile and licked his lips.

Ayman shook his head. His next few words came slowly and deliberately. "Your dick is going to fall off. When is the last time you had a woman you could be proud of? When have you had one? When have you had one that can spell 'cat,' instead of just showing you her kitty? Ever heard of a relationship, something real?"

"Are you Homeland Security? I feel as if I'm being interrogated. Damn!" Sterlin cocked his head to the side, and squinted his eyes. His tone was irritated. "Yeah, I do have more needs other than booty, but I ain't trying to be like you. You and countless others lay their hearts out, their money out, and their time. For what? Crying in my pillow? Oh hell no! I did that shit, and you know it. I begged someone to love me who did not…want me. I love listening to the blues, but not having them over some woman."

Ayman fired a shot at Sterlin's attitude. "Man, how many full moons will you need to get over one bad woman from twenty years ago back in college? You can't hold every sista accountable for her sins. You have the nerve to talk about me tripping over my divorce of a few years ago. Come on." Ayman sneered.

"Look, I'm not tripping. I'm just living to keep the bullshit to a minimum. I say to love, 'No thanks, I'll pass.' The woman for me, she don't walk on this planet. Now do us both a favor and go talk to that woman over there." Sterlin took a deep breath.

"Okay, my bad. You do your thing, but you know I'm gonna tell you about yourself sometimes."

"Oh, I know you've made a point of always telling me. But I seem to remember a time back in the day your ass was dropping panties like raindrops in Seattle." Both men laughed and held out their fists, slamming them together.

"Man, you read that in a book, and yeah, I had my day. Some of the things I did back then, I still wake up scared." The house band had resumed playing, so the guys had to lean forward again.

"Ayman, you need to let the pleasures of life be part of your work. Every arena and city we play in, women know you're single now. They've read your profile and are waving action your way. I see 'em, and you know I see 'em."

"First of all, I like my coffee black, and Barbie Doll ain't marrying me. I'm too Black in attitude; I don't have enough rainbow Docker-wearing BS flowing through my veins. That liberal-acceptance-on-the-surface shit goes far in the great Northwest as long as you're a Rainbow Black person. Us living in Seattle, Black people are outnumbered greatly but accepted for the most part in the mainstream. Look at you and half the other brothers in Seattle, who are dating, sleeping with, or married to a white woman.

"You can't go nowhere without seeing an interracial couple or child. Quiet as it's kept, more and more sistas are dating and marrying men outside their race in Seattle. Everybody acts cool about it in the Northwest until a Black man acts too black. What I did, telling off the media; that was too black." Ayman grinned, proud of his statement.

Sterlin threw a verbal brick at his proclamation. "You're full of shit, Mr. Anti-Rainbow! I do seem to remember that fine little Latino sister in Puerto Rico during the Caribbean tournament." Sterlin bopped his head in a mocking motion as if to tell Ayman he had him.

The band finished a song and was inviting other musicians to the stage and doing some announcements.

Sterlin went to the men's room. Ayman ordered more drinks. He also sent a drink to the woman in the black dress. Along with the drink, he sent a note on the back of a team postcard. He wrote:

Dear Lady, you are surely one beautiful woman. I assume that you are just as beautiful on the inside. I'm a visitor to this city, and if I were in my home city, I would ask to get to know you. As you see on the card, I am a coach for a team, and I'm here only for the moment. Please think about calling me or e-mailing me in the future, and maybe we can get acquainted.

Sincerely,

Ayman Sparks

Ayman nodded his head in acknowledgment to the woman's responding smile, just as Sterlin returned. He looked at Ayman as if to say, *"Did I miss something?"* Ayman stared at the candle burning on the table.

Sterlin started back in on the same subject they were discussing before his restroom break. "Ah, that fine little Latino sister in Puerto Rico, the one with the sista booty and the bright light-brown eyes. Man, she had the sexiest, come-do-me walk. Coffee black—my ass!" Sterlin raised his eyebrows, waiting for a response.

"Sterlin Baylor, you are a trip. Puerto Rican is a Black person of Spanish descent; most people think of it as such. And if she had been my woman, what were you doing looking at my woman's behind?"

Ayman chuckled, but had an inner conversation. *Damn, he thinks he knows all my biz! I'm not chasing it like him. I just want one woman. I'll never get like him. He's plucking feathers from every chicken in the coop!* Ayman continued, "Anything I've had going with a woman was honest, and if I did sleep with them, it was only with them, one at a time. The woman you're referring to was my friend. You might try that concept with a woman sometime. I'm going back to the hotel to make sure our boys are all in for the night. You need to be in yourself before it gets too late. Don't show up at the team breakfast in the morning looking like you've been eating all the chicken in town." Ayman chuckled. "Oh, and let's get the record straight; the little Black Latino sister was just showing me around the island. I do enjoy the presence and the company of a woman; it's no crime."

Sterlin laughed with a toothpick rolling in the corner of his mouth and then spoke, "Maybe the Black Latino sister qualifies for the one-eighth drop of blood rule with that fine round bubble, but you rode her bubble butt all over that island."

Ayman's nostrils flared and his face wrinkled with lines in his forehead. His assistant coach and best friend could be crude. "You are straight-up Houston Fifth Ward ghetto. Like I said, she was just a friend; I don't sleep around. You know how I feel about that. If I'm not going to be with her, I'm not going to sleep with her. I don't want to sleep with just any woman if she's not going to be around for more than a booty fling."

"Okay, Mr. Morals, I do seem to remember you not coming in one of those nights while we were in Puerto Rico. No, wait! I remember quite a few nights of you not coming in. Or at least, you weren't there in the morning."

"How would you know? The music was always up loud in your room." Ayman laughed.

"Whatever! If you think that I believe you 'slept on the beach by yourself' crap, please, Negro. If it was true, then I just recruited a new player. His uncle is Shaq, his daddy is Michael Jordan, and Flo-Jo is his mama. He has promised not to go to the NBA until he graduates!" Sterlin laughed so hard he had to cover his mouth.

Ayman shook his head, trying not to laugh. He turned his chair toward the stage but soon turned his attention to the caramel-colored, shapely sister in black. He listened to a poet recite as the band grooved. Ayman's vision went past the woman's dress next to her skin. His mind drifted to a place he wanted to be as he listened.

Without her, I just am
Almost in the dark
Want to be next to her
About to lie down
Thoughts of her make me want to stand up
I stare down into dreams
I see her sensual allure
Almost in the dark
Fearing being alone in the dark
About to turn the light on
She whispers into my dream
I'll show you where everything is, here feel that
Yeah, everything is right
Her beauty shines bright

No longer hearing the poet or the band, he imagined hearing the woman breathing in his ear. He fantasized he was locking his lips on her collarbone, and she was kissing him on the side of his face. Her nails were making deep, but not painful, trails up and down his back. He felt himself going deep in between her legs as he placed both his hands underneath her ass. Her nails dug into the flesh of his ass. The pain she pushed into him made him thrust harder. He pulled his hands from under her and pushed his upper body up. He sensed he was about to jet his thick juices into her and pulled out. She put her hands around his hardened *outer vein* fist-tight and stroked the head. He grunted, and she said, "Come on, baby!" From the middle of her fist, a river of life flowed across her navel.

Breathing hard, he woke from his daydream, and then left to go back to the hotel. There, he drifted back to the dream. He awoke that morning with a hardening lonely thought. He told himself to focus on the task at hand.

After the game, he fell asleep on the plane heading back to Seattle. He dreamed of her again, but soon the dream burned a hole into the present. In his lap lay the newspaper:

USA TODAY SPORTS NOVEMBER 26, 2005
THIRD-RATED UNIVERSITY OF KENTUCKY WINS
87–77 OVER EAST SEATTLE CITY UNIVERSITY

2

All Woman

While driving in Seattle, wipers clearing the windshield of nothing one moment, and not keeping up the next, can frustrate your drive. Lois Mae pulled into the parking lot and immediately turned off her annoying wipers. She pulled the visor mirror down and saw her reflection of ruby red lips. She was a red lip gloss queen; it was almost her calling card.

Lois Mae Ilan had a habit of constantly checking her lipstick in her driving mirror. Chaka Khan's "Sweet Thing" finished playing on the radio. The Love Minister, the deejay, rhymed poetic words between songs:

"From my microphone to your heart, let me share some hot, steamy thoughts with you. Let my fantasies touch you like kisses. My thoughts, let them engulf you with scintillating visions of the kind of time I want to spend with you listening to Earth Wind & Fire singing, 'Can't Hide Love.'"

Lois Mae's bare foot tapped the carpet. No way was she driving and scuffing on her suede Jimmy Choo boots. When she'd worn her boots out to her car, she was upset with herself. It was damp, and definitely not suede boot weather.

On the way to meet her date, a car pulled up next to her at a red light. When she looked over, a much younger Black man, flirted with her. He had more chrome in his mouth than the grill of her car. He motioned for her to roll her window down and mouthed the words, "Can I call you?"

She smiled and shook her head no. Her Chrysler 300 had a custom grill and extra-large chrome wheels. The car made her feel physically smaller when she drove it. The black and burgundy Chrysler, with the dark gray leather interior, always received compliments.

Her body did not quite make her feel so self-assured. Lois Mae was not a small woman. She stood five-eleven, and always wore heels. Her physical presence commanded attention. Slender she was not; there were a few too many pounds on her frame. She called them her "extra, dangerous curves." She was an Amazon-like woman walking down the street with her thirty-eight-D breasts. She was full-figured and proud of her breasts, displaying them in whatever she wore.

If men had any complaints, they never said so. Lois was a tall glass of a woman, and most men could not drink a full glass of her mentally or physically. It had been a while since any man had closed her bedroom door behind him.

Some men and women felt intimidated by her, until she spoke; then you heard a soft-spoken, well-educated, cultured woman.

Circumstances in her life called for a gentle but mentally strong man to deal with the psychological pain of her former marriage to a cheating and physically abusive husband. A second husband came along, and he was a dead man living. He was murdered.

Married for ten years to her first husband, she called him "The Vampire." His name was Vance. He stayed in the streets chasing anything that stood still long enough to suck blood. She would say, "The vampire would hump a telephone pole if he thought it would get him off." Yet she stood fast by her man, believing in marriage to the point that she took more than a few backhands over the years. It marked her with emotional and physical scars. Long after the "Vampire" had bit her soul, and after many counseling sessions, her therapist told her she was ready for a relationship. Lois Mae set out to find a man who was mellow and solid in behavior.

A few years after the vampire ex-husband, she found a gentleman at a bookstore. Every Sunday after church, she would browse for books at the South Center Barnes & Noble. Reginald Ilan was always there reading the paper. With her big legs and Texas-size behind, one day she strutted in her classic Adriana Italian Matlisse' by Azalea. While on vacation in France, she had purchased the rare 1962 vintage dress suit for a mere $2,500. Her high salary allowed the spoilage, but for the rest of the year, she bought inexpensive knock-offs. She had the vintage dress suit tailored, and it was working on this man as he yanked his eyes over the top of the *Seattle Times* newspaper. She made the first move by accident.

She flirted by strolling by him three times in fifteen minutes. Finally, she stopped in front of him and dropped a book near his foot. When she squatted down to pick it up, he leaned forward to help. His knee knocked her coffee out of her hand and onto him.

The perfect introduction led she and Reginald to a year of dating of intellectual minds, and that led them to a perfect honeymoon in Brazil. One year later, sex was rare as a one-hundred degree day in Seattle. There was no sex, no passion for weeks at a time.

She had told him about what had happened while married to Vance. She figured he could not handle all she had dealt with.

Lying next to Reginald with no sex, had her fingers helping to relive her physical loneliness. She could not believe a man would turn down sex. She thought all men wanted sex, all the time.

Just before the second year of her sexless marriage, thunder and lightning and all hell busted through her front door. She received a call while teaching an evening class; someone had broken into their home, stolen possessions, and life. The police found her husband murdered in a home invasion robbery. Lois Mae now had another bad card dealt her way.

Two years later, she thought enough time had passed. She had sex a few times and even she thought of herself as damaged goods, but none of the men could put her into overdrive. Actually, they bored her in bed. She told a girlfriend, "Damn! I had to close my eyes and think about being with another man."

Her first husband was the man she thought about when having sex with someone else. Vance the Vampire had bitten her with the kind of sex she longed for. He had poisoned her, too, with many regrets.

One of the men that Lois Mae dated she liked, out of the bed, but not in. He wanted sex, and his libido was fine; he just lacked imagination and skill. She thought teaching him a thing or two or twenty would help. When the talk came around, he walked out. He could not handle a woman who knew more than his ego could stand.

He told her, "A man wants to be the one who designs the way a woman gets freaky in bed."

She told him, "Well, I'm not Whoopi Goldberg, and you aren't Danny Glover in *The Color Purple*. So, you don't get to do your business on me and leave me still unsatisfied."

Life in the Northwest when you're forty, fine, and single, leaves you with few choices and it intensifies if you're an African

American. With not many places to meet other forty-something singles, you try new things. She thought she would try Internet dating, hoping to increase her chances of finding a man. She could advertise for exactly what she wanted and hoped it would keep the drama kings and control freaks to a minimum. Her dating profile read:

Divorced, Age: 40, Children: none, Religion: Christian, Education: College degree, Body type and looks: 5'11" brickhouse.

What I want in a Man: Intelligence: Not measured by plaques on the wall or money in the bank, but how you handle and treat many different kinds of people

Humor: I can be silly, can you?

Romance: A walk in the night with rain misting and slow dances under the streetlight.

Know our Creator blesses us and we can do most anything through Him.

Gainfully employed: It is not how much you make as long as it is honest work.

That was her online ad. Still, the momma's boys, married men, and the game players knocked on her computer door. They kept coming through, no different from the men in the streets, social functions, workplace, and church.

As part of her search criteria, they had to post a full-body current picture. She had been fooled a few times. Men posted photos of headshots that hid a body of a sumo wrestler. She was not vain about what a man looked like, if the man was heavyset. She just deplored the man with the handsome facial profile who showed up all out of shape. Her thoughts were she would never do that to a man. Nevertheless, after sorting through the pretenders, a few e-mails, and a few phone conversations, if the vibe seemed good, a date would ensue.

Lois Mae arrived for her date early so she might be inside ahead of him. The Chrysler's large lighted vanity mirror almost had a permanent burned-in image of her. She tested her smile; it turned her cheeks into firm, round, big, cocoa-brown snow cones. Her lips shone brighter than red stop signs. The ex hated her red lipstick, and wanted her to wear only clear gloss because he was extremely jealous. She rolled her lips inward, smoothing her red gloss one more time. Then she blew herself a kiss, complete with sound effects.

When she opened her car door and swung her legs out, some of her confidence hit the ground. She looked down at her stylish footwear, but she wished she wore a size seven instead of eleven. She tugged at her dress, a size-sixteen silk Anne Klein. She had to keep tugging at the dress, because an eighteen would have fit better over her behind.

The dampness on the sidewalk hindered Lois Mae's normally long sexy stride and she took short careful steps. In the plate glass windows of the Lake Washington waterfront Starbucks, she could see a red phantom figure highlighted by the open-flamed fireplace.

That must be him. I wish he couldn't see me walking in here. She watched his head follow her. *Okay, relax. Why did he pick Starbucks? I know he said he didn't drink, but dang, I need a glass of wine.*

Unlike her other encounters with men, he seemed honest from the first email. They had similar lifestyles; both were in education. He taught seminars on cultural diversity in the workplace. She wished her own university would implement workshops.

She told him in a phone conversation, "If I have one more white so-called-educated fool ask me if I know another Black person from here or there, I'm going to show them another side of my Black side." Lois Mae's attitude and sarcastic tone was never evil, just to the point. He liked her down-home wit.

He had sent flowers to her classroom the day of their first date. She was a Romantic Literature professor at East Seattle City University. In all of her years of teaching, neither of her past husbands had ever sent flowers to her classroom.

When she entered, the tall man lifted his long frame from his seat. *He's as tall as he said he was, but he's thin. He looks like his online pictures, but a much lighter complexion. It must have been my computer screen. I was hoping for a darker chocolate. I know I'm a trip, but I like what I like.*

"Hello, Lois, Ms. Lois Mae Ilan. We finally meet. Look at you, and an educated sexy sista. I hope you had a good day."

"Well, hello, Marvin Mandrill." She let him hug her. *Hmm, his arms are long and reaching. I know he didn't just touch my butt. Damn, he does smell good.* Marvin's hug did not end when she thought it should, so she dropped him a hint.

"Okay now, you can let me fall." He stepped back as she said, "Thank you again for the flowers. You did get my email thanking you?" She looked around to see if anyone was watching.

"Yes, Lois Mae." He asked, "Ms. Lois Mae, can I get you some tea or a coffee drink?"

"Yes, and most people think that Lois is my first name, but Lois Mae is really one name. So, thank you for that. I'll have a latte with Irish cream, with whipped cream. I like it sweet."

"You do, huh?"

"Well." She smiled and scanned his body as he walked away. *Look at them long legs, but as tight as those jeans are there should be something showing upfront. Damn, I'm bad; I need to get my mind out of his pants.*

They sat on the loveseat by the fire and they talked and laughed on all the subjects they had spoken about in their emails and phone conversations.

"So, pretty lady, you've been single for quite some time, and I know you told me before why, but it is strange to find a beautiful, intellectual and accomplished woman and you're available? You have the image of a great life. I Googled you, and you were recently featured in *Seattle's Fine Living* magazine; what an impressive life. I saw the pictures of your condominium on the lake."

His forefinger touched her smiling cheek. "You drive a nice car, and the article mentioned a closet full of New York City boutique shoes. Not bad for a Black woman, not bad for any woman in a man's world."

"Well, the image is fine, but sharing my life with someone special is what I would prefer. And I'm not one of these women who goes around saying there are no good men, and for sure, I'll never say I don't need a man. I'm kind of a victim of my surroundings being in the Northwest. Black love here in the Northwest; we are small in numbers. Anyway, that's enough about me, so tell me about those eyes."

She wanted to deflect the attention away from her, as his hands were touching her a lot. She repositioned herself. "Do you have green or brown eyes, or are we both wearing contacts and yours are colored?" They both laughed. *It was one thing for him to be running his hands up and down my arm, but up in my hair and rubbing my back? Is he moving too fast, or am I late?*

Marvin said, "My eyes are green and can sometimes look light brown. I guess my great, great, great, great-grandmother was tipping with the Irish master, or George Washington's wife was visiting the Mandingos' shack."

They shared a real hearty laugh at knowing it could be the truth. The laughing stopped, and an awkward moment sucked on the air in the room. Marvin made a reach and touched way too much for Lois Mae to ignore.

"What are you doing, unzipping my boot?"

"Well, I was going to massage—"

"What, massage my feet?"

"Ah, yeah," he slyly said.

"Do you do this with every woman you meet in public? I love it when a man fondles my feet, but twenty minutes into our first meeting? Slow down. We're out in public!" She forced a smile, and stood up.

"I have to go to the restroom." There was no anger in her voice, but the tone she used said enough was enough.

"Hey, Lois Mae, I meant no harm. Just trying to let you know I care about you."

"You care about me?" Her head jerked. "You don't know me. We just met two weeks ago on the Internet." *Maybe I'm being hard on the brother; let me lighten up.*

Marvin chuckled. "I do this every day. Can't you tell by my skills at getting you pissed off? Even though, I might be losing my touch."

Lois Mae admired his weak attempt to make light of what had just happened, and joked back. "Would you wait another fifteen minutes at least before you start rubbing anything? If you really care about me, wait two hours." They both laughed as she walked toward the restroom. She knew his eyes were beaming on her rear as she walked away.

I liked him better through his e-mails and his voice on the phone, but in ten more minutes, he would have been feeling all up in my booty. She giggled.

She took care of her business in the restroom, then stood in front of the mirror checking out her hair and her lipstick. She reached in her purse to pull out a little spray bottle of swap-meet imitation, high-priced perfume. It was unfitting of her financial status to use the cheap stuff, but her Joy by Jean Patou Perfume Deluxe cost $400 an ounce. She used the good stuff on her body, but her country girl ways sometimes would contradict her usual classy ways. Then she'd go cheap and use a swap-meet clone to scent her panties.

The good stuff was not in a squirt bottle like the clone. She lifted her dress, pulled back her panties and squirted the cheap stuff inside. *He's not going to get any of this tonight, but since he's trying to get his nose close...* She laughed as if she was laughing at someone else.

Before she finished laughing, she had to clamp her inner thighs tight. "Agh," she almost screamed and rolled her hips around. Her butt protruded even farther than it naturally did. The burn of too much alcohol in the cheap perfume made her squirm. "Damnit!" *I don't want to go out there and be twisting my big ass around with Mr. All-Hands out there waiting.* She checked her cell phone for messages while waiting for the burning sensation to dissipate. *Let me call Skillet.*

"Hello."

"Hey, girl, what are you doing?" Lois Mae squirmed while she spoke.

"Hey–hey, girlfriend, if you calling me this early I know your date did not work out. Get your butt over here and have a drink with me. Oh, that's right, you like Merlot. Well, pick some up and get here."

"I'm still on my date. I'm in the bathroom. You know that fake-ass swap meet perfume you gave me; it's burning my poo-tang."

"You silly, girl, you're not supposed to spray it right on your kitty."

"I know, but the spray applicator from this cheap mess sprays like a Windex bottle. The worst part of it is, I shaved off my hair down there last week, and it's starting to itch too."

"Well, Miss-Smell-So-Good-Up-The-Poo-Tang, it sounds as if you had plans for your date to—"

"No, he ain't getting any."

"If you did the double dose of smell-good on your coochie—"

"It's not like that, trust me. This date is going in the wrong direction. I sprayed myself by accident. Plus, I'm nothing like you; you're so nasty," Lois teased with a little chuckle.

"What are you trying to say?" Lois Mae could hear her friend laughing.

"You know exactly what I'm saying. I'm surprised you answered the phone. Your booty should be all up in the air by now." Lois Mae laughed hard.

"Oh, you think you know."

"I do and you know I do. Some brother will be making a booty call in a while. Maybe you're done already and you sent him out for some more wine?"

"Hey, I'm trying to slow down."

"Which one, wine or men?"

"Smartass! Men!" Both women laughed, knowing the real answer was wine.

Skillet's real name was Velvet Williams. Lois Mae had tagged her with the nickname, Skillet. Years ago they had met in the most awkward way. Out of nowhere, Velvet spoke to Lois Mae in a restroom of a dinner club one day while Lois Mae was having dinner with her husband, Vance. Food became the subject. Velvet ended up inviting Lois Mae to come over to her place for dinner. She found it a little strange that this tall, big-boned, Caucasian-toned, but Black-featured woman had invited her over. Later, Velvet identified herself as Brazilian and German.

Eventually, Lois Mae did go over for dinner; the two had a lot in common. Lois Mae found out Velvet knew her, not personally, but she knew of her. Velvet told Lois Mae she had been sleeping with her husband, Vance.

Lois Mae ended up grabbing a skillet Velvet was using. She almost hit Velvet upside the head with the skillet. Velvet knew she had been sleeping with a married man, but she never knew who the wife was. She stayed in a booty-fling relationship with Vance for years.

Velvet was an incredibly pretty woman. Men salivated over her exotic look. She only picked the wrong men or lost the good men due to her excessive drinking. Her high IQ baffled her friends, who wondered why her personal life was in constant turmoil.

Seeing Vance at dinner with Lois Mae, Velvet decided she couldn't take it anymore. There had been too many lonely holidays, too many excuses about why they didn't do this or couldn't go there.

The audacity of this man! Even as she was in the bathroom that day talking to Lois Mae, Velvet's cell phone vibrated, and it was Vance. He wanted to hook up that weekend.

Velvet had a revelation to clean up her life. She thought she would help save another woman, and at the same time free herself. She planned to end Vance's fun without much thought of what his wife might do.

With one bottle of wine down, Velvet got her nerve up to tell all while serving dinner. Lois Mae took the news calmly at first; but lost it. To hear what she already knew about her husband, and then from one of the women. A flash of emotion bolted her body across the kitchen, and she grabbed the full skillet from Velvet. Food went flying, Lois Mae cursed Velvet, and reached back to hit her with the skillet, but instead of slamming her head with the frying pan, she backhanded Velvet and she dropped to the floor like a sack of potatoes.

Lois Mae screamed, "Bitch, I should have flattened your face with this skillet!" Velvet was looking pitiful.

Lois Mae started to cry; one eye dripping rage, the other shedding tears of hurt. Her violent outburst scared her and made her feel guilty, somewhat embarrassed and exposed, yet still seething angry. She felt empathy for Velvet and for herself, so anger shifted to Vance, the vampire.

The two women sat down and cried together that night, talking and strangely laughing together. They shared their stories of Vance's evil twists. The evening was strange for sure; they even got down to the real dirt—the good sex—of the same skilled tricks he used on the both of them. They began to understand how he controlled them and made them dependent.

Lois Mae tagged her new friend "Skillet," from that evening's experience. She told her, "I'm so sorry to have threatened to hurt your beautiful face. I see why Vance was attracted to you."

"Girl, I attract men like flies with my face, but they always land on my ass."

They became friends that night; their lifestyles very different, but much the same when walking through the minefields in search of the right man.

"Lois Mae, I got wine and no man tonight. If you're on the phone talking to me, it tells me it's not going that good. So make your way over here."

"I don't know. Let me get back out here and see. I'll talk to you later."

"Yeah, well, at least get out of the bathroom or go invite him in."

"I told you I'm not a freak like you. I'll call you later."

"Marvin, I'm so sorry I was gone so long." As Lois Mae sat, he moved his body almost underneath her. It was a little loveseat with not much room in the first place. Lois Mae wanted to give herself a little space, but he was fast.

"Well, I'd love to get next to ya, baby, you know what I mean." *He thinks he's so smooth.* "I know what you mean." She stood up and moved in front of the fireplace. The background music led her to sway a little. The fire and her body flamed unknowing seduction. She told him, "I love this song. I love Angie Stone's music.

"Hey, baby, let me get next to you tonight and love you down!" There was cold silence from her as her sway slowed. Marvin stared lustfully at her. "Look, let's go someplace," his voice was testing.

"Like where? Her eyes widened. *He'd better not say something stupid.*

"Your place or mine?"

He's stupid. Lois Mae stared down at him. "I think we're both going home tonight to our own places, our own beds. I have never gone home with a man on the first date. Wait, yes, I have, but those days are over. They should be over for you too. But even if I still did, I would be telling you—no!"

"What's your problem? You said you can't meet a man."

She laughed a *how-dare-you* chuckle. "Oh, you have hearing and comprehension difficulties. I told you the kind of man I seek. I may not be a whole lot of things, but I am all woman. That to you, sir, is a woman who is never going to be weak for you." Her tone had no anger as she spoke softly, but assuredly.

"All you had to do was treat me like a lady and show me your intelligence, make me laugh a little. Your hands move faster than your mouth, and what comes out of your mouth is childish." She shook her head. *He's got booty first, passion doubtful values. He thinks of my intelligence as if it was a first-class upgrade, but coach is fine.*

Marvin stood up and towered over Lois Mae. "You're a trip. I could be someplace else tonight; instead I'm with your uptight ass."

Lois Mae lifted one eyebrow, looked up at the man who was making an ass of himself. Her lips rolled inward, then slowly outward. "Then, ahh…you need to go." She smiled with her lips pressed tight. *I hope I do not have to spray that cheap swap meet perfume in this man's face since it burns like mace.*

Marvin, feeling rebuffed, started walking away, but he turned around after a few steps. He parted his lips to speak with an *I'm-sorry* look. Lois Mae raised both eyebrows and shook her head no.

She made her way to her car. She pulled out her cell phone.

"Girl, I'm on my way over."

"Huh?"

"Skillet, I'm on my way over."

"Ah-huh."

Lois Mae hung up the phone and turned up the radio. The deejay, "The Love Minister," was slippery smooth.

"To all those who need love, have lost love or are missing the love of that special someone, here is a poem for you."

Wanting to see my love
Missing the scent,
Absent of the look
Desiring
Craving
Yearning
Drives my mind into a fog of memories
I'm waiting to see my love
The love that's meant for me

"Now let me play a little Toni Braxton for you, 'Another Sad Love Song.'"

3
Faith and Fate

Passing headlights from cars filtered through the stained-glass windows of the Mt. Baker Tabernacle Church and reflected off the bifocals of the deacons who sat behind the pastor. A deep bass voice sang out between the gold teeth flashing from Pastor Glasper's mouth while he Holy Ghost danced. Some of the children had no patience from two Sunday services and pointed and played with the light show while the pastor sang.

Vanita Irving sat with her Bible open but unable to focus on the words. Her mind strayed, no matter what the pastor preached. This sermon did help with her troubles.

"My sistas, I'm-ah, speaking to all the Eves, Esthers, and Ruths of the Bible. I have a message to all the Mary Magdalenes, Deborahs, all, deez Sarahs of the Bible of the Bible, here-ah in modern times God has someone waiting for ya. For those of you who are single, and trying to find a mate, let me tell ya how the Lord feels about-cha."

The congregation shouted, "Thank ya, Jesus."

"Some of ya are happy, but-ah, you know-ah, there are those among us who are miserable. Ya see, there is no in between;

either ya happily married or you're not, either ya happily single or not."

"Amen, brotha." A woman jumped up. She was sitting in front of Vanita and her son. The woman rose so fast it was as if a coil spring had let loose under her heavenly heavy rear end. The woman stood, shouting, and pointed with her stocky fingers; her gold and black nails long and curling.

"I don't need no mans! I got God; thank ya, Jesus." She stomped the floor and sat down hard. A man sitting on the same pew slid away.

The pastor responded, "No, my sista, you don't need no man. All you need is our Lord and Savior, Je-e-e-sus Christ. But I must tell ya, God gave Eve to Adam, and it's in His plan for you to have a mate."

Vanita Irving's emotions boxed with the preacher's words. Her soul spun like a loose hubcap on the highway, bouncing and jumping from lane to lane.

The pastor's voice boomed above the choir. The music could have been Saturday night swing-your-hips blues. Pastor Glasper did a sanctified version of James Brown's Mashed Potato with a 360-degree spin. It was all in the name of the Spirit.

Vanita's runaway mind interfered with her worship. *Why am I alone, alone with my son? Why did God let my husband leave me? What did I do wrong, Lord?*

She closed her eyes, squeezing them tightly, holding back tears. The church was hot as hell. Beads of sweat mixed with her tears. *Moms say menopause feels like this. Oh Lord, please don't let it be.*

A year and a half had passed since her husband had left, with no real explanation. He'd said that he couldn't take it anymore.

"I Surrender All" chorused over the pews from the choir. The church was full of women, in their thirties, forties, and fifties, mostly single, divorced, or separated. The other women in the pews had husbands who did not come to church often.

Vanita Irving removed her reading glasses and wiped under her eyes. Her nutmeg-colored skin felt irritated from wiping dry tearstains. She pulled out some coconut oil lotion and moistened her face. It brought back to life her almost unnoticeable black beauty marks and slightly raised dark freckles. They accented her soft elegant beauty. White men told her she looked like the Vivica A. Fox who fought Uma Thurman in the movie, *Kill Bill*. Vanita never assumed her beauty was an asset.

She had married JW Irving, a man somewhat like her father. All she wanted was a man like her father. JW worked hard and made a good living. He was a good provider, father and lover, while they were married. She did everything she thought a woman should do to please her husband, yet he left her, leaving her to raise their son on her own.

"Talk, preacher," the repeated plea came from all corners of the church.

"God urges you all to find a mate, my lilies of the valley."

"Amen, brother, I know that's right." Mt. Baker Tabernacle Church confirmed with praises for what Pastor was saying.

"Stop and sit still, Joshua." Vanita's seven-year-old son was restless; he was playing with another young boy. They were pointing at the beams of light reflecting in the church, including off the pastor's teeth. Raising a son alone added to her frustration.

Pastor preached on, "If ya show faith in God, he will lead ya to a glorious fate. God's way is never late; he's always on time. Your special soulmate is on his way."

"Joshua, sit still." Vanita popped her son on the back of the head with a forefinger. She heard her own sermon in her head. *Who wants to come into a ready-made family? Men I run into think*

I'm desperate. But I need some sex, ugh. I'm up in church lusting. But I want a God-fearing man lusting after me too. Maybe I want too much?

The pastor's words cut back into her distracted mind. "Turn your-ah Bibles to Psalms 65:4. It says, 'Blessed is the man you choose and causes to approach you.' My lilies of the valley, are you being chosen, or are you choosing? Then do the things you need to do to keep a man. How dare you withhold what God has given you. Give it up!" Pastor shouted, and shouted again as he jumped down from the pulpit.

The drummer and the bass player started playing a low-volume, thump-and-bump, soulful groove. "Give it up and stop blowing in the wind, riding the fence; commit to God's plan. Now hear what-ah I'm saying; don't get mad at the messenger."

The sermon went on with Vanita staring at the stained-glass windows. Her eyes could not see out, but a part of her was on the other side of the glass.

After service, Brother Jett made his way over to Vanita. He had no shame and no couth. She saw him coming and smiled to keep from laughing at his dead-grass, thin hair. She moved faster toward the parking lot.

With a tap on her shoulder, she knew it was him. "Sister Irving, it is good to see one of the finest sisters to grace God's earth." His nasally rasp did not match his burly body.

Vanita kept walking. "You need to stop, Brother Jett." *I don't know if any woman wants this momma's boy. I'm sorry, Lord, let me stop. I'm just getting out of church.*

"How about I pick up some dessert, meet at your place, and we can talk."

"Talk about what? It's already late; it's a school night."

"Ah, you know what time it is, and why you calling me 'Brother Jett' unless that's like you're calling me Big Daddy?" He chuckled. Vanita laughed at him, not with him.

"Excuse me, Brother Jett, Lord would only know why I'd call you Big Daddy. We've known each other since we were teenagers. I know almost every woman you've been with, but I'm not implying you've been fornicating." They both laughed as she kept walking. Vanita stopped and waved to her good friend, Alicia, who stared with a raised eyebrow a few cars away. "Oscar, I'm not going out and dating anyone right now for good reasons."

"Well, didn't you hear what preacher said about man and woman are not supposed to be alone?

"I can tell you didn't listen to the whole sermon. As a matter of fact, didn't you ask Alicia out a couple of Sundays ago?"

"Ah, you guys be doggin' a brother out. I just asked her if she wanted to go hang out for a while. It wasn't like I was hitting on her."

"But you hitting on me?"

"Well, we could talk."

"Sorry. Just let it be, please." Vanita turned and walked away. Almost on autopilot, she headed to her mom and dad's. She would have Alicia drop Joshua off over there. She did not want to go home to an empty house.

A tear rolled from the corner of her eye. It ran down her cheek and all the way to her lips. She tasted of her own emotions. She turned on the radio while more of her liquid soul ran down her cheeks.

The Love Minister was at it again, reciting his charms:

"The journey of falling

Falling in love

When we feel it

It's the sweetest of feelings
And it was at one time or more
Then we learn
The feeling of falling can mean something else
Other than being in love
The unforeseen
A heart feels it has been unplugged from life support
Grabbing, for what we don't know
We question inside, did I do wrong
Doesn't matter
A heart has been broken
Has fallen but we wise up
With eyes wide open
We know that old pains can help us grow
And weren't meant to harden us
That even suffering has its place

"Okay, with those words in mind, I'm gonna reach back into my old vinyl and play The Spinners 'Love Don't Love No Nobody.'"

Vanita chuckled at the sounds of pops and clicks from a record coming through her truck stereo. She pulled into the driveway of her parents' house and sat listening to classic melancholy soul.

4

Played and Played Out

The summer before the current season, deep into the night, the phone rang. "Damn!" Sterlin was instantly irritated. His eyes burned from lack of sleep, and he was exhausted. He reached for the phone.

"Hmm, hello."

"Hey, whatcha doing?"

"I was asleep."

"And in your dreams I'm touching you, right?"

Can't get it through her thick head to understand her time has come and gone. "Look, my plane got in late; I'm tired." He looked over at the clock. "Shit, it's three a.m."

"Do you want some company?"

"No!"

"How was Mexico, I mean, New Mexico?"

"Hey, I'll call you tomorrow. I got to go, bye."

"Wait—wait. Can I come over around nine and cook you breakfast? Even better, let's go down to Ballard, and hit Anthony's Homeport for brunch. It will be my treat."

"Just let me get some sleep." Sterlin hung the phone up. *Freak.*

He was awake now. He cleared his throat, ran his tongue around his mouth, and swallowed hard. Something was tickling his throat. He tried to place his finger in his mouth, but a woman's head was lying on his chest, and one of her long hairs tickled his throat. He smiled as he sniffed a finger on his other hand.

Warmth from her mouth floated across his chest. "Do I need to go? I don't want to cause any problems." Her lips brushed his chest. He felt her hand rubbing his thigh.

"It's okay, you just lay here and go back to sleep."

Her voice teased, "Do I have to just lay here?" Her hand slid up to the head of his semi-hardness. She played with the slippery drip. He wrapped his leg around her thigh, squeezed, and humped upward.

The covers slid back, exposing her ivory-toned shoulders. Sterlin put his hands on her waist and helped her squat over him. The skylight above highlighted their bodies. His powerful body was a pedestal for her amply curved figure.

"Damn, girl, these round mounds of yours are bigger than my hands."

"My round mounds." She laughed. "You make them sound like a candy bar, so could you suck them for me?" His hand squeezed her gumdrop-sized nipples, and he felt them spring back. She leaned over and helped her nipple into his mouth. "Yeah, bite it, bite me, I like that." He sucked and held her between his teeth lightly.

She repositioned her body. "Feel me. I'm so wet." She splayed her fingers on his chest to support her weight, allowing her to smear her wetness over his navel.

Sterlin's hard-on reached above his navel, her grinding ass bumping into it. He worked the mushroomed tip on her pubic hair.

"Can I sit on it?" she asked.

He reached for his condom box on the nightstand. It was empty.

"I guess I have to sit on those big juicy lips," she said.

"Ah-huh."

He wanted to be inside her fire but he was out of protection. *Damn, well, pussy sitting on my face is not a bad option.* He laughed louder than intended.

"What, what's so funny?"

"Nothing, baby, come on."

She spun around slowly; backed her ass up over his face. She grabbed his drooling mushroom head. She ground her ass nastily over his face, while his tongue parted her, sliding in and out. He kept licking her, probing her from end to end.

His large hands grabbed, squeezed, and spread her cheeks over his face, then he slapped her ass while his tongue licked. She heard the nasty sound of him eating her.

Sterlin's lips found her round marble of sensitivity. He took his time and licked, licked, and in a circling motion. He slid the tip of a finger into her ass and held it there. He kept licking her clit with a slow circular motion. He felt her asshole start to have spasms and he knew she was about to cum. She screamed in low tones. She froze for a moment until her legs began to tremble and quiver. Her juices covered his lips and jaw. She leaned forward, catching her breath. It gave him a chance to relax his jaw muscles.

She held his long shaft with one hand. Her forefinger and thumb was tight around the head. She began to suck and lick the shaft near his balls as she stroked the head as if she were milking it. He shook, and grunted. With a few more strokes, her hand jerked as if it was being forced open and closed; she felt warm thick, creamy liquid flow over her fisted hand. An animal-like grunting sound bellowed against her ass.

Sterlin helped her body off his chest. She leaned over him, kissing and licking all her feminine stream off his chin, lips, cheeks, and nose.

They lay motionless for a few minutes, until she told him, "Next time, don't run out of rubbers; I need to feel you inside me."

"Don't be greedy; we went through three of them."

"No we didn't; you broke one of them putting it on. But I understand you damn near stretched me and broke me too." They laughed and closed their eyes.

They relaxed back into the position where they were earlier before the awaking phone call.

Sterlin awoke and found himself alone in bed. Sitting up, he smelled food cooking. He scanned his room; he could tell she had dressed already, and he smiled.

Oh shit, the freak can cook, I think? Whew, when she stepped out of them panties last night, the girl had a stream of juice running down her leg, and damn that booty, damn! It will be nice if she's in the kitchen naked with just her heels. Sterlin laughed aloud.

"Hey, baby, you up?"

"What the hell?" Sterlin jumped up from his bed, grabbing and stepping into his sweatpants almost in one motion. He entered his front room and saw a woman he knew on the couch but not the one he'd slept with last night.

"Your food is almost ready," the woman said calmly.

Not quite sure of the what and where, Sterlin spoke softly and slowly, "Bobbie, what are you doing here?"

"When I called last night—"

"No, when you called early this morning," he reminded her.

"When I called, you sounded so tired. I thought I'd come over and take care of you. You should make sure you lock your door, honey. When I knocked—"

"Knocked?"

"The door just came open." He stared at her, cocking his head. She blew him a kiss, while her fingers with brown-reddish freckles toyed with her red hair.

He rolled his eyes, and walked through his house, looking for signs of last night and what was going on. *Damn, I forgot to turn the alarm on; I would've heard someone leaving and this knucklehead coming in. Where in the hell did that girl go and when? How long ago? Bobbie has been here for a while.*

Sterlin walked into his bathroom to relieve himself and found a note laying on the counter. *I guess Bobbie didn't go into my bathroom even though I know she's here to catch a brother. This is what I get for messing around with her silly ass.*

Sterlin had slept with Bobbie and her bisexual roommate. He broke it off with the two, but Bobbie kept coming by to get serviced. She thought it was a relationship by playing maid, and cooking. He told her long ago he didn't want her around anymore. He always felt she was up to no good.

Sterlin stood in front of his bathroom mirror looking up from the note written by the woman from last night. She wanted him to come over to her place later that night. She had apologized to him for having to be at work at seven. *Timing is everything.*

Bobbie called out, "Hey, babe, why don't you go back to bed, and I'll bring you your food. Then you can have some dessert, if you want me."

"I have some things to do; you have to go and I have to go. I need you to stop coming over here. We're through!" He walked into his kitchen and spoke firmly, "Respect my place; stop coming over here. It was fun while it lasted, but we are done."

"Oh we are? You sure you want it like that? I don't ask you for much. I know you screw other women. You didn't want me to come over last night, huh." Bobbie's red hair and brownish freckles blended with the extra redness coming to her face.

Sterlin was not one for confrontation. He tried to soften his approach. "Look, I'm just not into you. Okay, let's just move on."

She had three things cooking on the stove. She grabbed her purse. She pushed past him even though he wasn't in the way. When she got to the front door, she turned and winked at him, not a flirting wink. She reached into her purse, pulled out a used condom, and dropped it on the floor. She slammed the door.

He locked the door, then turned on his stereo. T-Bone Walker wailed on his guitar and sang the blues, *Can't live with a woman, and can't do without them.* He went into his bedroom, and did not see last night's condoms on the floor or in the trash. "Fuck it!"

Sterlin went back into the kitchen and finished what she had started. He laughed. *Well, I don't think she poisoned my food.* Then he thought about the missing used condoms, and threw the food out.

After showering and dressing, he headed out of the front door. There lay the condom Bobbie had tossed. He shook his head. *I let her hang around way too long.*

Upsetting women happened often, because he slept with women he had no intention of loving. It was his way of not letting a woman get close to him. Yet he hated the end game. When a woman wanted more than a bedroom affair, he never knew how to handle the end or the drama it brought. He played and played himself out, feeling bad about their hurt feelings, but not bad enough not to do it all over again.

5

Funny How Times Change

Joshua and I have to wake up earlier. As Vanita left her apartment the sun was trying to burn through the low-lying fog; the full moon had not hid itself yet. She pulled out of her driveway and drove onto Renton Avenue. The southern part of the Skyway area caused her to drive into blinding morning sun. She reached for her sunglasses.

It seemed everybody was running late to join the daily commute. Bad traffic nightmares could be another new mental disorder in the Northwest.

A rainbow-painted, old Volkswagen bus pulled out and could not make it up to speed quickly enough. An automatic reflex made her reach back to restrain Joshua. Her arms were not long enough, but her quick deceleration was smooth.

It was the late fall Seattle morning that was nice and clear, but with a chill in the air. With the heater on, blowing up her legs and into Vanita's face, it put her into a hypnotic state. The artificial heat and not enough sleep made her crave her bed. Her pillow was now at least sixteen hours away.

I need more sleep. I need a coffeemaker with a timer. I could wake up with no problem when I had a man. I'm not sure what I miss more: the smell of coffee or my man. She came back to reality as she pulled into Joshua's school parking lot in the dropoff zone. She looked back and saw his handsome face express the joy of being at school.

He unbuckled his seat belt. "Okay, Mr. Joshua Irving, give me a kiss goodbye."

"Okay, Mom, have a good day."

She hit I-405 smiling at the vision in her daydreaming, helping to blot out the commuting nightmare. She reached for her coffee. The warmth of liquid on her lips and tongue evoked memories of her lips pestering different parts of her man's body until he awoke with a hard-on. She wanted no foreplay in the morning. She wanted just the slow pushing of his thickness into her awaiting moistness. The thought of having him inside her made her wet. While inside, he would reach, find her clit, and rub it with the speed of a microwave turntable circling slowly.

Her foot pressed the gas pedal as her daydream vividly tailgated into the physical desire of that feeling of penetration. She gripped the steering wheel tightly. Her foot wiggled out of control as she drove. She envisioned his hands in the middle of her back, and him riding her from behind. The light back pains she had now were reminiscent of his hands squeezing tight on her waist. As she drove she pulled her skirt up just far enough and rubbed her clit through her panties. She had a mini-orgasm. She sped up involuntarily, reliving him grunting and feeling his warm release.

Now on I-90, on the floating bridge, she was heading west to downtown. The water was calm on the south side and rough on the north. The wide open view of Lake Washington woke Vanita from her rapturous past.

She smiled wide. *Damn! I want some so bad.* Vanita's period was a few days away; that always had her on automatic horny with full force every month.

She turned up a new flavor in music for the rest of the drive. *The Rhythm Country and Blues* CD played. A while later she pulled into the parking garage at work; she hit the repeat button again. Aaron Neville and Trisha Yearwood sang "I Fall to Pieces," sweetly. She loved the song so and bought the original by Patsy Cline. The song made her feel better knowing someone must have felt the same way she did.

The previous night left a chill in her that her heated daydreams could not thaw. After church, Vanita went to her parents' home. When she arrived, her ex-husband, JW, was sitting at the kitchen table. Mom and Dad never showed any ill will toward her ex. They kept the door open for JW who came there to see his son, trying to avoid Vanita.

He was sitting in the kitchen. Vanita said, "Why don't you just come over to where your son lives to visit him?"

"Your place...we've been down this road too many times," JW responded.

"My place...your son lives there, and do you think I'm going to keep you there against your will? Do you think Joshua is going to know his daddy from these little moments at his grandparents'?" She did not let him answer. "I see a plate of food in front of you. Maybe that's the real reason you're here." Her eyes rolled, and a deep long breath traveled past her lips with a message attached. *Kiss my ass!*

"Vanita, you're looking good, baby," JW said.

"Yeah, whatever. As you can see, your son is not here. He's with someone else."

"Where is he? Who is he with?"

"Oh, the concerned parent!"

JW stood up, leaned over into Vanita's face, and voiced a monotone response. "I just want to know where Josh is."

"As I've said many times before, I prefer you don't call him an abbreviated version of his name. You would be better to back up out of my face. Remember, as you have said all too many times, I'm crazy."

"Hey, baby, this is not about our son, and you know it!" He pulled back, and Vanita looked away. "I don't want to live with you or be married to you. Now, if you just want to hook up?"

Her head turn back toward him slowly. *He doesn't love me, but he'd love to screw me.* She hoped he could read her mind, because she really wanted to say her religion would not let her. "Your son is with Alicia, and I'm going to call her and tell her to bring Joshua to my place. Enjoy your visit with my folks." She made sure he saw the switch of her behind as she exited the kitchen without saying a word.

Vanita sat in her SUV in the parking garage; the heater felt good, better than last night's chill. She sat and sipped some more coffee and was about to take what she called her "happy" pill. If she took the pill, it would slow her mind down from thinking about too much. It also made her sleepy. She laughed at the thought that she called it a happy pill. The doctor called it a neuroleptic episode when she went from high to low. He said one Thioridazine pill a day would keep her on an even keel, when in fact it dulled her senses. It also suppressed her sex drive into a corner of her mind—sometimes. That was not a bad thing since she thought about sex all the time. She put her happy pill back into the bottle. *I'll take a pill tomorrow.* She prayed for healing.

Before heading up to her job, she listened to one more song. She took the CD player out of the repeat mode and listened to Al Green and Lyle Lovett's "Funny How Time Slips Away."

"Hey, Coach, how does it feel to beat your old team?" Larentzo yelled.

Coach Sparks said in a monotone, "All wins feel good. You had a real good game, but I told you that last night. Today is a new day. Work on your free throws. I don't want to lose a game because you didn't hit the game-winning free throw."

It was the morning after a win over the coach's alma mater, the University of New Mexico. Coach Sparks and Coach Baylor were mulling over the game plan for the next game against cross-town rival, University of Washington.

After losing to Kentucky a week ago, he changed the lineup. For the next game against the University of New Mexico, Coach Sparks scrapped his big lineup and went with smaller quicker players. The change resulted in an impressive win. The University of Washington game would be their last before the start of the regular season.

The athletic director had left a message for Coach Sparks, letting him know he was coming by to talk. A fragile relationship existed between the director and Coach Sparks. Athletic Director Bucket had been the head coach for the previous ten, mostly losing years. He had hopes that his son would take over the basketball program when he retired, but others worked behind the scene to have Coach Sparks hired. AD Bucket resented Coach Sparks.

Coach Ayman Sparks was a strong-willed, no-nonsense, in-your-face Black man at a predominately white college. Winning can smooth over perceived thoughts in the sports arena.

Ayman came to East Seattle City University (ESCU) with his own ideas. He knew how he wanted his team to play and the type of players who would play for him.

He had taken ESCU to the Sweet Sixteen of the NCAA Tournament the last two seasons. However, Ayman was perceptive to the game played behind the game. Ayman had a poster on his office wall that pictured a hundred Black men—all who'd fought some kind of struggle, from the likes of Malcolm X to then Senator Barack Obama to Richard Pryor and other Black men. The poster read:

DO YOUR JOB. DO YOUR JOB BETTER THAN OTHERS. BE PREPARED TO FIGHT, WHEN YOU ARE BETTER.

The athletic director walked in. Balls were bouncing, and the boys were shooting when AD Bucket reached Coach Sparks.

"Coach Sparks, could I talk to you?"

"I'm about to start practice. Can't this wait till later?"

"Coach, it seems there is a problem with a player's grade in a class."

Ayman gave Sterlin a look. Sterlin said, "I'll get practice started." He looked at Ayman in return, as if to say, "Don't lose your cool."

Ayman's face was deadpan. "Which player and what class? We have an academic department that handles these kinds of problems. The athletic director coming down to tell me of this alleged problem is a little strange."

"Well, Coach, it is my job also. We don't want an ineligible player who could cause us to forfeit a game, or even sanctions."

Ayman rolled his tongue inside his mouth, giving him time to think before he spoke. "Which player and which class?"

"That kid you recruited from out of the country. He's failing an English class. You need to look into it before he plays the next game."

"That player's name is Larentzo Sir John, which you should know. He's in his third year."

AD Bucket tried to act unfazed by Ayman standing up to him. "Well, yes, I should know the name of the twenty-three-year-old junior, the foreigner from the Bahamas."

Ayman laughed in the man's face. *Unintelligent man.* "Well, for the record, Larentzo Sir John is from a small island named St. Lucia, which is nearer to Brazil, not North America, where the Bahamas are. But if you like, I'll go recruiting in the Bahamas, and spend some time there after the season. Maybe I'll find some more players who look like him."

Ayman held a straight face but wanted to laugh again. *He doesn't think I can see through his tired ass.* "And as Larentzo leads our conference in assists and steals, and scoring, that's good, right? That happens to make him one of the best guards in college."

The AD tried a weak comeback. "Well, he hasn't helped you play well this year so far."

"Oh, so you do follow his progress. Good. In any case, you'll see his development in the score sheets. He has not scored a lot this season as of yet, because I had him focus on being the best defensive guard in the country first. The last of the big, slow kids, the seniors you recruited and gave scholarships, they might not play much this year."

"I hope it doesn't backfire on you. The classroom situation needs to be addressed now." AD Bucket turned and abruptly walked away. Ayman chuckled in amazement at how some men acted out their jealousy.

The team was still going through warm-up drills when Sterlin rejoined Ayman.

"What's that about?"

"Bucket thinks he's slick. I wonder what ESPN-TV, and the other media would say about a coach choking his athletic director?" Both men laughed. "I need you to go check on one of Larentzo's grades. Bucket claims there is a problem."

"Yeah, but it don't sound right. Since when does he come personally to tell you about something like this?"

"Since he became a rust bucket who can't hold his own piss." The two coaches pressed their fists together, and held them there for a long moment.

"Better to be cautious. I'll find out about the grade thing first thing in the morning. I'm sure his teacher is already gone for the day."

"Well, first thing in the morning, Sterlin. We need Larentzo to beat Washington. They're playing pretty well."

"I want to recruit that kid out of Garfield High School. If we can beat them, like I think we should, it will give us an inside track on that kid."

After Coach spoke to the players about the upcoming game, they held a scrimmage. The graduate coaches coached while Coach Sparks watched.

Sterlin, sitting with Ayman, said, "This game is big, and with the changes you've made, I sense a different attitude. A smaller, faster lineup fits their attitude to play harder. The hell with that slow-ass, big kid, let him whine. Your affirmative action plan is paying off too. Lorrie is good; she's sharp. What made you think of bringing on a female grad coach?"

"She played at BYU for three years, and then her religion and sexual preference crossed paths. She lost her scholarship and she lost her religion. She's older than most graduate coaches so she commands respect. Watching her run drills, she could make a good head coach."

"Maybe she can get hired to run a men's program," Sterlin said and nodded. "A woman in control of men; I can see that."

"I don't believe what I just heard you say. I'll leave that one alone in trying to believe you believe that," Ayman said.

Sterlin forced a sinister smirk.

Ayman asked, "What you got, them freaks of yours, tying you

up with bras and panties, and beating your ass?" He laughed hard at his own comment.

"Don't knock it until you've tried it."

"Ah nah, I don't think I want my booty stuck up in the air getting beat with anything."

Practice ended, and Ayman reminded Sterlin to look into the grades as soon as possible.

I can taste some teriyaki right now. She laughed. *Let me keep my big booty on this machine like I'm supposed to.* Lois Mae was staring out the big window of the Redmond twenty-four-hour fitness center. Her mouth was dry, her body sweated. Chaka Khan's "I Feel For You" blared as a woman's voice led people doing aerobics.

Working out was something she had always done since her days as a high school athlete and as a cheerleader. She was used to sweating growing up in the Houston, Texas heat. Up until she was thirty-four, she was a size fourteen at five-eleven. Clothes covered her body well, but her breasts and behind always pushed the threads to the limits.

At forty, her body still had that sex appeal, but the road was wider and rounder now. Men loved to be behind her; no matter what she wore, she could hot hide her sexy sway. A stair stepper machine and Lois Mae Ilan in a body suit had the men moving about for a better view. She was aware.

"Ms. Lois Mae, it's time for you to lift some weights. Head on over, and I'll be right over there to check on you," her trainer said.

Lois Mae smiled, protruded her big bottom lip, and rolled her eyes up. *How can a man be so fine and so gay? Look at his ass and thighs.* Lois Mae loved looking at her finer-than-fine personal trainer.

The music changed to old school with Cameo's "Candy." Lois Mae scanned the room wishing for more Black women to come to the gym and get healthy.

She told her trainer, "I may be a size sixteen, well, size eighteen in some things, but I'll never let myself go too far downhill. Plus, it tells a man you're motivated to stay with something important. Hell, I don't want no fat-ass man laying up on me. I like to eat too much. My thickness curves with some flare. I'm more than just a pretty face."

When Lois Mae started doing her squats, a smile came across her face; a fantasy played in her mind. The vision of her squatting over a man was her favorite position. She could get on top and keep going for a long time, blowing a man's mind.

"Ms. Lois Mae, let's do one set of leg lifts before you go, you pretty, fine Black thing, you. You know the men in here just go crazy over you." Her trainer fawned over her every time, and they had become very good friends. She joked with him that he was her secret lover.

"Now, Ms. Thing, you know if I was straight, you and I would starve to death because we'd never get out of the bed."

"When I was married, I loved and craved sex. Enough was never enough. It would amaze me how much I needed to do the nasty."

"Girl, you should be skinny up in here just thinking about the nasty as much as you do."

She laughed. "I was thinner when I was getting some. Now it's vibrators taking up the slack. As a matter of fact, it's time for me to make a Costco run to buy a pallet load of batteries. I have to admit, the toys and the videos help a little, but the feel of a man cannot be replaced."

"Honey, you keep working out to help relieve some of that sexual tension."

6
Back and Forth

The wins on the court never overshadowed Ayman's empty-house feeling. The heart versus the brain was a game played ever since his divorce.

After practice, Ayman flew to the Bay Area. A two-hour flight to see his aging grandfather would relieve some stress. He would also scout two players for possible recruiting.

One player attended his old high school, Balboa High, in San Francisco. The other player was in Oakland at Skyline High School, and that had Ayman's stomach twitching.

Oakland was where Vanessa, his ex, resided. They had only spoken maybe ten words since a judge had said they were no longer man and wife. She lived near the high school he would be visiting.

His mind bounced like a pogo stick. *Should I call her? Should I go by?* Ayman called, well, he dialed, but he could not hit the talk button. Back and forth, his heart petitioned his brain to tell him what to do. *Maybe she's thinking about me? Maybe she ain't. Maybe I need to wake up and smell the coffee. Maybe I'm not her flavor anymore.*

Ayman's heart was in check, not knowing what to do. He drove

by her house, his heart slowed, but the car sped up. He even ran
a stop sign.

Ayman grew up in Daly City, California, just south of downtown San Francisco. He was born to fifteen-year-old parents
who had to live with Ayman's grandparents after he was born.
His granddad was a preacher, whose own son had made a boyish
decision. Granddad would make sure his grandson made manly
decisions and so named his grandson *Ay-man*.

Ayman's dad went into the service at sixteen and his mother at
seventeen—different branches, separate lives, distant from their
child, so Ayman grandparents' raised him.

He was a good student and a great athlete in high school, while
setting records in track, basketball, and football. He entered high
school with a six-foot-two frame, natural lean muscles, and blessed
with athletic ability. He often heard that he was like a coach on
the playing courts from his coaches. Friends called him "Coach,"
because he understood what everybody should be doing.

Young male-stud athletes draw accolades, privileges and
female attention. Ayman was humble by nature, but was not shy
with the girls. The one woman who would not chase him was
Vanessa Davis. She was a young woman he had to pursue. They
met when Ayman's high school basketball team came across the
Bay to play her school. During warm-ups, she walked into the
gym with her girlfriends, and he rolled a ball in front of her to
stop her.

He stopped to pick the ball up in front of her in a flirtatious
manner. The girlfriends swooned. Vanessa said nothing. She
didn't fall for his velvet-smooth, well-done-steak-colored skin, in
his thigh-high 1980s basketball shorts. As he ran down the court,

he looked at her in the stands after each one of his power dunks, and forty-two points later, she barely lifted an eyebrow.

After playing the high school flirting game for a while, they dated, but she never took Ayman seriously as a future mate. He was the one who thought it was more serious. He loved her and wanted her.

She lived in a household where her highly educated parents made it a point that she'd have a highly successful man to care for her. In their eyes, a professional man was a doctor or lawyer, or maybe even a preacher, but not an athlete.

While she dated other men her parents approved of, she only slept with Ayman, sharing that part of her soul with him only.

Ayman went away to college to play basketball for the University of New Mexico, and for the next three years, they stayed connected. It was before the days of frequent flyer miles, but they earned enough miles to fly free if they had been available.

On a flight to see Ayman, Vanessa was carrying news: a missed period. On her flight home, as he watched her plane lift off, she was carrying his child. He thought about his mother and father, how he never knew where they were. He had love from his grandparents, but he always wanted the love of his mom and dad; that impacted his decision of what to do.

Ayman flew home one day after she had left and asked Vanessa to marry him. She wasn't certain, but the option of raising a child as a single mother, and coming from her household that she'd grown up in did not seem to be right. They were in their early twenties, and starting a family together was not the worst thing she could do. Her answer was yes to marrying Ayman. She had grown to love him.

Two months after their wedding, Vanessa lost the baby. Ayman's senior season had started, and he was either at practices, games, or in class. She felt alone in New Mexico, and was there only because of Ayman. Depression sapped her inner strength and with that hollow feeling, she made the decision to never have another child. It was an instant wall between her and Ayman. He wanted children; he loved the thought of having their child to raise, but it was no longer in Vanessa's life plan. She could not face the thought of ever losing another child.

Vanessa just wanted to be Ayman's wife at that point; she wanted to be his only interest in life. As a married couple, they both finished college at New Mexico. Ayman was not drafted by the NBA, so they moved to Spain where Ayman played European Pro Basketball for two years.

Living abroad was a joy for the young couple. They learned enough Spanish to talk passionately and nastily to each other when they made love. It was something they did until the very last time they made love.

In time they became homesick, and returned to the Bay Area, where Ayman returned to school to get his teaching credentials. Vanessa went to work for her father's friend's law firm. Her father reminded her often that she should be in graduate school herself, so she could have her own firm.

A year later, Ayman started teaching at an inner-city school, and joined the coaching staff of the school basketball team as an assistant. Two years later, the head coach stepped down after clearly seeing that Ayman Sparks was a success. Within two seasons, the team was winning city titles and competing in the state championship tournaments.

Life was good, teaching and coaching, but the home front had more ups and downs than a ball bounced in a game. Ayman wanted children, and at first he was patient, thinking that after a few years, Vanessa would feel differently.

Vanessa took things into her own hands. She and a girlfriend said they were flying to Canada to go skiing for the weekend. She left on a Thursday night and returned on Monday. She claimed she fell and injured her lower abdomen, and she spent a few days in bed.

Ayman was concerned for his wife's health. For the first time, he missed coaching a basketball game to be with his wife. Ayman carried some guilt that she had miscarried before. From then on, whenever she didn't feel good for any reason, he waited on her hand and foot.

Sterlin, already his best friend and assistant coach, replaced Ayman for one game. Ayman kept asking her to let him take her to the doctor, but she would not go. She was out of bed a few days later, but he noticed something out of character for her—no sex; she wasn't interested.

If there was one thing that Vanessa did want from Ayman, it was plenty of sex. They were like lovers born in a fire with un-limited fuel when it came to loving each other's body. Sex was always passionate and aggressive and sometimes sounded like a street fight, spoken in a mixture of English and Spanish:

"*Besar mi culo*! Yeah, right there, daddy. You know I'm mad at you, Bésame, and lick me, yeah, ah huh, right there."

"*Entregar ese culo, ahora*. I'm gonna slap that ass again."

"Then hurt me; come on me, *dolía*!"

"Spread them legs and get that big *culo* up in the air!"

"Do it to me, baby. Oh, baby, oh baby, I'm sorry, I'll be good. Spank me harder, daddy. *Te quiero*, owe, ooh, baby."

That kind of sex was not happening after the skiing injury she said she'd suffered. Three weeks later, she wanted him inside but told him to take it easy. He was puzzled; she always wanted the pleasurable pain. He slowed down to please her as she liked. She cried during and after sex, and she wouldn't say why.

He held her tightly after they had made love, thinking she might be near her period and was just emotional, or she cried had tears of joy during an intense orgasm. He fell asleep, but she awoke him in the middle of the night.

"I had my tubes tied," she confessed

Ayman's inner essence froze. His wife. She had deceived him and stolen from him.

In return he shared things he had done in his past. He told her about other women he had been with while in college and whenever she had visited home while they were in Europe. She knew he was not Mr. Clean, but it wasn't in her face then, and it was in the past.

Hurt the one who hurts you; they turned into children acting out, "You hit me, I'm gonna hit you back." Verbal slaps to the face from two people who loved each other. They separated for all of a week, and both thought whatever happened, they still belonged to each other. What most folks do is they forgive but never forget. It kept a wedge of pain that disappeared and reappeared until the end.

Other problems began to take shape in their lives. Money became a problem. Ayman's teaching and coaching earned a nice salary, but it didn't provide the standard of living Vanessa wanted. She desired a showcase house and the adjoining lifestyle. As far as she was concerned, Ayman was the reason she was going without.

Ayman also stayed busy teaching, coaching, and maybe being distracted on purpose. Often when he did come home, it was more game film to review or out to the garage to tinker on an old car. She wanted his attention. She felt she was losing on all fronts. The only thing that kept them together were the threats of leaving each other, but that turned into foreplay and settling for the way things were.

In a short period of time, Ayman became known as one of the best coaches in the high school game. His teams, with or without great talent, won city titles and state championships.

A young Black kid, Goldlyn Mayfield, enrolled at Ayman's school, but not to play basketball. The school had a sign language program that Goldlyn needed because of hearing and speech problems.

His disabilities did not stop the young man from running track. He was great at running or jumping, but he was timid when it came to playing team sports. Kids teased him about his speech. He could not hear very well, and hearing-aids of the era were distracting while playing sports. He, also being a self-conscious teenager, wanted to avoid any more notice.

A few times someone threw a ball at the back of his head to get his attention when he played basketball, but the shy young man did very well in Ayman's physical education class. Ayman spent time teaching Goldlyn how to compensate for his lack of team basketball skills.

It did not hurt that Goldlyn was an incredible athlete, six-foot-four and two hundred pounds, and still growing. Ayman taught the shy kid tricks and secrets to make basketball easier and fun to play.

With newfound confidence Goldlyn Mayfield turned out for the basketball team—his game awkward at times—but the team rode his great athletic gifts to many wins. The team worked with Goldlyn, learning some sign language and developing signals the other teams did not understand.

In time, the student body had special hand signs they used after one of Goldlyn's high-flying dunks. They signed, then sat in total silence for about three seconds before they exploded with a big roar of approval. He could feel the gym vibrate, and his smile lit up the gym.

Ayman also helped with Goldlyn's personal life. The kid lived with his mother; he'd lost his father in a tragic accident when he was in first grade. His mother had turned into an alcoholic, leaving Goldlyn on his own often. Coach Sparks became more than a coach; he became the male mentor the young man needed. Goldlyn asked if he could live with Coach Sparks, and Vanessa actually promoted the idea helping with the legal issues. They took him in with pleasure. A solid home life gave Goldlyn even more confidence in the classroom and on the court.

The troubles between Ayman and Vanessa faded into the background. Ayman had a child in the home, even if he was older. Vanessa found herself in Goldlyn's life as a joyful responsibility. They even talked of adopting a child in the future.

The success and uniqueness of the team became front-page news along with winning more state championships. In Goldlyn's senior season, the team went undefeated, but the big schools did not come recruiting. Despite Ayman's attempts to get the big Division One schools to give him a scholarship, none stepped up. No one said it was because of his disability, but it could not have been anything else. In all-star games, Goldlyn Mayfield dominated. He highlighted with great dunks, a sweet jump shot, and with hardnosed, in-your-face defense.

The kid scored well on his SAT test, yet no big-name schools offered him a chance. Coach Bucket at East Seattle City University had seen Goldlyn play in an all-star game, and dominate a player Bucket had recruited. He approached Coach Sparks with the idea of sending Goldlyn to a junior college, one near Seattle that had a hearing and speech program. Coach Bucket promised to give Goldlyn a scholarship to ESCU in two years.

Ayman and Vanessa had become like real parents to Goldlyn, and had concerns about a promise that could be broken and sending him so far away from home.

Before a decision was made, Ayman got a call and an offer to become the head coach at that junior college. Ayman knew Coach Bucket had something to do with the job offer. It was an added attempt to get Goldlyn.

Vanessa said *hell no!* Their happiness had been a temporary thing brought on by having Goldlyn in their home. To pick up and move, when Goldlyn soon would be on his own, did not sit well with Vanessa.

She did not want to go to the Northwest. She inquired and found the Northwest had limited Black social life, entertainment and arts, as well as having no Black adult radio stations. Being in the Bay Area helped her cope with her husband's busy life as a teacher and a coach. Ayman took the job anyway; Vanessa loved Ayman and supported him by going along.

At Everett Junior College, thirty miles north of Seattle, things went like a dream. Coach Sparks won his national Junior College Championship the first year and the next. Goldlyn led the nation's junior colleges in scoring, playing like a man among boys throughout the season.

Pro agents called, assuring Coach Sparks and Goldlyn he would be a first-round draft pick if he decided to turn pro, which Ayman advised Goldlyn to do, foregoing East Seattle City University for his last two years.

On the east side of Seattle, the news was bad for Coach Bucket. East Seattle City University alumni were screaming for Coach Bucket to step down. Coach Bucket had been grooming his son to become the next head coach. Since he was also the athletic director, he'd figured it would not be a problem sliding his son into the head coaching position.

The chancellor and the alumni pleaded with Ayman to apply for the job to try to change the future of the team. Taking over a major program that needed a complete overhaul didn't cause

Ayman to question his own ability, but what would be the attitude of the watchful eyes in the Northwest community? Questions swirled and swelled like the waves of water blowing over the floating bridges during a Seattle storm.

Then there was Vanessa, the wife, who couldn't understand. She threatened to leave again. He told her that if she took some interest, she would gain the benefits of traveling, and a big bump in income. He promised to involve her in more of his life.

Ayman applied for the job, but the selection committee, for some reason, took a real long time to select a coach. Later, Ayman found out that Athletic Director Bucket had fabricated an allegation that Ayman had an ineligible player on his team. The truth prevailed, and Ayman took over as the head coach at East Seattle City University. It was the first time Coach Sparks and former Coach Bucket crossed paths in a negative way, and not the last. Vanessa left him, but she came back.

On the trip back to Washington, the plane flew over Puget Sound. Ayman adjusted the volume of his headphones, he was trying to block out his thoughts. Natalie Cole screamed, "Love is always right on time. Love is you, love is me."

While his recruiting trip went well, the mental trip kept going back and forth. Natalie could not scream loud enough, and Ayman's inner conversation stayed a notch louder. *I miss her. I know life moves on. I need to move on.* The plane banked toward Mount Rainier. Ayman looked out the window at the snowcapped rise in the sky, and he wished his loneliness would tumble down the mountainside.

7

Good Morning, No Heartache

Lois Mae sipped on her hot ginger tea in her car and waited patiently. The morning campus traffic of cars and walking students was crazy. She gave a group of students the evil eye when their horseplay almost bumped into her car.

She turned up the volume of Roberta Flack's "The First Time Ever I Saw Your Face." Lois Mae was dressed in a dark-blue, ultrasuede pantsuit. The peekaboo open-toe pumps showed off clear French toenails. She felt sexy and professional.

After inspecting her perfectly painted blood-red lips in the mirror, she picked up a book and began to read, going over her class notes as traffic moved at a snail's pace.

She looked up from her book to check if cars were moving. Her almond-shaped eyes suddenly became like round blackberries. A man as fine as she had ever visualized strolled in front of her car with a self-assured stride.

Lois Mae didn't even have to think twice about whether he was a student athlete. She knew he was a man! Her awestruck eyes followed. He wore black knit gym shorts highlighting his high on his back protruding behind. His immensely muscled calves flexed with each step.

Cars began to move, and Lois Mae was able to pull into the faculty parking lot. Her car seemed to park itself because Lois Mae never took her eyes off of the man. His face had baby-boy features but he was mature and handsome.

My, my, my, his caramel forearms look like they're models for the Black Arm and Hammer box.

When she parked, the man walked in front of her car again. The sun silhouetted the man into a huge shadow. *Damn, he looks like an Ethiopian Hercules.* She chuckled. He walked in front of where Lois Mae had parked.

Lois Mae clamped her legs tight. She was already horny, and her jackrabbit vibrator switch had broken. The new one she'd ordered had not arrived.

The man looked around, turning full circle in slow motion. Lois Mae smiled to herself. His gym short drawstrings hung on the outside and swung like a pendulum on a big clock. *Damn, I need to get my mind out of his pants.*

The man walked away. She would have a lasting memory of him and a damp panty liner to remind her. *Let me go in here and try to teach class.*

In the faculty room, a fellow teacher friend met Lois Mae for coffee.

"Good morning, Lois Mae."

"Hey, Lydia, how are you doing?"

"I'm well. You're looking good, girl, all in blue."

"Honey, you dress well, you feel good, and you never know who or what you might run into. Just like a minute ago, I was coming into the parking lot, and the perfect vision of a man came strolling across the campus. He was beautiful. I need to go in the ladies' room and dry myself off."

Lois Mae thought, *I never tell my business, but he was too fine for my own good.*

"Ooh, that fine, huh?"

A long sigh escaped from Lois Mae, she patted her chest, and nodded yes.

"Lois Mae Ilan, I know why you teach Romantic Literature. You sound like you should be writing a poem about what you saw."

They laughed and kept talking until Lois Mae decided she wanted some quiet time before class started.

She headed to the ladies' room first, then to her classroom. Her head was down reading over her class notes as she walked into her classroom.

"Excuse me, Ms.," a warm bass note vibrated in her ear. The voice tried not to startle Lois Mae, but she gasped and spread her hand across her chest in shock. The man standing in front of her was the one from the parking lot. Lois Mae's eyes became bright blackberries again, and her lips parted and held still.

The man spoke, sensing Lois Mae was overwhelmed with his unexpected presence. "Hi, my name is Sterlin Baylor, the assistant basketball coach. Are you Ms. Ilan, the professor of Romantic Literature?"

Lois Mae tried to gather herself into her professional mode. "Yes, how are you and what can I do for you, Mr. Baylor, or should I say Coach Baylor?" Lois Mae's voice floated even though she tried not to. She had to pass in front of Sterlin and turn her back to him in order to get to her desk and sit.

Sterlin thought, *Damn, she's a fine sister with some serious booty.* "I…I'm here to check on a grade. The student's name is Larentzo Sir John. There seems to be a problem, or maybe not? I just came over from the academic office, and they couldn't help me with some incomplete information listed for your class.

"Yes, Larentzo writes very good essays, but he's slow to hand in his assignments at times. I don't think he's failing, but if I remember right, he wasn't here for a few days."

Sterlin moved over in front of Lois Mae's desk. "We did have three games back to back on the road. It's a rare occurrence when we don't come back to campus after one game, but we were gone four or five days."

Lois Mae pulled her eyes off of the drawstring and looked up at the handsome face. She focused maintaining her teacher role and listened. As an educator, she always tried to lend a helping hand to students who had extracurricular activities.

Her brothers had played sports in college, and she knew the workload could be overwhelming. Lois Mae had her principles too. She would reach to help most students of color, but she knew she was not doing them any favors if she cut corners for them. "Give me a second to check my computer, and we might be able to clear this up."

"Take your time." Sterlin did not think about asking or wanting anything done that was not right. Coach Sparks thought like a teacher first, and he believed in all his players getting an education. Often Coach Sparks insisted that a kid study for a test before coming on the court for practice. The graduate student coaches' staff all had to have tutoring skills to help while on the road.

A nervous Lois Mae felt that Sterlin was standing over her, when in reality, he was standing back several feet from her desk.

His eyes scanned a Langston Hughes poster on the wall. "I haven't read any Langston Hughes in a while. I had a teacher who quoted,

It's such a

Bore

Being always

Poor..."

"Yes, his poem 'Ennui'; it's about laughing at what you haven't got when you ought to have it." She kept her eyes on her computer.

"Yeah, that's the one." He admired her fit and finish. He wished he'd worn some long pants. He felt inappropriately dressed standing before a beautiful professional woman. Ayman always accused him of never looking at a sister, but Sterlin, in fact, loved looking at Black women when they had Lois Mae's kind of beauty. She was tall, shapely and voluptuous.

Early in his life a Black woman had used him and abused him and then another one had him crawl on the ground for her every breath. She toyed with him and embarrassed him greatly, and that made him insecure. Ayman and Sterlin debated and analyzed Sterlin's unforgiving attitude about why he felt the way he did.

"Your mama was black; why would you turn your back on all sisters? Why would you judge all Black women the same, when you don't do that with other women?"

The stereotypical lines flew at him. The one line Black folks threw at him the most was: "You only with them white women because they will do anything and a sista won't."

He laughed at that one. His experience with women was, whatever the race, they were all the same, when it came to what a woman would or would not say or do. He knew almost all his white male friends were dominated by their wives.

Now he chose women he would never take home to Momma on purpose. He chose women he had no chance of falling in love with. He could find the same in any woman, no matter the race, but he played into the same stereotyping he was so often accused of.

The kind of woman who woke up in Sterlin's bed was most of the time, fine, voluptuous, and non-Black. Sterlin was conflicted. Since coming to Seattle, he had gone into overdrive. It was just as he joked about something he had read: "Women dropped their panties, like raindrops fall in Seattle."

Sterlin always sensed or had a paranoid feeling that Black women knew he was into white women. Lois Mae had not given

him that look of contempt he usually got from Black women...
yet. It did seem that sisters knew his preference, and gave him
that sorry son-of-a-bitch eye-roll. *Well, I'm here on a professional
situation. But then again, that never stopped a sista from giving me the
stank-eye.*

Ayman's ex-wife, Vanessa, who still treated Sterlin as part of
her family, told him, "A Black woman is not going to treat you
funky, if you at least acknowledge her presence. It's when Black
men are with a woman of a different race, and you act as if you
don't see us. That pushes our buttons. If you're acting as if you
love the woman you're with and don't disrespect a sista in the
mix of it, we don't care who you're with. We are still your aunties,
sisters, and other relations to you."

"How long have you been on staff, Ms. Ilan?"

"I've been here since '99."

"I came here in '02 with Coach Sparks when he took over the
team. I'm surprised we haven't met before, or at least seen each
other around campus."

"Well, it is a sprawling campus. It has been something else ever
since they built the three strip-mall alleys running through the
campus."

"Yeah, only in America, a major college has shopping malls and
food courts all through its campus grounds." They both chuckled
as Lois Mae began writing some notes.

"I believe, I met the head coach's wife at a couple of functions
before."

"Yeah, you may have."

"The team has been doing very good the last couple of years."

"Oh, you follow the team?"

"Being rather tall myself I'm very well-versed at the game, but
I have to admit, I haven't followed the team much this year. How's
the team doing?"

"We're getting better. You should support your team sometime, maybe even this Saturday when we play Washington. It's for bragging rights in the city. If there are no ineligibility problems for Larentzo, it will help keep us on the right track."

Lois Mae kept her eyes on her computer screen and writing to keep from looking at the man standing at her desk. She thought she picked up the scent of cocoa butter, and she had visions of her rubbing his body down. She shook as if she had a chill.

"You cold?" he asked.

Out of the corner of her eye, she caught the two drawstrings on his shorts again. "No, but should you be walking around in shorts in winter?" *Why did I say that? Ugh.*

"Ooh."

She thought about what was behind the swinging drawstrings. *Have mercy!* "I'm sorry, this computer is slow." The computer wasn't slow, but her mind was on overload.

"It's okay. Were you driving a Chrysler 300, black and burgundy?"

"Ah, yes." *Oh shit, he saw me watching him.*

"Nice grill. I drive a Dodge Magnum with the hemi in black."

"Magnum, huh? With a big motor? Oh, does that ever sound so manly." An awkward silence followed, then they both laughed. "I'm sorry, I should not have said that." Now she felt she could look at him since they had shared some humor.

"Yeah, yeah, I heard that comment a few times before. Your front license plate holder reads '*Player for Life.*'" Sterlin flashed his big grin exposing two big dimples.

"Everybody has a story."

"And yours is? Concerning the license-plate holder, if you don't mind." He was smiling in a way that made her relax.

She inhaled a big breath. "My ex-husband had it on the car that went to me in our divorce…a few years ago. I have since traded in two cars, but have kept the plate holder. *'Player for Life'* has a different meaning than what my ex had in mind."

"I guess that's why he became an ex, huh…you don't have to answer that." Instantly Sterlin sensed he had made Lois Mae a bit uncomfortable.

"Thank you. Oh, here it is. I see where Larentzo has not done a very important essay, and I can't pass him until I have the paper in my hand."

"Well, in all honesty, I don't want you to make any special allowances."

"Oh, I won't, but if I can have the essay in hand by noon Friday, I'll pass him, and I'll make sure the academic office will be notified. I must say, though, you should check with the system administrator over there. In no way should he be declared in-eligible because of this one grade not being registered."

"Thank you so much. He'll have his essay in on time. I'll make sure of it."

"That's good, I'm glad I could help. If I come to a game, I'd like to see a win."

"Cool, thank you. Maybe I'll see you at the game." Lois Mae rolled her lips in and out hoping her lipgloss was smooth. Sterlin stared for a moment. There was silence between them. Sterlin was not flirting, an hoped she did not think he was. That made him nervous.

She was nervous; she wanted to flirt with him. A couple of students walked into the classroom. "Well, do you guys—the coach and his wife, your staff, do you hang out somewhere in town after games?"

Sterlin started to say that Ayman and Vanessa had divorced, but he avoided the subject. "If we win we have been known to show up at Gracie's in Bothell. It's a nice little Mexican cantina and lounge with live jazz. Ms. Lois Mae Ilan, it's been my pleasure. We will make sure you have that essay on time."

Sterlin walked from the door. She watched out the corner of her eye, his butt riding high on his back. She started to sing in a low volume, "Good Morning Heartache" by Billie Holiday, then she replaced a line with, "Good Morning No Heartache, what's new?"

She smiled, and because she felt damp, she decided to go to the restroom again before class started. She also wanted to write a poem first before the inspiration changed. Her short interaction with Sterlin was her inspiration, but she wanted to express her interpretation of the perfect man. She typed:

MAN ON FIRE
He's a hot man
His image alone makes a woman sweat
He's smooth, but not a criminal
He inspires daydreams
A walk, intense eyes, a sideways glance, the rollin' of his lips, his build
He's hot
Visualizing viral power in how he steps
His shoulders wide enough to carry any woman's load
When a woman closes her eyes she sees him in her sleep
Them lips, the visual of his lips melts mamas and daughters with his apple curves, and fulfilling-is-ness'
His creativity, a woman knows God made that man differently and specially
His touch, a woman knows he's got proficiencies that other men lack
He's hot, so damn hot
And when he opens his mouth, his voice is magic, His voice, it slides into a woman and makes her heart beat fast, and takes her breath away
He's hot

8
Love and Happiness

"Ah, Vanita, I...I was wondering would join me for the Al Green concert? It would be such a waste of tickets if I don't have a date."

"William, you and I both know you don't have any problem finding someone to hang on your arm." *Why do all these lawyers flirt with me all day, then they go right over to Alicia's courtroom and do the same with her?* "I saw you last week having lunch in a booth with Doreen, our muscle-bound security guard. Is that who you wanted last week?

William avoided her comment. "Ah, Vanita, a brother finding a good woman is not all that easy." The assistant prosecutor gave Vanita his standard smooth-operator BS that included starting each sentence with "ah," because he was lying or searching for what to say. She had witnessed him in court.

She mocked him. "Ah, ah, I know it's hard to find a good man."

"So let us go hear Al Green talking about a little Love and Happiness. 'Someone's on the phone. Three o' clock in the morning... Talkin' about how she can make it right.'"

She laughed. *That would be another reason I wouldn't want to go to the concert with him and take a chance he'd sing along out of key at the same time as Al Green.* "Ah, I see you like that part."

"Ah, that's the only part I know."

He straightened his suit while he looked over Vanita's shoulder. She turned her body to the side to look at whatever he was trying to look at; she raised her eyebrows, but not in shock. Doreen, the security guard down the hall, was waving at William.

Vanita walked toward the elevator, and William walked in the direction of the object in his eyes.

Men just know there's another one more willing, but what they don't comprehend is more willing does not mean more able.

All kinds of men did double-takes as she walked through the courthouse. Political men and men in trouble with the law, from traffic infractions. *Men everywhere! You would think there's one for me.* A smile stayed on her face, but she was not happy

Vanita grew up seeing all the things she wanted and dreamed of having. Her father treated her mother like a queen. It seemed her father was always doing something for her; from polishing her shoes, washing and waxing Mom's car, to rubbing her feet.

Vanita often caught Mom and Dad making out with long passionate kisses anywhere all the time. She liked to tease her mom and dad, even trying to pull them apart while they were kissing.

Vanita told them one day, "I can't believe that I'm an only child, with you and Daddy all over each other all the time."

Dad responded, "Baby, me and your mama wanted all the time we could have being next to each other."

Vanita witnessed both her mom and dad dealing with a changing America, Northwest style. Living and growing up in the sixties and seventies, her dad worked at Boeing Aerospace as a welder. He encountered volumes of racism but Vanita noticed he never let it show that it bothered him. He would tell her, "It's their problem, not mine."

Living in a mostly white community, neighbors feared Vanita's mom, because Mom would get in the face of snooty poop-butt kids and scare the crap out of them; the same went for their parents.

Mom would tell anyone who threatened to call the police, "Remember, I will get out." No one ever called the police. Vanita herself dealt with the ignorance of whites, especially white boys or men, in how they spoke with disrespect, but she had learned how to handle it all because of the example set by her parents.

Just outside the big doors of the downtown Seattle Courthouse, light raindrops fell, but that did not stop Vanita from waiting for her best friend, Alicia, a courthouse reporter too. She and Alicia made it to the park, and they began to eat their lunches. Alicia was excited. She paced in front of Vanita when she spoke, "Girl, there was this new attorney in my courtroom today. He played the shy thing to an Academy Award, though."

Alicia wore a huge '70s throwback Afro. It flopped around when she spoke, using her body and hand. She had an excitable voice. "Honey, I had to go up to him and introduce myself. He smelled so good, felt like I was tasting vanilla extract every time I opened my mouth." Alicia smacked her lips loudly.

"You're bad. It sounds to me like he might be married."

A man walked by in an oversized hoodie and pressed name-brand baggy jeans. He and Alicia checked each other. He flashed a "What's up" smile and nod. She sucked in her bottom lip, looked over the top of her eyeglasses, and finger-combed her 'fro.

"He's too old to be wearing 'thug-ery' clothes." Vanita scolded Alicia for paying too much attention to the man. "That man has to be damn near forty, and he's sagging harder than a teenager. And the plaid Timberlands...please, somebody. And you looking at him like he something to eat, stop."

"I was just looking, not jaywalking, officer. Please don't give me a ticket." Alicia's lips went to the side. "Now, as I was saying before you pulled out your badge, nah, if he were married, he would have hit on me like it was his job. Oh, and I checked for ring marks. Besides, he's a lawyer; he would never lie…right?" She and Vanita laughed. "Anyway, the truth for me is his Visa, and Nordstrom card maxed out." Alicia smiled while nodding approval to her train of thought

"That was not pretty." Vanita gave Alicia her *you know better* stare. Alicia took a deep breath, and pouted.

"Yer right, but if I'm gonna get played, I wanna get paid."

"It's not what they can do for you, honey, or what they can buy. For me, I need a man who's going to be crazy about me," Vanita said.

"Well, what is wrong with a brother being able to take care of you? After all that candlelight and bubble bath has run down the drain, what does he do for you? You should at least have a man who can buy you a Sealy Posturepedic mattress, and silk sheets. And then he should be able to rock your world on them sheets."

"You need to learn a thing or two. I need more than a man showing off his athletic skills, or his wallet. I don't want to talk about it."

A long silence passed while the two women ate their lunches. Vanita's and Alicia's minds traveled away and came back.

"Vanita, I always let you tell me about myself, so let me tell you something. You're going to have to trust a man again, and you don't trust men. I know your vision of the perfect love fell through. That ex-husband, he didn't know what was going on with you. I know you don't want to talk about it, but, you're getting better, right? You take your meds, right? All you have to be is honest about what you need.

"You yourself have said, it's hard to find the kind of man you want at church. It's because men at church are all about control.

Shoot, half the married men at church try tired-ass lines on me. Some of those 'married' church brothers see all this butt and lose their minds to see if I'll give some up."

Vanita looked up at the clouds moving back in, and said, "Two things: I don't want to feel bad because I'm a woman who can be emotional sometimes. And yes, I think I'm getting better. Also, I'm not apologizing for wanting a man who at least has a spiritual soul.

"I know that many of the men at church treat their wives like second-class citizens. When the sisters at church get together and let their hair down, that's all you hear. A lot of men come on with charm and the reverence of the Lord. Then they either become stiff as a board or act like they're your god after they've signed and sealed the deal."

Alicia shook her head, sending her hair into a frenzy. "Then why are you so hardcore about finding a churchgoing man? What if he's a good-hearted man, and he believes in God? Couldn't you work with that?"

Vanita smiled for a long moment. "Yes, that would work, and some good sex, too, because I need some. I need some bad. My fingers are getting tired!" Vanita laughed and peered through the trees watching the clouds stir and spoke to the sky. "God, you and me, we okay, right?"

"Girl, God knows what time it is. He ain't mad at ya. He put those feelings in you. God ain't mean like that, to have your body and mind craving. You and I and most other women are sitting up in church fanning ourselves and shaking our legs." Vanita knew it was the truth and kept listening.

"I understand how you feel, I do. My man needs to be warm, understanding, affectionate, and he needs to talk to me. And yeah, if he wants to be a freak, I'll be his." Vanita smiled. "You feel better to get that out? Now, can I finish my lunch? I have to go back to work, with you making me think about sex and too much about everything else. You are not helping me when I already admitted that I need some."

"I want you to be happy. We'll just have to keep praying for a man to fulfill all your needs. Okay?"

"All right, now let me finish my lunch. This conversation is way too hot, when it's so cool out here."

Alicia reached over and hugged Vanita before she responded. "Maybe I'm taking out some of my frustration on you. I guess I'm still mad at that fool who ripped my heart a new—"

"Alicia, your mouth, ooh. Now it's my turn to tell you about yourself. I have to say there is no reason to be blaming him for what you already knew. Jerome is a paralegal, not a lawyer. He had the warning signs written all over him. All over him!"

"His image should have told you to run; muscles bulging in an untailored suit. He's still wearing the Kiddie Curl on top of his head and shaved sides. You met the brother at a bar where lawyers hang out. Hmm, I guess that was close enough, huh?"

Alicia deflected and finger-combed her Afro again, as Vanita finished her rant, "You picked one of the wannabes."

Alicia pouted her lips and let her words crawl. "I know, I know. But, well, he didn't really say he was a lawyer. He said he worked for the legal department at Microsoft, and I just ran with it."

"Yes, you did let him misrepresent," Vanita said. "The only bar exam he knows about is the bar he bought you drinks at. I know a lot of women start calling men dogs just because one fake brother sucked them emotionally and sometimes financially dry. I got my issues with men, but sometimes we do this to ourselves. We set the drama in play with our own insecurities." Alicia looked at her with dismay.

"Yes, that includes me. I got my issues." Vanita's mind floated away to the last time she tried to have a relationship. *I tortured that man. I hope one day he forgives me. But his thing didn't get hard. It made me feel…as if I didn't turn him on.*

Vanita enjoyed the last few minutes in silence; she could revisit parts of her past. She tried to make sense out of the one relationship she'd had after her divorce. It was confusing: was it him or was it her? She had maddening thoughts. *When I asked him to get the blue pill, he called me a nymphomaniac. I just wanted to do it every day—all day.*

Vanita smiled wide and then chuckled as if someone had cracked a good joke. Alicia looked at her to let her in on the joke.

The women stood and headed back into the courthouse. Vanita looked in the direction of the King Street Station. She was thinking she and her son should catch the train to Canada for the weekend. She had read a good book about a man who found love in Vancouver after he had ridden the train there. Alicia broke her concentration. "Girl, you know the lawyer I was telling you about who was in my court today?"

"Yes, you scoped him out. So, when are you two going out?"

"Well, I told him to meet us for drinks at The Musicquarium Lounge this Friday."

"Wait, what's this 'us' thing?"

"You might like this guy. He's nice."

Vanita stopped her walk and shook her head. "Why are you not going after this man who graced your courtroom with such splendor?"

"I think he might be more your type."

"You do, huh?"

"You know how you like your men all soft-spoken, bald, tall and athletic-looking."

They started walking again. "What kind of mess are you trying to start?" Vanita glanced at Alicia's smirk.

"Come on, you'll see he's cute. Trust me."

"Trust you, huh? I don't understand why you and him are not going for a drink."

"You know I like 'em short and stocky, the kind of man with no neck. You know I like me some left tackle or inside linebacker. Those linemen who bend over and their big booties and thighs spread in them shiny football pants. I just want to wrestle 'em and get pinned underneath."

"Why is that?"

"'Cause I got all this junk in the trunk, and I need a man strong enough and low enough. I need a man low to the ground to pick up all this behind, and wide enough to cover it." Both women stopped to laugh. Vanita had to cover her face behind a magazine she was laughing so hard. Alicia looked behind her to make sure no one was looking. She slapped her protruding butt hard and started singing, "So high you can't get over it, so low you can't get under, bow-wow-wow-yeppie-yi-ya-bow-wow-wow-yeppie-yi-yo yeppie-yi-ya."

Vanita looked around to see if anybody was watching. "To think at one time you wore hot pants on all that," Vanita teased.

"Shoot, I still can. You just ain't gonna see me, but my next down lineman will. My backside keeps 'em howling."

"Girl, you do need a man!"

"Come on, we haven't gone out after work in a long time. So, Friday, huh?"

"I'll tell you what; you go with me to the women's Christian conference, and I'll go with you for a drink. But hey, no promises about me and this man you're talking about."

"All you have to do is just meet him."

9

If You Don't Know Me By Now

Ayman sat on a stool in his garage. The NPR radio program, "Fresh Air," had just run a show on the Philadelphia Sound. The show ended with Harold Melvin & the Blue Notes singing "If You Don't Know Me By Now." Ayman turned up the sounds.

He sat admiring his brand-new Kawasaki ZX14 motorcycle. The bike was one of the benefits of having a good friend—a college buddy who owned a dealership had allowed Ayman to purchase the bike at dealer cost. Ayman now owned a Harley V-Rod and a Kawasaki ZX14. The car he drove was a classic 1967 Jaguar. Playing in the garage with his toys was his relaxation outlet away from basketball.

His friend who owned the dealership, Tylowe Dandridge, had called and let him know he had some concert tickets he could not use. Ayman thought about whom he might like to take with him. He decided to call Sonya, an old friend.

"Hey, it's me, Ayman. Speak up; I can't hear you, old lady." Sonya was one of the friends Ayman and Vanessa had shared while they were married. Sonya was the real estate agent who had helped them find a house when Ayman took over the coaching job.

She and Ayman were like play cousins because they had grown up in the same neighborhood. They teased one another about everything and hung out from time to time.

"If you clean out your ears, you could hear."

"What are you talking about?" Ayman asked.

"You got selective hearing and memory."

"Whatever! If you weren't a woman, I'd kick your butt for being a butt."

"Yeah well, I got God in my corner," she said, "and you and all the world's army can't touch this. Hell, got one arm behind my back, so does it sound like I'm scared?"

They were good friends and teased each other. He trusted her to give him her female opinions without the personal attachment. He also trusted Sonya because she did not hit on him after Vanessa left, like many of her other female friends had.

"Hey, I need a woman to come do something with me. You were last on the list."

"Last, my ass!"

"Oh, if you're one of the Lord's soldiers, you might want to use words other than 'ass,' but maybe all you have to do is say a Hail Mary."

"Don't be trying to judge me, mister, with all that BS you be talking."

"Ooh, such words from a sweet little churchgoing girl, but then you know what they say about those women?"

"No, what do they say, smart ass?"

"All the freaks are at church."

"Then you should be going to somebody's church, being the freak you are."

"Freak? You think you know me? Please." He sat back on his stool in the garage and listened to Sonya.

"What part am I wrong about, church or you being the freak?" Sonya laughed hard. "You and Vanessa couldn't keep your hands off each other. It's a wonder you two didn't stay married for that nasty sex. Oops, I just let you know I know your business."

"Yeah, I know women kiss and tell. You really think you know me. By the way, are there any fine ladies at church?"

"You need to come to see for yourself."

Sonya, Ayman and Vanessa all went to the same church when Ayman was married and he wasn't involved in a basketball activity on Sunday. They attended the World Peace Faith Center in Seattle's Central District, where at one time, most of the Blacks lived in the fifties through the eighties.

As in most cities, gentrification changed the face of a community. Black churches, a few Black businesses and fewer and fewer Black families now resided in the Central District. Sonya lived in the Central District; Ayman would have chosen to live on the Eastside near the school.

Outside, the rain started to pound, and he had to press the phone closer to his ear. "I told you I have a couple of reasons I don't make it to church; one, I live on the Eastside."

Sonya's voice went up a notch. "Three hundred-plus people find their way there from all over Seattle so you don't have an excuse. Now come on back to church."

"I'll think about it."

"You're a lying ass!"

"Speak up; I'm having trouble hearing you. Speak loud enough for the Lord to hear you." He listened to Sonya rant some more about him coming to church while he opened the Jaguar car doors to look for a book.

"You wanna meet a woman; there are a bunch of new interesting women who joined the church since you last visited. Come back to church and I'll look into hooking you up. See, I'm trying a new game plan with you."

Ayman looked up at the wall around his garage at all the posters of beautiful women. His eyes fixed on posters of a young Jayne Kennedy and Pam Grier and other beauties of that period, then his eyes admired the newer classic beauties Regina King, Nia Long, Sanaa Lathan, and Sade.

"Answer this question," he said. "When you say 'interesting,' do these interesting women sit a little wide or have a bunch of babies by different daddies?"

Sonya's sarcastic tone deactivated, and she sounded hurt. "That is so sad you would think such about people at church, serving the Lord. What you just said was awful. It's not something I thought I would hear from your mouth. Strange I've always known you to be accepting of people, no matter what their situation was in life. Are you that miserable because you're lonely?"

Ayman felt the self-inflicted sting of his hurtful, ignorant and not funny joke. "I know that was bad. I think maybe I've been watching too many bad comedians."

"Who you saying sorry to, me or the Lord? Maybe if you had been married to one of these slightly imperfect sisters from church, you might be happy right now. I know Vanessa was picture-perfect. Her good looks didn't do anything for the longevity of your marriage, now did it; nor did you not having children." There was a long numbing silence on the phone. If Ayman had had a dog's tail, he would have tucked it under.

"Look, Ayman, I'm sorry if I hurt your feelings. You know your ex was all the things most men want, fine and all that, but—"

"Stop, please and cut me some slack. I loved my wife, but it just didn't work out. Also, I do like women who might be a little extra wide or thick, and I don't mind children if they are well-behaved.

But I did say something really stupid. I don't feel that way about any woman. I'm not Mr. Perfect."

Sonya's tone became less hostile. "You know I don't have anything against her or you. You just pissed me off with your negative comment about the women."

"So where's your Christian motto, 'turn the other cheek'?"

"I'm going to use your sometime hearing affliction, and ignore you on that one. But I have to get in your butt—women having a bunch of babies by different daddies; that's some stereotypical BS I expect to hear from a less-educated person."

"Like I said, I'm sorry."

"Ayman, how do you think it makes a woman feel to hear that? At the end of your insult, the word 'daddy' came into play. Ain't none of us women made a baby by ourselves. You could have been one of those daddies, who were not around being a husband and father. I'll take that back, not you; I'll give you credit up front, because I know you wanted children. But us women—some of us, wanting to be loved, end up with men who run away from their responsibility. Some of us keep trying to find Mr. Right, and we can end up having children by more than one of Mr. Wrong." Sonya knew she had kicked his butt enough, and joked herself. "Thank goodness somebody's having children. Otherwise, where would you get your basketball players? Now get your butt to church so some woman can spank your bad butt."

"You shouldn't be calling the kettle black. I think I remember you saying something about, somebody was spankin' your booty good. Ah, what's his name, the Rastafarian brother you said had you speakin' in tongues and doing all kinds of nasty."

Sonya screamed, "Stop and leave me alone!" Ayman's laugh became sinister.

"Oh, keep laughing. Forget you! You think you're gonna turn this around on me? I'm not telling you anything anymore. Don't let me tell you how I know you're a freak."

"What?"

"You do remember Vanessa and I went to the same hairdresser. She spread all your freaky-ass highlights while she was getting some hair highlights." Sonya had her own little sinister laugh. "Ooh boy, she told on you. Shit, every woman in there getting her hair fried wanted to be laid by you." Ayman got another good dose of her laughter.

Feeling a bit embarrassed, Ayman tried to change the subject again. "Okay, let me try this again. Are there any fine ladies at church, no matter their status in life?"

"Ayman, I know women are checking you out wherever you go. A good-looking single brother with a job? Please!"

"Oh there you go, talking about brothers without jobs."

"And I add to that, an opinionated man." They both chuckled.

"You should know Sterlin called me and told me you wouldn't make a move if a woman was standing butt-naked in front of you with a million dollars."

"What kind of stupid crap is that? I'd take her and the millions!"

"Spoken like a true man."

"Yeah, well, I suppose if I was like Sterlin, you'd be okay with that."

"No, I pray one day he gets saved."

"Don't count on it. He still has a hang-up about the spankin' that girl put on his heart twenty years ago. He scares away from anything darker than a fading tan."

"But it could have been a Roseanne Barr, Madonna, or Olive Oyl to hurt his little feelings." Sonya had contempt in her voice.

Ayman laughed and snorted. "Olive Oyl, no, I don't think so. Sterlin likes Sasquatch-size booties of the female kind."

"Just like a brother, looking at the butt as if it's brain-size, but damn, Sasquatch?"

Ayman laughed hard before he spoke again. "Well, my dear, is that why you're so smart because of the size of your butt?"

"Then you need to grow a bigger butt, to find a woman to whip your butt."

"That is a bit dramatic. Hey, I'd like a woman in my life, but don't need a woman messing with my focus. She's got to be put together in reality, not just a pretty poster."

"Get off your high horse."

"Hey, we're both in our forties, and that changed everything to a numbers game of who's left that you're compatible with."

"That's life. Do you think the woman you want is going to knock on your door? How about you go knock on her door? Get past looks and the infatuation."

"I wasn't born yesterday. All you're saying is elementary. I'm just saying I need to avoid women that are bitter about their past experiences with men."

Sonya said slowly, "Don't you think women are going through the same thing? Most grown men don't act grown-up."

"Point taken."

"Then you need to keep an open mind."

There was silence for a moment before Ayman remembered why he'd called. "Anyway, as usual, we end up talking about the same thing all the time. I called because I have some tickets. Would you and a friend like to see Nona Hendryx, the woman from the LaBelle days? Also, opening for Nona is another funky soul sister, N'dambi."

"I'd love to see Nona. I think I heard of the other woman when I was in L.A. Where are they going to be?"

"The Triple Door, this Friday, which is good, because the season will be getting crazy starting Saturday night."

"You guys play Washington this Saturday, right? You know, my son is bugging me to take him and his friends to the game. Can you help get us some good seats?"

"I'll have some tickets at will-call. What about the concert?"

"Yeah, it sounds good. I'll drum up a lady friend."

10

Love Me Like a Man

Sterlin drove down the road listening to Bonnie Raitt's guitar rocking a blues-like funk. Her voice professed the blues over a man:

The men that I've been seeing, baby

Got their soul up on a shelf

His Texas roots dipped deep into blues music. He didn't really listen to the words in the verses, but he loved the chorus.

Love Me Like a Man

His foot stomped the gas pedal, and the hemi engine roared; the sound of power fed more of his ego. The black Dodge Magnum passed its reflection in a window. Sterlin watched as if he was flexing his muscles in a mirror. He cut off a car to make a turn into the school's sports complex. Sterlin rolled up the window and continued to listen.

Jamming along, he pulled out his cell phone. "Dora, hey, it's me, Sterlin. So we are all clear; the teacher has sent over her grade. Cool. Could I have a copy of some documentation that the academic office has put on their seal of approval? We can't play Larentzo Sir John under any cloud of suspicion.

"Yes, Dora, I do remember. Yeah, it was about this time last year. Oh yeah, I can still feel that ass." Sterlin listened to the woman as he got out of his car. He grabbed his gym bag from the back of his car. While closing down the back hatch, another conversation entered his ears.

"Coach, you almost ran me over." It was a senior on the team, Hafeez Rasheed.

Sterlin nodded at the young man, keeping his conversation on the phone. "How about you deliver the proof? Yeah, the same place as last year." He lightly chuckled. "I only got a few minutes. Cool, I'll see you in about fifteen."

Sterlin turned his attention to Hafeez, who had walked on. He jogged up behind the young man. "Hafeez, hey, your coach just set a bad example, driving like that. This would be one of those 'Do as I say, and not what I do moments.'"

The young man was one of the team leaders, and could have been the star if not for Larentzo. Hafeez's nature allowed him to take a back seat and be a *team player* first. "Coach Baylor, I should not question your driving. It is nearing the end of Ramadan, and I can be a bit on edge. Many blessings to you, Coach."

Sterlin was reminded of how it used to be that youth were that respectful of their elders. It made him feel old and morally bankrupt for all the things that he was about.

"Hafeez, is there something I can do for you? How can I help? I know you're tired and somewhat weak from fasting along with games and practices."

"Coach, we Muslims have our best energy after our morning meal before dawn. With our games usually being after sunset, I have not been at full strength."

"Let me look into a few things. You are family, and family comes first."

"Thank you, sir."

Sterlin nodded and walked ahead hurriedly. He entered the rear of the sports complex. At the end of the hallway, he unlocked the field sound-booth door.

Moments later, the door reopened slowly, and in walked a tallish Asian woman. She smiled with her eyes and soft expression, then she kissed Sterlin. Without saying a word, she lifted Sterlin's shirt and ran her tongue across his abs for a bumpy ride.

Her skirt dropped while her tongue kept bathing his firm stomach. Her body's curvaceous hips were spread; her breasts— her bra was losing the battle of support.

She squatted, and pulled down everything he had on, then she took him into her hands fist over fist; she stroked and milked him. He was thick, and she could feel his pulse when she cupped his balls, but he was not hard. She wanted to relive last year's quickie behind the gym bleachers, but he wasn't hard. She sucked and licked harder, mechanically, with no rhythm, while she jerked on the shaft awkwardly.

He looked down, annoyed. She wasn't skilled, and it didn't feel good. But in the past, lack of skills from a woman had never stopped him from getting a hard-on.

Why am I doing this? I'm stuck with her ass behind some bleachers like I'm in high school. Damn, I'm a sorry-ass ho!

She was not going to give up as he began hardening.

Damn, let me get this over.

He lifted her up from her knees and spun her around. He ripped open a condom, and then stroked his dick to make it even harder. It helped to watch her showing off her ass, spreading her cheeks and watching her getting nasty playing with her openings while making grunting sounds. He slid the condom on with still some difficulty, because his dick was not very hungry for her.

He put his hands on her hips, and slapped her ass. He was

pissed at himself, but still pushed into her wetness. Her grunt was a nasty growl. He humped hard feeling his hard-on turning log stiff. She liked it rough and she got it with him going faster and harder. She was massaging her clit in a rapid motion, matching his aggression.

She started holding a long note that led to her saying two words: "I'm Cumm-inng." She lost what little rhythm she had. She moved the wrong way and with her already being much shorter, her awkward move made his manhood pop out; he was done anyway.

A moment later, with him taking off the rubber, he said, "Dora, we're going to have to do this another time. I have to go."

"Oh, I came so hard, but you didn't get a chance to."

"Hey, another time."

She left but not before she tried to plan another rendezvous. Sterlin blew her off.

I wasn't even horny; I did it to be doing it. This babe didn't even turn me on, but as soon as she offered it, I hit it. He shook his head. *Damn.*

Sterlin walked slowly with his head down as if someone had hurt his feelings. He was empty at the moment. He walked toward the gym as if he were marching to a date with the hangman. He'd had a few too many of those moments lately.

11

Meeting in the Ladies Room

Lois Mae opened the fridge door, and if leftovers could talk, they said, "No, you don't want to eat me." She closed the fridge and reached for the phone, then pushed auto-dial.

"What's on the stove?" Lois Mae's voice sang through the phone.

A freezer-burn voice returned, "Damn, don't you ever cook?"

"Skillet, I just asked. What's wrong with you? I thought we'd hang out. I'll bring a salmon I got in the freezer." One of the things that cemented the ladies' friendship—food.

"I said, do you ever cook? It seems to me I'm always the one cooking."

Why is she talking like this? "Okay, tell me what's really going on. You're having a bad day, for sure. Is it your period, or did some man get his, and you didn't get yours? Because…nah, wait a minute. It can't be your period, because we both had our periods at the same time last week. "What's going on?" Lois Mae asked.

"Well, I haven't had my period." Silence of still air blocked the phone line. Lois Mae waited for Skillet to talk. "Lois Mae, I'm in trouble, I know it. This is the second month in a row. There are times I'll miss a month, but it always comes on time the next month. I'm on edge, and my nerves are shot. I didn't mean to go off on you, but..." A low volume-wailing cry entered into Lois Mae's ear.

"I assume you were on some kind of protection. More than one if it's not a regular dude!"

A feeble voice warbled. "Umm, I ah" is all Lois Mae got in return.

"Didn't you go on that Depo-Provera shot and..." Searing verbal heat flew into Skillet's ear. "You're not fourteen and humping in the backseat of some car."

A crying plea insisted it wasn't like that. "Lois Mae, I did go on the birth control injection, but maybe I didn't wait long enough before it would stop pregnancy. And shit, I told you how big Bbwadene is. Sometimes rubbers would break."

"Sometimes? Bbwadene. The African?" *What is wrong with this girl?* "I thought you stopped seeing him, because he got..." Lois Mae screamed, "Married!" With anger spewing out, she had the recollection of being on the wrong side of Skillet's past. "And ain't he the one that hit you or threatened you?"

"It was my fault, he saw me with another man." Her words tumbled.

"What the hell, that's okay, huh? You know we're friends. I didn't need to hear this." Lois Mae had an uncomfortable feeling while talking. She had long since forgiven Skillet, and forgiven herself, too, for letting herself be a victim. Her friend was walking down the wrong path again. She had not learned, and listening to her stupidity hurt.

"And Bbwadene don't live with his wife anymore. They're separated," Skillet pleaded for understanding.

"Ah, huh, right, how many times have you gone to his place?

You haven't, right, I'm sure of it. I suppose he comes to see you right after work, eats your food, and breaks rubbers off in your ass, and never stays the night, right?" Lois Mae laughed at the rules of the player's game. "Didn't you tell me his African name means 'big dog'?"

Lois Mae let up on her scolding. "Okay, okay, I know you're hurting. Look, come over. I'll cook. We'll sit down and talk about this problem. But let me warn you, you know what I'm going to say, and you know what you need to do if it isn't too late."

Dead air plugged the phone line again.

"Please don't go off on me anymore. I know you care, but please, I'm already freaking out. My old friend Roberta is here at my place, in the bathroom at the moment."

"Who?" Lois Mae knew of whom she was speaking.

Skillet knew Lois Mae knew too. "Yeah, Roberta. You used to say she would do Smokey the Bear because he was big and dark."

"Oh her—yeah."

"She might be coming with me."

"Ah-huh." Lois Mae had a little devil on one shoulder who spoke for her real feelings inside her head. *Trifling, inconsiderate, man-chasing bitch. She was all over every Black…dick or wallet. All the while she claimed she had a man.*

"I remember how she acted at the Prince concert after-party," Lois Mae said as a reminder.

"Yeah, it was pitiful."

Damn, I don't want her in my place.

"Is it okay if she came with me?"

"Hey, have her come on over. We'll all sit down together and help you with this."

Skillet revealed some more news. "Roberta is five, almost six months' pregnant, and you can hardly tell."

Lois Mae snickered. The bad devil on her shoulder finally spoke aloud through Lois Mae. "That woman is a ticking time bomb waiting to blow up someone's life. One would hope her biological clock would never have started ticking. I hope the daddy's genetics is better than hers. Otherwise, it will be one slow, chubby, confused kid. Boy, I hope the daddy got a brain. Then again, he had sex with her. Damn, another child with an uphill battle coming into the world. I assume the daddy's Black?"

"Mae, that is all so mean. That was so un-you. Stop! If that child needed your help, you would be the first to help."

Lois Mae wished she could rewind her words. Feeling ugly inside, her mind clicked over to the angel on her other shoulder.

Dear God, what's wrong with me? That was pure ugly. I don't know what to say. Please forgive me. You know I wish no child ill will. Sometimes the thought of some people having a child is hard on my soul.

"Skillet, my real issue is I'm hurting for you and I'm deflecting. I'm sorry for saying those things about your friend. I don't always talk and think like an angel. God will forgive me! Will you? Now come on over. Let me share some interesting news; not like what's going on with you, though."

"What?"

"I met a man."

Skillet's voice sang out and through the phone, "Who, another one of your computer dates? Tell me."

"Hey, don't let that woman hear my business. My dating life is A and B conversation, and I don't want the woman to hear or see any of my business."

"Relax. She's still in the bathroom. Now do you have something to drink?"

"I have some wine, but maybe you don't need to drink, but get on over here." Lois Mae pushed the hang-up button. She shook her head in disbelief. *She is my friend, and I need to be there for her. Anyone who knew how we became friends would think my head is full of Cheerios. But I can't let her drama get in my way too much.*

Since Lois Mae's introductory chat with Sterlin, his voice resonated in her thoughts non-stop. She wanted to talk to him but he just had been offered an invitation to watch a game. *I guess that's not really an invitation. Maybe I should have checked directly with him to see if the grade registered, even though I know I received an email from the office that it did in fact. What the hell am I thinking? A man that fine like most likely has a showpiece or two to hang on his arm.*

She walked over to her campus calendar, which had a picture of the men's basketball team in action. There were no pictures of the coaching staff. *I could call over to the athletic department and ask for him. I'm tripping. Stop being a dazed little girl.* She laughed at herself.

Lois Mae went to advance her iTunes from playing Marvin Gaye and Tammi Terrell's "If This World Were Mine" but she waited for the song to end. She advanced to Ledisi and turned up the song, "In The Morning." She walked out onto her patio. The condo was built over a water channel on the east side of Lake Washington.

She could see a couple in a little boat on the lake in some rare afternoon sun. A silhouette of the couple floated. The blowing wind made little red ripples. The romance of it made her feel warm, but lonely.

A cloud blew under the sun bringing the temperature down, and a minute later she was holding herself against the chill and she came back inside. The iTunes player changed to Teena Marie's "Portuguese Love." She pulled a sweater on, picked up her computer tablet, walked back outside and sat down on a lawn-chair recliner. The couple in the boat was still there. Lois Mae watched them in a dreamlike vision. Sun still peeked through, shining directly on her patio. A gentle cool breeze blew up under her long dress, and she shivered but she wanted the outside air swirling around her. It was a stimulating feeling. She typed a poem:

I walk alone
In a crowded world
I just want to kiss those one pair of lips that stand alone
As long as I breathe
Hope is in sunrises and sunsets
He will not come as perfect, as I want
He will enter my life as perfect as I need
Pure of heart he will arrive
What can I do, until then?
Wait-Look-Ask-Pray
Give thanks for how it will be
Give thought of what I will do with him
For him
Because
Gentle is his soul
Mindful is his way
Passion for me, is her joy
Beauty is his soul and flows through his heart
Why is he for me?
God said, he will be me
In knowing how to love me

She saw herself and the man she'd met in her classroom, walking together around the lake just as the sun set. She imagined that they would be listening to "If This World Were Mine." The doorbell rang, and her perfect mirage disappeared. At the door a sad-faced Skillet, and Roberta walked in acting as if she was on a reality show. Lois Mae closed her eyes for a moment and prayed for Skillet. Lois Mae also prayed she herself could deal with Roberta for however long the visit.

After grilled salmon and avoiding any negative conversations, Skillet told both women she wasn't sure what to do. "I need for both of you to let me take care of this my way. I got myself into this, and I need to be the one handling my business."

Lois Mae reached out and wiped Skillet's face with a napkin. There were long, black mascara tears running down her face. She looked like a raccoon.

Roberta said in a raspy voice, "As I told you, you can give it up for adoption. I'm all set. Can I go out on your deck and have a cigarette?"

Skillet knew the answer and cut in front of Lois Mae, who responded, "Girl, not here. Nobody does anything unhealthy near these walls."

"So, you're giving your child up for adoption, huh?" Lois Mae's tone was Pacific Ocean cold as she stared at Roberta.

"Yeah, I thought it would be cool at first to have a child. The first couple of months I was mentally into it, but it stopped feeling like it was the thing to do. It was already too late for an abortion, so full-term it is."

Lois Mae's mind was turning, and hot as a clothes dryer. *This poor excuse for a woman should not be having a baby or the ability to reproduce anything.*

"The adoption agency is paying me pretty good." Roberta snapped her finger.

Lois Mae's tone went to the South Pole. "And why would they do that?"

"Well, pure white babies are the top adoptable requests, and then mine is next, a child that is half-Black or mixed race because of their lighter color."

Velvet's mascara started to run all over again as she slowly got up and went out on the deck. It was just as dark and cold outside, as it was inside.

"How does the daddy feel about this?" Lois Mae was eyeballing Roberta like a panther in a tree, ready to pounce for the kill.

"He's a scrub, and wouldn't or don't care." Roberta chuckled. "Girl, I need a cigarette." Roberta hollered out to Skillet. "Hey, Velvet, come on, we got to go. Let's go down to the Fremont District; the clubs are going to be jumpin'."

"Leave! She's not going with you; she's staying here." Lois Mae's voice slammed like a sledgehammer. She said it again but even slower. "Leave!" Lois Mae almost growled at the end of the word. Both women stood up—Roberta backed up and Lois Mae stood five-eleven, tall and angry.

Roberta left, and Lois drew a hot bath for Skillet in her extra-large spa tub. She prepared the spare bed, and after Skillet had soaked, the two never said a word. They had chamomile tea and started to watch *Disappearing Acts*. They both went to bed after Wesley seduced Sanaa against the refrigerator door. Both had dreams some would call nightmares.

12

A Woman's Worth

A window to the outside world of The Musicquarium Lounge was just above Vanita and Alicia's table. The view showed women strolling in heels as early winter showers created slick streets, and that equaled a flood of broken heels.

Inside the lounge, a man said to Vanita, "Excuse me, miss, may I sit down and have a drink with you? You are so fine." Vanita was alone as she waited for Alicia who had gone to the restroom. The man had a thin face and a wide body. He crowded Vanita's space standing over her. His wide-legged jeans with the built-in sagging look were touching her chair. The thirty-or forty-something man wore a tight-knit body shirt. Apparently, he lifted weights and wanted everybody to notice.

Vanita was instantly irritated. She was dressed in her business suit, and to think this was the kind of man she attracted. She had arranged Joshua's care for the evening so she could try to relax. The man at her table wasn't making it any easier.

"Lady, I never see a woman as fine as you are. Anyone ever tell you—?"

"Yes, I've heard it before; thank you, but how about you let me and my friend have a drink in peace." *Dang, the man didn't even ask how my day was.*

"Okay, I'll let you chill." The man turned, walked, and scanned for other landing spots. Alicia was working her way through the bar patrons. Vanita knew she had done more than just make a pit stop at the restroom. Throngs of men were strutting and preening and nodding their head at her as she made it back to her seat.

"Girl, who was that talking to you?" Alicia asked.

"I think he was here for you."

"Do I know him?"

"He was just another man who cannot dress like a grown man, and wear cheap bling-bling."

"Relax, honey, you're out to meet a real man."

Vanita finished her virgin strawberry daiquiri and was ready for the sweet taste of another. The after-work Friday crowd was getting thick. Vanita and Alicia shook their heads no to requests for their unused chairs.

Alicia sat half-listening to Vanita talk about cases in her court, and was swiveling her head 180 degrees like a rotating fan. She finger-combed her huge Afro, sending out flirting invitations with her eyes.

"Girl, you are a mess. Slow your roll," Vanita said and poked her friend on the arm.

Alicia stared at her. "I know you're not over there drinking. Ain't no alcohol in your drink, is there?"

"No, I'm not drinking. I took my happy pill and can't mix the two, or I'll be snoring and drooling in your lap." They laughed.

The waiter made his way through all the smooth operators and Friday-cleavage. "Would you ladies like to order any food to go with your drinks?"

The ladies shook their heads no, and he left the table smiling at Vanita for as long as he could without knocking someone over.

"When is this man going to get here?" There was almost a nervous wavering in Vanita's voice. A lounge band started playing and the crowd ramped up the volume. Glasses clinked, while laughter and endless multiple conversations clashed.

"He had to go to a late bail hearing, but he'll be here," Alicia answered.

"Well, while we're waiting, I'll tell you about the Woman's Worth Conference." Vanita did not see Alicia roll her eyes, as she did not want to hear about it right then.

The corner window table gave them a little privacy, allowing them to talk freely. "The church conference helps us to be happily single or more joyfully married."

Alicia's head moved around like a bobble-head. "So, what made the last conference so interesting?" She asked the question, but her attention strayed.

Vanita avoided another man trying to get her to make eye contact. "Sometimes churchgoing women play right into the myth of the holier-than-thou mess that men want us to believe in. When they do, they want to guilt us into feeling like heathens.

"At the last woman's Christian conference, it got crazy. Sister Collins, from Greater Southside Baptist, got all uptight and just about lost her wig. Sister Judy, from our church, was in our Christian women's relationships class."

"The lady who moved here from Austin, Texas?" Alicia asked.

"Yeah, that's her. She told us when she was married, she tried to spice up her sex life by showering with her husband, soaping him all up and down. When she stooped down and started to go down on him, while she played with herself, he got all twisted up and said, 'A woman shouldn't be touching herself,' and he called her a Jezebel."

Alicia's head jerked and she frowned as if she had swallowed sour milk. "No he didn't!" She laughed so hard she dribbled a few drops of her third lime Margarita. "Look at what you made me do, telling me some crazy mess like that."

"Oh, honey, that's not the funniest part. When Sister Collins heard that, she told Sister Judy that only a woman on the streets would do such a thing as to touch herself and put her lips on a man's thing!"

"Yeah right." Alicia was still laughing and mocking, "Oh, you know she don't have a problem with her husband embedding his face in her pooh-tang. What woman doesn't touch herself? Please!"

Vanita pointed toward herself, joking, and said, "Not me."

"Ooh, stop lying; you got more toys than downtown got pigeons."

"I don't quite have that many," Vanita exclaimed, her eyes watering from giggling so much.

"Well, you got more than I do." Alicia tried to sound serious.

With a straight face, Vanita said, "Alicia, you're doing it live, and I'm doing it by Memorex." Both of their heads flew back as they laughed.

"On the serious side, the moderator at our conference brought some real insight for women to know about sex. Many women, she said, make an effort to satisfy a man with the things they want to do as women. In some cases, that's good enough, but it leaves men shaking their head at times."

"What? I don't understand what you mean." Alicia turned her head to hear and focus on what Vanita was saying.

Vanita leaned in. "Well, we want a man to have an ejaculation to prove to us that we have satisfied him. Men can do this physical release with or without us."

"Huh? Please, I can make a man bark when he cums."

"That may be true, but that don't mean he really got off. The woman went on to explain, there are elements beyond a man feeling the pleasure of releasing fluid through his penis.

"We often try to satisfy men by doing what we like to do to them. We assume because he is grunting and sighing or whatever, he's satisfied. Some women put limits on what we think men need; they generally take what we give them. Many women tell men they don't need this or that. And some women tell their man something must be wrong with him for wanting it freakier, nastier. Some women are sarcastic, and demeaning with questions like, why do you need that, and asking why does that turn you on? Or ask, did some other woman do that and now you want me to?

"Also, she made it known that we set ourselves up to compete against strip clubs, XXX-this, and that. We should be the ones that bring all that into the bedroom. Men are visual creatures. They want to see, they want to look at us moving our bodies about, they want to smell us, and they want to hear us talk in primal lustful ways."

"Shoot, honey, I know I'm free in the mind with my man," Alicia said. "Once I was dating this guy, he wanted to watch the animal channel while we got our freak on. Well, I didn't have cable at my house, so I had him pay for my cable. I let him watch them lions do it up to a hundred times a day while he was humping me. I told him he was king of my jungle, and I wanted to growl and roar when he had his orgasm he'd never forget."

Vanita covered her eyes and shook her head. "Girl, you are a mess, but I guess you got the concept." Vanita tried to ease the visual from her mind, but couldn't and started laughing.

Alicia kept telling of her exploits. "Girl, I take my man to a strip club and buy him a lap dance. That's right, and then I take him home and do him nastier than the freak on the stripper pole.

I always pay for the stripper who ain't fine, the skinniest girl in the house, bucktooth, and ain't got no breasts!"

"You need to stop. You're making my side hurt." Vanita tried to hold her laughter.

"Shoot, I know I rock my man's world. I do whatever he wants, any place, anytime, any way." Alicia popped her fingers to the music. "Tell more of what this lady said. 'Cause I be cummin' three and four times in a row. Most men I know cum once, and want to take a nap." Alicia had the most serious look on her face as she allowed Vanita to continue talking.

"Sometimes women in his past life may have ridiculed him for his wants, but when our men know we don't have boundaries, they will feel more than a just physical release. His brain will shake, just as his body does.

"You know that intense orgasm that makes you want to be held, or you almost cry; a man will do the same. He might not cry, but he'll cry inside. A woman who puts out the visuals, and her pheromonal scents of her body in his nose, and talks that nasty stuff while he's humping will make a man go crazy."

Vanita's vision drifted to a time she had cried in her man's arms right while making love. Alicia interrupted her trip down memory lane.

"You're right, or that lady was right, because I know a whole lot of women say if my man needs all that, then he needs to go find another woman. And we all know those women don't have a man, or can't keep a man, or their man is sniffing on me. Me, I'm gonna give 'em a double dose of this freaky-funky stuff."

"Freaky-funky stuff, huh. You're too funny, girl." Vanita excused herself to the restroom. "When I get back, I'll have to tell you the rest of the story, the best part."

With her conservative blue pinstriped suit, her tall frame made the pinstripes longer and more prominent. Her family trait—the high-on-her-back derriere—protruded well beyond the small of her back. It made the rear vent of her sport coat nearly horizontal. As she walked past the bar, the men in every direction made eye-goggling a sport. Some classless men pointed at her, nodded, hissed, or said, "Hey, baby."

Some women admired; others went into hater mode. Vanita, in her two-tone black leather and gray suede boots, took her time striding. She was not showing off; it was just her walk. After walking back through the rudeness, fresh drinks were waiting when she made it back to her table.

"Girl, you know you need to slow down on the gin and juice," Vanita said to Alicia as she sat down.

"This ain't gin. If I had been drinking gin, there would be a man sitting here ready to take me to a motel, or somewhere. Robert Lamont, the lawyer, is over there. You can't see him, but he's talking to that idiot lawyer, William, the worst lawyer in the courthouse. He'll be back around in a minute. Now, tell me the rest of the story about what happened at the conference."

"Okay, like I said, Sister Collins told Sister Judy that only a woman on the streets would touch herself sexually, especially in front of a man. She said a Christian woman would never touch herself in such a fashion, and never, never ever put her mouth on a man's thing. Sister Judy was good-natured, just smiled, and said matter-of-factly, 'Well, Brother Collins, your husband, always tells me he likes the shape of my big lips, says it reminds him of something. And when I ask him what does that mean, he just sticks his long tongue out and smiles.'"

Vanita and Alicia laughed to the point they didn't notice the tall smiling redbone brother standing behind them.

"Alicia, I hope you weren't telling your friend about that judge who laughed at my motions and didn't dismiss the jaywalking tickets against my blind client." Alicia laughed, but Vanita just smiled, never parting her lips. She did a slow scan of the man who looked like a skinny version of Sinbad the comic. He had red freckles, with sparse reddish hair, almost burgundy. He was balding badly, and the hair above his lip was reddish. The man was not Vanita's kind of attractiveness; it was not how she had pictured him. Alicia had said the man was tall, dark, bald, and athletic, she thought.

"You know that man was not blind." Alicia chuckled as she spoke. "He may have looked like Mister Magoo, but the two of you were perpetrating a fraud against the court." Vanita laughed.

A man approached their table. "Robert Lamont, meet Vanita Irving. She's my girl from way back," Alicia said.

He reached down and lifted Vanita's extended hand. "Hello, Vanita, it's very nice to meet you. Are you as crazy as your friend here? She cracks me up."

"No, I'm not crazy."

"Well, if you are by chance, it will be okay if you take just one pill, and you're not required to take ten." He laughed at his own joke way too hard. Alicia cringed, and Vanita's face became stone. The lawyer sensed he might have stepped where there was a missing manhole cover. "I'm ah...headed to the restroom; be back."

They watched him disappear through the crowd. Vanita and Alicia turned and faced each other. No words were exchanged.

Moments later, Vanita ordered an apple martini. Alicia wanted to ask if she really wanted a drink, but she refrained. The drink sat on the table untouched.

The lounge band switched from playing a smooth jazz groove to a variety of reggae, salsa, and old-school R&B. With the daylight gone, light beamed in from car headlights and streetlights.

The band played in front of a large aquarium, giving it a nice blue glow. A small dance floor appeared to have feet moving on every square foot.

Mr. Lawyer Guy never came back. They saw him talking to another woman. The ladies people-watched and small-talked. Earlier, anyone who bought multiple drinks had a chance to enter to win two free dinners and concert tickets. Alicia had entered. They announced the winners, and Alicia was one. The concert started in an hour, downstairs in the same building. Vanita volunteered to let Alicia and one of the men who was already there go to the concert. She would call it a day, but no way was Alicia going to let their female bonding time end. The venue downstairs was a dinner cabaret with a beautiful stage and seating area. Inside they found seats on one of the lower tiers.

"The first woman, do you know what kind of music she plays?" Vanita asked.

"Honey, I don't know anything, but what I do know is we eating for free."

Vanita shook her head and watched the people coming in. "I saw Nona Hendryx at the Bumbershoot Festival some years ago. It will be nice to see her again."

Alicia picked up the flyer and read the story aloud about the history of Nona and LaBelle. On the other side, she read about the diva name of N'dambi. The opening act was labeled as "sexy, funky, and jazzy." "It sounds like it's going to be real nice."

13

Soul from the Abyss

"I'll be there in ten," Ayman said into his cell phone. "Be ready, you and whoever. Who is whoever?"

"It's my friend Arleen," Sonya said. "You met her before, and she's walking through the door right now."

"Oh, yeah, I remember her from when we played Spades over at your house. She's the one who claimed all her failed relationships have always been the man's fault." Ayman laughed. "All two hundred! There's something about a person who makes claims like that; it might be a clue to run for the hills."

"A man with an opinion!" Sonya had an exasperated tone.

"A woman with an opinion!" Ayman said back to her.

Ayman heard a question from the background. "What's he saying about me, girl?"

Sonya answered Arleen. "Oh girl, he's talking about you were the curvy sexy one." She spoke back into the phone. "I'll see you when you get here."

Ayman laughed as he clicked the phone off.

The women met Ayman at his car and he opened the front and rear doors of his classic Jaguar. Sonya took the rear, while he was hoping she would have sat in front. Arleen was of medium height, and a medium-thick build. This evening she flaunted something too short and too loud for Ayman's taste. Her shiny gold blazer and money-green skirt, screamed wrong threads for the evening, as far as he was concerned. *Her spiked boots laced up to her knees and that skirt, with the split in back, is almost short enough to show her back door. Somebody's gonna think I'm pimping.*

He looked down at Sonya before he closed her door. She could read his eyes and shrugged her shoulders.

The Jaguar doors were light, and shut without much effort. Arleen inadvertently slammed the door, never giving him a chance to close it for her. His teeth grated. *Damn, she plopped her big butt down as if she were diving into a pool from the high-dive.*

They passed a billboard that advertised the East Seattle City University basketball team. The billboard pictured the team, Ayman, and his coaches, and a picture of a huge shark with a basketball in its teeth:

WATCH THE SHARKS HUNT AND FINISH OFF THE COMPETITION

Arleen turned and faced Ayman. His attention was on the road, but he sensed her stare and cut his eyes over to her. "With all that money you make, why drive this old thing? It looks like it has wood on the dash. Shoot, if I was you, I'd be in a Lexus or Benz."

Donny Hathaway's smooth voice was singing a live version of "A Song for You" on the Jaguar's sound system. "Dang, even the music is old in this car. Can't you play Usher or Beyoncé? Do you have that song 'Sista Big Bones' by Anthony Hamilton?"

Ayman rolled his eyes up, and thought why would he listen to Usher or Beyoncé. He exhaled a long breath before he spoke, "I like Anthony Hamilton; this just happens to be playing."

Ayman looked in the rearview mirror, and made eye contact

with Sonya. She rolled her eyes at him, realizing her friend lacked sophistication.

When he pulled into the underground parking garage, he paid the valet to park the car in two spots, and gave him a healthy tip. The young man recognized Coach Ayman Sparks, and let him know he would take good care of the car. He also wished him good luck in the upcoming game against Washington.

It was a dreary evening, sprinkling on and off. Ayman broke out the umbrella, and both women huddled close to him as they walked up the hill to the Triple Door. Arleen huddled next to Ayman. She made him feel as if he was sharing a rib bone with her. *I don't need someone to think I'm with her on a date.* Sonya kept close but respectful space under the umbrella.

Once inside, the seating host also recognized Coach Sparks and sat them at a good table. Their seats were perfect, up front and personal. Ayman positioned his seat so Sonya and Arleen sat close to each other. It appeared he sat alone and was just sharing the table. Sonya had pulled Arleen aside and told her to lighten. The man was not her style, and she was not his.

A few people recognized Coach Sparks and came by the table and held short conversations. One woman asked if he was having a summer camp again for youth. Her body language and other trivial exchange suggested she wanted to talk more. When she left, he avoided eye contact with Sonya. He knew she had something to say, since he claimed no women came on to him.

There was an opening act, a spoken-word artist flowing over a jazz trio. His narration was erotic and metaphorically imaginative, in a smooth and deep voice:

"As I'm down, I admit, I submit
From being whipped
Turned into a licker

Addicted to your sweets
Internal sweets cummin' outward
Knees burn, floor burned backsides
I find myself back inside in charge
My sweat falls on the tip of your nose
You don't blink too damn intense
Big legs offer support, but little restriction
Imposing rhythm
Deep and wide it flows with aching and bliss
You hold mountains for me to dip my face
Angled I hit that G-spot
Reoccurring sliding comin' in and pulling out
Perfect you and I know what's cummin'
I huff and puff deep and down
I hold you tight
I squeeze your backside
Trembling travels from your toes and reaches your fingers
Now I dance on your reared paradise
My face goes to beautiful ugly
I grunt sounds that make no sense
Because I am being
Whipped and you are turned out"

After he finished, women erupted with loud "oohs" and "aahs." When that part of the show was over, Ayman headed to the bathroom, then to get some hot tea. He felt tightness in his throat and thought, *No, don't let me have a sore throat before tomorrow's game.*

After a trip to the bar for tea, he mingled with a few people. He turned a corner to walk back inside and he saw a beautiful profile standing alone. She was tall with a dark caramel complexion. She wore a blue pinstripe pantsuit that accentuated her curves. *Damn, she's fine. She's beautiful. She was sitting inside, but I didn't see her clearly as I see her now.* He blinked his eyes. More than anything, he noticed she had a pleasant expression on her face. At ten feet away, he felt strange; as if he were a lost boy standing there naked to the world, feeling exposed and stuck in quicksand.

He had an inner chuckle. Somehow he lost that little lost boy feeling when she turned her head in his direction and smiled. He walked up to her without a thought of what he was going to say.

He walked in front of her, and she looked up at him. "As I'm down, I admit, I submit from being whipped, and I don't know the rest of the poem, but I wish I could find the right words," he said with a half-laugh. She laughed too. "Now if I have made a fool of myself, could you let me down real easy?"

She smiled. "Are you trying to huff and puff and blow my house down?" He dropped his head partly to hide his big smile.

"Touché." They quickly fell into an easy but nervous where-is-this-going chat. After a couple minutes of chatting about the spoken-word performance, the conversation went another direction.

"Are you here to hear N'dambi and Nona or just one of them?" Ayman asked.

"Well, my girlfriend who seems lost—or maybe she went back upstairs—she and I won tickets. I'm familiar with Nona Hendryx, and looking forward to seeing her, but I haven't seen the other lady."

Ayman tried to inform her about the style of N'dambi, which led to the subject of old school music. Soon they were reminiscing, which led them to when had they graduated from high school.

Ayman commented with a smile, "I'm starting to feel a little weird about letting on that I'm forty-something, and I graduated in 1980."

"I'm around from the same time." She smiled. As they kept

talking, she mentioned that she had seen people sitting at his table. He explained that they were friends from the church he attended sometimes. His mind raced. *Was she watching me? I hope I don't have to tell her I haven't been to church in over a year.*

"Ooh, a man who goes to church, or at least knows what one looks like inside." She had an impressed look on her face. The subject changed to his relief, and it became apparent she did not know who he was by facial recognition, when she asked, "And kind sir, to whom am I talking?"

He thought, *You idiot, introduce yourself.* Nervously, he said, "Ayman...I'm Ayman Sparks. And you?"

She mocked him, teased him to ease her own nervousness. "Vanita...I'm Vanita Irving, and it's nice to meet you." They shook hands. Ayman had a fetish for hands. Her fingers were slender, warm, and smooth. He noted that she wore no wedding ring on her other hand. He released her hand gently as she pulled away slowly.

Another woman approached and introduced herself abruptly. Her pear-shaped body practically stepped in between Vanita and Ayman. Her huge Afro made her taller than she was. "I'm Alicia," she teased. "And why are you over here talkin' to my friend? I know you. You're that coach that was on ESPN, talking about you ain't no Black preacher." She turned her back to Ayman and spoke right into her friend's face, "Girl you should have seen him." She mouthed to Vanita, "*Hot.*"

Vanita laughed. "Since when you do you watch ESPN?"

"Honey, you know I have to keep up on who's who. And if I can watch the animal channel, I can watch—" The lights dimmed, and cut her off.

Ayman wanted to ask where they were sitting. He popped his fingers in frustration. *I can't leave Sonya and...* He could not remember the other woman's name. There was a hesitation from all three.

Walking away, Alicia said, "Enjoy the show." Vanita followed, but stopped.

Ayman said, "I hope you like the show. Maybe I'll see you before Nona takes the stage. I assume there will be a break."

"That would be nice." A soft, inviting look came across her face as she turned away and walked ahead of Ayman.

Before he sat down, he went into total fixation, watching her.

She looked at him out of the corner of her eyes. Their glances turned into a long pause before she took her seat.

Sonya caught the play in action, tipped her head, and opened her eyes wide in a questioning look. He smiled sheepishly.

The place was ready and full of Friday night energy as crescendos of drumrolls and cymbals crashed along with rising volume from the band. A beautiful Amazon-like, copper-brown woman sauntered onto the stage. Dressed in a beautiful, pink, ruffled baby doll dress in her bare feet, her presence grabbed everyone's attention, and applause.

She started to sing "Everybody Loves the Sunshine." The party was on, the old school song was an original by Seattle native, Roy Ayers, and the Seattle people had crazy-love for the song. The band played the song with a funkier beat. People rose and danced or swayed. N'dambi had a Nina Simone neo-soul voice, earthy and pure.

The band played several jams until "Soul From The Abyss." That led into a low-volume groove while N'dambi spoke about love and loneliness. "I ask that you close your eyes for a moment and see yourself holding a lover. Maybe their face is not clear. Whatever it may be, look around you. Others just like you are bewildered about this thing called love. For those whose lover is sitting next to you, kiss them; let them know you care." Then she joked, "If you're on a blind date, it's okay to kiss them on the cheek. Keep it short now, but don't be shy. If there is no one, look deep within the abyss of that love you will share from deep within your soul one day."

Arleen wanted to make a move on Ayman, but he gave her a disapproving eye. To his right and down a row, Vanita Irving peeked his way often.

His eyes honed in as a hawk would. The candles on her table flickered off her face, and he could see her eyelashes batting in slow motion, and her lips parting.

N'dambi massaged the crowd's ears singing about her mood indigo. Her earthy voice and words made Ayman's emotions stand to attention. The lyrics fed an allure into the woman sitting near. The band played another song titled "The Meeting."

Vanita was in a trance. In a matter of less than two hours, she went from being highly disappointed in one man to being high on another. He was sitting behind her, and out of the corner of her eye, she could see this man, handsome and refined.

His voice…She could hear him in her head at the same time N'dambi spoke. "We all live with mood indigo, feeling so alone; the blues turn black when your lover is not there."

The blue lights from the stage cast a hue down low, but the gold lights above were like the sun rising over the theater.

"You can do to change that mood indigo. Wave your hands in the air if you understand a man and woman are not supposed to be alone. Just how do you find the one, the one that's meant for you? I know, let your soul come up from the abyss. Open your eyes and let a new vision come in."

Vanita turned in Ayman's direction. His expression was as clear as the crystal glass on his table. She felt his connection to her own feelings at that moment. *He is just like me: alone, alone, alone.*

N'dambi and the band started in on a song called "Crazy World." During intermission, Vanita had become apprehensive about turning around and seeing him. Her bladder was asking for the restroom. She turned the other way and went up the center aisle without looking over.

Returning from the restroom, she tried to look as if she was not searching for him. He was wearing a black leather blazer, with a black no-collar shirt that had some type of image on the front. He looked good in a stylish leather blazer and black jeans. It was obvious that he had large thighs and a small waist. She waited in the foyer among all the people refilling drinks and mingling. She hoped to see those black jeans approaching her.

The house lights came down, and Vanita returned to her seat, and looked over at his table. The other women were there on one side, but he wasn't.

The audience was audibly showing its excitement as the band members walked out and picked up their instruments. The emcee screamed, "Here she is, Nona Hendryx!" The band went in a turbo funk mood, and she sang, "Why Should I Cry?"

Nona was great, but after half a song, Vanita looked again to see if Ayman had returned to his seat. He was there enjoying himself, dancing in his seat. *He's cute, look at him jamming.* Vanita felt some sense of relief to know he was still there. She was already worrying if she would get a chance to talk to him after the show.

Nona and her band played a relentless groove for ninety minutes. The place was a party pushing at the walls to fall down. Nona, in her black body suit, exuded sexiness that both men and women could see and feel.

A slower tune with a long intro played while two female back-up singers stood on each side of Nona. They went into harmony singing, "Come into My Life." The trio had the sound of the old LaBelle.

It had a haunting overtone for Vanita. The lyrics she heard resonated what she wanted and needed—a good man to come into her life. She glanced behind her. In her head she heard, *He is just like me: alone, alone, alone.*

14
After the Dance

After the concert, Ayman's anxieties ran like storm run-off and flooded his mind. *Do I ask her for her number? She was just passing time when she was talking to me.*

He and Sonya waited for Arleen to return from the restroom. He did not see Vanita, but he was scanning for her until he had to walk the ladies to the car. He spoke to Sonya as if Arleen weren't there, while huddled under the umbrella as he left the building.

"I kind of met a woman in there."

"Yep, there was no doubt. She was watching you every chance she could. I'd be surprised if she ain't got a crook in her neck." Arleen moved away and walked in the rain.

"You saw her lookin', huh?"

"I saw you lookin' too."

Ayman opened the car doors. "I didn't get her number," he told Sonya. Arleen climbed into the backseat and closed the door firmly. Ayman ignored her.

Sonya nodded her head back toward the direction of the lounge. "Give me the keys to start the car for some heat. Go back. She was pretty, if I have to say so myself." He stood there. "Go, before she leaves, or you'll be wondering what if."

He ran back without the umbrella; a smile came across his face. He was tripping about him being this big strong man who stood in front of thousands cheering or booing people sitting in an arena, but he was scared to talk to a woman. He stopped by the aquarium and wiped the rain from his face. He peered through the aquarium to see if she was at the bar.

"Did you enjoy the show?" Her voice was behind him.

He turned and looked into instant visual intoxication. His smile went from medium to high, and got stuck. "Yeah, it was all great."

"When N'dambi spoke about having mood indigo and the poem, I could feel all that," he said.

"Let me make sure I have this right. Your name is Vanita, right?" She nodded.

"I would love to talk. I really would, but I have my friends in my car waiting. Could I have your number? Here's my card." He handed her two, which read: *East Seattle City University, Coach Ayman Sparks* with his photo.

She hesitated, and an awkward silence passed in a noisy place. "Those were your friends at the table you were sitting with, right?"

He chuckled to disarm her. "Yes, they're just good friends; well, only one is my friend, and she brought along her friend. I escorted them back to my car and came back hoping you hadn't left." She took the cards from his hand without taking her eyes off his face, as if she were reading the fine print of a disclaimer.

She reached into her purse, pulled out a pen, wrote on one of the cards, and handed it back to him.

As they stood there, the place was loud with conversation, laughter, and glasses clinking. People passed, and one person wanted Coach Sparks's attention. "Hey, Coach, you guys going to win tomorrow?"

Ayman turned to the man, trying to be cordial. "We'll give it a good run."

"Good luck, Coach." The man extended his hand, and they shook hands.

"How popular are you?" Vanita asked, smiling.

"Well, people know me, but I rarely know them. I can call you, right?"

"You can call me."

"You lose your friend? You okay? You're not stuck down here? My friends live up in the Central District. I can drop them off and be back here in about twenty minutes if you need a ride. I'm not the Green River Killer; as you can tell, a lot of people know me."

She laughed. "Time out, Lone Ranger."

"Time out?"

"Yes, you must be good during timeouts with your basketball team, with how much you can say in five seconds. I play a little basketball myself in high school." They smiled and gazed at each other. "My friend, she's running around here somewhere. It's like a candy store to her. However, thanks for the offer, Lone Ranger. Do you come to the rescue of all women?"

I'd rather be Tonto, Ayman thought and smiled wide.

She reached out and put a pretty finger on his chest. "Go take your friends home, and you go home and get ready for your game." He nodded, reached out for the finger, held it and said good-bye.

He was walking away when Alicia approached Vanita. "Let's go somewhere else for drinks, so we can talk about his fine behind." Vanita said nothing as she watched him walk away. "Girl, that's how a man should look like in jeans." Alicia sucked her lips in. Vanita nodded, as people seemed to part to make a path for him as he walked.

After dropping Sonya and Arleen off, Ayman headed toward a place to chill and think. As he drove, many questions came to mind, and he answered them. *How long should I wait before I call her? Damn, she can hit the Internet and check me out for anything she wants to know.* He remembered something he'd heard once: "For a moment or two everybody is perfect."

The one upgrade he was not able to make to his classic Jaguar was the sound of the loud wipers. The drizzle turned to pouring rain. He killed two birds at the same time; he put the wipers on fast and cranked the volume of the stereo. He disliked most remakes, but he grooved to Queen Latifah's remake of "Simply Beautiful" with Al Green.

After he pulled into the parking lot of Gracias Restaurant he turned off the ignition, then he sat and listened to one more remake by Queen Latifah: "Hello Stranger."

Inside the lounge Ayman walked past the bar full of sitting Dockers and dresses. Sports Northwest Channel was showing the preview of tomorrow's game, the showdown between East Seattle City University and the University of Washington.

A prerecorded interview with Coach Sparks had just finished giving his analysis of the game. "Coachie, how are you?" Baldomero, the bartender, asked. People looked up from the bar, and others in the place buzzed at attention.

"Baldomero, good to see you, my friend, as always." Ayman looked around for a place to sit. There was a place at the bar, but he wanted a space for himself. He did not want to hold court and talk basketball with anyone.

The bartender's Hispanic accent mixed with a happy singsong way of speaking. "Good to see you tonight. You want your regular drink?"

"No, *amigo querido, dame algo* hot for my throat." Since living in Spain, he used the Spanish he knew as often as he could.

"Senior Coachie, how about B & B? It go down real well, and warms you up."

Ayman knocked on the bar, nodded his head, and took a seat

at a table near the corner. A woman vocalist was walking around holding CDs of her music. Ayman removed his leather coat, and the vocalist saw Ayman's shirt. She pointed and said, "I love your shirt with Billie Holiday's face singing as if she's in a smoke-filled place. Where can I find one, if you don't mind me asking?"

"I found it in my travel. I travel a lot."

"Well, how about I sing a Billie Holiday song for you?" she asked.

"'Lover Man'?"

"I can do that."

The woman came to the bandstand, made a gesture in Ayman's direction and said, "For the last set of the night, I'm going to start with a request from the shirt on the body of that handsome man dressed in black. I'm going to sing Billie Holiday's "Lover Man." Ayman lifted his glass in salute. The TV volume was off, but game highlights were showing. He laughed at how distracted he was with a big game hours away.

He finished his drink and then a glass of warm water. He waited to make sure he could pass a driving test, and headed home. He switched the music over to Marvin Gaye's "After the Dance." The song increased Ayman's mind game, envisioning Vanita's beauty. He glanced in the rearview mirror and caught himself smiling, and thought, *Focus, man, focus.*

15

Sideshow

Skillet snored in the other room while Lois Mae drank her coffee at 7:00 a.m. She watched the rain hit Lake Washington from her deck, and then moved inside to watch old cartoons, an old childhood enjoyment.

Foghorn Leghorn, the oversized rooster, was trying to woo the widowed hen, Miss Prissy, by babysitting her bookish son, Egghead Jr. *Even in cartoons, males try to get in the henhouse.* She laughed out loud.

"What are you laughing about?" Skillet's snoring had stopped, and a moment later, she walked into the living room. With a sheet tied above her bosom and draped down to the floor, she looked like a full-figured Roman goddess.

"I'm just laughing at these cartoons. There's coffee ready, and how about you cook this morning? I want a cheese omelet with the leftover salmon. Oh, and don't be having your naked ass in my kitchen."

"Hey, if my big ass touches anything, it will add flavoring. I'll hook you up an omelet, but I don't know if I can take the smell of food. Girl, I'm starting to get that queasy feeling." She chuckled, but it sounded regretful.

Hearing Skillet, Lois Mae feared for her friend. Lois ran her hand through her thick mane, while watching her friend turn the corner into the kitchen.

"Velvet?"

"Oh no, you haven't called me by my name in a long time. Does that mean I'm in trouble?" They shared a laugh from separate rooms.

"I am not going to call you Skillet anymore. You know we were going through a tough time in our lives when I started calling you Skillet. Now we are...you are...you're at a point you need the most secure and mature atmosphere around you."

Velvet returned holding the coffee pot; a long pensive stare at the hardwood floor cast her thoughts downward like a young child avoiding eye contact. She opened her mouth, but no words came out. She nodded her head.

Lois scratched her scalp, reminding her that it was dry. "I have a hair appointment at ten. What are your plans for today?"

Velvet turned back toward the kitchen. "You can drop me off at home."

"Would you like to go to a basketball game?"

"What game would you be going to? And your coffee needs a Mr. Yuck sticker! This stuff is so weak. It might have to rub my big ass on this pot to add some strength."

"You just like your coffee black as a cast iron skillet."

"Funny, ha, ha. Remember, I'm in here making your food." After the laughter died down, Velvet said, "Lois, I love you for being there for me.

"That's what friends are for. And about the game, it's a big one, I guess.

"East Side versus the West Side," Velvet said. "Yeah, the men at work were talking about it when they weren't making comments about my butt. It sounds like fun. I'll go, but first thing," Velvet's voice growled, "I need some real coffee, yuk."

"Well, make it your way and hurry with the food. Let me ask you something. Does Foghorn Leghorn ever win over the widowed hen, *Miss Prissy?*"

"You need to leave them cartoons alone, Ms. English Teacher."

Why does he always take my spot? I got mine, he's got his. Ayman had to park in Sterlin's parking spot. It was not a big deal; it was just something Sterlin did when he got to the gym before Ayman.

He went to his office, rechecked the day's schedule, and walked into the gym The players, other coaches, and the trainers were gathering. He and Sterlin touched bases on what everybody was saying about the game. They were both relieved that their main player, Larentzo Sir John, was eligible to play.

"I think we're ready for the game," Sterlin said.

"It's going to be a long day, I'm glad we booked hotel rooms near the Key Arena this afternoon, so the kids can rest away from everybody before the game."

"Hey, how was the concert last night?"

"It was nice. As a matter of fact, I'll tell you something, I met a woman there last night, and she seemed...nice." Ayman was forcing back a smile. He hollered out to a player, "Get your elbow under you, and follow through on your shot."

"Stop multi-tasking, thinking about this woman, and trying to coach. Pick one. You're always telling me to focus. So, what about this woman? What makes her special, if that's what you're saying."

"If it was just one thing, I could tell you, I would. Maybe it was a full moon, and she put a spell on me."

"I assume she's fine." It was Sterlin's turn to coach before

Ayman could answer. "Hey, Hafeez, don't step back from that freethrow line when you miss. Practice your form right after you miss, on the line. Yeah, that's better; now stop missing." The kid nodded and made the next free throw. Turning his attention back to Ayman, Sterlin asked, "Now, is she fine?" He was running his hands down an imaginary woman's figure, with emphasis on the bottom as he acted like he was spanking a butt.

Ayman stared at him. "See, that's your problem, you and that booty addiction. You need a twelve-step booty program and therapy."

"Maybe…maybe you're right. I love booty. I may have a problem." Sterlin chuckled, but there was sadness to it.

"What?" Ayman raised an eyebrow. "Did you get a woman pregnant?"

"No! Stop tripping; I guard my sperm like Prince makes people dance—constantly and consistently. But on a serious note, listen, yesterday, I did this freak and—" A whistle blew from across the court. It was time for Ayman to take over—first with a team talk, and then a walk-through practice.

"We'll talk later." Ayman read Sterlin's face and understood he wanted to talk now. He blew his whistle, told the team to stretch some more, and gave his attention to Sterlin. "What's going on, man?"

"I'm just sick of the same old thing. Women! It's gotten old."

It was Ayman's turn for his jaw to drop. "What happened to you?"

"Hear me out. I did this woman, and had to work to get my dick hard. I thought I wanted to freak with her, but when it came time, I was bored before I got started."

Ayman stood tall in front of his confused friend and shook his head. He wanted to laugh, but did not and said, "It was bound to happen one day. Your dick didn't turn on when you hit the switch.

You have been sitting at the all-you-can-do booty table, gorging yourself with all the booty you want. You've grown tired, man. Put your dick away, roll it up, and put it in the back of your sock drawer. Don't pull it out for everything unless she turns you on, not just your usual horny urges."

"What about holidays?" Sterlin chuckled at his joke. Ayman didn't like that.

"Negro, I'm holding up practice listening to your dilemma." Ayman started to walk off.

"Man, my bad. I hear ya."

Ayman stopped and spoke. "Do you know what it means to say, 'There are too many freaks, and the circus is leaving town'?"

"What's that supposed to mean?" The two men stared at each other, two best friends who never had a problem challenging each other and trusting at the same time.

"Sterlin, you are not a weak man, but you play yourself to be weak by letting yourself be chased and caught by every freak in sight, and now the tent in your circus ain't rising to the occasion."

"What in the hell? Who told you that?"

"My granddad, and you need to make a commitment to yourself. Any woman you decide to be with…she needs to come from rarefied air. Otherwise, you're being played when you think you're the player.

"I'm not saying it would be okay to be a pimp, but at least a pimp gets something out of the game. You don't get anything, not even a good nut. I guess it's good?"

"Yeah." Sterlin felt disgusted hearing what he already knew, but he kept listening.

"With you, ever since you were last in love with…" Ayman wanted to avoid bringing up the sore subject of a past love affair. "Anyway, you have to grow up, or be swallowed up. Sex is all the same when you live like you live.

"Women may like you for the stud you are, but that gets old, right? Most of all, when you go through as many women as you do, you belittle women and yourself. I hate to say it, but it comes down to the simplest thing: you make yourself lower than pussy. You go around thinking you're turning them out. You might want to rethink who's really being turned out." Sterlin's eyes had anger dulling his vision and shame closing them.

Ayman did not let up on his friend. "Hell, half the women you sleep with don't respect you. When can you recall really looking into a woman's eyes when you're sexing her up and caring for how she really feels? For real man, tell me, come on, tell me, when was the last time?"

"You know it was Monica."

She was the last Black woman he had known Sterlin to have anything to do with. Twenty years ago, Monica Turner had turned Sterlin into a howling, crying fool. Now years later, she was almost an over-the-hill pop diva living her life in *Cougarville* dating young rappers.

Ayman softened his tone. "Ah-huh, almost twenty years ago." Ayman thought he should get back to practice, but he continued. "Vanessa and me, even when we weren't getting along, coming home and finding her there after each win or loss, she was my refuge from the world. She was my rock. What have you had? Hell, even with just a memory of Vanessa, I'm better off than going from woman to woman.

"As I see it, you need to take a break. Be a nun: don't need none, and don't want none for awhile. Leave the women alone. Grow up. Don't give me that look. I'm telling you and your dick need a break. Come on, we got a long day ahead of us." Ayman slapped his friend on the back.

He's right, Sterlin thought.

Ayman blew the whistle. "Huddle up at center court. Come on, Sharks, hustle like winners."

Sterlin's head echoed deep inside with hurt in a place that had been empty of feelings. He had been living skin deep. Ayman's words had penetrated nerves near his consciousness. For the first time in a long time, he felt pain from the painful truth.

He's just like every man, a liar. Vanita sighed. *I know he was with those other women I saw him with*. She puffed some air out, then sat up in bed. *Men*. She tossed her pillow across the room and put her feet on the floor, but she had gone to bed feeling better than she had felt in a long time.

As she walked to the bathroom, she felt uneasy in her head. Clarity spun like the spinning wheel with a woman tied to it and a magician throwing knife at the board. She had lied to Alicia. She hadn't taken her happy pill. If she didn't take her meds, she could stay awake forever. She was awake most of the night resulting in an irritable mood.

She sat on the toilet; her period had walked through the door minutes after she had walked in the door last night. Cramps and a heavy flow added to her attitude. Another sigh. *I'm glad Joshua's not here this morning*.

She sat back and relaxed on the stool, resting her head against the wall. Drowsy and dazed, she closed her eyes. Ayman Sparks, the six-two, handsome man with gumbo-brown skin came into her vision. Unlike a few minutes before, he was a good guy again, as she rested on the stool.

One way to ease her cramps was masturbation, a temporary fix, but that was something she did like breathing. After she made herself cum, it relaxed her to fall asleep. If anyone had seen her sitting there, they would have thought she had overdosed with her head leaning against the back wall. Her elbow slipped and hit the toilet handle, and the sound and a slight spray of the flush touched her and woke her.

She washed her hands and face; it made her want a shower. Vanita started running the shower and went downstairs for a minute waiting for the bathroom to steam up. Down in the kitchen, she checked her phone messages. Joshua wanted to know where she was. It was already 10:00 a.m. Vanita made hot tea and turned on the computer. She looked at Ayman's card, then the school basketball team website. *My shower!* Moving fast, she made her way back upstairs to find the shower running cold.

Damn! Thank goodness I have gas; it won't take too long for the hot water to heat up. Back downstairs, she studied Ayman Sparks, the coach of a major college basketball team. She read his bio on different sources; on Wikipedia, some information gave her more questions and thoughts. *It says he's divorced. It doesn't say anything about children; he's forty-five, so they could be grown. Am I crossing his mind?*

Trust and Vanita were worlds apart since her husband had left. With no clear understanding of why in her head, it was like climbing a mountain naked at the foot of Mt. Rainier, fourteen-thousand feet high in the sky.

Hours later, with Joshua in her SUV, she asked him if he knew about the East Seattle City University Sharks basketball team.

"Uh-huh, Dad took me to a game before." Vanita's face tightened. "Dad said he wants me to play for the Sharks when I go to college." Her seven-year-old son asked, "When do I go to college, Mom?"

"Honey, too soon."

"Mom, could you ask Dad to take me again?" She did not answer, and he asked again. "Mom—"

"Can I take you? Would you like that?"

"Okay, can you buy me another Shark shirt? The coach signed my other one. It's at Dad's house, and then I'll have two."

"The coach signed it." *Small world we live in.* "Joshua, if I can get tickets, we're going to a game tonight."

"Yea!"

"I have to see if I can get tickets, and maybe the coach can sign another shirt for you. And maybe sign his name on me."

"Huh?"

"*Huh* is not a word, and never mind."

16
Tell It Like It Is

The heat in the beauty shop, along with Jill Scott singing her melodic soul, set off a relaxing drift for Lois Mae. The warm rinse felt good while she lay back in the contoured chair.

Her hairdresser, Bonnie, slipped the hair dryer over her head, and the nail lady prepared her feet for a pedicure and for an extra-long massage from the lower calves down and in between each toe. For the service, Lois Mae always gave the lady a sizeable tip.

With hair drying and the massage going on, she was drifting into daydream land. *What would it feel like if a man with big, soft, gentle hands were doing my feet and wearing nothing but a G-string?* She opened her eyes, feeling embarrassed about her thoughts, but she quickly closed her eyes again and smiled.

The imaginary man stepped over her long legs, exposing his thick muscled ass in front of her face. He reached down to massage her feet.

The hot air around her head relaxed her deeper into her fantasy. Lois Mae imagined watching the man squatting and acting as if he was humping her feet. She became damp high up between her thighs. She adjusted herself in the chair. The visual of his ass was perfect, as was his fully rounded ball sac leading into his thick growing manhood, hanging down; it was getting hard, and harder.

He dripped a long stream of clear pre-cum and rubbed it on her feet from heel to arch, and in between her toes. She was sweating from the neck down. Her mouth was dry. She needed a Brita pitcher full of water. The imaginary man turned his back and she wanted to reach out and touch his firm ass.

Her lungs pushed her breasts up, and her nipples hardened and almost ached. Lois Mae shifted in her seat. She was envisaging him turning and facing her. He was aggressively stroking his erection while staring into her eyes. He pointed his hardness toward her toes, and she heard a deep grunt. It was her grunting as she felt warm, thick cream shooting on her toes. She jerked in her chair, curling her toes tightly.

The woman massaging her feet threw up her hand, and dropped the heated lotion.

"Lois Mae, is it too hot? You want me to turn down the heat? You look uncomfortable. Girl, the way you're over here squeezing the armrests," Bonnie said as she came over to check on her.

"Miss, I do sum-ding wrong?" The nail lady doing her feet was puzzled.

"No, I'm fine. Could you pass me that fitness magazine and some water?"

Magazine in hand, she thumbed through and stopped at a feature story about enjoying sex when you're not having sex.

After practice, the team bus headed for Seattle's Rainier Valley area to the Bronze Fork & Knife Restaurant, for the team breakfast.

After breakfast, the team would go to Pike Place Market. At breakfast, the two coaches had time to talk some more. Ayman spoke about meeting Vanita at the concert. Sterlin listened, but he was in a distant place. Ayman reminded him he needed his head together for the game.

For publicity, ESCU and Washington were meeting at the market for photos in their team colors. There was a fish-throwing contest between the two teams, always referred to as the East Side versus the West Side Stink. The public and fans weighed in with lots of trash talk and the players did their part as well. It was load and ruckus, but all in fun. As a coach, Ayman hated this part of the sideshow, yet he knew public relations was part of his job. The one redeeming grace was he could talk to the guys as a friend or a brother, and sometimes as a father for what they lacked in their everyday lives.

From his earliest years of coaching to now, he had seen young men entering into adulthood from a hip-hop world, unaware of any conscious core values. Ayman made a point to raise their understanding of responsibilities. He engaged them in present-day social issues. Often, when the team had a road game, he would have a team bus leave from the airport and tour each city. He hired local historians to give a narrative history of neighborhoods and schools; the bus traveling from the rich "hoods" to real ghettos, which were unlike the rap-video ghettos.

On the trip to Kentucky, the team went to the Muhammad Ali Museum and the boxer's childhood house. Every mind opened wide when they crossed over the bridge where Ali threw away his Olympic gold medal, because of racism.

Coach Sparks told them, "Material things are fool's gold if you don't do the right things in life. All the bling-bling, and gold and silver teeth may show how much money you've made, but have you made people respect what you stand for? If for some reason you lose all your bling-bling, nobody will want you when you're down and out.

"If you're shot nine times and live, it doesn't make you a man. It proves the fools who shot you are bad shots, and you're a dumb-ass for putting yourself in harm's way."

He asked each potential recruit, "Do you wear someone else's labels to promote what? What is your motivation in life, someone's label or how you're labeled?"

The young men on the East Seattle City University team did not sag their pants around the coach, or away on their own. There was one major rule in place: "Do nothing to embarrass yourself, and do nothing to embarrass your team."

When the fish-throwing contest was over, Larentzo came over to talk to Coach Sparks. "Coach, I know I scared you with my grade problem. It won't happen again."

"Son, let me tell you, I would be scared for you if I thought anything would keep you from being successful. If basketball got in the way of your education, I would advise you not to play basketball.

"Don't get me wrong, I need you on that floor. You have skills, but it's my job to bring out the best in you on and off the basketball court."

"Coach, how good was Goldlyn?"

The team fight song blasted through the sound system while the cheerleaders danced and cheered.

"He outworked the word 'work.' He's in the NBA because he understood focus. His hearing loss may have helped hone his focus, but he enjoyed the hard work. You and he, both have God's athletic gifts of size, speed, and strength, but those are just tools. Your drive has to stay in high gear every waking moment to use those tools.

"Often great college players don't make it in the pros. That final jump to the NBA is a completely separate ladder all to itself. Most of all, you need is awareness."

"Awareness?" Larentzo asked.

Coach Sparks had to stop to shake some hands and wave at a few people before he answered. "Son, your education from the classroom to walking in this world as a man is paramount. Look at some of the pros, how they walk and talk and act a fool. How much awareness do you think a person has when he takes some of his millions, buys a hundred thousand-dollar car, spends another twenty-thousand dollars on wheels and stereo, then doesn't pay his traffic tickets, child support, or taxes? Maybe he ended up gambling. Just how much awareness does one of them have when he carries a gun without a permit, and gets pulled over with drugs in his car?"

Some young women came by and asked the players for autographs. Larentzo stopped to sign a few before the conversation could continue.

"Coach, I have too much to live for. Back on the island, I live for many people."

The two took pictures with some fans. The market was loud where they were standing, so they moved away from the crowd. "You do come from a place where they look up to you as one who made it, but your life is just now starting, and you have some challenges ahead. As your coach and friend, I hope to help you not make a mistake that can travel with you the rest of your life."

"Coach, have you done anything you can tell me about that has stayed with you?"

"Well, I don't have any earthshaking news that I know of, but in relation to what I've been sharing with you...you have to be aware that little missteps can cause major sidesteps in your life. What you do today may not show up until later.

"Anyway, keep up with your schoolwork. It could have hurt the team, and hurt you now and in the future."

"I understand, Coach, but can I make it in the NBA if I work as hard as Goldlyn?"

Coach Sparks smiled, because no matter what he said, a young man's ambition to play pro basketball was his foremost thought.

Coach Sparks said nothing for a moment—on purpose—and thought, *Just how do I get these kids to think about their life as it is now?* "Son, can you maintain your drive every practice, every game? Can you be the first in the gym and the last to leave? Will you work hard enough to change the bad to the good? Can you handle your critics in a mature way? Can you be humble when everybody is telling you how good you are? You answer those questions, and you'll have your answer."

Ever since coming from the island of St. Lucia, he and Coach had developed a close relationship. Ayman felt he had to look out for the young man a little more than some of the other players. Even though Larentzo was a few years older than the other players, he was in many ways younger, because of his background.

After the Pike Place Market fun and games, Larentzo sat down on the bus next to Ayman, who said, "Don't stress yourself out over whether you'll make it to the NBA. Enjoy the life you're living right now, Youngblood, don't get caught up in all the hype. Most of all, don't fall for the okey-doke with the girls."

"Huh?" The look on Larentzo's face showed confusion.

The team bus started to pull away. Coach Sparks pointed out the window to the cheerleaders and other girls. "Too many boys leaving college for the pro game have babies to feed. We have one pro football player who took the life of his baby's momma because he didn't want to pay child support when he was making millions."

"Have you always respected women, Coach?" Larentzo did not look his coach in the face when he asked that question.

"I have, at times, failed and I wish I could take it back. But the question goes to my private life, so I'm not going down. I just have to say no man is perfect, and I've made mistakes. We all should hope that we're able to fix, or repent, or say we are sorry, and be forgiving before we leave this earth."

"Coach, I have a girlfriend I like a lot. She's not like some of the girls. She would not want my money if I had any, or if I ever do. She comes from a family that has money. She wants to do good in life without any man controlling her. I respect her for that."

"That's good. I'm not saying every girl is out to set you up, but a major part of this discussion is your need for awareness."

"I read that Goldlyn lived with you while he was in high school. Maybe you could help me keep my focus if I lived with you."

"Larentzo, that was a rare situation that came out of real need. Trust me, I keep a close eye on all you guys, and you can come talk to me anytime. I'll always be here for you, now and years down the road."

Larentzo turned his whole body and watched a ferry crossing the choppy waters of the Puget Sound.

By late Saturday afternoon, Alicia was on the phone wanting to know if Ayman had called Vanita.

"Girl, I've been calling you. Did he call you yet?"

"No, and you know it's one of two things. He's got other women and is tending to them, or he's playing that game of putting a woman on hold."

"Yeah, they can do that, calling a week later. But I didn't get the impression he's that kind of man."

"Oh, and what kind of man do you think he is from the thirty-second meeting you had with him? Do you know something I should know?" Vanita's tone was harsh.

"What's the problem? Why are you trip—" Alicia knew when Vanita went off, she was in or near one of her manic states. Vanita did not fall into that dark world as she used to, and all too few understood.

Medication and some therapy had changed the effects of the sky-high to dark-hellish attitudes that used to come like weather changes in Seattle. Going to work, church, home, and a few friends' homes had kept her somewhat grounded.

The reason her husband had left was he thought she was crazy, and she was driving him crazy. She still had never come to grips with that. What had kept him from leaving for years was plenty of nasty sex, before it became unbearable to be near her.

Some manic-depressive, bipolar people have an aggressive sexual nature. Even when their bodies do not want, the mind can stay in overdrive. Vanita had worn out every man sexually. It was not just how often; it was once sex started, she could not stop. Her fingers and toys kept going, masturbating for hours while men snored.

If she were going into a manic mode, she would let a man have it verbally if he did not want sex. The last man had some getting-it-up problems and she about made him jump off a bridge. When in a deep manic mode, a part of her mind lied to her that she did not do certain things. Yet, in the corners of her mind, it never happened.

The sweetest woman normally could get fixated on something and appear to lose all her common sense and comprehension. The only viewpoint that made sense to her, no one else could deal with.

The worst part of it all, she went undiagnosed for too many years. Friends and family who didn't know better either steered clear or patronized her erratic and often volatile behavior. The person who did finally stand up to Vanita and help her was Alicia.

Confronting Vanita was not easy. Alicia educated herself first and gathered pamphlets, therapist contacts, and mental body armor before approaching her friend.

With today's attitude, Alicia was trying to recall whether Vanita had drunk last night. That was a no-no, along with no sleep. Those two factors, plus some form of stress, could be triggers to send her to the dark side.

"I'm sorry, I'm sorry. I'm tired, I guess," Vanita apologized.

"Where's Joshua?" Alicia asked firmly.

"He's in his room."

"Tell me, and tell me the truth. Did you drink last night?"

"I..."

Alicia knew the answer was yes; she also knew she had to stay in front of Vanita verbally and never let her start defending herself.

"Never mind, I'm coming to get Joshua. You go to bed and relax. I'll rent some movies for him and Calie to watch."

"Your daughter doesn't want to be bothered with my son. All they do is fight over what video game to play. Besides, I'm taking my son to the basketball game. I was able to find some tickets, even though they're not very good seats."

Alicia sounded almost desperate. "Do you think it's a good idea? Think about this. I know you're tired."

"I'm fine, and you worry too much. It's not what you think. You even brought it to my attention that I need to start meeting men again; really, I'm fine."

"You're fine?"

"Yes, I'm fine."

"I don't mean to push, but you need to do one thing. You need to be honest with this man. You have to let him know how things have been, and what you are doing now to keep your health. After that, it's his choice to work with you and understand you."

"Not to worry. I want someone to be honest with too. Okay, this phone is beeping. I hate trying to click over, and we have to get ready to go. We're going to dinner first, then to the game. You know traffic and parking is going to be crazy."

"Okay, have a good time."

The bus pulled up to the hotel where the team would rest and hang out until game time. Ayman was glad to get his room, because he needed some downtime away from Sterlin with his female dilemmas, and from the kids.

He closed the curtains to the Seattle skyline. He stripped down to take a nap. A mirror reflected a tattoo on the cheek of his ass. On his brown skin was the image of a woman's red lips. His ex-wife had convinced him to get the tattoo when they were living in Spain. She modeled her lips, so her name was there in spirit for a lifetime. Vanessa had thickly put on lipstick and kissed his bared ass to leave a perfect lip print for the artist to use as an outline.

Since the divorce, only a few women had seen his naked body. When they asked about the tattoo, he told them he loved to be kissed there, and when they did kiss his butt, his egos smiled.

He turned on his side and reached for the TV remote. The hotel had some Sirius Satellite Radio stations. He heard Lalah Hathaway's voice. It made his ears feel like what his nose and mouth would feel from the sweet taste of hot cocoa; she was vocalizing "Forever, For Always, For Love."

He lay down and as soon as his eyes closed, a beautiful woman appeared. It was Vanita from the previous night, and she was picture-perfect. Ayman rolled onto his back, and placed his hands behind his head. Lalah's groove stole the show for a moment, but

Vanita came back to the forefront when he closed his eyes again.

Will Downing's voice took over the sound waves with "Hey There Lonely Girl." Ayman sat up on the bed, reached in his wallet, and pulled out Vanita's phone number. He dialed. The phone went right to voicemail, catching him off-guard. It beeped before he was ready to leave a message. He stammered, "Ah, this is…Ayman, from last night, Um, I'll try you later." His mind held court. *How is it, I can be out in front of thousands of people and be fine, but just one phone call to a woman and I freak?* He chuckled.

Tired, he finally went to sleep. He dreamed of Vanita's dancing slowly and approaching his waiting body. He awoke later to Michael Henderson's "You Are My Starship." He arose and took a shower until the hotel should have run out of hot water.

17

It's All in the Game

Horns blared, and mini-megaphones intensified the screams. The Key Arena seats were filled with fans wearing the deep-purple colors of the Huskies or the red-plum purple of the Sharks. It was a full house for the Eastside-Westside rivalry. With tipoff time twenty minutes away, both teams were in the locker room.

Coach Sparks pointed to sections on the board of the plays to run when the other team made a change in defense. The last point: never back down.

Coach said in an intense tone, "I know you have some friends over there, but this is your family here, and blood is thicker than water. A shark can make any dog disappear in one bite."

The kids screamed motivating chants, fist-pounded, and slapped hi-fives. It was rare that their coach used the battle cry of spirited inspirations, but for this game he felt after losing two years in a row to the University of Washington, he needed to show more rallying cry emotions.

Coach had one more stimulus to get the kids fired up. "Boys, turn around." The team managers were holding up new uniforms. The locker room erupted and shook. An even deeper purple than the Husky purple glistened. The uniforms had silver trim that almost reflected, but the biggest highlight were the warmup jackets with a silver shark with a dog in its mouth, a grin showing all its teeth. The dog appeared to be a scared, miniature Scooby Doo. Ayman knew he would receive a reprimand from the conference. Ayman also understood it would be light slap on the wrist. The conference would be happy if they beat Washington who is in another conference.

The kids went crazy. They ran back onto the court, pumped. The kids acted as if they could run faster and jump higher.

The Husky players did not see the humor in the rivals' celebration. They were the home team for the game and had to wear plain white jerseys.

The game was a war, the two teams hit the floor tussling and hustling for every ball, even blood ran from cut lips. Exciting plays had the arena at deafening levels. Right before halftime, with ESCU down by six points, Larentzo stole a ball, went the length of the floor, and dunked in the middle of three Husky players. One of them shoved Larentzo, and he turned as if he was going to hit the player, but he just ran back up the floor. Coach Sparks jumped off the bench and screamed at the referees.

Larentzo ran by his coach. "I got this, Coach. I'll make 'em pay." Ayman nodded, but still gave the referee a piece of his mind. Larentzo kept his word and took control of the game, making a three-pointer, a shot he didn't take often. His shooting percentage was low from the three-point line, a part of his game he needed to work on. But he made this one. The next time down on offense, Ayman called out a play with only twenty seconds left before half.

The team passed the ball around, cutting back and forth until Larentzo passed, cut to the basket, caught a perfect pass in midair, and threw down a Seattle wind-storming, thundering dunk. Now the place was too loud for anyone to bear. Halftime, with ESCU up by three and momentum going their direction, it put the Dogs to sleep. In the second half, the Sharks ran all over the Huskies who were beat, losing by fifteen.

A young man Coach Sparks had tried to recruit but who was leaning toward going to the University of Washington came over. His mind was made up; he committed to ESCU.

After the game, the players and coaches debriefed and spoke with the media. A meet and greet to sign autographs for fans in the foyer was next. All players, whether or not they played, had to participate. Since it was a home game, they did not have to ride the team bus back to the campus. There were a few players missing, and Ayman knew who they were without his assistants bringing it to his attention. He would handle it later. Fans and supporters wanted him to sign objects, make comments or ask questions. He charmingly responded quickly to keep the line moving.

Tables were staggered to facilitate picking the players or coach the fans wanted to meet. Sterlin was down at one end, with Ayman at another table.

Sterlin supervised the summer basketball camps, so many young players who had participated in the camps came over to his table to say, "Hi, do you remember me?" He gave generic responses, until two mature women stood in front of his table.

"Oh wow, you made it to the game. How did you like it?" Sterlin rose from his seat and reached for Lois Mae's hand.

"It was exciting; I had forgotten how intense the game can be. This is my friend, Velvet Williams." Sterlin's eyes focused on a flawless face. Her skin was a watered-down cream tone. He could not tell if she was a white woman. She was slightly shorter and wider than Lois, but her curves did not turn the wrong way. Her beauty had his attention, but more than that, he thought he knew her. *I hope she's not someone I slept with.*

Lois Mae scanned Velvet and Sterlin checking each other out. "You two know each other?" *Please tell me she hasn't slept with him.*

Velvet thought, *Where do I know him?* "You used to play pool downtown at Cue It Up?" she asked.

"Yeah, it's been awhile. They closed," Sterlin answered.

Lois Mae said, "Well, we should keep moving. Just wanted to come by and say hi." She was insecure about Velvet's presence. A man she had a crush on from the first sight stood, fine and dressed in a black pinstriped suit that hung off his broad shoulders, like palace drapes. He was checking out her friend as far as she could tell, and that made Lois Mae feel little.

"Why don't you guys meet me and Coach Sparks at Gracias? Do you know where it is?" Sterlin gave an honest invite as his mind had other thoughts. *Yeah, that will be cool. It's one thing for me to try to go without some booty; it's a whole another thing not be around a fine-ass women.*

"Maybe we'll do that," Lois Mae answered curtly. Her eyes signaled for Velvet to move along.

Sterlin had a split-second to watch two stunning big-boned females walk away. *Damn, and I'm in a self-imposed lockdown!*

Down the hall, Ayman stood behind a table and extended his hand to the dream girl from the previous night. Vanita stood alongside her smiling son, who had a new Sharks jersey. He wanted Coach Sparks's signature. His grin widened when his mother seemed to know the coach, because they fell into a conversation. The two seemed to forget that others were in line waiting. Coach Sparks had not let go of Vanita's hand a full minute later.

Vanita nodded her head toward her son. "This is my young

man, Joshua. He wanted you to sign his new jersey, an early Christmas gift."

"Hello, young sir, let me sign that for you. I hope you come back, and I hope you come back often." Ayman bent over to sign his name but looked up at Vanita. Her soft smile made him freeze and stare long after he had signed Joshua's jersey.

"So, you didn't lose the number?" Vanita asked.

"No, I did call and leave a message."

"Oh, I'm sorry. I guess I just didn't check my messages. I wish I had."

Face-to-face with only a table separating them, their eyes hugged what they both wished they could reach and hold.

"Coach, great game. My kid wants your autograph if you don't mind." A fan broke up the shameless game going on in his eyes.

She waved good-bye and mouthed the words, "I'll call you." She turned and sauntered away with her son's hand in tow. His eyes caught her rear in her jeans; his lust ripped off her jeans and imagined her *Good & Plenty* striding naked in her black pumps. She looked back at him and her pretty face stole his heart. They were alone in the mix of many.

"What the hell was that about?" Velvet asked Lois Mae. "You spoke to him as if you didn't want to see him, and he wants to see you." Outside on the way to the car, Velvet wanted to know why Lois Mae was so abrupt.

"I brought competition to the game."

"Game? What?" She laughed and looked at the side of Lois Mae's face. She saw eyes that could have sliced open sharkskin. Her laugh quickly waned. "I ain't slept with him. I just thought I knew him from somewhere. Maybe it was like I said: we crossed paths at the pool hall. Do you really think a fine Black man like that can walk around and no one can see him but you? How about you move into a cave in the hills with him to keep the rest of us man-stealing cavewomen away from him?"

Lois Mae was walking faster. "Stop!" Velvet demanded. Both women turned and faced each other. "You can dish it out, but you can't take the heat in the kitchen when the hot grease is popping your ass! You don't trust me; okay, I understand. But we can't keep doing this."

Lois Mae spoke two words that took about four seconds. "Doing what?"

Velvet lowered her eyes. "I have made too many mistakes. I've danced naked with too many men. I'm dealing with the outcome of that now, but I am no ho. I'm not just a wet spot for a man. I've tried to keep one man in my bed, but my naïve horny ass and too many glasses of wine, have led to fortuitous situations. I have fallen for bullshit. Am I a tramp, a slut, a bitch, or whatever? Do you really want to know what I am? I'm a woman just like you. I make mistakes, just like you. I'm human. What happened back there was innocent, but we're out here acting like children. No, wait, not this time; I'll not take the blame. It's all on you, Lois Mae. You're acting childish."

There was an awkward silence as people passed by on a dark Seattle sidewalk. Wind kicked up and made noises like a horror movie soundtrack.

Lois Mae stared into the dark, avoiding looking at her friend while Velvet continued to talk. "I did not hit on that man; I don't believe he was hitting on me. If you're interested in him, then you should meet him at that place, and you can drop me off." Velvet walked to the parking lot and Lois Mae followed.

The two still had not talked as they drove on for miles. The stereo played Anita Baker's "Fairy Tales." Lois Mae turned down the music and said, "I just made a fool out of myself." Velvet opened her mouth to talk. "No, listen to me. As I get older, I should be more secure, instead of insecure. With or without you, I had no way of knowing what the man wants or doesn't want. My mind has been doing a bump and grind with hopes and dreams, replacing my common sense.

"I had a short professional meeting with him, and since then I've been acting like a young girl with a crush. Just like fairy tales, my daydreaming mind put me on a stage, and my emotions got me booed off. I apologize; let's go have a drink."

Five minutes later, Velvet said, "Sometimes you have to let things fall into place with a man. We both want what most women want: a good man to call our own. Do you think it might be possible we scare off good men by fitting them for a tux and start thinking about bridesmaids just as soon as we meet? We mark them as our man because of our view of an early impression."

Maxwell's live version of "The Lady Suite" was playing when Velvet asked, "Do you think he has a friend for me?" They both chuckled.

They arrived at Gracias Restaurant and hugged before they entered the lounge.

18

Smooth Operator

Baldomero, the bartender, reached over the bar and shook Sterlin's hand. "Good game, Coach. You want the usual?"

"Thanks, I'll wait a minute." Sterlin scanned the club, and the women in the club scanned him. The new age version of *Looking for Mr. Goodbar* stared in awe, batted eyes, pursed lips, and adjusted cleavage. Painted nails combed through blonde, brunette, and the various shades and blends of dyed hair. The regulars (females) held fake smiles well past cutoff time, in hopes that this time he'd come to their table.

Velvet and Lois Mae sat at a back table observing. They knew the play very well. The great Northwest was an interracial haven where mixed couples flourish, and ethnic love blending was as common as the flavored coffee in almost everyone's hand.

Velvet leaned over to Lois's ear. "Well, a cave or fairy tale? You know the deal. Any attractive Black man, shoot, I'm probably too dark, too."

The band played elevator jazz, and patrons chattered louder than the music. Sterlin twisted and turned his body to make his way through the tables until he stood in front of their table. "I assume you two saved this seat for me?" He sat across from them before they answered. They were stunned.

He pulled out his phone and answered a call. "Okay, I'll see you at practice." He flipped his phone closed, and lifted his finger. The bartender nodded his head.

"We weren't sure you were coming," Lois Mae said.

"Oh, there's a lot of end-of-game stuff to do. Sorry about that."

"No problem. We've just been sitting here relaxing, talking about people."

"Talking about people, huh?" Sterlin laughed.

"So we're in here acting like we're better than everybody," Lois Mae said. They all laughed, and kept talking.

Three drinks arrived. The waiter leaned over and whispered into Sterlin's ear. Sterlin shook his head with a firm "no," as he looked across the room. The waiter patted him on the shoulder and walked away.

"Well, we can tell you're a regular here." Lois Mae batted her eyes at Sterlin.

"Yeah, maybe I do come here too much, but I'm happy to be sitting with you two beautiful ladies."

"Ah, isn't that sweet. You keep that up, and I might pay for those three cherries in your drink," Lois Mae teased.

"Too late, your drinks are paid for the rest of the night. Try another night."

Baldomero and Sterlin had a cherry-in-the-drink code. Three cherries in his Whisky Sour meant the company at his table was top shelf. Two cherries meant pretty, and one meant, "Come on, you know better."

A major difference between Sterlin and Ayman was their confidence in social settings and coaching poise. Sterlin's outgoing persona was easygoing, and he could talk to anyone anytime.

Ayman, on the other hand, would blend in with the wallpaper in the middle of a party. A one-on-one intimate conversation was more suited to his personality.

Sterlin had the women laughing and talking as if they had known him for years. Their lively discussion revealed that Lois Mae and Sterlin were both born in Texas only miles apart, and for ten years lived less than twenty miles apart in Houston, until Sterlin moved to New Mexico. Lois Mae's aunt had been Sterlin's Sunday school teacher.

"Yeah, it's a small world we live in. Ask your aunt about the kid with the big head who used to ask those uncomfortable questions."

"What kind of questions did you torture my aunt with?"

"Ah, I asked her, did Adam have wet dreams like me when he saw Eve naked?"

"What? No, you did *not* do that." The next table over laughed as hard as Velvet, Lois Mae, and Sterlin. "What kind of little boy were you?" Lois Mae asked.

"Hey, I was playing hide-and-g-get as soon as I could crawl."

Both women went stereo. "Ooooh, I'm-a-tell."

"Of course, you're reformed, right?" Lois Mae joked.

"Well, I'm on probation."

"What did you say; you're doing some kind of mastur-ahhh-bation." Velvet elbowed Lois Mae in the side and they covered their mouths, laughing.

"You think you're funny. Cute. So, you wanna go back to the playground and play in the dirt, huh? Well, you show me yours and I'll show you mine, as I did with the girls in Sunday school." Sterlin smirked.

"I betcha you were terrible." Lois Mae playfully sneered and reached over and punched Sterlin in his arm, and her hand bounced off. He laughed, as her eyes widened in amazement. The boring, smooth jazz band allowed conversation and Lois Mae told Sterlin she had met Ayman's wife.

"He's like my brother, and she's like my sister, but they're not married anymore." He changed the subject back to them getting to know each other and then more laughs.

One-thirty in the morning, and Ayman was at home talking with Vanita on the phone for an hour and a half. Ayman was going to meet up with Sterlin after the game, but he had something more pressing on his mind—Vanita.

Ayman's slow baritone harmonized with Vanita's sweet alto. The duet was working like verbal Novocain. Each wanted to hear what the other had to say.

"You know, we've been on the phone awhile, and I should be sleepy, but you have me wide awake," Ayman said. Vanita had her eyes closed as she lay back on her bed smiling. "I wish I knew everything there is to know about you, right now."

An hour later, after talking about some of their past, family, friends, her child, and about his coaching life, the tone changed. "Whatcha listening to?" Vanita asked.

"'Pretty Baby' by—"

"Eric Benet, I love his music." She asked bluntly, "Is she still around, your ex-wife?"

"No. She don't park in the Northwest anymore."

"What do you miss about having someone around? I'm not just talking about your wife—in general."

"What I do miss, that quiet interaction where you seem to be working as one mind, one soul, and the affection. What about you? Where's your ex?"

"I hate his ass!" Vanita's soft, sexy voice took a fire and brimstone tone. "My ex, my son is my only connection. He treats me like a condom he'd pull off his dick." Her response threw Ayman. She quickly explained, "I'm sorry; It's kind of a sore spot."

He changed the subject. "So, how do you fill the time…alone?"

"My son is near me all the time, but he's no man. I go to church, and I have a few good friends. You met Alicia."

"Yeah, she's funny."

"My girl has helped me a lot. She thinks you are so handsome."

"And what do you think?"

"Amm, well, I heard an English woman say once in a movie, 'You are gorgeous, darling.'"

"I'm not going to touch that."

"Oh, well, what do you want to touch?"

"Oh, hold on; the line is clicking."

"What, do you have other women calling you at—" Vanita was instantly irate.

"Hold on! If somebody is calling my private line, there's a good reason." Ayman answered and was on the line less than ninety seconds writing down information. He clicked back; Vanita was gone. At the moment he could not be concerned.

Dressed and out of the door in another ninety seconds, he dialed Sterlin while driving well over the speed limit.

Sterlin held the door for Lois and Velvet to exit. Both were still laughing and talking. Velvet stumbled a bit on the way to the car; she'd had too much to drink. They were all going to meet at the IHOP to put some food in Velvet's stomach. Lois Mae was slightly pissed at her, knowing her condition. Sterlin pulled his phone out of his pocket, looked at the number vibrating his cell, and answered.

"What's going on?" He turned away from the ladies. "What?" His voice had volume and slight panic. "I'll meet you there. Yeah, I know where it's at." Sterlin pushed the end button, and faced his female friends. "I have to cut out. We might have some team troubles. I'm sorry, I got to go. We'll get together soon." He hugged both of them in one motion, then ran to his car.

"In his black suit he looks like the Black Superman." Lois Mae smacked her lips. "But Superman isn't into me. But, he still seems like good people."

"I think I know what it is."

"What? And don't tell me you think he's an undercover brother. Please don't let that fine man...ah, no, he's not pitching or catching for the same team."

"That's nasty. Get in the car, and I'll tell you what I think."

Back on the freeway, Velvet said, "He's not into you, because he's into white women."

"If that was true, he had every woman in there besides us to pop the pimples on his booty. Nah, I don't think he would have invited us and then sat at our table."

"Girl, look, I'm not Black; I'm not white. I'm that color they call *other* on the little check box. I see things from a different angle. So many brothers gravitate my way because they can't catch some *Sex in the City* ass. They would screw Carrie Bradshaw's skinny ass or hump Vanna White behind curtain number three if they could. I don't know why he spent time hangin' out on our island, but honey, I could smell Ginger's perfume from *Gilligan's Island* all over him."

"And you talk about me watching too many cartoons. You might want to change channels from the reruns. Personally, I don't think any Black man is totally one way when it comes to a woman's race. It's easy for us to say that a man chases one race or another when we see them with another race."

"I can't believe I'm hearing this from a Black woman. A Black woman like you."

"Like me? Honey, I'm not going to be a hating sista, screaming every Black man who has a white woman is messing up my world. I've been played on, peed on by all kinds of men. I can't concern myself with whether he is with a white woman.

"Too many brothers are in jail, and not enough in school or not working. Some are always reaching up to pull a good woman down. Yet, I know there are plenty of good Black men who I have just not had the pleasure of meeting yet. That's how I choose to look at it."

"So you don't think some men chase one race over another?"

"Don't matter."

"Why?"

"If they don't want me, they will find any number of reasons to avoid me. If a man is gay, there's a straight man looking for me, we just haven't met. If a brother is shady, there's a moral brother out here wanting me, we just haven't met. My saying a man wants a woman of another race instead of me, is saying another woman is better than me. Honey, I'm nearly six feet tall, with every woman who loses weight, her weight relocates to my butt. A man, if he don't want you, he just don't want you!"

"But wouldn't you think that the history of Blacks in America would keep Black men from crossing over?"

"Some people seem to have made uncomplicated choices that are complicated."

Velvet teased, "Honey, you're talking like a sociology professor instead of a literature professor." They both laughed.

"Many Black men have let down the ones who have kissed their skinned knees and soothed their wounded historical pride. The simple truth of our long failing history of *brothers gone bad*; we know about the players and wannabes, the addicts, the criminals, the deadbeat fathers, and other failings. Bad men make it hard on good men to be trusted. And now we hear about the under-cover brother.

"Well, there are *women gone badly*, too. The women who chase after the bad boys. Do we women run away from the soft-spoken, mild-mannered, hardworking, low-income man? You know we have. Do women have the same problems as men? Yes! The drink and drugs infect us as much as anyone, but it is highly ignored. There is a need for some of us to be medicated. Bad mothers; there are some women who should have never dropped their drawers. No offense."

Velvet responded quickly, "None taken. I haven't proved to be a bad mother yet."

Lois Mae wanted to stay on point and moved to another point to avoid going deeper into Velvet's problem.

"Men—all men, not just Black men, have problems. White men are some of the biggest whores to walk this earth; history shows that. Those founding fathers, like Thomas Jefferson, had his favorite little slave girl. Look at that shades of Black people. It doesn't take a rocket scientist to figure out how that came about. You and I get hit on by white men as if it's a sport. I know a little something about race mixing.

"I'm from Texas, and you would think that white women and Black men would avoid each other. They don't. The same could be said about Black women and white men avoiding each other. They don't. I didn't."

"What? You dated white men?" Velvet said it loud enough for people two thousand miles away in Texas to hear.

"In college."

"Hmm, look at you, dipping Mr. Marshmallow in your hot chocolate."

"Once. My first."

Velvet's eyes widened as she studied the side of Lois Mae's face. The Chrysler 300 digital dash lights flickered in her eyes, and off of her skin. "Was it just sex?"

"Loved him." The tension in her voice stretched the two words into a poem.

"I'm listening."

"I was a freshman in college, and he was a basketball player."

"That's a different twist: a black female and a white jock."

"It happens. Sistas cross over under the sheets or live in the suburbs with their Caucasian husbands. The other part of Black history is, how do I tell some brother with a light complexion whom he can date when he may have a white mother, grandmother, or great-grandfather?"

Velvet shook her head. "Yeah, but a lot of these brothers, I watch them ignore Black women when they are with a white woman."

"And I can assume sometimes that these brothers avoid inter-action because they've received the third degree from a sista. And maybe some brothers act a fool because they are fools. I hate that shit too, but I don't want his ass, either. I also hate that another Black woman will look at my big black ass, and think I might be a threat to steal her man. I say all this, because there are too many damn reasons."

Velvet chuckled. "I understand."

Lois Mae sounded apologetic as she said, "I'm not trying to be funny, but you're not Black, but only date brothers. Why?" Lois Mae took her eyes off of the road for a quick glance and smiled at Velvet to reassure her she meant no harm.

Velvet stroked her chin as if she were a man with a goatee, and shrugged her shoulders. "I attended Rainier Beach High School when my parents moved to Seattle. It was a racially mixed school, and for the most part everybody got along. And you know I was the finest thing to ever walk on the halls."

"Girl, please."

"Well, most of the white boys were scared of me. The nice ones would flirt but would never date me. The other white boys could be so rude and crass. The Black boys were smoother. They saw my booty and my pretty face, and they said sweet things in what sounded poetic. You know, like Teddy Pendergrass talking to you. It just seemed the Black boys were more confident in how they carried themselves; that was attractive and sexy before I knew what sexy was. And to this day, when I see chocolate milk in the store, I cream. Sonny Glass, my first—he was midnight, pitch-black, chocolate sweet to look at and listen to. I would start stepping out of my panties, when he walked by. We did it in his daddy's Cadillac up in Seward Park."

Lois Mae laughed and teased Velvet, "Damn, up in the park in daddy's caddy. You had your big legs all gapped open. I see one foot tangled up in the steering wheel, and your other foot hanging over the back of the front seat. Damn, you a freak." Lois Mae laughed, and drove her car into the other lane. A car honked at her for cutting them off.

"My legs weren't as big back then." They giggled. "But it sounds like you know all about humping in a car."

"Only after I was married, girl, did I do anything like that, and that was in a van."

"I hope you don't think I chase a Black man because of so-called jungle fever."

"No, I don't. I'm aware that jungle fever exists, but I think in most cases, it's much deeper than an animalistic attraction."

"Animalistic." Velvet laughed hard and put her finger to her lips as if someone else might hear what she had to say. "Don't you ever tell anybody, but while Sonny was going down on me, his dog was in the backseat and started licking my toes. I came so hard."

"What the fuck…You, you, you, are so nasteee. And, hell no, I would never tell anybody, and claim I knew you." They both laughed until tears rolled as Lois Mae pulled into Velvet's driveway.

"Tell me about your first, this white basketball player?"

"My grandfather is white," Lois Mae said.

"Oh."

"My complexion, it doesn't show my white blood, because my grandmother and my momma were purple black, but these brown eyes are not fake." Lois Mae put the car in park and laid her head back. "I went to my grandfather's farm almost every summer in a place called North Texas County. My cousins would all come. As Black as we were, we loved being there with our white granddaddy. He loved us. My grandmother, his wife, died when I was a teenager.

"That part of Texas had many Black farmers. There might have been more Blacks than whites in that part of the county, but rednecks still ruled. One day while walking home from town, a few of the redneck, teenage boys got stupid. They called me and a young white girlfriend names. You know, 'nigger-lover' and 'nigger-bitch.' My shining white knight pedaled up on his bike and beat the crap out of one of the boys. He didn't say much then, or much after. Later he went on to be the local sports star stud.

"We crossed paths when I was going to the University of Houston. He wasn't one of the star studs anymore, just one of the players on the bench. It was the glory years of the Houston teams. His name is August. We connected at a party when I was in my freshman year. We ended up laughing and talking about the old times back when we were kids in North Texas County. We spent time together, acting as if we had no interest in each other. I assumed it was because he was white. We saw each other always with other people around. I was still a virgin; had that stupid thought it was time to give it up. I picked him. He picked me, as time would tell. I loved him in a way that was immature and simple.

"Believe it or not, I smoked reefer back then, and acted like I had smoked and drank too much one night."

"Oh no, you lost your virginity like so many of us pure maidens do; acting a fool to hide our shameful desires."

"Yep, that was me. We had sex in his dorm room. The next day he acted as if he didn't know me, and that was fine. I knew the end of the story before I lay down despite the fact I thought I loved him. It was about losing my cherry. I just wished I hadn't developed feelings for him."

"Well, most women can't brag about the first time. How many can claim they gave up the booty in a five-star hotel to romantic music and champagne? How many women can say the first time they put their booty up in the air for Prince Charming, he stayed Prince Charming for the rest of their life?" Velvet laughed when she started to exit the car.

"He was…is my cousin."

"What the hell!" Velvet sat back down and closed the door. "Honey, a dog licking my toes versus you…"

"He knew, but I didn't find out until my grandfather passed that next year. You know how sometimes kinfolk dying brings families together for as long as the fried chicken lasts. My father was speaking to August's mother at the gravesite. Come to find out, she's on the other side of my grandfather's family that had a problem with Granddaddy having a Black wife, my grandmother.

Dad introduced me to his white first cousin. I can still hear so cheerfully, the sarcastic Texas drawl."

Lois Mae did a vocal impression. "You're so pretty. You look like your grandmother with those big bones and lovely hair. You know my son says he sees you at school. I remind him to look out for his cousin all the time."

"I'm sorry. That had to be a harsh time in your life. As you said, we've all been played on, peed on. It's all in the past, honey, and it don't matter now."

The story was not over for Lois Mae. "Ten years later, one of my brothers bought the farm from another family member, and he moved there. I went to visit, and ran into August in town. He had his wife and two children with him—his Black wife and mixed daughters. I can only imagine what his momma was feeling. I try to fool myself, and remind my soul he was only my second cousin, as if it makes a difference. Needless to say, I know the other side of a few things."

Velvet squeezed Lois Mae's hand and got out, but before she closed the door, she said, "Chocolate pudding, honey, he got a taste of your pudding. Whenever you write your book one day, a chapter should be named, 'Chocolate Pudding,' the cure for racist bullshit."

Back on the road, Lois Mae put in Minnie Riperton's *Greatest Hits* CD. The song "Perfect Angel" flowed, and then faded into "Back Down Memory Lane."

19

Do the Right Thing

Sterlin arrived at the Pole in the Hole Gentleman's Club minutes ahead of Ayman. The strip club on Aurora Avenue was near several clubs. They both parked in the back of the club. Sterlin got into Ayman's Jag and they watched police car lights flashing.

"A couple of our kids had fake ID's and were inside the strip club. They had a beef with a U-Dub fan outside the club, and are drunk," Ayman said.

"Who? Dumb-Ass Meredith and Kevin?"

Ayman nodded. "Earl was on duty. He got the call and called me. He has our kids in his car, and the other cops got the other boys." Earl, a Seattle police officer, lived on the Eastside and often worked out in the ESCU campus gym. The former champion weightlifter had befriended Ayman and Sterlin.

Sterlin slowed his words. "Here's what I know; it's the blues man." Ayman looked at Sterlin. "Across the street there's an under twenty-one dance club. We had some other kids over there. One of them was Larentzo. He was leaving the club and saw Dumb-Ass and Kevin from across the street, fighting."

"Tell me this is not going to be a nightmare?" Ayman blew out a long breath, as he noticed local TV news vans setting up shop across the street.

"So far, what I do know, Larentzo and his girlfriend came across the street and his girlfriend was assaulted by a U-Dub fan. Larentzo punched the fan and knocked him the fuck out."

"Oh, man, no."

"Yeah, this is a mess." It was Sterlin's turn to blow out a chest full of air.

A couple of strippers were hanging out by the back door, half-ass naked. More police arrived to block off the parking lot. Three graduate coaches' staff approached his car, and he rolled down his window.

"We got here as soon as we could," one of them said.

Ayman gave directions. "Two of you find all team members and centralize them, then move them away from here. They are not to speak to anyone; no TV or radio people. Call a team meeting for seven in the morning.

"Lorrie, I want you to gather information on who they might have in custody, or are just holding for questioning. Earl, the real big cop, you might recognize him from working out in our weight room. Tell him you want to check for any injuries that might have occurred to any of the players. When you talk to the players, tell them not to give any information to the police until I or a lawyer is present. I mean name only. There's a young lady involved; get her name, and if you can, tell her the same thing."

"Got it, Coach." Ayman rolled up the window.

"Why did you send her over there, instead of the other guys?" Sterlin asked.

"Earl has a crush on her," Ayman responded with no inflection.

"But she's a lesbian, right?"

Ayman turned toward Sterlin, but stopped from completely

staring at him; his eyes were fixed on the passenger side mirror.

"Okay, it doesn't matter." Sterlin had one of the answers that Ayman wanted to know. "It's Tyreene, Tylowe's daughter, that Larentzo has been seeing."

Tyreene Dandridge was the daughter of one of their best friends, Tylowe Dandridge. Tylowe, Ayman, and Sterlin had become friends in college at the University of New Mexico. When Ayman came to the Northwest, he and his old college friends reconnected and rode motorcycles. Tylowe owned the motorcycle dealership where he purchased his motorcycles.

While Ayman was still married, the two guys would put their wives on the back of their bikes and take couples road trips to Canada. Ayman and Sterlin were like uncles to Tylowe's two daughters. Tyreene, a star basketball player, was on the women's team at East Seattle City University.

"The media would love to shove the camera in your face." Sterlin looked out the back window as he spoke. Ayman answered his cell phone.

"I'm gathering information. I will update as soon as I can." He flipped his phone close. "That was Buckett. You know it would make his day if we had kids in jail."

"Yeah, our wonderful athletic director, he'll blame you no matter what." Sterlin kept staring and talking to the back window. "Here comes Lorrie."

Ayman rolled his window down. "They are arresting Meredith and Kevin for drunken and disorderly conduct and for having fake ID," Lorrie said. "It appears Larentzo is not in trouble, but the kid he hit is screaming bloody murder. Several witnesses have come forward and are saying the man got in Larentzo's face, took a swing at him, and got knocked out. The police are charging the guy, but not Larentzo. Officer Earl said he will personally take Larentzo and his girlfriend, Tyreene, to her home."

Ayman nodded his head. "Good job. Seven in the morning, team meeting." He rolled the window up, then drove over to Sterlin's car. "Meet me over at Tylowe's."

Four stoplights down the road, away from the troubles and unforeseen repercussions, Ayman's thoughts gave way to the hour before. He dialed Vanita's number and it went straight to voicemail. *"I'm not available. Please leave a message."* Her voice, soft, but businesslike, left him feeling as if he had done her a grievous wrong.

I did leave her hanging. Damn, I'd rather be on the phone with her than dealing with this mess. He turned on the radio. Michael Powers's guitar was strumming "Frosty the Bluesman." It was two weeks before Christmas. Basketball season consumed most of the seasonal holiday joy. Now it was doubtful there would be any holiday cheer.

A beautiful woman with unique facial features and the skin tone of a brown fall leaf smiled at Ayman and Sterlin. It was a beautiful smile to see on a difficult night. They were at the home of Tylowe Dandridge.

"Come in," Tylowe's wife said. "He's in the den. I'm making coffee."

"Meeah, if there is any woman I want to open a door right now, it would be you," Ayman said. He hugged her, and Sterlin kissed her on the cheek on the way to the den.

Tylowe rose from his seat, and without saying a word, he grabbed Sterlin and hugged him, while a young woman with watery eyes hugged Ayman tightly.

Ayman put both hands on her shoulders and squatted down to her eye level. "Mia, everything is going to be okay. Your sister will be here shortly. She's fine." The four people in the room switched places to hug.

"I woke Mia up," Tylowe said, "because we work everything out in this house together. I didn't know how before I gained a family, but that's how we do it now."

Ayman nodded.

Meeah walked in, carrying a tray of cups loaded with coffee and slices of cake and pie. The doorbell rang, and Tylowe motioned for Ayman to go to the door with him. A five-minute conversation took place at the door before it closed.

Tyreene Pearlene Dandridge entered the den and was rushed and hugged by her sister, Mia. Larentzo followed, and Meeah hugged him and held him for a long while. She'd already heard that he had stood up and tried to protect her daughter.

He laid his head on her shoulder, his soft eyes blurry with tears.

The doorbell rang again, and a moment later, the ESCU women's basketball coach walked into the room with Tylowe and Ayman.

"Coach Newton," Tyreene said in an apologetic tone. The coach nodded.

Ayman led the meeting. He first wanted to know all the details the two young people could tell him.

Larentzo and Tyreene were leaving from the under twenty-one dance club. They saw his teammate involved in a scuffle across the street in the adult club parking lot. Larentzo ran over to help with the intention of getting his teammate out of there. Tyreene followed, and a Washington State Cougar fan—not a U-Dub Husky fan, got in her face and called her an East-stink-like-a-fish-bitch in reference to her ladies Sharks jersey. He then told her she should go into the strip club, and get hooked on the stripper pole and flop like a fish on stage.

Larentzo said he was trying to walk away with his teammates and Tyreene when the idiot tried to put a dollar bill down Tyreene's jersey. The women's team had badly beaten the Washington State Cougars the previous week.

The inebriated idiot threw a punch at Larentzo, but missed, however, Larentzo did not. The Washington State fan lost some dental work.

Ayman wanted to give the young man a high-five, but he had to be coach. The adults agreed how to address the media, and legal issues from their end of the situation.

Larentzo asked Ayman, "Coach, am I suspended?"

"No, not as far as I'm concerned. The university may have something to say about all this, but I think you're in the clear. You're in the clear with me, and I'll push that."

Tyreene looked over at her coach wanting to know was she in any trouble, and her coach told her no.

Ayman handed his keys to Larentzo. "Go wait in my car."

Tyreene and her sister, Mia, headed to another part of the house.

"How did it get past me that they were dating?" Ayman asked. He had a smile on his face for the first time in hours.

Meeah answered, "When they did a photo shoot for all those team billboards, they became close. He's a good kid, and he respects her. He told me he was raised in an orphanage in St. Lucia because his mother was so poor and had substance abuse problems. It proves good things about the human spirit when they want better for themselves. He's very fond of you, Ayman. He talks about you like you're a god." Ayman's lips pressed tight and into a closed-mouth grin.

Ayman had another stop at the police station. When he got there, he had Larentzo stay in the car. When Ayman walked in, he saw Coach Leassler, Meredith's father, who was also the school's women's softball coach. The man had his hand on his hips, accentuating a gut hanging lower than the zipper of his pants. The two coaches had no love for each other. Ayman viewed him as a man with a tail.

"Coach," Meredith's father said, even though the greeting was disdainful.

"Coach." Ayman's greeting might as well have said, *"Go screw yourself."*

"I understand your foreign boy hit and hurt someone, but my son is here and that violent boy is not."

Sterlin walked up behind Coach Leassler and drew his attention. There was silence in the hall. The three men adjusted their positions to form a triangle.

Coach Leassler was slightly taller than Ayman, but had the belly girth of a woman long past the due date of her pregnancy. Ayman's facial expression at that moment made him exceedingly dangerous-looking, but he chuckled coolly.

"You think all this is funny?" Coach Leassler asked.

Ayman, the man of cool said, "Coach Leassler, this is a time you might want to put yourself into coaching mode and forget about being an overprotective daddy blinded by ignorance. You don't have the facts, and I will not discuss any of the details with you until you are willing to converse with the best interest of the team and the school. I will tell you this, though. If your son is less than truthful at anytime, he will never play another minute at ESCU. Your son is drunk, and I'm sure they are taking a blood test right now to confirm it. You might want to suck in your gut and get a dose of reality, and a good lawyer." Ayman took away all the man's personal space and got nose to nose with Coach Leassler. He was so close he was stealing the air from going up the man's nose. "And if I hear you use the words, 'foreign' or 'violent,' with a negative connotation, or anything derogatory about any of the kids I coach, I will gut you like a dead pig. That is not a threat!" Ayman pushed his finger into the man's bulbous belly, and poked deep into his flesh. Coach Leassler tried to show resistance, but lost the battle and moved back.

It was now five in the morning, and change-of-shift police were milling about. Ayman did not see them or care if they heard him. Mr. Cool was hot, but under control. Ayman continued to talk, while Coach Leassler stood petrified. "I will defend any player on my team. I don't give a damn if his name is Ted-F-ing-Bundy, and that includes your son." Ayman stepped around him and went to the main desk.

Forty minutes later, Coach Sparks, Coach Leassler, his son, Meredith, and the other player, Kevin, walked out of the police station. There would be more to deal with later, but for now, Coach Ayman Sparks had enough influence to help release his players.

20

Justice For All

7:00 a.m. All ESCU basketball team coaches and the athletic director attended an earlier morning emergency team meeting. Coach Sparks dispelled rumors and reminded them they were equally team and family.

"We must respect each other when we do well in life, and when we fail, on or off the court. You are going to have TV and radio media in your face. Keep our family business in the family. If you let strangers in your home, you will not have a home. The Bible says, 'A kingdom at war with itself will collapse.'"

At 10:00 a.m. in the conference room, Athletic Director Buckett headed a meeting with Coach Sparks. Also in the meeting were Coach Leassler and two university legal consultants along with Meredith and Kevin. Kevin's parents lived in Montana and were on speakerphone during the meeting.

The legal consultants made it clear that Meredith and Kevin had to be suspended. The criminal charges hanging over their heads were not the school's problem until they were found either guilty or innocent. However, the young men had been involved in behavior unbecoming of the school's rules of conduct for students on scholarship.

This made Coach Sparks's job a lot easier. It took him out of the discipline loop; the system would control the punishment and any penalties. Coach Leassler sat heavy in his chair. A press conference was called to inform the public that the school would not tolerate its student athletes crossing the line. The TV cameras from local sports news and ESPN rolled as Coach Sparks stepped to the microphone.

He remained cool and calm at the microphone stand, answering mindless questions that anyone could answer, whether you coached marbles or a major college basketball program.

"Coach, will this affect your season?"

"We'll adjust."

"Coach Sparks, do you think this reflects on the team maybe needing more rules?"

"Locks are to keep honest people honest. If the temptation to do something wrong overwhelms someone, no amount of rules will help." Ayman even handled the purposely ignorant reporter.

"Coach, I understand that a Black player was involved in a fight at the club at the same time. Why isn't he suspended, yet two white players who don't play much anymore have been suspended? There's some rumor that these two players have not been happy lately."

Coach Sparks did not flinch and responded with a smile, "This is where you might want to do your homework. If it's important for you to make yourself feel important, that makes you appear to be an incompetent reporter who would rather make newfangled news. The facts of the night and the people involved at the clubs are being handled by the university.

"This great university would never allow any coach to make consciously ridiculous decisions of the type implied by your statements. However, for the record, look around the room. I see your fellow reporters looking at you with disdain.

"A coach of a major college program who has had successes cannot play favorites where race is concerned. Any reasonably educated person would have that much understanding. A deliberately deceptive statement such as the one you have made in front of your colleagues, show us you are the one with a major issue." The room full of media people chuckled while Coach Sparks made a fool of the reporter.

By 2 p.m., the drama had quieted. Even the athletic director had to let his head basketball coach know he appreciated his professionalism. Ayman needed to handle another situation. He needed sleep. He also needed to make contact with a woman.

Sterlin's voice boomed, "I need for you to leave me alone! Let me repeat this for you again, and for the umpteenth time, I don't want you, but you keep bringing your silly ass around—un-announced." Sterlin's anger was piledriving into Bobbie's reddening face as she stood in his doorway.

Since summer, she had showed up anytime at his doorstep, and Sterlin would end up slamming the door with orders not to return. A few women were doing similar things. Ayman would tease, telling Sterlin to put his lawyer on speed dial to expedite restraining orders. It had never reached that level, because they normally moved on, eventually. In the past month he had two other women show up and the same scene as now had happened.

"You don't understand," Bobbie pleaded.

"Step!" A bass note from Sterlin roared deep from his chest, and he closed the door. After talking to Ayman and some self-examination, he realized he was the one who was fooled into thinking he was the shit, and now he had craziness showing up at his door.

I'm a forty-three-year-old man still playing twenty-year-old games.

Ayman is right. I need to chill. He laughed aloud in the middle of his inner conversation. *Damn, I'll have to start jacking off like a teen-age boy. A man's got to do what he's got to do.* He laughed, walking through his place.

He thought a little ride might help relieve all that had happened. He went down to his garage and started up his motorcycle. He wiped it down, checked the air pressure. It had been awhile.

The weather was clear and crisp. He rolled the bike down the driveway while the motor was warming up. He ran back into the house to put on his insulated riding pants and was gone for about three minutes. When he walked back into the garage, he heard the motorcycle rev extremely high, and then came metal and plastic crashing sounds. He ran down the driveway to see his two-wheel cruiser lying on its side and a yellow Porsche Boxster screeching its tires, as it sped away.

"Bobbie!" His voice was like a harpoon. She stopped. He ran toward her car and had almost reached her when she burned rubber again. She was not going forward but in reverse and he had to jump out of the way. He lived on a quiet tree-lined street. The two of them made it freeway loud.

The reality of his motorcycle being knocked over gave him the highest dose of anger-fed adrenaline. Sterlin was many ways wrong when it came to women, but he was not ignorant of knowing he was a Black man chasing a white woman down a city street. She stopped her car, sneered at him, and screamed, "This ain't over!"

He cursed her under his breath while he stood on the curb, then walked back to his house. She drove away slowly.

The motorcycle was still running. He turned the key off, picked up his toy, and wheeled it back into the garage. He did not care about the damage at that moment. He closed the garage door and pulled off his riding clothes, then turned on the house alarm.

Ten minutes later, with a shot of whisky in hand, he sat in his hot tub. He needed to decompress. His mind forced thoughts that he spoke aloud to the bubbling water.

What in the hell am I doing? I could have killed her. It's not the first time I've let an oversized Barbie doll get too much and then want too much. Shit, last night's mess with the kids and now this. I could have ended up on the wrong end of the news. If Ayman heard about this, damn, I don't even want to think about his reaction. Damn. I'm a grown-ass man. I need to act grown up. Hot steam and whiskey helped soothe his psyche.

"I wasn't sure what to make of you having to get off the phone so abruptly. Then I saw the news reports and the press conference. Is everything going to be okay?" Vanita's call awoke Ayman.

"We had to move quickly to bring things under control, I believe." He started moving around and dropped the phone. "Excuse me, I have a bit of a headache, and I'm headed down to my kitchen to get some water and see what I can find to eat. Aspirin sours my stomach without food."

"Poor baby. You have been through a lot." Her voice was lessening his pain.

"I am really sorry about leaving you hanging last night. Can I make it up to you?"

"Yes, you can, if only you let me do something for you."

"What might that be?" he asked.

"Let me bring you a plate of food."

"No, nah, you don't need to do that."

"Are you the kind of man that can't let a woman do something for him?" She chuckled.

"I don't have any fight in me right now."

"No need to fight me, but naked wrestling is okay."

"You're funny," Ayman said in a hushed voice through the phone. "I know you have a son to tend to, so how are you going to get away to bring me a plate?"

"My friend Alicia took him to the movies."

"Okay." They spoke a while longer, and he gave her directions to get to his house.

The phone rang. Lois hated answering the phone while watching *Cold Case*. The Black detective reminded her of her favorite uncle. The caller ID read "private."

"Hello."

"How's my juicy fruit?" Vance the Vampire, her first ex-husband, was on the line.

Lois spoke into the phone as if she were bored, "What do you want?"

"I was just thinking about your sweet ass."

"Yeah, and everything that has an ass from a jackass to a dead ass. Please, Negro, give it a rest. The only reason you called me is to see if you can get some ass. It ain't that kind of party no more."

"Dead ass? Aren't you the one with one dead-ass husband six feet in the ground? I'm the living ex-husband with the big dick, remember?"

Her mind seized, her eyes dulled, her lungs froze, and not even blood pumped for a moment. The verbal punch from her first ex floored her but he didn't knock her out.

"That hurt Vance, but you have always been a punk. God loves you, but He don't like the ugly you have always done to me. As I said, you called testing the waters to see if you could get some. Well, get this." Lois quietly hung up the phone.

After the murder of Lois's second husband during a home robbery, Vance helped during the early emotionally trying times. He spent time with her, acting like he was her friend. Lois's soul dripped pain; she needed closeness. He wanted booty, and she had sex with him. Every now and then, he called hoping for another taste. That would never happen again, and she made it clear. He had become verbally mean and had said she would never have another man and other spiteful things each time she rebuffed him.

A minute later the phone rang again. She answered by putting the receiver on the coffee table and turning up the TV volume. A smile returned to her face.

21
Reasons

Ayman peeked out of the front window, waiting. Earth Wind & Fire's *Greatest Hits* CD was playing throughout the house. With his black, silk smoking jacket, and red, silk pajama bottoms, he could pass for a black British prince. All he needed was a pipe the shape of an upside-down question mark.

The house was always presentable to company but he walked around for a final inspection. Back in the bedroom, he stopped at the mirror. *Look at me, dressing to impress.* He laughed. The door-bell rang. He jumped out of his red silks, pulled on some jeans, and hurried to the door.

A shivering smiling face rushed in when Ayman opened the door. A plate covered with foil was in Vanita's hand.

"Hi, let me take that," he said.

"I can't believe you got me over." She smiled.

"I got you over here? What you talking about? I didn't invite you. Thanks for the food, good-bye." He tried to keep a straight face but couldn't. He burst out laughing.

"Ah, a smart-butt, I see." She laughed with him. Then she stared at him. His scent, his eyes, his smile with the perfect goatee wrapped around his full lips, his voice, and his presence froze her in time. Seeing him so close and in a different light, with no one around, he was even sexier than usual. Embarrassed by her reaction, she hoped he wouldn't say anything, and she smiled apologetically. "You should take this plate to the kitchen," Vanita said, leaning her head to one side. He tilted her head the other way to tease her. "Funny man."

He nodded in the direction he wanted her to go.

He walked behind her, observing her blue calf-length leather coat, which flexed around her hips with each step. Her black slingback shoes clicked on the hardwood floor with her long strides.

Vanita stopped after taking four steps into the kitchen. Gray slate floors expanded into a room the size of her living room, dining room, and kitchen. There was a breakfast nook in a glass sunroom at the end, with double doors that opened onto a patio. A center island of twenty feet or more had two sinks, two ovens, and two cook tops, with food prep areas on both ends highlighting the room. Alternatively, it might have been the black marble countertops and the frosted glass windows in dark mahogany wood kitchen cabinets encircling the whole room that stole the show.

After her Home Improvement TV moment, she walked over to the center island and set the plate down. Vanita spoke with no inflection and said, "She cooked!"

No sense in playing dumb, he thought, and answered, "Yeah."

She was keenly aware of her surroundings as she viewed more of the kitchen. The kitchen was a chef's dream. He broke concentration. "I appreciate you bringing me some home-cooked food. This place hasn't seen any real food other than take-out or cold cereal in awhile. I don't cook that much except grits and eggs." Ayman sensed it might be a problem for her to have seen his kitchen, which used to be another woman's kitchen.

Vanita walked around the island, admiring the complete layout. As she approached Ayman, her eyes fixed on his. "Do you get lonely here?"

"Yeah, but this is just where I lay my head." It sounded like he was apologizing.

"I have to go," she said. It was his turn to tilt his head in wonderment. She continued, "My friend will be bringing my son home soon."

"Okay, I understand."

"Mr. Ayman," her voice teased, "you within, a short time, have me so into you. From our first meeting and our late-night phone call, which was unfortunately cut short—although, I do now understand—anyway, I like you." She kept talking as she walked toward the front door. He followed her and listened, watching the blue animal skin move with each step she took. "I'm not sure this is a good thing—me liking you. I have my young son to care for. If I let someone in…I can't believe I'm saying all this, and I'm sure you don't want to hear it."

The sound of her heels became a fast-paced click-clacking. When she reached the door, Ayman reached over her shoulder and held the door from opening. He did not do it in a threatening manner. Her head lowered. He removed his hand from the door and gently turned her as if he were turning back the hands of time. Two of his fingers lifted her chin. Her eyes closed with nervous tension. He leaned over to let his lips touch each of her eyelids with feather-light kisses. His lips found their way to the tip of her nose. He had been admiring her cute little nose, which he kissed. It flared and anxiety shook her body. He kissed the freckles under her eyes.

Ayman placed his hands on her upper arms, holding her. He leaned in and turned his head to kiss her lips. His lips touched hers ever so lightly to where a soft breeze could pass through. His touch was radiantly warm. He waited for her to initiate more pressure. She waited for him, absorbing the mesmerizing numbness of his closeness.

She pulled her lips away and leaned her forehead on his shoulder. Her feet shuffled to the song, "Be Ever Wonderful." She kept her head on his shoulder and slow-danced. He wrapped his arms around her and let her lead. The song was near the end when their lips touched again and this time she pressed her lips against his. Slowly, they let their lips gently touch. The slow dance slipped into another song, "Reasons."

Right at the point of parting their lips, she said, "Oh, this is too good, I should go." Vanita turned to open the door but turned back. She kissed him, their tongues dancing for the time the high voice and saxophone called and answered, back and forth. Their lips rested on each other, before they fully parted. A long stare promised there would be more to come.Vanita left, and Ayman watched her trot to her vehicle, her heels click-clacking.

It was one in the morning again. Ayman and Vanita had been on the phone for three hours. They were having another smooth conversation much like the other night. It started out as friendly talk about basketball and the media things he dealt with as a coach.

The conversation moved along, and as the night progressed, they became playful and teasing. In the last half-hour, they kept toeing over the flirtation line. Vanita opened the door to her bedroom through the phone line. She had been touching herself for the last half-hour, listening to his voice. He had that magic tone that made her body tingle when his voice flowed in her ears. At a certain point, Vanita had a short, light orgasm, rushing her honey all in between her fingers as she kept squeezing her nipples, and sliding her fingers over and into her wetness.

Ayman thought her sighs were sexy, and she sighed a lot when they were on the phone. Vanita almost gave herself away, but Ayman didn't catch on. He asked her if everything was all right. She said she just needed some water. She put the phone down, went into her dresser drawer, and pulled out a three-pronged Rabbit vibrator. When she got back in the bed, she placed a towel under her hips, then pushed and slid the toy inside her wetness. The phone receiver mouthpiece was lying facedown on a pillow, but even then Ayman heard a faint non-painful grunt-groan.

She picked up the phone. "I'm back. Sorry it took me so long."

"Are you okay?"

"Yes, I'm fine. Ayman, I love your voice. It is so...tell me a bedtime story."

"A bedtime story?"

"I want to hear your voice in my ear as I lie here in the dark."

"Hmp, what kind of story are you talking about?"

"The kind of story that starts with the way you kissed me earlier."

"Well, that kind of story would have juicy, sexy kinds of things going on."

She spoke to him in a soft pleading tone, "Please tell me!" She placed a pillow over the vibrator to muffle the sound as she pushed the "on" button to high.

"Are you sure?" he asked.

"I'm all ears, talk to me."

"Well, let me think."

"Make me feel you want me...please!"

"I do, but I don't want to scare you away."

"You know we are grown, and we can say what we feel, so if I was to let you do anything to me, what would you do?"

Ayman was turned on hearing her speak, but some concern drifted through his mind. Was he leading her on? Would she turn off if he went too deep? Was there a line to be crossed with their short acquaintance?

"Ayman, I want you to tell me what you want to feel, if you could have me." She was doing a lot of sighing and taking deep breaths that Ayman could hear.

"Close your eyes and think about my lips raining down kisses onto your chocolate skin like a warm shower. Against the entry door where we have already kissed, I wanted to pin you to the door with my body pressing you tight."

"I wanted you to pull my hair," Vanita cooed.

"I will pull your hair so I can lick and kiss you on your neck. When I do pull your hair, you feel my demands, my wants and needs. I'll put my hands on your hips and squat down and as I pass by your breasts, I'll lick and suck your breasts."

"Damn! I would like that. My nipples are hard right now… ooh, baby."

"I noticed your nipples say hello through whatever I've seen you wear."

"You like that?"

"I love it."

"I have a nipple in between my fingers right now and if you were here, I would lick them for you to watch, or hold them for you to suck."

Ayman was lying on his own bed, back in his red silk pants, squirming.

"I would like to see that. What are you doing?" he asked. Ayman could hear the buzzing in the background. Her sighs and long breaths told him what she was doing, but he wanted her to say it.

"I'm letting my hands and a little friend do to me what I want you to do."

"Wish I could watch." Ayman had eased out of his silk pants. He held his hardness, but did not stroke it. Talking to her was his first priority. He wanted to hear her get off. There were no more thoughts of, *Is there a line to cross?*

"You wanna watch me lie here with my toy in me? It's going in me like I want you to. Baby, talk to me...please."

"As I was squatting down, I lift your dress and go under. My hands will squeeze that perfect ass of yours." It seemed for a moment that Vanita stopped breathing while Ayman told her more. "I'm licking your thighs, both sides, getting closer to your panties. When I get there, you spread your legs and place your hands on my bald head as I slide my tongue in you. You hold my tongue like you're holding that toy inside now. I sniff you. I taste you. You taste like sugar, I'm sure. My tongue becomes your toy, doing nasty things to your wetness. Because you have squatted far enough and spread your legs wide enough, I am able to lick you in one long, slow, tongue drag, and I keep licking you like that over and over."

Ayman could hear her panting hard. She was cursing underneath her breath. He thought about what it must look like as her vibrator made her legs quiver and squirm.

"I suck your clit into my mouth and run my tongue in a circular motion in a nasty constant rhythm. Can you feel it, baby? Can you feel my tongue licking you?"

"Yeah, yeah, yeah." He heard her faintly.

"I'm licking you, I'm licking you," he teased.

Vanita repeated, "oh, oh, oh." Each time she said the word it became louder.

"Come on, baby, come on now, cum on my tongue." He heard a primal moan, a deep intake of air, and a bellowing wind.

The phone transmitted only breathing. Ayman waited for her to recover. He hoped she would treat him to her own verbal, lustful, erotic style to complete his night. He yawned, quickly reminding him he had not slept much the past couple of nights. He envisaged Vanita lying there, her long body slowly stirring, inviting him in between her legs, if only he was there. The thought of entering her body, feeling her warm wetness made Ayman horny, his hardness dripping in his hand. A minute had passed, and he called out to her. No answer.

"Vanita," he repeated. Still no answer. He listened carefully and heard a quiet snore. He waited another thirty seconds to see if she would awake, then hung up the phone. He turned over and drifted off to sleep with a smile on his face.

22

This Christmas

The nightclub incident might have had an influence on the team. The regular season started with one loss and four wins. They lost a close game on the road, and two of the wins were against lesser foes. In the fourth game, ESCU beat the University of Las Vegas, number ten in the nation at the time. It helped the team get its bearings and gain confidence.

Ayman seeing Vanita made losing feel less stressful. They saw each other every day he was in town, even if it was just for a few minutes. They went walking along the Green River behind the Boeing Renton Plant at night listening to the river pour into Lake Washington. Sometimes they barely spoke a word, but they held hands, as planes took off from the air field across from them. They had late nights on the phone almost every night. He had to make sure he got some sleep in order to keep his focus.

Ayman went over for dinner after a practice one evening. After dinner, Ayman, Vanita, and her son, Joshua, were watching a rerun of the movie *The Five Heartbeats.* The little man fell asleep leaning on Ayman a few minutes into the movie. Ayman carried her son upstairs, and laid him on his bed.

He could have taken Vanita upstairs and done anything he wanted. She let him know he could. "I care for you and I want you to know me. You need to know since you may already see I'm busy. Running a college basketball program demands my full attention. We need to know before we go too far that you can handle my world.

"You have a son who is a sweet kid. I don't want Joshua to get too attached to me and then find out...well. But don't worry; I will spank that booty good and plenty when it's time."

"Sure you will, Mr. Big Talker." She turned around and moved her hips around. He slapped her on her butt. "Oh, daddy," she said. He lifted the back of her hair, kissed her on her neck, and licked and sucked on her collarbone. She reached behind her and felt his hardness. "Oooh." He started grinding against her. She reached down into her panties. She played. She groaned, and then turned for him to see her pull her finger up slowly. She painted his lips with her juices and held her finger under his nose.

He thought, *Should I leave? Should I go?* He turned and opened the door, and she slapped him on his butt.

Three days before Christmas, Ayman had a slight headache and was relaxing with his head in Vanita's lap. "My friends and I do this thing on every Christmas Day. We go out a few hours on our motorcycles. I'd like to put you on the back of my bike."

"How long have you been riding? Do you need training wheels? You got an extra helmet, and if you do, is it a helmet another woman has worn?"

Her question made him laugh louder than his head could stand. "Ouch, hold on. You're supposed to make my head feel better. You want all your questions answered in order? Is there a point system?"

"Sounds like you're avoiding my questions."

"I have positive responses to all your reservations, I mean questions."

She kissed him. "I'm free by noon Christmas Day. My son will go to his father's."

Christmas Eve morning, Vanita had called and woke him up early to ask if she snored in his ear, again. She had found the phone on the floor in the morning. Sometimes her medication would kick in, and she could go to sleep within a breath. It was worse when she didn't take her meds on a regular basis, and she wasn't. That could cause her emotions to rise and fall as if she hadn't taken her meds at all.

Her favorite colors were black and gold, and after practice Ayman headed over to Tylowe's motorcycle dealership to do some Christmas shopping. She called later that evening. He was at home going over game film, so they did not stay on the phone long, but they spoke about the ride on Christmas. "Okay, yeah. As far as tomorrow, remember, a helmet that another woman has not worn."

"Gotcha covered, talk to you later."

"I'm keeping the baby." Those were the first words out of Velvet's mouth, right after she had put down some gifts. She had arrived at Lois Mae's house before a Christmas Eve gift exchange party. "I'm going to my parents' house tomorrow to tell them. I'm feeling like this is the best gift I can give them. This isn't happening under the right situation, but having this baby is not the wrong thing to do. There's a baby in me, which will change my life for the positive, I have to believe," she almost whispered.

Lois Mae nodded her head from across a table. Both women's

eyes were misting, and they took deep breaths. The doorbell rang; partygoers were arriving.

The gift exchange was for a smattering of a few friends and work colleagues from ESCU. Velvet said a few hellos and good-byes, then headed out the door to her car, her mind thinking about this time next year and her child's first Christmas.

"Nice ass," a man said when she was outside the door of her car.

Velvet's body jerked with enough force to almost dislodge her left breast from her bra. Her keys hit the ground. "What the hell are you doing here?"

Vance, Lois Mae's ex-husband, stood on the other side of her silver Volkswagen, retro style. It made tall men appear even taller. A cheap cigar in his mouth, he moved the plastic tip around. He did not answer her, but he asked her questions.

"So did you tell her? Are you going to?" Velvet lowered her head and adjusted her bra. "Did you tell her the baby in your belly is mine?"

"Why you here? And it might be yours. Why you wanna hurt her any more than you have?"

"Hurt? Why'd ya give up the booty long after you two have become such good friends?" He laughed and slapped the top of her car. "Shit, friends like you..." He made a hand gesture pointing his finger to his temple, and mimicked pulling a trigger.

"Kiss my ass. You took my ass, and it's called rape, you mother—"

"Bitch, shut up. I took what you wanted to give up."

"Give up? I was drunk or something."

"Yeah, or something." Vance laughed. "Yeah you were kissing my ass while you were drunk on something." He smiled an evil grin at her.

"Yes, I was drunk that night, but I did not want to sleep with you. I told you to leave me alone. I don't know what happened that night."

"Oh, you were drunk on this good dick. That's what happened."

Velvet trembled and pressed her lips together so tight she could have squeezed blood out, but a tear rolled down her cheek. "You are an asshole who's out to hurt people."

Two months earlier, Velvet was having a glass of wine at the Esquire Club. The African had stood her up, and Vance just happened to walk in and sit down next to her. Velvet drank, but not as much she thought, but for sure, something happened that night.

At first, she told Vance to get lost, but as the night went on, she lost control. She woke up at his place, naked and with a dry stickiness between her legs. Vance acted indifferent and made her catch a cab back to her car.

Now she had issues about who was the baby's father. The African had avoided her since he stood her up. She thought it better to tell Vance that she was pregnant, but she was unsure of the father. He told her he couldn't care less because he figured she would never tell Lois Mae it was him, so he would never have to pay child support.

"Vance, why are you here? Get away from me!" Vance started to move away, but not from Velvet's demand.

"Hello, Happy Holiday, Feliz Navidad, or whatever applies." A male's voice was approaching. Velvet fixed her eyes. The streetlight revealed his identity. He was carrying several small boxes under his arm.

"Hi." She gave the best greeting she could at the moment. Vance kept moving and gave no greeting as he left. "What are you doing here?" she asked Sterlin.

"Well, I felt bad about how I had to leave you guys that night, and I have not been able to get back with you two ever since. Anyway, when I called to see if you guys wanted to meet me out somewhere and Lois Mae invited me to you all's…" He laughed. "Twenty-dollar-plus-but-no-more-than-forty-dollars gift exchange.

Damn, whatever happened to the five-dollar white elephant gift exchange?

"When you guys make all that higher education taxpayer money, you should spend it." Velvet laughed for the first time that night.

"Sorry, I scared your friend away." They both watched a Corvette roar away.

"He needed to go," she muttered as she squatted to pick up her keys from her original scare. Sterlin stopped her from picking up the keys by moving much faster.

"I'm sorry, what did you say?"

"Never mind, he was leaving. Go on up; her place is on the right."

"You're not coming in?"

"Oh, I have some other plans."

"That's too bad. I wanted to make it up to you guys for bailing out that night. I came bearing gifts." Sterlin pointed to the boxes under his arms. "You sure you have to go? I had a good time with you guys." Other people were arriving; some waved or spoke Christmas greetings. "Hey, join me so I know more than one person."

"If you do me a favor, I'll stay for a while."

"What might this favor be?" Sterlin raised his eyebrows.

Velvet drew in a big breath. "I think I know a few things about you." He drew his head back. She continued, "I assume you don't date sistas, Right?"

"You know this about me, how? And if it's true, what is the favor you want?" His voice was monotone.

"Look, I know I'm out of place. I don't know you at all. What I do know is my friend likes you. So, I ask if you're not into her, please be kind. Don't be a jerk. She has known one too many. Too many people have let her down. I'm one of them." Velvet pressed her lips tight momentarily, then said, "She needs someone to be for real."

Sterlin smiled, but it was not a happy one. "Ah-huh. I'm not dating anyone right now, and I don't want to at this time. It's kind of a long story, but I'm not trying to go there right now, either."

"So you're just tapping that ass here and there?"

"Ooh, you don't mince words, do you?"

"I'm just showing my frustration with men. It has nothing to do with you. As I said, I don't know you."

"Well, since we're all being all honest. As far as my personal tastes in women, I don't want to be rude, but that's my business. I will give you credit for speaking up. Look, I just want good friends in my life right now. I'm not looking for friends with benefits. Lois Mae is beautiful; she's a sexy woman, but me...I'm in chill mode right now."

"Hmm, did some woman break your heart?" Sterlin gave her a distress look; he'd had enough of her intrusions.

She gave a contrite smile, then nodded. "Sorry, I apologize. I'll come back up with you; I really don't have anywhere to go."

Later that evening, half the partygoers left after drinking Christmas cheer and exchanging gifts in a blind draw of names. The ones that stayed decided to wait until midnight before leaving. Laughter and conversation filled the living room.

WDAS, an Internet radio station from Philadelphia, played through the stereo. Tony Brown's "The Quiet Storm" was playing extended hours of Christmas music. There had been a little dancing and swaying to old- and new-school, soulful Christmas music. Donny Hathaway's "This Christmas" had just finished playing. Some people were discussing relationships, to love or not to love. A roundtable of opinions brought everyone in the conversation among one married Black couple, a married Hispanic couple, two single Black women, two single Black men, one single white woman who was Lois Mae's fellow English teacher friend, one married male, one single white male who might have been gay, and Velvet, who jokingly referred to herself as "other."

Wesley, a short, stout man, the ESCU grounds supervisor, and a single man had drawn the ear of most. Wesley spoke in a listen-to-me and look-at-me volume.

"Let me say this, and please let me finish before you make any assumptions or draw any opinion. I am not looking for gender equality in a relationship. The thought of a woman forcing her wants and needs on me to be my so-called equal partner by going against me that makes me uncomfortable. Relationships fail, because women think the money they make now allows them to run things and wear the pants in the house." All the women cut their eyes. The other men looked at the women's hands as if nails would turn into claws, but they let him talk.

"I look at things in an old-fashioned way, when the man was the head of his house. I don't seek to dominate my partner, but I wish for her to let me be the one who makes the final decisions in the house until I prove consistently that I can't."

"What? What planet have you been living on?" a married Black woman asked. Her husband shook his head and said, "You done asked for it now, buddy." Everybody in the room laughed.

The married Black woman had reddish-gold skin. Even though she was smiling, her skin had lost the gold and flushed crimson. "Oh, I'm in the Christmas spirit, so I'm gonna give a pass on his old-fashioned ways."

Wesley spoke, "I really don't need a pass, sister, no disrespect to anyone." He looked over at her husband, who lifted an eyebrow. "The lines are blurred between men and women. This is where… well, I don't understand. Okay, someone tell me. When there is a bump in the middle of the night, who gets up? And why is it okay for a woman to act helpless in order to get a man's help? Oh, we know they do this to catch a man or simply because they need a

Mr. Fix-It-Man. Then, once they hook a man they pull the feminist treat-me-as-an-equal mess." He spoke with a smile on his face.

All the men looked away. The women cocked their heads and stared at him like he was crazy.

The single white guy who might be gay said, "I think relationships are hard enough without putting us on different levels. I want to be fair in love, because I want love to be fair to me."

The Hispanic husband responded, "My wife and I, we do believe in the old-fashioned way, but I make sure I hear what's important to her. I believe she sets out to make me happy, because I care about what she thinks."

His wife nodded her head and said, "Yes, that is true."

The other single woman sitting next to Lois Mae was Darnelle; a smallish Black woman who chuckled before she spoke to Wesley. "It's not all that complex. Your train of thought is really quite Neanderthal. Yet I understand men who think like you. I'll tell you what, I'll help you with your coat when you leave, and open the doors for you. If I ever see you out, I'll buy you a drink, pat you on the ass, and send you home alone, being the perfect gentlewoman." That brought more laughter to the room. Wesley laughed, too.

Darnelle had whispered to Lois Mae, "He was so nice earlier; sounds like he's got small dick problems. I was thinking I was going to let him come down my chimney tonight and get some cookies and milk. Why'd he open his mouth and put his little dick in it?" Lois Mae had to bite her lips to keep from falling out laughing.

With midnight only minutes away, the conversation changed with drinks refilling as the mistletoe came out. Sterlin made an effort to steer clear. He ended up giving the single women pecks on the cheek. After midnight, the crowd shrank down to four, the cleanup crew: Lois Mae, Sterlin, Darnelle, and Velvet.

Sterlin, the manpower, moved a few items that had been set up for the party, and he carried out the trash and recycling. As he went back up to get some more disposables, he passed Darnelle and Velvet. They all said their good-byes, and Sterlin felt a setup, when Velvet gave him a nod and the eye.

He walked back in and had it in mind to tell Lois Mae up front that he was not on the market. He was going to tell her he just needed friends and that it had nothing to do with her. After his conversation with Ayman, his motorcycle being knocked over, and almost being run over, he was committed.

Back in the kitchen, she faced him, and he could not get his words out fast enough. Lois Mae beat him to it. "I understand you aren't interested in any kind of relationship." He opened his mouth, but she cut him off. "Velvet tipped me off about how you feel, and it's okay, really it is. You don't have to explain.

"I can face whatever comes my way. Life has taught me that. For me, as a woman to find a man who's not out to hit it and quit it is rare. In the few times I have been in your presence, you've made the-all-gentleman team. I can deal with that and be happy. Yes, I have wondered if you're available." She turned her head in slight embarrassment from her disclosure. "But I know how to be a friend too."

"Thanks for the gift," Sterlin said.

"What gift?"

"The gift of not making it personal."

"Well, I'm about being your friend."

"And I'm a man who doesn't mind taking the trash out, opening doors, or getting up in the middle of the night when you hear a bump." They laughed, hugged briefly and said, "Merry Christmas."

23

Two-Wheel Funk

Riders pulled in at the All World Motorcycle Dealership. Tylowe and Meeah sponsored a Christmas Day motorcycle ride fundraiser for children's charities. A few of Seattle's well-known citizens participated, like Coach Ayman Sparks. Decent weather brought out over a hundred riders. Most rode with their mates on the back, or in sidecars.

Sterlin was trying to rub out the scratches on his bike that were never going to rub out. Tylowe looked and shook his head.

Meeah and her daughter, Mia, both had custom-painted, hot-pink motorcycles. Mom rode a Harley-Davidson V-Rod, too much bike for some men, but she had skills. Mia rode a Triumph Daytona 650. Tyreene and her team was away in Hawaii for a tournament. Mom and daughter were also dressed in red leather pants and coats with hot-pink helmets.

Ayman with Vanita pulled in on his ZX14 Kawasaki. Tylowe, Sterlin, and Meeah were in conversation at the time, and their mouths froze.

"Who is that?" Meeah asked, looking at Sterlin.

"I assume it's the woman he's been seeing."

"Hmm, he hasn't mentioned her to me," Meeah said.

Ayman put down the kickstand, dismounted, and helped his rider take off her black and gold leopard-print helmet. She also had on light-tan leather pants and coat, with other accessories.

"Mom, look at her boots; they're fierce. And the matching gloves; she is sharp." The boots were leopard-print suede up to her knees with stiletto heels. The gloves were leopard print. Vanita's long braids surrounded her face.

Meeah recognized the helmet and light-tan leathers; they came from their dealership. She ordered all the women's riding apparel. The two women stared at each other, scanning each other from head to boots. Their stares seem to carry telepathic thoughts. Vanita's signals might have said, *"I'm with him, and what's it to you?"* Meeah's Vulcan raised-eyebrow stare said, *"Yeah, but he's family, I'm gonna protect him if I have to."*

Ayman had a silly grin on his face. The last couple of years they had all ridden single because of him. They stopped doubling up in an unspoken gesture a few years back so Ayman wouldn't feel bad about his divorce.

The wife of another rider was standing behind Meeah and knew the group well. She whispered just loud enough for Meeah to hear, "Damn, you can hear the cow skin mooing. She must have parachuted into those pants." Meeah, not being of the catty nature, did not acknowledge the comment.

Ayman and Vanita walked over to the signup desk to check in, then approached the group. Tylowe and Meeah greeted them. "So, where've you been hiding this beautiful woman?" Meeah asked.

Ayman could not rid himself of his sheepish grin. "This is Vanita Irving, and this is Meeah and Tylowe Dandridge, my good friends."

"My daughter and I love your boots, honey," Meeah said as she reached out for her. The two touched their cheeks together. "And the matching gloves, ah yes, they are nice. Ayman, the lady has style." Vanita's eyes met Meeah's, neither friendly nor hostile, but far from warm.

"Well, I rarely have a chance to wear the boots and gloves. This sweet man…" She rubbed the back of her hand against Ayman's cheek. "He showed up with this helmet with the leopard print and these beautiful leathers. I had to accessorize." Vanita unzipped her coat and pulled out a leopard-print scarf wrapped around her neck. Both women smiled.

A swarm of riders took to the road, heading north on I-5, the destination, La Conner, a sleepy little town on a waterway channel about sixty miles away. On the road, it was a beautiful sight to see all the colors on two wheels. Meeah designed her own line of motorcycle wear. All riders knew to come to All World Motorcycles, to dress and accessorize.

Tylowe, Ayman, and Meeah led most of the way as all others followed. Sterlin looked at Ayman's date from the back. *Wow, her booty. The moon lowered itself into those leather pants, and it's gonna have a hell of a time trying to rise out of there.*

Out on the open road, Ayman shifted his bike to a lower gear and hit the throttle. The bike's engine revved high. Sex. Everybody but Vanita knew that she was about to have sex. Meeah shook her head, wishing she was riding with her husband so she could have a private vibrating moment.

A half mile down the road, Vanita started to squirm, spreading her legs wider and scooting up tight behind Ayman. He revved the bike up more. She held him tighter, the strong vibration going up through her body and centering between her legs. She could feel a warm wetness. His bike was loud, yet he thought he heard her moan. She squeezed her butt cheeks tight, and her right leg shook, making her foot almost come off the foot peg, then her body relaxed. He shifted the bike to release the high revs. With her breasts against his back, he felt her breathing at an exhilarating pace. He smiled wide, making his helmet feel too small for his big head.

Ayman and Sterlin had arranged a feast for the riders who rode to La Conner. They had a deep-fried turkey with all the side dishes anyone could eat. Jo & James Catering Service served plates full of great food at picnic tables set up near the waterway.

Sterlin had a moment to get to know Vanita while Ayman mixed with others.

"So, are you a Northwest native?" he asked.

"Yes, born and raised in the liquid sunshine. Ayman tells me you two are like brothers."

"We have known each other since college."

"Hmph, that means you could tell me about all the women he must have?"

"You're not serious?" He had a smile on his face, but was not happy being put on the spot. *Am I a magnet for personal intrusions, dang?*

She stared at him, and he read her stare. Yes, she was serious. "Hey, you need to get to know him. My brother, my friend, has the moral code of a nun." Ayman walked over. "You got a unique one here," Sterlin said to Ayman.

"Yeah, and she's beautiful too," Ayman said, reaching for Vanita's hand. They walked down by the river.

"I'm glad you could come along. How was the ride?" She playfully hit him on the arm but kissed him on the lips.

"I think I said the wrong thing to your friend." Ayman cocked his head. His facial expression was inquisitive. "I jokingly asked about your other women."

"My other women?" He was a bit annoyed. "Vanita, maybe an image comes across to you that I can or do have a freeway to the land of ladies. The truth is I'm isolated because of my job. When someone is in the public light, people come with hidden agendas. The last thing I need to do is get involved with some nut case." The tone of his voice seemed to come from deep in the ground. She blinked her eyes, and her body jerked. "I don't mean to make it sound so absolute, but I can't have a relationship blown up on the front page."

"I'm sorry if I crossed the line."

"It's all good, so just try to relax."

"Ayman, I do have something I should share with you, and maybe it might not be that big of a deal for you." *I hope.* She stared into his eyes, wishing she didn't have to tell him about her problem. She hesitated, and he waited. "I've been through a lot, and sometimes it was hard to deal with, and I…" She hesitated again, and Ayman broke her silence. He thought she wanted to share that her ex-husband played around on her, and it might have caused her to ask Sterlin a question based on her insecurity.

"Hey, baby, we've all been through a lot in the past. This is now, so don't worry about the past. I don't need to know all about the past. Maybe later you can tell me, and maybe later it won't matter."

She knew what she needed to say but took his lead to let it go for the moment—a big relief. Her mind raced. *I need to tell him, but he said he doesn't need a nut case. I'm not a nut case, and he's a good man.*

She told him, "Maybe because you seem so perfect, I can't believe I'm with you."

"I'm not perfect. I scratch my booty in public." He reached back behind as if he was going to scratch. She pushed his hand away, and lightly brushed her hand against his behind.

"That's nasty," her voice flirted.

"I thought you wanted a nasty man?"

"I do. I was just saying."

"Yeah, okay." He laughed.

"Come here and kiss me, nasty man." Their lips had hardly touched.

"Ayman!" Sterlin called out. "Turn on your cell phone." His voice sounded strained.

"It's in my bag, on my bike." He told Vanita to wait a second, and jogged away. Sterlin met him halfway. In the next moment, most of the riders sitting or walking around were captivated by the two men holding each other. Sterlin was more like holding Ayman up. His grandfather had passed, and family members had been calling Ayman until someone finally called Sterlin. Tylowe came over and a moment later, he held Ayman too.

It was a while before Ayman could compose himself. He took a walk through town alone and made phone calls to those who needed to hear from him. Every business was closed, and the old buildings helped make it feel like a ghost town. He understood Granddad was at the age when anytime he could go to join Ayman's grandmother. She had passed away a few years earlier.

As he kicked dirt and rocks while he wandered the lonely town, Vanita eventually found him sitting on a bench. She chose not to say a word, but she stood behind him and rubbed the back of his head.

Ayman, with the softest voice he might have ever used, talked to the lonely town and her. "I was going to call him when we got back. He turned ninety...today, on his last day, Christmas." She leaned over and placed her cheek alongside his, and reached for his hands. She felt him trembling and the tears touched her cheek.

Hours later, after the ride back, they were back at her place. Ayman sat on her couch, leaned over, his eyes closed. She came into the living room wearing a red silk Chinese print robe, the front open, nearly exposing the tip of her dark round nipples. He opened his eyes and closed them again.

"Sorry I was gone so long, but I took a long shower."

"I should be going; it's been a long day."

"You're not going anywhere," she told him, "unless you absolutely have to. Please stay. I ran you some bathwater. My son won't be back until noon tomorrow, and I just can't let you be alone tonight. You really shouldn't be alone." He opened his mouth to speak, but she stopped him with her finger across his lips. She shook her head.

He smiled a lifeless smile, his eyes dim, not a lot of emotional life in him. From his childhood to the last visit with his grandfather, his mind was seeing the past in black and white. Vanita pulled on his arm as if she could lift him. She led him to the bathroom, and left him alone. He stripped down and slipped into the hot bubble bath. She came back with a beer, and he flashed a thank-you smile as he took the glass. She soaped a towel and washed his chest and arms, before scrubbing his back. "I'll leave the rest to you." She smiled, kissed the top of his head, and closed the door behind her.

After his bath, he found her in the bed. He crawled in next to her. As if she were caring for a child, she pulled the covers over him. Ayman curled into the fetal position. She moved in next to him, spooning his body, and once again he felt her breasts against his back, this time there was no leather in between, just skin to skin. Her hand swept lightly over his chest, and he drifted off to sleep.

Vanita's eyelids fluttered, a little startled from her sleep. She heard Ayman relieving himself in the bathroom, and she smiled, thinking his bladder must have been near bursting. His stream was loud as it hit the water, and it seemed to go on forever. She had a vision of him standing with his legs apart. It aroused shameless feelings in her knowing he was either holding or letting his manhood hang. It made her thighs clamp tight, and her toes stirred. She had not seen his manhood yet, but she had felt it.

Temptation had her hand creeping while he was sleeping. He had moved about in his deep sleep, stimulated by her fingers sliding under the waistband of the sweats. She listened to his soft snoring. It sounded almost musical, and she did not fall asleep for hours.

The sound of him in the bathroom running water indicated he was brushing his teeth with the new toothbrush she'd left on the counter. She knew he was coming to kiss her. *Maybe I should get up and brush my teeth*, she thought as she pressed her lips against her hand. She decided to let him kiss her all over except her lips. She wanted his soft-pillow lips to travel over her body.

The thought of it already had her wet, thinking she would want him to slide his tongue down her neck, and to her breasts. She wanted him to press his hard body down on hers and to feel the heat of his hardness.

He walked out of the bathroom without the cutoff sweatpants. Her eyes opened wide in surprise. He was wearing his jeans, and he was putting on his shirt. She sat up and he sat down next to her, pulling on his socks.

"I need to go home; I have so much to do," he said.

"Can I help you with anything?" Her voice was unsympathetic.

He heard it but ignored it. "No, baby, you've already done a lot for me, and I slept like a baby. Thank you."

She got off the bed on the opposite side and went to the window. "It's barely light out and it's raining. It's not safe to be out there so early on that bike."

He walked over to her, with thoughts of holding her. She stiffened, and he noticed. "I'll be okay. Maybe we can have a quick cup of coffee before I go."

"I'm out." She walked by him, and he slowly followed her downstairs. She seemed to be the one in a hurry. Vanita pulled the rest of his riding gear out of the hall closet, while he put on his boots. He wanted to be concerned about her attitude, but he had other things on his mind. She let him kiss her on the forehead before he entered the garage to roll out his motorcycle, and Vanita stood in the door, watching him. When the motor roared to life, she hit the button, and the garage door rolled down.

Ayman felt his phone vibrate in his pocket as he was putting on his helmet. The idle of the motorcycle engine made it a bit hard to hear when he answered, so he spoke loudly. "Yes, I know who this is. No, it's not too early. I thank you for calling. I'm all right. He told me you came by to see him. I thank you for that too. Yes, that's my motorcycle. I'm headed out for a ride to clear my mind. Well, arrangements most likely will be finalized by tomorrow. Sure, I'll talk to you, when I see you. It's a going-home for my granddad. All else is moot." Ayman thought about where he was standing. "Hey, let me…ah, call you later. Okay, bye."

Ayman closed his eyes and visualized Vanessa. It was the first time they had spoken since the divorce. The ride home barely gave him time to process everything on his plate: Granddad and burying him, time restraints of travel, plus the season. How would it all work out?

25

Boys to Men and Women

Ayman buried his grandfather and still managed basketball operations. He was gone a total of twenty-four hours. A school booster owned a private jet, and offered to fly him and Sterlin to the Bay Area and back.

A rare crossing of paths with his dad at the funeral almost felt good. They had both lost a man they loved, and realized with the passing, they had to make more effort to spend time together.

During the funeral, he looked for Vanessa at the service and the after-dinner, but he never spotted her. At least she'd called to say she was sorry that he'd lost someone as important as his grandfather when he was standing outside Vanita's garage. Maybe it was all too much for her.

Back at practice at midday on New Year's Eve, his mind was in faraway places. He and Vanita had had a few short phone conversations during the past few days. They decided to have a sit-down talk. He had some concerns about moving ahead in a relationship.

They wanted to meet on New Year's Eve, but he was going to

have the team over to his place for the evening in an attempt to keep negative partying from happening. She did not have a problem with him not being available, since she normally went to Night Watch service at her church. She told him she thought she was falling in love with him, and he said he wanted to be in love with her.

At Night Watch service, Vanita prayed in the New Year, asking the Lord to give her the strength to deal with her problems. She and Alicia had a small falling-out about whether or not Ayman should know about her manic depression and meds. They sat next to each other, singing songs and listening to testimonials, but they might as well have been sitting on boxing stools in between rounds, waiting for the bell to ring.

At midnight, they hugged, but there was tension. After service in the parking lot, they tried to work it out. "Alicia, let me see where this is going with him first. I don't want to scare him away. Sheez, we are not moving that fast. We haven't even had sex yet, as bad as I need it. He didn't want it…yet."

"Maybe you're not supposed to until you are totally truthful."

"I almost told him, but his grandfather died, and it messed up the timing." Vanita lifted her chin. The moon was almost full, and it cast a long shadow behind her. She spoke toward the moon, "My doctor has cut my meds to less than half; he thinks I'm doing better and I may not need them much more."

Alicia knew better, and that Vanita had done this before, claiming her doctor was changing the levels of her meds. The numb feeling the medication gave her seemed to wear her down, and she would stop taking them. For awhile, she would feel perfect, but her world would fall apart. The most telling effect was that Vanita was always an honest person until she stopped taking her meds.

"Vanita, let's go see the doctor together like we did before."

"I'm telling you, I'm doing well now. Just…just give me some space on this?"

"No matter what, you need to tell this man. You need to be honest with what goes on in your life."

"I got to get my son home. We'll talk later."

The basketball radio-game announcer said, "That's it, East Seattle City University beats Nevada with a convincing blowout 75 to 50. What a way to start the New Year."

The radio blared through the gym loudspeakers while Lois Mae did her workout on the stair stepper. She, like many others, ate too much over the holidays, and she chose to do double duty in the gym. She and Sterlin had spoken a few times on the phone and had lunch once. They had fallen into a friendship total mode. She had even thought about introducing him to another lady friend. When she had tested the waters while joking with him, he had reiterated that he wanted to avoid dating.

Basketball was in full swing, but school was still out for Christmas break for another week, so Lois Mae planned to go to Houston for the weekend. That would put her and the ESCU basketball team in town at the same time. Her new team was going up against the school she attended, the University of Houston. She and Sterlin arranged to meet and hang out while in Houston.

The timing to go visit family in Houston came right in time to catch some winter sun. Planning the trip brought on a slight complication when Velvet gave her a dog for Christmas. Lois Mae had wanted a dog, but she'd never found her choice. She didn't want a puppy or a little dog, even though she lived in a condo. Her home was a large condo with a fenced backyard, and a gate that led to a trail down to the lake.

Velvet searched and found the perfect dog, maybe out of guilt for her other issues. The day after Christmas, Velvet walked into Lois Mae's condo and said, "Take this bitch." It was a two-year-old female Rottweiler. The dog, Selena, walked in and sat at her feet, and sealed the deal. Lois Mae did not want to leave her in a kennel just as the dog had become her new baby. She was able to find an in-house-dog-sitter at the last moment.

A giant platter of crawfish sat in front of Ayman, Sterlin, Lois Mae, and other people they all knew from the area. They were at Willie G's Seafood and Steak House in Houston. It was Friday night, and the place was packed and loud, a reunion moment for Ayman and Sterlin with some University of New Mexico alumni friends who lived in the area. Along with some people Lois Mae knew from Houston, everybody was having a good time.

Lois Mae engaged in a lively conversation with a cousin of Sterlin's. Ayman was not quite sure of the personal interaction between Sterlin and Lois Mae, but it had him quite amused. She was a Black woman hanging out with Sterlin, and interestingly, she bore a resemblance to someone from Sterlin's past—Monica Turner.

Sterlin sat uncomfortably; his laughter was not sincere. Ayman had a sports talk radio interview at 9 p.m. and soon left as others drifted out, leaving Lois Mae and Sterlin.

"Life is so funny. Here we are in Houston where we both were born, but we live and work in Seattle and never knew each other," she said.

Sterlin had his elbows on the table supporting his chin with his hands. He sat back and folded his arms.

"You're quiet. What's up, you guys nervous about tomorrow's game?" Lois Mae asked.

"Nah, we should be in good shape. This is not Houston of years ago. We're playing well, and Larentzo can smell the NBA. He's elevated his game to a level we didn't think he would reach until next year."

"Does he need to go to the NBA? What I mean is, so many of those boys are not mature enough. I'm no expert on skill, but I just hate hearing how these boys have people hanging all over them, using them, and have more tattoos than a zebra has stripes."

"Well, I agree with you some. In the case of Larentzo, he's a great kid. Ayman and I stay in the ear of the kids. We check out everyone who starts hanging around our kids, and we have our snitches. There is always the worry the NBA might swallow a kid and spit him out in a few years. A troubled kid at the UW left school early a couple of years ago, and he's out of the NBA already. We'll sit down, and talk to Larentzo about it at the end of the season."

"I see you're talkative about basketball tonight, but not much else." She tilted her head and smiled, while Sterlin pressed his lips tight. The waitress stopped and asked if they wanted their drinks refreshed. They both ordered water and the check. "Have I done or said something wrong?"

"No." Sterlin turned his head away. "I know you—I know a woman like you is what I mean. You're fine, smart, and you flirt with most men you meet."

"Excuse me?" Her voice rose to a level that made her cover her mouth, and her eyes scanned the room. "Could you tell me what's really going on with you? Even a slightly educated person can hear this is something deeper than your surface comments."

Sterlin avoided eye contact and said, "Forget it."

"Forget what, Sterlin? You make a jacked-up comment and then have nothing to say. I thought we were friends. I have not hit on you. You made it perfectly clear you are not into dating or anything related to it in your life right now. I respected that. We just happen to be sitting here while we're both in Houston to enjoy friends and relaxing.

"How about we pay the bill, go outside, and sit in the car and talk?" she said. "That way we can listen to the radio. I miss the radio down here. You know they jam the old-school jams."

Float, float on; the lyrics flowed in the car, as Sterlin sat back, his seat slightly reclined. Lois Mae relaxed in her seat, angled toward him. Her head rocked back and forth on the headrest.

"Many moons ago, I loved someone," Sterlin said. "It was the only time I have ever been in love. I'm forty-five, and I think, unlike most people, I'm almost a virgin at love, and what I do know about it, I don't like."

"How many moons?" Lois asked.

"In college. I don't want you to think I'm a weak-ass punk."

"Macho or crybaby, I know how to be your friend and take you as you are. If you knew some of the people I let into my life and accepted their—" She shook her head and shuddered. "So." She pushed her finger into what felt like a horse's hip of a shoulder. Her finger folded from the resistance. A chuckle met her smile.

The warm winter breeze of the Houston night crawled through the rolled-down window. His words met the breeze as he spoke, "You being my friend helps."

She thought, *Oooh, I'm definitely on the friend list.* "Well, I'm here. I can be that big or little sister."

"Thanks. One of the reasons I moved to Hobbs, New Mexico is when I was ten, my mom passed away. My mom, I got my size from her. She was a big lady, over six feet tall, and she supervised in the oil fields. She was the smartest, strongest and the softest woman on this earth, but I lost her. So I went to live with my long-haul truck-driving dad. He was cool, but he was on the road. I rode along sometimes but stayed alone most of the time."

"You were so young to stay alone."

"He had the blue light special going on with women, a different cheap woman from another city or town or from another part of the state every week. They all wore blue by his demand. They needed a place to stay, and he always needed a babysitter."

"He had them wear blue? What kind of fetish is that?"

Sterlin smiled, and almost laughed. "My mom wore blue a lot, and when they divorced, he held on to her emotionally, loving her through seeing a woman in blue. She was a physical creature, but her intellect, even I as a child could see that it was something special. You should have heard her recite poetry. I can still hear her, even now. Anyway, my dad, he'd come off the road, I'd get a new pair of shoes, and he'd bring Ms. Whoever a new blue dress, blue sweater, blue panties, or blue whatever."

"I suppose you don't like blue?" Lois Mae's voice teased.

"Nah, it's cool. I saw you in some blue shoes the first day I saw you. They looked nice with your big legs." Sterlin turned toward her and chuckled.

"Don't be looking at my legs. Remember, we're just friends."

"Please, if you were an eighty-year-old nun, I'd still check to see if you had big legs and—"

"Stop. You know you ain't right."

"Yeah, just like an English teacher should not use 'ain't.'" They both laughed.

"Hmph, as long as I'm in this car talking to you, while in Houston I'll use *ain't*."

Sterlin's chest expanded, then a short but deep exhale followed. Ten seconds passed before he spoke again. "Lois Mae, I have a troubling past." She let him take his time.

"I was built like a man at fourteen, and six-foot-three, but I was only a boy when Ms. Red moved in. Ms. Red…" He shook his head, his eyes closed and visited another time and place before he said, "Tall and curves, dark brown skin, coal black hair, with blood-red lipstick, just like yours.

"She had perfectly painted red nails on her fingers and toes. She was shiny beyond a diamond. She became more than a blue light special; she was my dad's arm-piece. She was the closest image to my mom that Dad had found, only she was polished like fool's gold. She never wore blue, always red, or nothing." Another long silent period went by.

"She became more than my babysitter when my dad was on the road. I became her boy toy. I knew about sex, the kind of stupid knowledge a fourteen-year-old knows. That means nothing. I hadn't even masturbated yet…well, I mean I had not cum yet.

"One day she knocked on the bathroom door while I was in the shower and said she needed to use the toilet. I told her to wait a minute. Her response was that the shower curtain would hide us from each other, and with the shower running, it would block out the sound of her peeing. So she came in, but I didn't hear her pee. Her shadow squatting, sitting on the toilet…" He laughed as he kept reproducing the past. "This went on every day for a couple of weeks. I really didn't think anything was wrong. She and Dad were always in the bathroom at the same time.

"It was a summer day when Ms. Red became my first, and I became her pet dog who sniffed behind her twenty-four-seven. I had been playing basketball all day at the park, and I was taking a shower. She had gotten to the point she didn't even knock anymore. She just walked in and sat on the toilet. I knew she wasn't peeing most of the time. I could see enough shadow to know her hand was doing something between her legs besides wiping."

Sterlin pressed his lips tight, drew a deep breath, and held it before he let it out. The music on the radio made him stop for a moment. It was a double play of Sly and the Family Stone's "Everybody is a Star" and "Family Affair."

"Maybe I helped in a way for it to happen. After awhile I would soap up my, my, ah…"

"It's okay, say it whatever way you want, I use the word, *pussy*, so you can use whatever you want," Lois Mae whispered.

"Okay, I would stroke my dick, while I watched her silhouette, her arm moving fast between her legs. I'm not sure if I ever thought about her watching me. Anyway, I became more than curious."

"At fourteen, what boy wouldn't?" Lois Mae smiled, and touched his arm.

"I guess." He thought in silence while they both watched the last of the patrons enter their cars and leave. "That day, she pulled the shower curtain back, and I was, was…hard. She got in, soaped me up and stroked it a lot better than I knew how. She washed every inch of my body like I was a baby, and I stood there. I knew it was wrong. Her hands were all over me as she stroked it and I shot a load of cum for the first time in my life." He chuckled. "I can remember freaking, and tripping, being scared shitless, as my stuff ran all over her breasts.

"I had never seen a woman naked other than in magazines, with skinny white women. She was dark, big, and had curves.

"She got out of the shower like nothing had happened. The water ran cold. I was frozen. I couldn't move for what seemed like forever. As time went on, whenever Dad was gone, she showered with me and taught me what she wanted me to do. My hands, my lips, my dick, my innocence, she molded me into her live human tool.

"Eventually, the whole house became her playground to have

me as she wanted. I never said no. Not sure I wanted to. We did what some people call nasty, freaky. I touched and played with every inch of her body, even where the sun don't shine. She did the same to me. I thought it was all normal since that's what she wanted, and for sure I did enjoy it." Sterlin's facial expression shrank his eyes tight.

"I don't have any judgment of you," Lois Mae said as she smiled. "You were a child, and she took you to a place two grown folks can hardly run from. I appreciate you baring your pain with me. I truly do mean, no judgments from me, is the word of the day, the year, and this life we should live."

"In some ways, I'm not mad about the fact she taught me how to please a woman and enjoy making a woman go places they don't think they could go."

Lois Mae uncrossed her feet, shifted her hips, and then crossed her feet the other way. "Well, I guess you can't be mad about that."

"Yeah." Sterlin turned his head away to avoid eye contact and blew another long breath out the window. "This went on for two years, until I was in high school and I got a real girlfriend. She looked like her and was built like her. I thought I was supposed to share everything with the one you're with. Well, that's some crazy shit. She freaked out and told her mother that I had been having sex with my dad's girlfriend, a woman twenty years older than me. She left out the part that she and I were having sex.

"Back then, things were different. The school police officer and his cop buddies showed up at the house while my dad wasn't there. I was already the school sports stud. If I participated in whatever sport, we won. So I believe he saved her and my life from my dad. They took her down to the Greyhound bus station and told her not to come back. I heard from her a few days later. She called to let me know she was in Houston and I could visit anytime."

"Wow, did she ever come back?"

"Nah, she knew better. She said the police warned her they would rape her with their gun barrels if she came back to town."

"Texas justice, a rape for a rape," Lois Mae said.

He chuckled, but there was no humor in it. "Raped. I was raped. What do you think? No, don't answer. That was the last I heard from her. My dad told me he stayed with her when he'd go through Houston.

"Just a few years ago before my dad died, he told me that she was the best pussy he ever had. Said that woman was so nasty it made his head spin. I asked him if that was why he kept seeing her for so long after she left Hobbs. His response was she used to tell him he had the biggest dick in the world." Sterlin chuckled in silence, almost. "She used to tell me the same thing."

Lois Mae sighed, feeling his pain.

"We should get going, because this is only part one of my woman drama. Gotta get back to the team hotel. Need to make sure the boys don't become men before their time. Plus, I need some sleep to live for another day; I'm drowning in the past right now."

"You know you can call me anytime, right?"

"You're all right, I don't care what they say about you." Sterlin laughed.

"Oh, now you wanna be a funny-man. You get back to your team, and keep your day job. Make sure you beat my old school, or I'll have bragging rights." She wanted to show some form of I-understand affection. Sterlin moved quickly and exited his side of the car. He opened her door before she could blink.

He took her car keys from her hand and opened the door of her rental. The chivalry felt good, but she also felt rushed or avoided as they said good-bye.

"I'll see you sometime later in the season," he said.

26

As I Lay There

After Ayman's radio interview on a Houston sports station, he retired to his room, knowing he should go to bed, but thoughts of Vanita invaded his rest. She had some quirks about her, but maybe she just was nervous about him in a way that had her acting strange at times. He thought about how she'd acted so cold the morning he'd left from her place and her questioning of Sterlin at the picnic. He had to settle this because he did like her; he thought he could be falling in love with her good side, so he called her.

Vanita was sound asleep. She had started back taking her meds, which made her tired and lethargic, but her attitude was changing back to how it was when she and Ayman had first met. After they had exchanged greetings and current events in their lives, Ayman had jumped right into the subject on his mind.

"My position in life is not more important than the people in my life, but when it comes to a relationship, I need to be in a stable situation. I can't have bad days in the office because I have been fighting with my woman. I'm in the public, and my inter-actions, they affect young men and their futures, the university, the city, and possibly on a very small scale, the whole sports world. All that being said, I want to be clear as we think about moving forward.

"I'm sorry, but this may come off too harsh." Ayman's breathing sounded like ocean air going into Vanita's ear. "I can't do drama with you."

"Okay, Ayman, please tell me what's on your mind, but could you not use your coaching voice, Coach Sparks." She laughed.

"Sorry, I can get intense when I'm talking. Old habits die hard."

"Ayman, I understand. I stepped across the line with what I said to Sterlin. I know you don't have time for other women, and you have given me every moment you have. The morning you left from here, well, I wanted to feel important to you at a crucial time in your life. Please let me explain what I was feeling that morning when you left from my place."

"Please do," Ayman said coolly.

"Please be patient with me. I'm not perfect, and I have some emotional insecurities that come from…" Vanita went silent, and it made Ayman think they had been disconnected.

"Hello, are you there?" he asked.

She wanted to tell him about her manic-depression issues. It was the second time she had tried, but she froze up with fear. Vanita moved her conversation to his emotions.

"When you found out your granddad had passed, of course I wanted to be there for you. You are so much man, but you turned into almost like a little boy. I sensed fragility that I'm sure you don't want people to know you have. I can respect how you feel. I understand where you're coming from. I want to know you, and support you. Do you want to know what I like, what I want, and what bothers me?"

"Vanita, I want to give and receive, so talk to me."

"I might sound stereotypical in my wants. I'm sure I'm asking for the same things as any woman asks. For sure, I don't want a man in my face demanding anything. I like to let my man lead, but talk to me with care in your eyes, and out of your mouth."

"I can do and want to do that."

"There's one thing for sure I want. I like sex; I'm at an age where my hormones are raging. So please tell me you're a man who likes to do it."

Ayman was laughing hard as he responded. "Hold up. Timeout. Woman, I love sex. Don't we talk about it all the time?"

"Ah yeah-a, but-ah, we ain't done it, yet."

"It's coming."

"When you get back here, it's on, and that's a demand."

"I surrender; you can have all I got." He laughed.

"Okay, that's what I wanted to hear," she said, and laughed herself. "That morning, as I lay next to your body, I wanted to make love to you in hopes it would ease your mind for the moment and relax you. You tossed and turned all night. A selfish desire in me needed you to touch me and want me. I wanted you to take me and use my body like a rag doll if it would have helped you relax. It would have satisfied me to no end.

"I wanted to make love to you, Ayman. At one point in the middle of the night I put two fingers into my pussy, doing it to myself at first, and then I took my fingers and placed them near your nose when you turned over onto your back. There was a smile on your face. When I heard you in the bathroom, I just knew you were coming back to bed to melt me; my mind went there to a place; I had to have you."

Ayman was sleepy, but his body was alert, hearing her voice. He kept listening.

Vanita made no effort to hide the fact she was touching herself.

"That morning, I held my breasts, wanting you to spank my nipples and rub your hardness between my breasts." Ayman's Hardness was oozing right then, but he had rubbed the head dry and needed more lubricant. He reached in his travel bag for massage oil. He wasn't saying a word, just listening to her while she whispered seductively through the phone.

"As I talk to you right now, if you're not hard, that would be good for putting all of you in my mouth to suck you hard." Her voice became a verbal porn movie as she tried to push Ayman off an orgasmic cliff. "I would have held my ass up high just so you could see everything from behind. I hoped you would lick me first from behind, then go inside me.

"I wanted you to ram me deep, deep enough to come out the other side." Ayman lost his cool and groaned through the phone, and she kept talking. She knew she had him stroking hard and fast.

"I wanted to feel your tongue lick me between my legs like a cat licks his paw. I would have played with myself in front of you. I would have done anything to turn you on. I would have squeezed my breasts for you and inserted my fingers inside me and pumped hard—not just one hole, but two, just to see you stroke yourself."

Ayman shot a load all over his hand, but he kept it almost quiet, because he did not want her to hear him get off. Though he was breathing hard, he said, "So, this is why you were upset. When I get back, we'll handle this once and for all," They spoke for a while longer before he went into an orgasmic slumber.

27

Mid-Season Slump

In the game against Houston, Larentzo twisted an ankle early in the game but it was not a factor. East Seattle City University barely won a game they should have easy, with or without Larentzo. The next game, they upset Notre Dame. Larentzo played on the bad ankle. He was able to inspire his teammates with his never-say-die attitude. By midseason, the team was playing okay, but far from expectations.

Ayman was struggling with a number of issues. He and Vanita had a strange vibe going on between them. They finally made love the day after he returned to Seattle from Houston. The sex was as if they were ballroom dancers, dancing like most people wished they could. Once off the dance floor, she pulled on him with her up-and-down mood swings, sometimes with an aggressive attitude. She could go from sugar to vinegar in a matter of minutes.

He fought against the idea that it had to end, before it really got started. Her sweet side confused the issues about what to do. Ayman held the thought that his lifestyle once again must be the problem, as it was with the ex. Basketball, the need for total focus, and a bad relationship led to a conversation between Ayman and

Sterlin. It was not often that Sterlin had much to say to Ayman about his personal life.

The last time he spoke up to Ayman, it was about giving up on his marriage to Vanessa. Sterlin thought the two should have stayed together. The two of them were his family. He knew they loved harder then they fought and that they should have tried harder to stay together. Sterlin could sense the tension tightly wrapping Ayman. On their way to the barbershop after practice, they were stuck in Northbound 405 traffic.

"At practice yesterday, she sat in the stands not looking happy," Sterlin said, "while the boys were shooting free throws. You two were beefing hard. What's that about? You two have only been dating, for what…a minute? How long can that last? In all those years, Vanessa never brought any drama near your job."

"Sterlin, I hear what you're saying. I also know that Vanita rubbed you the wrong way from day one, but I'm not defending her actions."

"Yeah. When you were done talking to her at practice, you came back down to the floor and yelled at the team for the rest of practice."

"Did I?"

"Shit yeah, yeah you did!" Sterlin changed lanes as traffic opened up. He turned down the music with Robert Cray singing "Blues Ain't Nothing but a Woman."

"Look, man, you told me a long time ago, you can only yell so much as a coach. You said, if you yell too much, the kids will tune you out, and you end up yelling even more. By the end of practice yesterday, the kids…" Sterlin could not find the words to express, so he turned the music back up.

The conversation started up again outside the door of the barbershop.

"I'm going to say it again: you have been coming to practice with an attitude. You're not patient when the boys make mistakes at practice," Sterlin said.

Ayman responded, "I'm the same man. I can't let them make any mistakes. We aren't good enough to make up for them while Larentzo is nursing his bad ankle."

"We are good enough. Let some of the other kids be more offensive. The other boys are walking around on pins and needles if they take a shot and don't make it. Besides, I know you and this woman are like fire and ice. Ever since you've been dating her, she twists you ass-tight, as if she has your balls in a vise."

"I have not brought my personal life to the gym, the team, or even to you."

"Oh, and why in the hell are we having this conversation? I am a part of your personal life," Sterlin said as he and Ayman stared at each other for a moment. They were brothers of different mothers and fathers, but brothers they were. Ayman closed the door behind them as they entered the shop.

"Hey, coaches. How you guys doing?" They exchanged greetings with Rube, the owner. The shop had three chairs and two barbers working. The timing worked out that both barbers were about done with other customers. After awhile Ayman and Sterlin sat in the chairs for shaves and facial trims.

Rube laughed and spoke. "You two were having quite a conversation outside. I was thinking you guys didn't want to come on in."

"Oh, it's all good. We were talking about the facts of life." Everybody laughed.

Rube waved Ayman into a chair. "Ah-huh, women. Well, just as long as it's not about basketball. I'm sure you get tired of talking about basketball twenty-four-seven."

Sterlin said, "Well then, women should be off limits, too, during the season."

Ayman looked over and said, "Look who's talking. Just because you're taking a so-called break, if in fact that is what you're doing."

"Do I need to referee?" Rube laughed and whistled as if he was calling a foul.

"Rube, you understand that you have to be patient with a woman in the beginning of a relationship?" Ayman said.

"The way I see it, it's true we want women to be soft, warm, maybe even nurturing toward us men. However, there can be a price to pay—the fact that men such as you two, striving for excellence, well, that adds confusion and stress to a woman."

"How is that, Dr. Ruben?" Ayman joked.

Rube laughed and semi-mocked his assertions. "In my studies of female psychology, all men pose a problem for women in how they can best support us. Add in the fact that you guys have occupations that call for perfection. You are somewhat public figures with public responsibilities. Some women might be apprehensive about the task of representing you as your mate. Some women might feel intimidated and feel unable to support you enough in her own way. All in all, it can give a woman a case of cramps in the head, otherwise known as insecurities."

Sterlin spoke up, "Hey, even I know better than to call them cramps in the head. I'm glad there are no women around to hear you put it like that. If there were, I'd act like I didn't know you." The men laughed.

"Hey, I got the term from a woman I used to date, but you're right. Insecurities in a woman; we, as men, sometimes are victimized by how women act out their insecurities.

"A woman can whoop your butt with seemingly out-of-control erratic emotions. Whether we want a woman to support us or not, they try, and we end up feeling good when we see and feel them going the extra mile for us. But the problem is, she develops intense feelings that we hardly know how to support. Do you hear what I'm saying?"

"I hear ya," Ayman said through a hot towel, acknowledging what he already knew. Yet Ayman felt there was something more than apprehension with Vanita that he just could not put his finger on. He hoped her fluctuating negative emotions would dissipate. He wanted to change his mind about not wanting to be with her, because the other side of the mountain, her valley of peace, was a nice place to be.

To Ayman, it just seemed all too weird. One time they had been enjoying a bath with candles at his place, laughing and fore-playing and in less than a minute, she'd turned colder than if they'd bathed in the Pacific Ocean.

The one thing he could not complain about was her need for sex. She was on him for sex around the clock. It seemed her libido never shut down. They would have physical, intense, nasty sex for hours. Long after Ayman had fallen asleep, she would wake him up for any form of sex she could get. Sometimes he would awake, and hear her constantly masturbating while lying next to him.

He laughed aloud with the hot towel on his face. *At least I'm making up for lost time.* All of her escapades replayed in his head as he lay in the barber chair.

ESPN was on the TV in the barbershop, but no one talked sports. Sterlin spoke up. "Rube, you make it sound as if it's okay for a woman to send a man on a roller coaster because a woman loves hard. Men love hard too, right?" There was total silence, with sheepish grins on every face except Sterlin's.

Sterlin and Ayman had been going to the same barbershop

since they'd first moved up from the Bay Area, and the barber-shop was like a locker room where the boys let their hair down. Conversations about Sterlin and his escapades with women were like stuff of legend locker-room talk. Sterlin laughed at what he said. "Yeah, I know, I'm the last known man to be known for loving hard. Cut a brother some slack. Damn. What I should have said, if a man loves hard and starts to act crazy, they put his ass in jail." Sterlin thought about his motorcycle being knocked over, and almost being run over himself.

Rube responded, "Well, weird and crazy are two different things. I hope you guys are smart. I'd hate to turn on the TV or read in the sports section that some woman has one of you guys in a jam."

"Nah, nothing like that," Ayman said. The other barber turned on the stereo. Sly Stone jammed, "If You Want Me to Stay." Ayman's cell phone vibrated in his pocket. He was sure it was Vanita. He let the phone vibrate as the mellow mood of the hot shave fought against thoughts of what mood she would be in.

28

Edge-a-ma-ka-tion

"Class, as you can see in the handout, everyone by the end of the month must turn in two papers on two different romantic novelists. In addition you must write a 600-hundred-word poem. The poem can be a series of poems or an essay in the style of those novelists totaling 1,500 words." Lois Mae heard a little grumbling from her class as she finished explaining the requirements. "This is a part of the '*edge-a-ma-ka-tion,*' as some of you will go on to be great writers yourself one day." The key part of the word I said is, *edge.*"

She stood in front of the class with a smile. Winter sun shone through the back windows of her classroom. In her element, teaching her love of literature, she excelled. The students whined because they would rather hear her read or recite, as she mesmerized them. Her passionate style had students on a waiting list to take her class.

On occasion, she would perform at various open mics, or spoken-word venues, and her reciting skills would wow the crowds. She could recite Shakespeare, Langston Hughes, Zora Neale Hurston, and Alice Walker. Lois had read the entire book, *The Color Purple*, on the radio over a two-week period.

A program called "Books on Radio" broadcast on the school's radio station, and record numbers of listeners throughout the Northwest tuned in during the two weeks. At the beginning of each class, she read a Nikki Giovanni love poem or one of her own. She was asked by her students to end class with a poem.

She walked as she talked, stopping at the window, turning to let the sunlight cast a shadow as she recited.

"THE MOON & THE WATERFALL
I am the moon
Cresting at the point of your waterfall
Your crashes are like kisses
I feel your spray all over me
Now no one can say I'm dry of love
You make me become full of everlasting life
No, I can't contain you
You overflow
I rise up spilling
Overwhelmed by your soul
How deep you go
I'll never know
Wide and deep you are beautiful
I feel you in inner spaces & outer places
I come down on you
While the sun rises up
On my dark side I spread your banks
Waterfall love-I can't slow
But sometimes dam you up
When I'm gone too long
Sometimes I have to eclipse the sun, baby
But honey, I come back fuller and lower, and turn blood-orange-red
with desire

I move through the sky taking my time for hours
So we can go back to the beginning of time
I stay up longer from dark skies into daylight hours
I cool the mountain snow from melting too fast
So I, the moon, and you, the waterfall, can slow dance"

The students snapped their fingers for Lois Mae's work as they always showed appreciation for her poetry. After the class, a young lady with an exotic complexion approached Lois Mae's desk.

"Ms. Ilan, my mother has a coffee shop over in North Seattle. I was hoping you could come sometime to the spoken-word, open-mic nights we have there on Fridays."

"Thank you for inviting me, Meko. Is this the place they call Flava Coffee?"

"Yes."

"I understand Alexandria Cornet performs there from time to time."

"Oh, I call him Uncle Alexandria. He and my mom are good friends, so when he comes to town he recites."

"I'd like to hear him sometime, and maybe I'll recite a piece or two."

"Great, we'll be looking forward to it. I told my mom about you; she heard you on the radio reading *The Color Purple*, and she can't wait for you to come to her place."

"Meko, I hope you don't mind if I ask you about your ethnic makeup?"

"No, I don't mind. I'm Black, Japanese, and German."

"Well, you are very beautiful and very Northwest, for sure."

"I know, huh?"

"*Huh* at the end of a sentence is not allowed in my class." Lois Mae chuckled.

The young lady laughed, and shook her head. "It's so Seattle, huh?"

The refrigerator door slammed shut. Vanita stared at the picture of her son on the door in his baseball uniform. She cooled her thoughts. It had been one of those days when anger kept showing up. First, she had to cover her own courtroom; plus, another coworker was ill. Then her son's teacher called and said Joshua was having problems getting along with other students. Vanita was infuriated, not with her son, but with the teacher.

The teacher felt that Joshua's behavior had started to change about two weeks earlier, and asked if anything had changed at home that might have Joshua off-balance. Vanita went on defense and offense. She told the teacher it had to be how she ran her classroom, and maybe she needed to go back to school to learn to teach. She warned the teacher that she hoped her son wasn't being singled out because he was Black. The school had a high percentage of Black students; it was unlikely that racism was a factor, and the teacher was Black. Joshua was acting out, just like his unmedicated mother.

Vanita opened the refrigerator again for some chilled wine. She had another problem; she'd self-medicated with something other than her meds, which were collecting dust in the medicine cabinet.

As happy as she was about Ayman being in her life, she was unaware of her fluctuating moods. The distress on others, though, could be anywhere from mental needle prick, to all-out pit bull of an attack, especially to those closest to her. Joshua was reacting to her unstable behavior, from a loving mother one moment and a bully the next.

The phone rang, and she checked the caller ID, choosing not to answer. A moment later, her cell phone rattled against her keys in her purse, and again she did not answer. The truth was on the other end. It was best to avoid Alicia.

Bipolar behavior could be intimidating and confusing, even to those who understood the symptoms and the diagnoses. Alicia did not shy away from Vanita's issues. She cared about her friend, and was in all the way when it came to being there.

Ayman had spent time with Vanita's son and enjoyed Joshua, but he had noticed the boy wanted to leave the house with him every time, and he didn't want to go home anytime soon. It might have been normal for a child having a good time, but the boy seemed sad, and a bit angry. Now the boy was having problems at school.

Vanita's unmedicated life turned everything to chaos; she was another woman, not the woman Ayman first met, and she changed fast—real fast.

Ayman's phone rang. "Hello." He did not recognize the number on the caller ID.

"Ayman, this is Alicia, Vanita's friend. We met the first night you two did at the concert."

"Yeah, Vanita has spoken about you being her best friend." He was puzzled. Had something happened to Vanita or her son? How did Alicia get his home number? Why was she calling? "How are you? Is there something wrong?"

"Do you have a minute? Is this a good time?"

"What's going on?"

"I got your number from Vanita when she was going to be at your house, and her son was staying with me. I'm calling you, and I really wish I didn't have to."

"Why are you calling?" There was caution in his voice. He was skeptical of another woman calling him, who was the friend of another woman. A few female friends of his ex-wife had tried to make a move on him when the two had broken up. He knew Sterlin encountered situations of that kind often.

"You and Vanita, when I saw you two standing next to each other, it was as beautiful as a couple can get. But what looks right isn't always right. I don't want to get in your business, but my friend has a problem."

"And you don't think she'll share this problem with me?"

"No. That is the problem. This is something she should have talked to you about early on. I asked her to tell you so you two could have an honest relationship."

"What, is she still hooked up with her ex somehow?"

"No, he's out of the picture." There was a long silence on the phone.

"What is it? If you have taken it upon yourself to call on behalf of your close friend, I have to believe this is pretty serious."

"Vanita is bipolar. She is not well because many times she is off her medication. I feel I'm forced to tell you this because it can be pretty serious for all of us who come in contact with her. Right now I'm worried about her son. He is hurting from her change. The change is her not taking her pills."

"Bipolar? I don't know much about bipolar, but I'm hesitant to discuss her problem, even with her best friend. I'm a private person for a number of reasons."

Alicia felt she was doing him a big favor, and her voice let him know it as she went monotone. "I respect your privacy, but I have to tell you, if you don't know a lot about her problem, and you continue to have a relationship with her, it will become bigger than any of your privacy issues. Let me ask you this. Have you noticed she has frequent shifts between episodes of extreme highs and deep depression? I know you must have noticed it by now. Sometimes verbal aggression, and other times she shuts down. Have you not seen her go from a kitten to a wild lion?"

Ayman wanted to say yes, but instead said, "hmm" into the phone. He sat down on a barstool in the kitchen and thought about how Vanita appeared to have such a good time cooking in his kitchen, but the next time she would just stare at him while she had a big knife in her hand, chopping food. Her stare was chilling, though. She never took her eyes off of him, and it seemed she never looked down at the food she was chopping.

Alicia sighed. "This has been a recurring problem. I told her from the start to tell you. The woman loves you, and this problem has clouded her judgment about being honest with you and herself."

Ayman listened to about fifteen minutes of Alicia revealing background on Vanita. As he did in most situations, he listened and did not reveal much in return, mostly to protect himself from his words coming back.

After talking with Alicia, he understood better what was going on, and he understood he had to leave Vanita alone. It was too much for him to handle or do anything about. Alone in his kitchen, he felt lost, but strangely felt better to have been educated, but so sad at the same time.

Lois Mae checked all her dating subscriptions: *Black Singles*, *Ebony Singles*, and *Yahoo Singles*. She had a good laugh with one of the hits on an e-mail was titled "It's Hard Out Here On an ex *Gladys Knight Pip*, I Can't Get a Date."

Sitting on her couch with her computer tablet, she almost spilled her sugar-free butter pecan ice cream on the keyboard. She opened the e-mail addressed to her dating profile moniker, Miss Love, Will Love On.

It read: *To Miss Love, Will Love On, I'm not a pip or pimp, just a man who can't find a date with a smart, lonely, loving, not hurting too badly, and recovering, funny, intellectual, spiritual, and joyful woman. What I'm trying to say, I'm looking for a whole woman, whose troubles in life don't outweigh her smile.*

Lois Mae tilted her head as if her screen turned sideways. She liked his wit, so typed: *Enough said. Either you are sweet and for real, or you have great lines that you use on the weak and defenseless. Not to say I am a weak woman, so send a picture, please. Make sure it is a picture of you and not a picture of Denzel, unless you're him.* She clicked "send," and smiled.

She spoke to her dog, Selena, who was sitting at her feet. "Selena, let's go for a walk instead of reading about men who have reinvented themselves as Mr. Right." She laughed, as she reached down to rub Selena's head, and kept talking as if the dog understood. "I might start thinking good men are only in books." She laughed and stood. Selena wagged her body, including her cropped tail. Lois put on a sweater, then dog and master went for a spirited walk along the lake.

When she returned, she had mail but she ran some bathwater first and poured a glass of wine. Wine in hand, she picked up her tablet.

There was an e-mail from the young lady in her class, letting Lois Mae know that it would be great if she could come that Friday to her mother's coffee shop for open mic night. She wrote that Alexandria Cornet would be featured that evening. She also asked Lois Mae to recite that night as her mother had requested.

Lois Mae wrote back that she would do her best to be there. The next e-mail was a response from the man she had answered earlier. He had sent a picture, was good-looking, and his phone number came along with a note that said, "Sorry, *I'm not* Denzel, but I am attainable and just as charming."

She wrote down his number, went into the bathroom, and lit candles. She pulled off her sweats and walked nude through her place. In the kitchen, she put a pound of strawberries in her blender along with a half-cup of virgin olive oil, and a cup of heavy whipping cream. She hit "blend" to concoct her special body scrub. After pouring the mix into her bathwater, she submerged her body in the fragrant, relaxing elixir.

Lois Mae soaked while Selena rested in the doorway. Was it strange that having a dog made her feel less lonely—a heartbeat to hear what she had to say besides the four walls? She laughed at the thought; she wanted someone beside her when she walked her protector dog. *Am I going crazy? Let me call this man.* Her headset connected to her cell phone allowed her to voice-dial.

"Hello, may I speak to Mr. Attainable and Charming?"

The voice at the other end laughed and said, "You have me." His voice was nasally, and it did not charm Lois Mae, but they spoke on the phone for a half-hour while she relaxed in her tub. The conversation went well, and they set a meeting. The man, whose name was Esquire, said he was Black and Puerto Rican, and was born and raised in Spanish Harlem. He loved poetry and knew of a few poets, so Lois Mae invited him to meet her at the open mic she planned to attend that Friday. From the phone conversation, she doubted it was going to be a love interest, but she thought, *At least I have a date.*

"Selena," she called out to her dog. "I should wait a little more before meeting him but it will be in public."

30

Practice Against the Bad Things

Tylowe hugged his friend, and it wasn't the half-hug, brotha shoulder bump. "Hey-hey, man, whatcha doin' down here?" Sterlin asked. He was sitting in the film room, breaking down game footage when Tylowe walked through the door in his riding leathers.

"I thought I'd come on down and see if you guys wanted to come to my latest photo expo tomorrow night. I know you have a game Saturday night, so I thought you might be free on Friday."

"I'll come down for a minute, but I think I'm coming down with a cold. I hope it's not the flu. I don't think Ayman will show up; he's got the blues over a woman." Sterlin shook his head and shrugged his shoulders.

"The woman we met on Christmas day? We all need love. You might try it again one day." Tylowe smiled at Sterlin with wide eyes while pushing his lips to the side.

"It seems this woman he was hooked up with has some mental problems. He had to break it off, meat-cleaver quick. When he did, she threatened him ten different ways."

"Nah. Are you serious?"

"Yep, he's trippin'. He's hoping she'll come to her senses and just mellow out. She blows up his phone with hang-ups, and then she calls back and calls him names. The next phone call she threatens to call the newspapers or the police, and say he did some crap. Then the next phone call, she says she's sorry and just wants to be with him.

"He let me hear the messages and see the text messages. She has a bipolar disorder; that's what her friend said who called Ayman to let him know."

Tylowe stared in disbelief. "Wow! He needs to make sure his lawyer knows what's going on and transfer all her calls and text messages to the lawyer. I hope he doesn't speak to her at all. She might try to set him up some kind of way."

"He has called his lawyer." Sterlin chuckled as he thought about his own motorcycle incident. As he put his feet up on his desk, Tylowe sat down. "I have had my share of odd situations," Sterlin said.

"Tell Ayman to call me. I have resources," Tylowe said.

"He left from here about twenty minutes ago, headed for the doctor. He's also staying at the Residence Inn for awhile to make sure this crazy-ass woman don't come over to his house while he's at home."

"That serious?" It puzzled Tylowe to hear the news.

"Could be."

"Well, not to change the subject, but I want to see you for my showing, all right? It will be a little different."

Sterlin reached into his pocket for his cell phone. "Damn! I don't have Ayman's problem, but I have an ex-booty fling that trips out from time to time. You know how they can be when you cut them off. I will never understand why it becomes, 'I hate you,' when it's over, when they knew it was only for fun in the first place."

"Well, my brother, I can't tell you I understand. I'm married, and never really got into that part of the game."

"You got lucky and found Ms. Perfect."

"She is not perfect, but Mrs. Right, and you know I got hurt before, but that should tell you're capable of finding the one who God designed for you if you close your eyes," Tylowe said.

"Close my eyes?"

"Yeah, close them. You've had your eyes on everything, so you can't tell the difference between what is for you and not for you. Close your eyes metaphorically. Close your eyes and you will see what is good for you. Your other senses will kick in and replace your eyes, you'll hear better, and the right scent of *the woman* will enter into you when she's there. Then, maybe what comes out of your mouth will draw in the right woman for you. When you do open your eyes, you'll feel and understand what I've come to know. A woman is a king maker, a man is a queen keeper. A sun rises, but the moon never sets on their kingdom. The queen is rich; the king protects her heart of gold. Her king leaves his legacy; his queen is his authentication."

"Man, you have always had a way with words to say some deep shit like that. But yeah, I'll come through and check out your photos for a quick minute, but I'll be out of there early. As the season goes on, man, the slightest cold can drop you to your knees. What I got now I don't want it to get any worse, because we go on the road next week," Sterlin said.

"I hear ya. I'll tell Meeah that you'll be there." Tylowe turned to go but turned back. "I really don't know how you two handle the pressure of running a major college basketball program as two Black men in a majority white population. The odds of nothing ever happening are not good. There's always something, but that goes to show just how strong we have to be. Not often do we get to enjoy the fruits of our labor when we walk in the public light."

Sterlin shook his head. "You're right, but that's how it always has been, so we don't know what it's like to let our guard down and find nothing gone wrong."

"Is all that stuff over with your boys and the strip club? I'm so grateful my daughter didn't get a black eye over that," Tylowe said.

"The prosecutor's office let us know that all charges will be dropped with some community services. It just hasn't hit the paper. The two idiot boys will be at practice and they'll be able to play in a week. It's not like they were playing a lot of minutes anyway, but in practice it helped to practice against the height."

"It's too bad you can't practice against the bad things that can happen in our personal lives. I'll e-mail you more info on the show."

"Yeah, you be careful out there on the bike." They pounded fists.

31

Doctor's Advice

In the doctor's office lobby, an ESCU basketball poster hung on the wall. Ayman sat reading a sports magazine as a boy of about twelve asked him for an autograph.

The boy's mother told Ayman her son was pretty good and played on his school team. Her son was teased often because they were from Mexico and they lived in cheap apartments adjacent to a white neighborhood. She cleaned houses of some the students in his school. Ayman asked for the postcard back, and jotted a number to call for her son to receive a basketball-camp scholarship.

Ayman's doctor ran a free or low-cost medical clinic. He could go anywhere for medical service, but he chose Dr. Ron, as everyone called him. When Ayman first took over the ESCU basketball program, Dr. Ron, an alum player from the University of Washington, welcomed him. The two became friends, and Ayman had helped with some fundraisers to keep the clinic going. Ayman's blood pressure could ride a little high during the season, and this season, with the drama of Vanita, team troubles, and the passing of his grandfather, his blood pressure became an issue.

The two men hugged when Dr. Ron closed the door behind them. "So, I heard your message. You have a woman causing you some problems?"

"Whew, I don't even know where to start. It's all so crazy. I can recognize the other team's defense in basketball, but this woman with mental issues, I was blind." Ayman seemed to run out of breath. "I liked her."

"I don't think checking your blood pressure will help right now. Relax for a minute." Ayman moved down from the examination table and sat in a chair across from his doctor friend. "Coach, you are in the majority of people who unknowingly find themselves involved with a person who has what sounds as you were told a bipolar disorder. Quite often, people cannot figure out why their relationship is in constant turmoil. Depression and some forms of bipolar disorder, often referred to as manic-depressive, are unpredictable. In the case of this woman, as you have described her, her behavior might be in ultra-rapid cycling, where moods change several times per week. It's rare, but it could be. I strongly advise you to avoid her. When they are in a cycling mode, they run a relatively high risk of committing suicide."

"Wow." Ayman eyes widened.

Dr. Ron chuckled. "I guess I'm going to have to wait a bit longer to check your blood pressure. Do you know if she's being treated with medications and/or therapy or counseling?"

"Her friend said she goes on and off her meds."

"That's the worst a patient can do, because it takes time for meds to take full effect. Enough about her. How are you doing otherwise?" As the subject changed, Dr. Ron finally checked the blood pressure.

"Coach, if you don't find some peace with some of the things you're going through and lose a few pounds, you'll be on meds for your blood pressure. It's a bit high. Do you hear me?"

"I should be able to lose a few pounds now. Her home cooking was good." Ayman laughed but it was not a happy one.

At 2:00 a.m., Ayman's cell phone rang. The caller ID read "private." He knew it was Vanita, as it had been every night. He had stopped answering and just listened to her nasty phone messages the next day. He hoped she was not coming by his house since he was moving back home soon.

He hoped she would never show up at his door. Her threats had moved to the level of, *I'm going to hurt you, embarrass you.* Ayman had forwarded all voice mails and text messages to his lawyer.

The two of them decided to hold off on a restraining order. A judicial order would be a matter of public information; local news services would have a field day. His lawyer educated Ayman to the fact that public figures on all levels dealt with threats. It was something that most of the time played itself out. Ayman hoped so. His blood pressure was riding high through it all.

32

Moving Forward

Practice had a guest stop by, and give the team a pep talk. Goldlyn Mayfield, Coach Sparks's former star player and adopted son, and now one of the best players in the NBA, was in town. Goldlyn's team was playing in Portland later that evening, so he flew into nearby Seattle for a few hours.

Goldlyn spoke to the team about focus, sacrifice, enjoying their success, and learning from failures. It was going to be a big game for the ESCU team Saturday against Georgetown on national TV. With Goldlyn Mayfield watching, practice was spirited.

Spending time with his adopted son had Ayman in good spirits. He was going to let the kids out of running the normal amount of wind sprints if they ran a few hard. Ayman was a tough coach insisting his team run full-speed wind sprints. Coach Sparks reminded the team, "I never ask you to do something that you cannot do." The two suspended boys were back at practice.

Before the team ran, the team captain, Larentzo, came over to the sideline to speak to the coaches.

"Coach, my ankle is at full strength again. I want to personally bet you."

"What is it you want to bet?" Ayman cut his eyes over to Sterlin. Both he and Sterlin knew the kid obsessed with trying to impress Ayman. He always wanted to show the coach what he could or would do to please him.

"I will break the record for the fastest time for four complete lines, and I will touch each line."

Ayman, with a smile on his face, looked over at Sterlin and Goldlyn. Sterlin responded, "You want to break Goldlyn's record?" Sterlin's uncomfortable throat was itching, and he coughed several times while he spoke. He was starting to lose a battle with a cold coming on.

Larentzo addressed the record holder, looking him in the eyes. "I will break your record, Mr. Mayfield."

Goldlyn could read lips. He was the only player in the NBA who was deaf, but he had overcome his disability with Ayman's help but still spoke with a thick tongue. He spoke to Larentzo slowly, as he had spoken to the team earlier. "Please call me by my first name. You make me feel old, and I'm not. You have a lot of talent, but will breaking my record help your team?"

Larentzo stared at the best athlete Coach Sparks had ever coached. He wanted to be on Goldyn's level. What Larentzo wanted most was to be as close as Goldlyn was to Coach Sparks. He had asked Coach Sparks several times if he could move in and be around him more. Ayman always thought it was best not.

"I need to know how good I am, and that will let me help my team."

Coach Sparks said, "I understand what you think this will do for you, but you don't have anything to offer if you lose. Oh, yeah, there is another part of the record—"

Goldlyn interrupted his mentor with his slow, thick speech, "I made sixteen free throws in a row right after I ran the wind sprints in that record time."

Larentzo turned and faced Coach Sparks. "I have nothing to offer but my shame if I can't break the record. But if I do, I want to live with you, in your house."

Coach Ayman Sparks stared a long time at the young man, then nodded. Larentzo trotted over to the end line to position himself for the challenge. Coach shouted out to everyone in the gym what Larentzo was going to attempt in front of the current record holder. The kids and a few spectators whooped it up.

With an assistant holding a stopwatch, and another coach blowing the whistle, Larentzo leaped into blazing movement. He did what he said he would. He broke the old record and sprinted over to the free throw line. He made six in a row, four more, then four more. The gym was loud after each basket, and then quiet while he prepared to shoot another. He almost missed number fifteen but made twenty-one in a row before he missed.

Goldlyn was as excited as Larentzo and ran over to the new record holder and hugged him. When practice was over, Coach Sparks drove Larentzo to his dorm room and helped him pack all he needed to move.

After Ayman helped Larentzo move into his new room in his house and gave him a key, he settled into his own room. Someone living in the house made him reflect on how he missed another heartbeat in the house. The feeling of missing his ex had waned with time, but there were moments.

He reached for the phone to check messages. Another nasty message and threat came from the voice of a woman he thought he loved just weeks ago. He took a short nap and woke to the phone ringing. It was Sterlin sounding sick. "I'm headed out later to meet Tylowe for some kind of artsy thing. You want to meet me?"

"You sound awful. You need to keep your butt home so you're ready for the game tomorrow." Ayman sounded like he was trying to give an order for Sterlin's well-being.

"Ah, I'm cool. I'll only be out a minute. I told him I would be there, and he did want you to come. I forgot to tell you."

"Damn, you sound like shit. Keep your ass home."

Sterlin ignored his friend. "Anyway, now you got another wannabe son living under your roof. How's it feel?"

"Ask me in a month or so. I'm used to living by myself."

"Larentzo will never give you any trouble. This might be a way to keep the sports agents from trying to talk to him."

"It might help. He was something else today, with the pressure of Goldlyn looking on. I'm proud of his willingness to put it on the line."

Sterlin coughed deep down in his chest. It made Ayman pull the phone from his ear before he heard Sterlin say, "Well, he looks up to you as someone who saved him from living on an island in near poverty. Who knows what he would be doing right now if you hadn't given him a scholarship here in the States. No mother, no father, an orphanage—you're his hero, maybe the first man in his life." Another harsh cough came from Sterlin.

"I had a strange feeling watching Goldlyn and Larentzo walking out of the gym together. You know, we have had a good effect on a lot of young men."

"Yeah, we have."

"Goldlyn stays with Vanessa when his team is in the Bay Area," Ayman said in a fading voice. "You talk to her?"

"From time to time, but you know this. She's my little sis. I check on her, and she checks on me. She is just like you, though, always telling me to stop doing this and start doing that." Sterlin managed a laugh along with another deep cough. "Don't worry, we don't talk about you. She only asks if you're doing okay. Besides, anything else about you would be boring." He tried to laugh again but another cough produced something nasty in his mouth. Sterlin was wheezing and constantly clearing his throat.

"You need to go to bed; you sound awful. I got to go. I have a twenty-three-year-old, six-six athlete living here, and I'm sure he's hungry."

Sterlin sneezed in the phone and hung up.

Spoken Word

Lois Mae and her date met outside the door of the coffee house, Creative Tastes & Expressions. She was going to meet him at her place but thought better. He opened the door for her. As she walked past him, she noticed she was at least four inches taller. *He had lied about his height. Why do they lie? Oh well, it's just a date.*

The coffee house was like being in a large, open, cozy living room. They sat at a table near the windows. The tall windows and sheer curtains filtered the streetlights and passing headlights.

The growing crowd of people relaxed, drinking coffee, tea, and specialty waters. The stage held a stand-up bass and a conga player jazzing up the place. Esquire asked Lois Mae what she wanted to drink, went over to the counter, and placed an order with a warm-faced, long-silver-haired woman. She had on an apron that read "Lady Flava." A handsome cocoa-brown man with a clipboard stopped at Lois Mae's table and asked if she wanted to sign up for the open mic.

"Yes, I'm here for the open mic. Please let me sign up. What a beautiful place."

"I'm your host. My name is Tylowe. Welcome to a night of

poetry." He reached for her hand. Lois Mae responded with her name and shook his hand warmly.

She scanned several easels placed throughout the coffeehouse. Beautiful photos and paintings sat on the easels. She asked, "Is any of the art for sale? They are magnificent!"

He smiled. He had the kind of smile an artist would draw. "We'll have an auction later. The art is my wife's paintings and my photography." Tylowe patted the back of someone passing by; it was Sterlin. He turned and smiled with tired eyes. He and Lois Mae had spoken a few times since Houston.

"You know this pretty woman?" Sterlin asked Tylowe.

Sterlin's questions caught Tylowe off-guard. Both he and Ayman teased Sterlin, doubting that he personally knew any Black women.

Lois Mae asked Tylowe about Sterlin. "Do you know this handsome man?"

Tylowe looked in both directions, play-acting as Lois Mae and Sterlin nearly spoke at the same time.

"We—," she said.

"She—," he said.

Esquire interrupted, returning with coffee and tea. Introductions and a small amount of conversation ensued. People were arriving, and the noise level kicked up. Tylowe excused himself to meet and greet and sign people up for the open mic.

Sterlin stayed and dominated the conversation with basketball. Esquire seemed disinterested in engaging in the banter. Lois Mae flashed her poetry journal and said she was going to recite some of her work. Maybe Sterlin didn't notice the discomfort that Lois Mae's date was having, but she did.

"You need to take care of that cold, and don't be spreading cold germs around. You should be at home, or at least go over there and get yourself some hot tea." She raised her eyebrows and nodded her head toward her date for Sterlin to take notice.

He took the hint and started to back away. "Yeah, I don't feel real good." He rubbed his chest, then his throat. "But I wanted to support my friend. Now that I know you're reciting, I have to stay long enough to hear you." Sterlin backed into a woman. "Oh, excuse me," he said. Her blue eyes flirted. She scanned down his body adorned in black slacks. Her expression said she was quite pleased. Lois Mae heard Sterlin say, "Oh, Ann, I would give you a hug, but I have a cold. I'll make it up to you next time, I promise." Ann still gave him a short hug.

The coffeehouse was full of people mingling and checking out the photo art. A piano player joined the bass and conga player. The jazz was funky, people socialized, and the espresso machine let off steam.

Sterlin and Tylowe met up again by the serving counter. Tylowe noticed that his friend was in bad condition and waved his wife, Meeah, over. He whispered in her ear. She took Sterlin by the arm and led him to a couch near the rear. She told him she would bring him something to drink. She returned with hot tea just as Tylowe spoke from the microphone on stage. He announced that the sign-up sheet was full.

Lois Mae pulled out her poetry journal. She flipped through the pages, even though she knew what she wanted to recite. She was trying to ignore her date because he was irritating her. Esquire displayed some verbal and body language insecurities and childish jealousy that a first date had no rights.

After Sterlin left their table, he acted angry and made in-sinuating remarks. He said that Lois Mae must have a bunch of men in waiting or a bunch of old lovers everywhere. His tone was condescending, along with his nasally voice. She invited him to leave, but he stayed. She was on a bad date, repeating history.

The evening proceeded and the poets had the crowd thinking, laughing, and clapping their hands. Tylowe introduced the featured poet of the night, Alexandria Cornet. As he graced the stage, he spoke to the bass player before he recited a story poem, with the kind of voice you would recognize twenty years later—passionate-rich-deep. The musicians layered a groove. The coffeehouse hushed. The music and Alexandria Cornet held every eye and ear as he recited.

"The groove of the music made his body want to move
He wanted to move to the dance floor, but not alone
He looked, and he sought
He turned in different directions
So he waited poised for the one
He passed on those who danced out of step
He had a style that was hard to match
It had to be a special dancer
He passed on those who only wanted to dance one dance
He wanted someone who could feel the rhythm of life
Then he saw the most beautiful eyes and they held him in focus
Her eyes said, 'Do you see me? I want to dance with you. Please let
* me move with you.'*
His eyes floated an answer, 'Yes.'
A ballet of syllables and a waltz of adjectives escorted them
They danced
They were in the present, and the past times was just that, in the past
Soul to soul, quickly they found no words could communicate what
they already knew
His dancing slowed her heart and brought liquid to her skin and
glistened her beauty
She elevated into his space and he guided her to a new day
She let him be a man, and he let her be a woman
They danced a dance unlike no other dance

They moved around the interruption of the world
They both had been waiting to dance to feel a sweet warming the
  center of their groove
They found what others only dream of, an openness to express wants
  with no judgments
He wanted her and she had him to her own
With nothing in the way of their dance, they got into a love of their
  own zone
A Soul Train *line parted and they danced, danced and danced*
Forever"

He stepped down from the stage. The Night of Creative Tastes & Expressions audience cheered and asked for more. Tylowe came to the microphone and let everyone know Alexandria Cornet would bless the stage again later. He went on to talk about the photographs displayed. They were from his new poetry book, and he was auctioning off limited-edition prints of his work. The proceeds would go to a drug rehab center he and his wife Meeah supported. Meeah stood alongside her husband.

Tylowe gazed at his wife when he spoke about how good it felt to have his best friend, lover, and soul mate to help maintain a worthy cause. Lois Mae looked at the couple and wished she had a love of her own.

Meeah began the auction as Tylowe brought each photo to the stage. Lois Mae tried to engage Esquire in small talk as a peace offering. She was going to bid on a piece of art and asked for his opinion. A dismissive attitude flew in her face. She turned away at first, but then she turned back. Her eyes became rocket launchers of contempt. She'd had enough of his funk, and she told him, "Leave. Don't call me, and forget you ever heard my name. Please get away from me!"

"Screw you, bitch!" He smiled with an evil expression.

She was glad the music was up in volume. She smiled with disdain, "That will never happen." He responded with a scowl that felt violent. Her history of an ex, who had been violent, set off red lights. Lois Mae quickly grabbed her shoulder bag, her poetry journal, and stood. She spun in every direction.

Her movement had an emergency feel to those within her vision. Sterlin noticed and she saw his quizzical eyes and pointed to a space next to him on the couch. He was dealing with his own uneasiness. Cold medicine was not keeping up with his cold, and he was miserable. He waved his hand for her to come over, and she hurriedly made her way to him. She quickly sat and took a deep breath. She was slightly embarrassed, feeling as if everyone knew her business, but no one did. Her five-eleven height disappeared behind Sterlin's mass. Her breasts rose fast, hesitated, and fell slowly.

Sterlin looked sideways over his broad shoulder. He saw distress in her face, but her body language showed a sense of relief. He cut his eyes over to her date. Esquire stared, but Sterlin's stare loomed destructive. Esquire tucked his tail and looked away.

Sterlin turned toward Lois, and his face softened as he leaned into her. He whispered, "Don't let him ruin your night." His throat felt like sand as he swallowed hard. "Will I still hear you recite?" She nodded.

The auction continued, lively and loud. Lois Mae wanted to bid. She finally spoke to Sterlin, her voice buried under the coffeehouse noise. She reached for his arm, always amazed that her hand felt like a baby's touching his bicep. He turned and lifted his eyebrows. *He communicates a lot with his facial expressions.* She smiled, "I want to bid on the next piece, but could you do it for me?"

He smiled and said, "How high do you want to go?"

"Oh, it doesn't matter. I like that picture of the couple sitting in front of a fireplace. I want to put it over my own fireplace. Plus, it's for a good cause."

Sterlin nodded. Meeah told the audience that the silhouetted nude bodies in the photo were her and her husband. People "oohed."

Lois Mae and Sterlin overheard the couple sitting in front of them. The man said, "She looks good, but you can't put that buffed brother on my wall."

The woman poked him in the side, blew him a kiss, and said, "Well, we might have to talk about all those naked women car posters in your garage, huh?" He had a surrendering expression while chuckling. His woman joined in on the bidding. The photo was the hot piece of the night, and the price went high quickly. Lois Mae squeezed Sterlin's forearm each time to signal him to bid. Twice she squeezed, and she was already the current high bidder.

Lois Mae flashed her spread hand in front of Sterlin, and then flashed four more fingers. His eyebrows and facial expression asked, *are you sure?* She nodded, then smiled, loving that they were communicating and hardly needed any words.

He stood up and tried to speak over everyone, but his throat hurt when he swallowed. The room spun for a moment, and he felt short of breath. He cleared his throat and raised his hand. Meeah pointed at him. He flashed five fingers and four more fingers. It was two hundred dollars over all the other bidders. Lois Mae won her art piece. People cheered, and Sterlin pointed to Lois Mae, the winner. Esquire walked out, and she felt pleasure and relief. With the auction over, it was time for more poetry. Tylowe read a short poem he said he had written for the love of his life. The women in the audience all voiced a collective "oooh."

"Her expression of beauty overwhelms

I gaze at her expressions of internal joy and outward pleasures
I'm addicted to her love
A spiritual love
I never want to live without her love
An unmatched attractiveness is a fixture on her face
My desire is to please her to let more of her unfiltered sensitivity rise
Her emotional hold on me is my strength,
She is the key to my joy
I'm addicted to her love
A spiritual love
I never want to live without her love
Expressions of ecstasy glow on her body
I refuse to take my eyes off her no matter the angle of my vision
She and I have entered into a spiritual love
The essence of her exquisite soul brings me home
I'm addicted to her love
A spiritual love
I never want to live without her"

Lois thought, *He is proud of the love he has found.* She had a happy feeling, but felt sad within moments, thinking about her own life. She pulled out her poetry journal and wrote while other poets recited. Lois wrote in her journal faster than most could type. She was inspired. A vocalist and the bass player teamed up for an emotional duet of "St. Louis Blues," and their intensity of the performance mesmerized the audience. Lois wrote and erased lines of a new poem until a smile said she was done.

Meeah came by to check on Sterlin and introduce herself to Lois Mae to alert her where she could pay and collect the art she'd won. Lois Mae told Meeah she had to know where she could find the *I Dream of Jeannie* silk and chiffon pants she was wearing. The two women spoke quietly while the poets recited.

Before Meeah walked away, she felt Sterlin's forehead, and shook her head disapprovingly. She leaned over and said to Lois, "Girl, please take this sick man home and put him to bed. He's really not doing too well." Lois Mae nodded and smiled, not knowing what to say. She caught herself staring too long at the side of Sterlin's face, wishing she could go inside his head.

Lady Flava introduced Lois Mae and called her to the stage, and told the house they were all in for a treat. "Ms. Lois Mae Ilan is our local distinguished literature professor at East Seattle City University. Many of you have heard her voice on the local radio theater version of *The Color Purple*. Here she is!"

Lois had on a red and pearl Ralph Lauren knee-length dress, her long strides accented by her maroon calfskin knee-high boots. Her flowing walk said she had regained her composure after the earlier bad-date experience.

Sterlin smiled at the visual of her sway. *I'm all ready feeling seasick; don't look.*

"I want to thank my student for inviting me to bless this stage. What a wonderful night to see and hear such great talent. To have read Mr. Alexandria Cornet's work in my class and to have heard him tonight is an honor. I am going to stay with his theme, a dance, I present you my poem."

She looked over at the piano player and asked, "Can you do a little Donny Hathaway type of slow chord progression? I have never recited along with music, but I would like to try." He nodded and filled the room with a slow, electric-piano-layered groove. Her voice, sultry and Southern, pulled in and held every soul in the house.

"Dance with me
I am worthy of a dance with you

Even though I'm Fatigued
Seen better days, I'm alive in my soul
I'm injured but not dead
I see you looking for that perfect dance
Maybe reasons from the past, you looked past me
If you dance with me
I'll heal
You'll heal
We hurt, because the jazz of the past had no soul
Let me dance with you
It will be therapeutic and healing
Years of spinning and jumping in the wrong directions
Dealing with other's imperfections
I can see you are wondering, can life be pain free
I look at your sweet but sweat-drenched face...and I say
One more dance
Let that dance be with me
I will stop the bleeding in your soul and bandage the damages of
    missteps
And if you hold me tight, I will feel the heat I need to help my sore
    soul, move the way you need me to move
Yes, we are old dancers
Tired, drained and aching
This world cuts deep
Scars remain
Questions... sometimes they hurt more than answers until the needle
    breaks off for that last screech
One more dance, please, I ask you to dance with me
I know others have stepped on your toes
I have thought a time or two I was the prize in the show
My past dancers they threw me into the air

All too often they have failed to catch me
We are in pain from others tap-dancing on our spirits
Yet I am willing to leap into your arms
Dance with me
In time, our love could be the hottest ballroom dances
Your dry tears
My wet tears
We must push aside tears and never dance alone, again
Love and trust will help us perfect our steps
Whom you have tangoed with, I judge not the past
Understand I do have fear, but I will follow your lead
On wobbly legs and with tattered heart, I ask you to take my hand
*   and I say*
One more dance
A dance meant to last forever as friends and lovers"

Lois Mae dipped her head and the audience clapped and roared. Some stood and applauded. Alexandria Cornet walked over, bowed to her, and led her back to her seat. The people clapped her all the way.

Sterlin stood to make room for her to sit. He reached for her hand and saw she had tears rolling down her cheek. Another dizzy spell hit him. He had to sit, and he did, quickly. The back of the couch was high and he laid his head back abruptly. She put her hand on his forehead.

She told him, "We are going, now. Let's go." Sterlin's face was blank. Lois Mae stood up and walked over to Tylowe. The band was playing for a short intermission. Tylowe and Meeah both came over to Sterlin, and Tylowe helped his friend outside. Lois Mae walked down the street to her car and opened the passenger door. Tylowe and Sterlin had a short conversation. Sterlin gave his car keys to his friend and told him he would pick up his car tomorrow. Tylowe was able to get a little laugh out of Sterlin by telling him he would let Meeah drive and burn rubber in his car. Both Ayman and Tylowe teased Sterlin about being over forty, and owning a hot rod Dodge Magnum with all that horsepower.

Sterlin whispered to Tylowe, "My car is my woman; she rolls like I like to roll. My car makes me feel good when all else fails."

Tylowe looked over at Lois Mae holding her car door open for a sick Sterlin. *If only he would open his eyes.*

33

Fever in the Funk House

Lois Mae pulled away from the curb and started asking medical questions without letting Sterlin answer. "Who's your doctor? What medicines are you taking? Did you eat? What did you eat?"

"Jeez, woman." He tried twice to clear his throat. "Where's your little white uniform, white stockings, and the little white hat with the red cross? I hope you don't plan on sticking a thermometer up my butt."

Her smile was devious. "I'm not sure of the inflection you used. Was that a request or a demand?"

"I'm sick, and you're picking on me after I gave you a safe haven from your date."

"Oh, okay, I'm going to let that one slide because you're sick. I guess you're one of those men who try to play tougher than they are when they're sick. I'll kick your butt!" Lois Mae sent him a sideways glance.

He tilted his head back. "Where are you taking me? And, do you have butt fetish? First you want to put something up mine, and now you want to kick my butt."

"Whatever. Taking you to my place, I'll doctor you up, make

you all brand-new, and then put you on the curb, like a little lost child."

"Hmm, and I'm supposed to feel better? I got a better idea. Would you mind taking me to my place? It feels like I've been sweating in my clothes. I do appreciate you looking out for me, but I'd rather you'd take me home. The way I feel, I should have stayed home, but then I would not have heard your poem. That was special. Can I have a copy?"

She ignored his request, but couldn't hide a smile. "Where do you live?"

He directed her to Eastlake area overlooking Lake Union. She turned on some music and turned left. Al Jarreau sang "Fire and Rain."

She pulled into a twenty-four-hour Walgreens pharmacy. Sterlin stayed in the car, nearly asleep, while she shopped at the pharmacy and the grocery store next door. She had to wake Sterlin to get more directions. He mumbled the directions, and added in a surrendering line. "I'm sick."

Sterlin opened his eyes, sensing he was near home. He pointed to his driveway. As she pulled into the driveway, he said, "Hold on." He dialed his cell phone.

Lois Mae cut her eyes his direction, her nose flared. *He's checking to see if the coast is clear. Oh wow, the nerve to have me come here.*

He never spoke into the phone; he just dialed a number. The garage door opened. "Pull in," he said. She was reluctant but she drove forward.

Due to the recent events with a spiteful ex-booty-call knocking his motorcycle over, and other fretful history, Sterlin had the new security system installed. He also bought one for Ayman as a gift to protect him.

He was proud of his useful toy and explained the best he could with his strained voice that through a cell phone app, he could control the house alarm, garage, door locks and lights, and other amenities.

"I like that. I want one for my garage and condo," Lois Mae said while feeling slightly ashamed of her original thought.

"Stop trying to keep up with the Joneses." He fought back choking and laughing.

"That's what you get, colored man, for trying to be funny. You remember, I told you I'll kick your butt."

Coughing and laughing, he said, "Woman, please."

They walked up the stairs. Sterlin barely made it. He threw himself across his bed, laboring to rest. She made herself at home, and then drew a bath, pouring and sprinkling in ingredients she had purchased. Some other ingredients she mixed into a boiling pot and put face towels in the mix to simmer. She took out of a box a digital thermometer she had purchased and chuckled at what he had said earlier about putting it in his butt. For a moment, her thoughts went to a feverish funk house.

"Go get in the bath," she ordered.

"Okay," Sterlin answered, but did not respond physically.

"Come on, while this water is hot."

"Damn, my nose is plugged up, but I can smell something. What is that?"

"Sugar and spice and everything to make you feel nice." She laughed.

He turned on his side, his big body curled into a fetal position. Her eyes widened watching a huge man being broke. The bed was an oversized king, large like everything in his bedroom. The dresser was tall, and the curtains hung from windows stretching from ceiling to floor. Lois Mae sat in a corner next to the bed and watched Sterlin's upper body expanding with labored breaths. She sat in an overstuffed chair with a huge footstool. At the side of the chair were end tables with reading lights. She walked through his house and was impressed. He was a manly man but with a good sense of style.

"Sterlin, your bathwater is waiting." She pleaded as she sat on the bed behind him. "Come on, baby boy, go get in the bath, please." She was uncertain if she should touch him, and how he would perceive it, but she followed through and rubbed his back. The skylight above blended their shadows into one. She slowly leaned on her elbow next to him. He sat up and looked at her for a moment. He walked into the bathroom.

I hope he doesn't think I know. Maybe I shouldn't have sat on his bed. My mamma taught me better. She laughed to herself, rolled over onto her back, and looked up through the skylight. She almost fell asleep. His voice startled her when he called out.

"Lois Mae, thank you. I truly appreciate you taking time to help me. Whatever you put into this water, I think I remember this smell from when I was a kid."

"No problem. I have some tea you need to drink."

"It's not some mess they gave us as kids that gives you un-controlled runs, is it?"

She laughed. "Well, don't you want to feel better?"

"Yeah, well, if it is that mess they gave me as a kid to clean me out when I got a cold or flu, we're getting back in your car and going to your place, and I'm gonna blow your toilet up. So, think twice about what you're giving me." They both laughed.

"No, I won't give you Bigmama's special brew." She went to the kitchen and came back to the bathroom door. "Hey you, are you okay in there?"

"Yeah." He said it slow and long, and relaxed.

"Here, drink this tea for your throat."

"Bring it in. Just don't take any extra peeks."

"Well, if there is something to look at, I'm looking." She had lit the one candle he had in the bathroom, but the soft glow did little to light the big bathroom.

"I ain't got nothing to look at." His chuckle sounded almost sinister. "For sure you're a country girl with all these voodoo smells. My goodness."

She left and came back with a folded towel. "Here, put this over your nose, breathe in hard, and sip the tea. Keep the towel over your nose till I bring you another."

"Yes, *Nurse Ratched*."

Oh, funny; I remind you of the nurse in *One Flew Over the Cuckoo's Nest*, huh?"

"Ah, no, I was ah—"

"Don't try to clean it up now." She put the lid down on the toilet and sat down. Periodically, she went back for another towel.

She was bringing him more of the last of her towels when he walked out of the bathroom with a towel around his waist. They didn't see each other and Sterlin walked into her chin with his chest. It could have been bad for her lips, but she stopped him by placing her hand on his chest. *Damn, his chest is brick hard.* She wanted to squeeze. She felt fever in her funk house boiling again.

"Oh, I'm sorry, I didn't see ya."

"Get in the bed. You need rest, but drink some more tea first," she ordered.

"Is your dog going to be all right being left alone all this time?"

"Yeah, she's fine. If she needs to go out, I had a doggie door installed in the basement and the backyard is completely fenced and secure."

"Then, hey, look, you're staying here tonight. You can use my robe, or pull a T-shirt out of my dresser drawer. Please don't drive home tonight. It's really too late. I would feel so bad after all you've done for me. My spare bedroom has a nice bed, or my chairs recline into a soft, comfortable bed. The footstool at the end makes a nice little sleeper. You can find some bedding in the hallway closet." He pointed to the chair where she'd sat earlier. "No matter what, you're staying. I still run this asylum here."

He was looking down at her, and she was looking up into his still very tired eyes. The man told her what to do, and she loved it. There had been a few times in her life when it felt right. This was one of them. His tone was warm, but firm. She felt needed. She grinned and mused, about the fact that he gave her options as to where she could sleep. Lois Mae was charmed. *He didn't offer his bed...That's a good thing, I think.* She nodded and turned away, and headed out the bedroom with a smile glued in place.

She made herself some tea and sat in his kitchen, daydreaming in the night. She thought she heard noises out front. She went into the living room and peered through the big bay window. Bushes blew, and moved about. It reminded her she was in a strange house. He had a grandfather clock, which stuck 1:00 a.m. She took her tea into his room along with her poetry journal. She found the bedding in the hallway and fixed up the recliner. She sipped her tea and wrote in the dark with the help of a candle.

Sleep In Your Heart & Soul
His soul has me
Only if he could hear my whispers
I'd say to thee
I want to love thee
Love you for who you are
I blow kisses over
They are filled full of my desires
He turns his body to the sky

Exposing his heart, my love rains down
The universe sends healings to wherever there is pain
The sun and the moon lift my shadow to lie next to him
And under his dominion,
I'll always be by your side
Only if he could hear my whispers
I would assure him
I'll do for him what he can't do for himself
I'll walk the last mile for him
I'll never let him stand alone
He turns his powerful being and my eyes see the protection he can
*   provide for me*
Only if he could hear my whispers
He would hear me say
Let me live in your heart and soul

She put her book down as he turned over again, but kept the fetal position while facing her. She stood up next to his bed, and said her nighttime prayers. Looking up through the skylight, she rubbed his back as if he were a child. It was hard to pull away, but she moved back to the recliner, and she pulled the covers over her. A few slow tears crept down her cheek. She was not sad or hurt. She knew not where the tears came from as she drifted off to sleep.

"Wake up," Sterlin said. He stood in front of where Lois Mae was lying all covered up, looking peaceful. Sterlin reached down and touched her arm. "Hey, pretty lady. Wake up."

"What time is it, and how do you feel?" she asked, rubbing her neck. Sterlin was dressed, and he held a glass of orange juice for her.

"It's almost eight, and I feel so much better. I don't know what kind of voodoo you worked on me, but I feel like I can leap a tall building in a single bound."

She smirked and rolled her eyes. She was wearing one of his basketball jerseys, and under the covers, she could feel one of her breasts had fallen outside the jersey. It was also just long enough to barely cover her butt. She felt naked with him sitting across from her. "I need to use the bathroom." She gave him a look to say "leave."

"What, you don't have anything on? Hmm, it seems to me I heard you say if there is something to look at, I'm looking. It's fair play, right?" He gave her an all thirty-two-teeth grin.

"Oh, and you said you don't have anything to look at, so I didn't look. Besides, I have nothing you want to see." Her voice held a touch of embarrassment.

Sterlin clapped his hand and rubbed them together. "Girl, you had more twisting in that red dress last night than a tornado—a true Texas booty. I was sick but that cleared my vision up." He laughed with his mouth closed. Then he added, "Hmm, maybe that's why my head was spinning?" He kept laughing.

"Okay, I see you are feeling better, and what are you doing looking at my butt?" She fumbled under the cover, repositioning her breasts, then threw back the covers. She stood and proudly walked to the bathroom, with just enough jersey covering her rear. She didn't mind him peeking.

"I'm getting dizzy again," he teased.

"Okay, I have a voodoo doll. Don't make me have you running down the street naked and speaking in tongues."

"All right, I'll be good and do anything you say."

"Find me something I can wear. I do not want to walk out of your place wearing what I had on last night. Can I have some sweats or something?"

She cleaned up and dressed. They decided to go to breakfast and then go to Tylowe's house to get his car.

He backed her car out of the garage. The wind was blowing a bit to go along with overcast skies and misting. Lois Mae walked out of the garage wearing E.S.C.U. coach's warmups. She made them look as if they were hers. She was impressed that he had a new spare toothbrush.

She had spent the night, and it felt like he had no interest in her other than as a friend. He was almost too much of a gentleman, as if he were sending a signal: *Stop In the Name of "I Don't Want Love."* She told herself, *Let it go*. He opened the driver's side door for her. She insisted that he drive. It gave her that feeling of riding alongside a man.

He drove past his front door that was up a flight of stairs. Something caught his attention. He stopped and backed up.

"What's wrong; you forget something?"

He shook his head, parked, and jumped out. He strode up to his porch, then walked back down in hostile steps. An emotional fire burned at what he saw. Slowly, he entered the car.

She asked again, "What's wrong?"

"Nothing!" Nothing was his front door and porch vandalized with red paint.

"Wait!" she said firmly. She got out of the car and walked up the steps. The sight reminded her that she thought she'd heard a noise last night. She walked down the steps looking back, and got back in the car.

She let him be, not knowing what to say and how or why it had happened, and he drove straight to Tylowe's. He parked her car behind his, walked around, opened her door, and helped her out. The winds blew hard enough that the smaller trees waved. The grass was soft, and both their feet sank in.

"Glad I don't have on spiked heels," she said to the ground.

"It's a good thing I had my tennis shoes in the back." Sterlin had no response.

She looked at the view of their cars and kept speaking in an effort to break the ice, not wanting to ask questions about the vandalism. "Look at us, two grown folks running around here driving Hemi-engine hot rods in pretty paint." She thought she could get a smile out of him, but he didn't smile. She asked in an exasperated tone, "I don't know what to say. Am I making it worse? I should leave." She held herself and shivered in the cool breeze.

He faced her. "I'm sorry, but I have to skip breakfast. I need to take care of a few things before the game. I'll make it up to you. I would like to see you later...please. Can I come by your place... later?"

She placed the back of her hand on his forehead. "You don't feel warm, but are you sure you feel better?" She wiped mist from his face.

Her smile, her pretty lips, and bright brown eyes, eased some of the anger he felt from someone vandalizing his property. Lois Mae's teasing and sarcastic humor had an effect on him that he enjoyed.

Her touch last night had put him to sleep, unknown to her, but when she rubbed his back he felt something different that eased him to relax. He felt what he had been avoiding, a sincere woman who cared about what was going on with him. She was truly concerned about his well-being. She was a star in her belief of who she was in knowing her worth in herself. Unlike the weak, emotionally needy women Sterlin let walk in and out of his life like a shopping mall revolving door, Lois Mae seemed to be the kind of woman who was soft in heart and strong in pride. Fear was not there with him, when he was near her. Sterlin wanted more of her. He knew when he awoke that morning, sat on his bed, and watched her sleep. Now, with her touching his forehead, wiping dampness from his face, it injected trust he badly needed; he was feeling strong enough to deal with his fears.

A mist on her dark caramel skin and black hair made him stare and breathe deep. She had fixed her hair in one long ponytail. He saw her stunning beauty—her spirited soul turned her attractiveness into magnificence.

She had showed her realness, not coming on to him for sex first, as it usually happened. He smiled at her and put his hands on her arms as if to lift her. She stopped holding herself, unfolding her arms.

They were standing in front of Tylowe's when Meeah walked out and down the stairs. Sterlin, responding to Lois Mae's smiling nervousness, leaned over and kissed her lightly on the lips. He pulled back a little, looked into her apprehensive eyes, and kissed her again. She kissed him back. Their tongues moved like fingers on a saxophone.

Meeah approached and teased, "All right-tee now!" She giggled. "Sterlin, here are your keys. I'll be going back in and leave you two alone. I see you're feeling a whole lot better." She turned and started to walk away.

"Hold up," Sterlin said to Meeah but kept his eyes on Lois Mae. "Meeah, could you do me a favor? I owe this beautiful woman breakfast, or at least some coffee. She's been a godsend, taking very good care of me. Can you bail me out? I have to go."

Meeah kissed him on his cheek, and said, "Come on, girl. I'll take care of you."

Sterlin kissed Lois Mae on the forehead. "I'll call you later, sometime after the game." He got in his car, and she came to the passenger window while he warmed the engine.

"You are not well yet; please don't overdo it." He nodded and reached over and embraced her hand. He stared at her for a long while, until he said, "I'll dance with you."

The women stood and watched him leave. Both wore big smiles. Lois Mae had one big *ahhhhhhhhh* going on inside her. *He heard my poem.* Then she said it clearly for the blowing trees and everything above, "He heard my poem."

Meeah smiled wide and said, "Honey, he has a fever over you; that's the kind of medicine he's been needing."

34
Hot

Within a block, Sterlin realized he needed to slow down, and cool down. He was hot and headed over to Bobbie's place to shake the shit out of her. His mere physical size could put fear into anyone. Even during sex, his girth was not an easy thing for some women to deal with. He sometimes used that as an excuse to be with bigger women. The truth was he simply desired a bigger woman. Right now, he wanted to make Bobbie disappear underneath him in another way as he drove toward her place.

That woman is crazy. She tries to kill my motorcycle and damn near ran me over. Now my door and porch, dammit, I have red paint spread all over. It's a mess. I need to kick her ass. He laughed a painful laugh. *I don't need to end up on* Eyewitness News.

Red paint on his porch was challenging the sudden happiness he was feeling about Lois Mae. He awoke that morning ready for a new day, a new way. He was feeling like a little boy and wanted to tell everybody, but that for sure was not his style.

Sterlin pulled into a roadside coffee stand, then ordered tea. He found a residential cleanup company online using his phone, and made some calls. Then he called Vanessa, Ayman's ex, and he told her A to Z about Lois Mae.

"Little Sis, I had to call you to tell you, and I don't think I'd tell many others. No, I haven't told Ayman yet... He's doing all right. Yeah, we have a nationally televised game today. I betcha you'll be watching... Yeah, no, I just couldn't tell him that you were there and that I saw you and we had spoken...'cause he's mentioned it a few times he thought he would see you at Granddad's funeral. No, I'm getting into what you should have done. I know it was hard on both of you."

Sterlin told Vanessa about the troubles he'd had with the crazy woman. She told him he had to tell Lois Mae so they could have a clean start. He agreed he should let her know about the senseless-ass woman who had put red paint on his door. *Yep, I have unfinished business.* The thought kept repeating in his mind as if he was practicing.

Visions of the woman who made him feel better than he had in twenty years of full moons were powerful and soon blocked out the image of red paint on the porch. He laughed and turned his sound system on. A woman had slept in his house, but not with him. On the car stereo, Muddy Waters sang a happy blues tune about the love of a good woman.

His physical health was better than yesterday, thanks to Lois Mae, but he knew he needed food to keep his energy up. He called Ayman who was already planning to have breakfast with Tylowe. Tylowe had just taken off right before Sterlin had arrived to pick up his car.

Traveling across Lake Washington was rough that morning. High winds blew waves and spray over the floating bridge. Sterlin crossed over just before the Department of Transportation closed the bridge. He still had a ways to drive to Snoqualmie Falls to meet his friends for breakfast at Salish Lodge. He pulled into the parking lot at the same time Tylowe was getting out of his wife's Jaguar. Another friend who rarely came around escaped from the passenger door. Psalms Black, a fellow past University of New Mexico associate of Sterlin and Ayman, was more of a friend of Tylowe's.

Psalms Black was as wide as Sterlin but shorter, yet his neck made him look like the most powerful man Sterlin knew. Psalms had golden eyes and whose skin was almost the same color. He intimidated most other men because he was so handsome while looking like he could destroy. To Sterlin and Ayman, Psalms Black's ultra-reserved demeanor kept them from becoming chummy. He was not a criminal as far as they knew; he was a personal bodyguard to people who needed guarding, but there were hints of a secret life. Tylowe was close to him; he understood him better. Psalms was an original Seattle native as was Tylowe.

At breakfast, Ayman made light of the fact that four, well-built, well-dressed, Black men in this day and age still drew stares. "It's still about being Black in a white-controlled world," Ayman said.

Tylowe responded, "It can't always be about race. We all have white friends who respect us and care about what we go through. Okay, we just have a few white friends."

"It's not about race," Sterlin said. "It's about money; racism is just a tool for the almighty dollar." They all nodded. Both Tylowe and Ayman admired that Sterlin spoke up. He was usually the one to avoid saying anything too socially deep or political.

Psalms Black spoke with a voice as deep as all the guys put into one. "I'm Black, but I come from a white mother; so this world sees me as a Black man when it needs a bad person, an over-achiever, and overcomer, a jock, and one those Black men different and better in white societies eyes than my all my Black brothers. All of you have been that Black man at some time or another." Quiet sat at their table as others around would never feel like the four of them. The truth was that it was a different world for them, unlike the one for everybody else lifting a fork and smiling inside the restaurant.

The subject changed to Sterlin talking about the crazy woman and the red paint. "She kept coming by after I told her it was over, and then she damaged my motorcycle, and now the red paint on my porch. Or it might be a few past crazies as of late; it could be anyone of them."

Ayman stared at him, in a nonreadable message. That was the message.

Tylowe spoke to both of them, "The both of you don't need drama derailing your goals. I have a suggestion to help you be able to concentrate on the season and avoid predicaments that might ruin your careers or image. Let Psalms here do some private investigation, and bodyguard work if need be."

"Get Suzy Q, I'm overkill," Psalms Black said, like a hammered nail going in on one hit.

Tylowe nodded his head. "Yeah, you're right. You guys know my friend from Canada, Suzy Q? She left the Royal Canadian Mounted Police. She fought constant harassment for being a lesbian, and finally a jealous asshole detective drove her to knock him out." Tylowe laughed hard for a moment. "And they paid her a nice sum to keep it quiet. Anyway, she has moved down here to the States, and I think she might be able to help. She's doing a combination of bounty hunting, private investigation, and bodyguard work."

"Oh wow," Ayman said.

Sterlin glanced over at Psalms Black and took a big breath and blew it out.

Tylowe continued, "As I said, you two are in a visible arena. You cannot deny the recent effects of these women on your comfort level; vicious people who don't give a damn about you for any number of reasons.

"You don't need to be blindsided. I have both Psalms and Suzy Q do some work for me and my family"—my girls in college and my little business empire that had some criminals involved when I first took over. I purged them, but I still need safeguards.

"She can help you guys. She'll work behind the scenes, do background checks, scope out funky stuff, and keep you out of harm's way. Plus, you'll get the Tylowe good-buddy discount."

Sterlin said, "Set it up! I have someone special in my life."

Ayman stuck his fist out. Sterlin pounded both Ayman's and Tylowe's fists but said nothing. They knew Sterlin would want too much more. Psalms Black did say, "A good woman makes a man a king."

When their breakfast arrived, four beautiful Black men said grace and nourished their bodies and didn't care who saw them or heard them. Tylowe ribbed Ayman, "Now people are going to think we are preachers just like you."

Ayman tried to look hard, but ended up laughing.

35

Steppin' Up

There was not an empty seat in the house and the band was loud. Coach Ayman Sparks and all his assistants dressed for the big game in dark maroon suits—even the female assistant coach, Lorrie. She was interviewed about what it was like to be a female coach on a men's team.

The local sports radio station KJD, which most referred to as KJ Dumb or Stupid, asked questions for the small-minded, armchair jocks. "So, do you think the boys accept you because you're a pretty woman?"

Assistant Coach Lorrie responded, "I think the most accurate reason is they are respectful young men, and that is the type of young men that come to play here."

Coach Sparks did not like the negative banter the radio station frequently used. The station lacked depth about sports, and the worst part was they spoke harshly often in personal barbs about young men and women playing college sports. Coach Sparks sent them an open letter asking them to stop. He wrote: "Using kids in such negative unconstructive chatter just so you can have higher ratings is morally wrong." The sports radio jocks mocked his letter.

The Northwest sports bars were full and ready to watch the Georgetown Hoyas in Seattle to play the East Seattle City University Sharks.

After the coaches had gone over last-minute instructions and match-up assignments, Ayman told the team, "Hoyas will try to take us out of our game with their mouths. They will foul you hard, but you can't get caught up in all that. Your weapon is to play basketball with everything you got. Their mascot is a dog, and we can run that dog back to the nation's capital. Let's play!"

As in every game, the team circled into a tight formation for a moment of silent prayer. The ESCU team had players representing mainstream Christian faiths, Muslims, Jews, and other faiths. It seemed to work as a unit of respect.

When the team came out to start the game, sitting a few rows back, the coaches had their own cheering section. Tylowe, Meeah, and Lois Mae all had on team colors.

In the first half, the ESCU team was down nine points, but Larentzo was having a great game. He had eighteen of the team's forty-four points. He was also defending another future NBA player, Javahni Jordan, who had more media recognition. Larentzo was on a mission to prove he belonged in the top tier of college players.

Right before halftime, Larentzo dunked hard on a Georgetown player, and the ball hit the player embarrassingly hard on the head. Larentzo pumped his fist into the air and smiled at a row of cameras on the sideline. The Georgetown player ran up behind him and knocked him down right in front of the ESCU bench. When Larentzo hit the floor, everybody jumped up from the bench. Coach Sparks kept his seat, and yelled for everyone to sit down. Larentzo did a push-up in a pose that resembled the world's strongest man. From that position, he sprang up to a gymnastic handstand, and back-flipped to his feet, and ran down the floor as if nothing had happened. The arena exploded in a chorus of cheers.

The next play, Lindsey, the ESCU center known for his sharp elbows, nailed the Georgetown star player in the nose and blood poured. The Sharks were going to stand their ground against the Hoyas.

During halftime, Coach Sparks, pointed out, "We are so dead set on scoring. We're blowing it on defensive assignments." After five minutes of venting his displeasures, Coach threw his clipboard down. It shattered into pieces, and he walked out of the locker room. All the coaches followed. Coach Sparks was not above using a little theater to push his team. He was acting now, and Sterlin had a hard time keeping a straight face.

The second half was close. Georgetown's Javahni Jordan heated up and two of the best college players went toe-to-toe. They each scored point after point for their team.

With Georgetown ahead by four points and less than two minutes to go, Larentzo was fouled on a three-point shot. The Georgetown coach stormed onto the court, protesting the foul call and was called for a technical. The original foul call, plus the technical, added up to four free throws. Larentzo stepped up to the line, and just like at practice made all five as easy as blinking his eyes. He was on a roll when it came to making free throws, forty-seven in a row since he last missed nine games ago.

With the game tied, both teams missed their next shots. At twenty-four seconds left, Coach Sparks called a timeout, gathered his staff, and discussed their options. Sterlin's assignment was to set up the play they would use. Ayman would either agree or ask for another option.

"They are going to double-team Larentzo when he touches the

ball," Sterlin said. "He can handle the pressure if we have him get the ball at the top of the key. Let him run some time off the clock, and then we run a double screen. We'll screen left with Hafezz fading to the corner for the open shot, and Nomo will roll to the hoop. We'll keep Reiser on the wing as a third option."

Coach Sparks said, "Let's do it. Put in Shervey for the weak-side rebound and tell him not to foul. I'll talk to Larentzo."

The players sat drinking water while Sterlin diagrammed the play. Ayman squatted, looked into Larentzo's eyes, and said to him, "Son, you have done a good job leading your team today. You are everything you wanted to be today and more. I know you want to take the last shot." Larentzo's eyes drifted away from his coach's eyes. "Look at me," Ayman said firmly. Larentzo did. "I need for you to understand, the next level is you doing whatever it takes for your team to win. That's the next level. Goldlyn made a statement to you in the form of a question, about what you do, will it help your team." Ayman raised his eyebrows, asking "*do you understand*." Larentzo nodded.

Hafeez leaned over and told his teammate in a caring tone, "Let's do this."

The whole team clasped hands in a circle, and Larentzo yelled, "One, two, three!" The whole team yelled, "Shark Bite!"

The play worked, but when Larentzo passed to a wide-open Hafeez, a camera flashed in his eyes, causing him to hesitate taking the shot. The split-second delay allowed the Georgetown defense to recover back to Hafeez, and he was forced to dribble away from the defense. Nomo read the situation, and he knew what to do when a play broke down. He ran up behind the man guarding Larentzo and set a back screen. Larentzo took four steps toward the basket, and Hafeez passed the ball high above the rim. Larentzo made like Superman, leaping high above the rim. He caught the pass one-handed in mid-air and dunked the ball. This time flashing cameras did not matter.

The East Seattle City University Sharks defeated the Georgetown Hoyas 87-85 on national TV at the buzzer, and the crowd went crazy. Larentzo finished the game with thirty-eight points. CBS cornered Coach Sparks and Larentzo. Larentzo pulled in the other four players on the floor with him when the game ended.

The CBS interviewer asked, "Larentzo, is this your last year of college? Is the NBA next?"

"I love playing for my coach, and I love playing with my teammates. I'm focused at this point in the season on our team trying to make it to the national championship. That's all that matters right now."

"What is it like playing for Coach Sparks?"

"He is more than a coach. He teaches us life lessons. He's a mentor to all of us."

Ayman was proud that his players felt like that.

After the game, Lois Mae met Sterlin in the parking lot. She kissed him and said, "I'll see you later at my place."

36

Winners and Losers

"Mom, the Sharks won. I saw Coach on TV."

Vanita nodded when her son ran into the kitchen with his good news. Normally, she would have warned Joshua about running in the house, but was forgiving him as she hoped he would forgive her past for behaviors.

Alicia, with the help of another woman, a deaconess at her church, had provided intervention. They were able to sit her down and talk. It was a struggle, but as in previous times, they convinced her to go back on her medication.

Vanita's erratic behavior went beyond her relationship with Ayman. Vanita had shown signs of being bipolar since her early twenties, before marriage and a child. Her husband never knew what the problem was, but finally she drove him out of the door. After their divorce, Alicia was able to convince her to see a therapist. Now her relationships worked better, but only when she was on her meds.

The powerful drugs' side effects were most noticeable in the first weeks. Going on and off the drugs could add to the intensity of the side effects, like feeling extremely drowsy and disoriented. Clarity came in small increments.

"Mom, can we...can I call Coach?" Joshua and Ayman had gone to hit golf balls and some other boy stuff, but Ayman had not been around for awhile, and the young man often asked why. Vanita said that Coach was busy with basketball.

"Mom—"

"No!" Vanita's tone bruised Joshua's feelings, and his eyes began to well up. She took a deep breath and thought about her response. She stooped down, and apologized to her son. "Honey, listen. Coach and I were good friends, but sometimes people don't get to stay friends forever. Coach is a nice man and maybe when his season is over, he'll spend some time with you." She stood and turned quickly to keep her son from seeing her tears. The room turned vertigo. She grabbed a barstool and held it to keep from falling. She vomited.

After she calmed down and reassured a tearful, scared Joshua she was all right, she read up on her meds' side effects, and ate a bowl of butter pecan ice cream. It cooled her stomach.

Quite often after games, Coach Sparks had dinner with some of the players. Team members Larentzo, Shervey, Hafeez, Nomo, Reiser, and Foley sat at the table eating large burgers. The happy team wolfed down their food and made jokes. Hafeez had the largest burger, a veggie burger. With Ramadan past, he made the best of eating all he could eat. Coach Sparks had a supersize milkshake and fries that he dipped in the shake. The young men teased him, having a good time, when Tylowe's daughter, Tyreene, and a few other girls walked in. "Sorry, Coach, the party is over. We're out," Shervey said.

"Okay, guys, treat these ladies like ladies, and have them home before midnight." Ayman had a straight face. They all laughed.

Ayman left right after the group did. He started his car, and the stereo played The Spinners' "Love Don't Love Nobody." A sad smile stared back at him in his rearview mirror as his mind raced, *Winning isn't everything.* He sat back in his seat resting his eyes and slowed his mind from missing what he was not sure he was missing. He pulled out his cell phone. He thought, *Dammit, I miss her. I know it may not be the right thing, but...* He still had her on autodial.

39

Another Fine Night

Dinner was cooked and the table set. Sterlin was on his way over. Lois Mae had downloaded some blues music from iTunes. Meeah had told her that Sterlin was a big blues fan. Meeah also told her the story about how she met her husband, Tylowe. The story gave Lois Mae hope.

Shemekia Copeland played while she sat on her deck covered up with a blanket enjoying the nighttime lake view. Selena, the dog, lying against her legs had become a ritual.

She thought she heard someone come up the stairs to her place and she smiled, visualizing Sterlin. As she approached her front door, Selena walked in front of her and sat at the door, so Lois Mae could not open it.

"Selena, move. Move, girl, move." Lois Mae had to pull Selena's collar and yelled through the door, "Hold on." She barked, something her dog rarely did, and it startled Lois Mae.

Whoever was outside sounded like they jumped down the stairs. *Sterlin can't be scared of a dog.* She opened her door. Her stomach clenched, her throat closed. She slammed the door. Her heart raced, and beat hard.

Thrown red paint covered her front door and porch. She ran to her bedroom. She had a handgun, but kept it put away. After a couple of minutes she mustered the bravery to carefully open the door with Selena by her side. She said aloud, "Someone really wrote 'BITCH' on my door."

Selena almost walked out into the wet paint, but Lois Mae grabbed her collar. Sterlin called up the stairs, "Hey," and bounded up the short stairway. He froze and stared at the ruin. His eyes reflected the red funk as he slowly lifted his eyes to mirror the distraught, but beautiful brown skin of Lois Mae. He stepped around the paint, and the dog hummed deep in her throat.

"It's okay, girl, go," Lois Mae said to Selena, pointing for her to move away. Selena backed up a few feet; her fearsome look barely fazed Sterlin.

"Lois Mae," he said in an exasperated hush. He looked back at the vandalism and then focused back on her.

He thought he knew who had done the damage.

She thought she knew who had done the awful deed.

She reached out for Sterlin. Selena hummed again deep in her canine throat but backed up a few more feet. Sterlin, showing no fear, squatted down and extended his hand. Selena inched forward, sniffed and sat in front of him. Sterlin patted the dog's head.

"I need to call the police," Lois Mae said. "I thought the asshole might be a freak."

Sterlin stood, and she closed the door. "What?" he asked. She took his arm, and they walked over to the couch.

"That man I was out with last night called me a bitch. He had the most evil attitude when I wanted to end the date. Originally, I told him he could pick me up, so I gave him my address. He must have done this, and followed us last night to your place."

Sterlin's mind was whirling as words crawled out between his lips. "I'm not so sure he did it."

"Why?"

Sterlin explained, "I...ahhm...I got kind of a stalker."

Lois Mae pulled away and sat back as Sterlin continued explaining.

"I came over here to tell you about her." He felt the recoil in Lois Mae's body language. He tried to backpedal. "Maybe I'm wrong about the stalker thing. This guy threatened you, huh? Maybe it was him, who knows. Look, the paint all over my porch this morning. I assumed some woman I used to be involved with had done it. Now I just don't know what to think."

"Okay, tell me everything." Her tone was even, but her breathing was erratic. The fact was neither was sure whom to blame. "Some women, huh? And how do I get this paint off my door?"

Sterlin took a deep breath. "I know a twenty-four-hour vandalism cleanup company. They already have my place looking better. We'll call them in a minute. Look, I know this is not the way to start our..." Sterlin did not know what words to use.

"Our relationship, beyond us just being friends? Is that what you want to say?"

"Yeah. Whatever just happened, don't let it stop us before we start. You'll have to be patient with me. I'm almost a virgin at a one-on-one relationship."

"One-on-one? Are you sure that's what you want?" Her eyes asked at the same time as her voice. "Ready to put some, I mean, all other women away for a one-on-one?"

"Yes, one-on-one."

She smiled. "The day before, we were just casual friends, but you kissed me this morning as if you cared for me. That overrides everything. I should be ready to kick some ass, over my front door, but you're here, and I don't care. I'm happy you're here. I feel kinda safe. Maybe I'm crazy."

"Maybe!" he said.

"Yeah, maybe. Whatever happens is supposed to happen, excluding our doors looking jacked up. Sterlin, please talk to me as if I'm living inside your head and there is nowhere to hide. I promise you, I'll do the same. Have you heard of Nikki Giovanni?"

"Who hasn't?"

"Baby, a whole lot of folks. Anyway, she said, 'I really don't think life is about the I-could-have-beens. Life is only about the I-tried-to-do.'"

Sterlin pressed his lips to Lois Mae's forehead and kept them there.

"I still want to call the police, and I still want to feed you," Lois Mae said. "You're still not at full strength. I don't want you to relapse and be as sick as you were." She rubbed the back of her hand on his forehead.

"I could use some food," he said, "but I'm a little fearful about my car being out there. Let's call the police, then how about we go to my place? You can put your car in my garage if you want to drive. Or you can roll with me and leave your car in your garage."

Her voice had reservation. "I don't want to leave my dog here, not knowing who this person is out there."

"I'll help you pack up everything, and your dog comes with us."

"Okay, let me pack an overnight bag and put my kitchen in order."

"I upgraded my security to an outside intruder warning system. If anyone comes near the perimeter, lights come on, and a little beeper goes off inside."

"Are you taking me to your place or to prison?" She laughed as she walked toward her bedroom. Sterlin came up behind her and held her. She laid her head back on his shoulder.

"You want to escape me?"

"I may not want to leave." She turned and faced him. "I want to lie in your arms tonight. I don't want to sleep on a recliner across from you." She thickened her seductive Southern voice.

"Are you sure?" He kissed her neck.

"I've been sure."

After the police came and took a report, the couple went to his place. They ate and talked for awhile. It was not too late in the evening, but Sterlin was still fighting his cold. He was sleepy, and she prodded him to go to bed.

"I know, but..." He didn't finish what he wanted to say. Sterlin walked around the table, stood in front of her, and he reached for her hand. The look on his face was passionate and wanting.

"What?" she asked.

As he often did, he spoke with his eyes. Lois loved it because she could read his intentions in his facial expressions which were as penetratingly deep as his voice.

He led her through a sliding glass door. Out on his back deck, he put his hands on her hips and turned her in different directions. She gazed north, west, and south. In a panoramic view, she gazed at Lake Union, Queen Anne Hill, the Space Needle, and the downtown Seattle skyline lights. She felt mesmerized.

He removed a cover to a hot tub sunk in the deck. Steam and heat filled the night air in secluded privacy.

Lois Mae faced Sterlin, and her lips moved as if she had something to say, but she was in awe.

He said, "I'll be back in a sec." A moment later, she heard Sam Cooke singing, "Please Don't Drive Me Away."

He came back with a tray of towels and bottled water. Lois Mae was braiding her hair into ponytails and said, "Boy, I'm going to mess up my hair over you." He kissed her on top of her hair as she turned her head from side to side while finishing the last braid. He brushed his lips against her forehead between all her movements. "Stop messing," she teased. She wanted his lips to go anywhere he wanted to put them.

He placed his robe over her shoulders and stared into her eyes. Once again, she could read him loud and clear, but she told him, "I want you to tell me that you want me."

Sterlin did not speak immediately. He had her sit on a bench next to the hot tub. The steam made sitting outside comfortable in the late-winter air. She nestled her head into the hollow of his neck and shoulder. "I want you. I want you, Lois Mae, but I have to tell you...I have been with a lot of women...sexually." His chest rose, moving her head, and expanding the threads of his shirt.

She placed her hand on his chest. "Who you danced with before doesn't matter to me. We all have a past. I have a good feeling about us. Maybe our pasts will help us be patient with each other. I will not lie or cheat on your heart, but I won't ask you to do the same. If you're going to love me, you will. If you're going to play with my life, you just will. There is nothing I can do to stop you, so I'm not going to treat you as if you might do me wrong."

Sterlin nodded as he watched the steam rise before he said, "I woke up this morning looking at your sleeping beauty, and my heart was clear on what I want.

"I want to deposit my dreams in your soul and watch them grow. Things are clearer for me than they have been in a long time. You are that woman who became my friend first and didn't ask for more!"

"That woman."

"Yes, that woman. The kind of woman I want to try to make happy. I know this, and we don't even know much about each other, but I know enough."

They faced each other, and their lips rushed to each other as if life was going to escape. Their kisses seemed to generate their own steam, until they ran out of breath.

After a sip of water, Sterlin told her, "I know about love..." His mind drifted for a moment, then he continued, "I know about the wrong kind of love. The few who know me know it hurt me bad. It made me scared, and maybe I just bedded down women, instead of letting a woman get close to me."

"Sterlin, no one has the right to judge you. I'm not in any position to play high and mighty about your past. What concerns me is how you feel about me now." Lois Mae leaned in on his chest and heard his heart pump a steady beat.

"I imagine you wonder why I feel this way so soon? It's not as if we have been dating and hanging out a lot."

She kissed him on the ear and whispered, "No, I'm not wondering. I'm living in the moment. I'm living on faith. We can waste time wondering why and what if. I don't want to do that.

"What you are doing right now, talking and sharing your feelings, is rare. I'm not a male basher, but it's not often a man will get down to the bare bones of his feelings. Men just don't, but here you are exposing yourself to me."

She blew out a long breath. "Your naked soul is beautiful. With you exposing your soul, that makes you a fine man." She slid her tongue into his ear. "When are we going to get in this hot tub, or is it just for show?"

He took another deep breath and said, "Listen, I have always used protection. Hell, I don't even know what it feels like to be inside a woman and not have a condom on. I think the last time was twenty years ago. Well, I know it was twenty years ago."

"Ahh, that's a change of subject." She lightly giggled.

"Come on now, listen to me."

"Okay, okay, baby, I'm sorry. I know you're being serious about something that's important."

"A woman I once loved back in my college days, she ran my ass over. This woman tore my heart apart like a single-page news-paper. You bear a slight resemblance to her.

"For sure, I'm drawn to a pretty face, and a woman with large breasts and a big round booty. Add your height, and I'll howl at the moon, if she has some booty just like yours." He tried not to laugh.

She punched his arm and chuckled. "I thought you were trying to be serious, and you need to stop looking at my butt."

Sterlin spoke and moved his jaws as if he were a talking robot. "Not possible." He laughed, and she punched his arm again.

"Sterlin, tell me what happened with this woman. Tell me how she hurt you."

Sterlin told his sad story—how he loved someone who toyed with him and strung him along for games. She had other lovers, yet he always forgave her, and it would happen again. He tried to break away from her, but she had control of his heart. He was like a lost puppy she could lead home every time.

After all the interactions he'd had with women in his life, he simply did not know what it was like to have a healthy relationship with a female. He told Lois Mae the reasons he avoided Black women. He always felt out of control to a Black woman's wishes. First, his father's girlfriend, then again in college—he fell deeply under the control of both women. He knew it was a weak excuse, but he had never been strong enough to deal with it. He let her know he was ashamed of being so weak, partly because he had only been with a Black woman three times in his forty-two years of life.

"I look, I stare, I dream of women the color of my mother, but I just stopped reaching out. Does that pose a problem for you?"

"Do you or have you treated a Black woman badly?"

"No, never. I know there are some brothers who hate themselves, so they hate on everything chocolate. That's not who I am. Look, don't laugh at me, but…hmm, I'm just scared of Black women. Sistas have been dismissive toward me. I guess I have felt they could feel the weakness in me. Then I woke to your kindness and I see you as my friend."

In her head, silence overrode the bubbling water and the sounds of the city. She shook her head out of her trance. "You said you woke up feeling different today, right?"

"Yeah."

"Then, like I said, all that happened before me doesn't matter. The race thing, that's someone else's problem. No one has the right to judge you. It is tasteless and classless for anyone to stand in the way of someone's love."

They stared for a long moment before Sterlin nodded and said, "The deal is, I have always felt weak in the presence of most Black women. I can't explain it. If a sista said, skydive without a parachute, I'd smile and jump.

"My best female friend, Ayman's ex, Vanessa, always said a Black woman loves a strong Black man. I have never felt strong around a Black woman."

She thought as she listened to him, *His heart has been buried, but he's not dead.* She rubbed his chest and angled herself to look into his eyes. "I only care that you learn to love me, and that I can make you happy."

He nodded and continued to tell her of his past. He envied his best friend, Ayman, who had the love of his life while they were in college. Ayman and Vanessa were the happiest people on Earth, it seemed.

"I just wanted the kind of love I saw," he said. "Ayman and Vanessa were in love for life, and they told everyone and acted like it for years. Quiet as it's kept, they are still in love. I wanted to be like my friends, having someone who loved your funky socks and everything else."

"I don't know about the funky socks. We may have to talk about that." They both laughed.

"Ayman and Vanessa were the perfect circle, where two lovers live and breathe for each other. That's what I wanted, but I was thick as a brick in the head with a bad woman. I loved her. Ugh." He shook his head and looked up at the sky.

"You can use her name; it's cool," Lois Mae said, rubbing his chest, and kissing his cheek.

"Monica Turner, *the* Monica Turner; she's the one who turned me every which way but loose."

"Ah, are you talking about the singer, the movie actress?"

"Yeah, the ultimate celebrity drama queen." His laugh had sarcastic overtones. "She used me as a training bra for her first session of how to dog a man out. When we dated back in the day, she had her way with me."

"Yeah, I've been told more than a few times that I resemble her. The truth is, I don't think she can hold a candle to me. Right?"

"Yes, you're right." Sterlin knew to say yes, but he meant it.

Lois Mae shook her head. "The media has played her up as an innocent victim of choosing bad men. She married the baseball player and divorced him a year later. She dated that European prince, and then the TV sportscaster. She's in the news now, divorcing Kid Funk Dogg, that old-ass rapper, but she might be pregnant."

"I could have warned them all." Sterlin snorted a laugh. "I'm not really laughing."

Lois Mae thought about what Sterlin had told her in Houston— the story of his dad's girlfriend sexually abusing his youth. Adding all these issues together, she had a better understanding of why he avoided emotional closeness. In a strange way, his pain made her feel good. Sterlin trusted her. Her being and her style made him willing to move forward with her. She could feel his emotional arms around her; he needed her. Sterlin told the last part of his sad story of twenty years ago.

"She gave me VD." There was pain in his voice.

Lois Mae responded with a whisper, "I've been there. My ex brought it home...twice."

Silence ensued. Even the wind seemed to disappear for a few seconds. Sterlin's hand reached and touched the tip of her nose and lips. He let his finger slide down her chin past her neck, stopping at her breasts.

He said, "I want to make love to you. I wanna learn to love you like you need to be loved. I'm willing to give all of me, and I want to please you in every way."

"I've used protection since my last husband." *This is very different. Men I've known hate and avoid this conversation, but this man brings it to me. I knew there was a reason I liked him.*

Sterlin broke into her inner conversation. "I wanna feel all of you. Let's get tested, because sooner or later, we are going to lose our heads. It will be just a matter of time before I break a rubber off in you."

Lois Mae shifted in her seat. She made some expressions on her face he could not read.

"You all right?" He put his hands on her thighs and squeezed.

Lois Mae looked up into the nighttime sky and breathed in the air. "You should be kissing me."

He kissed her cheeks. She was broiling and baking from his touch. She rolled her head back, and he kissed her on her neck. She groaned so loud the people up in the Space Needle might have heard from miles away. From her neckline to her lips, his tongue danced. Her body was simmering. The hot tub was ice water compared to the heat between her thighs, and just as wet. Their tongue tips connected and fused. They kissed for a long while.

Finally, he let her catch her breath.

"You know how to kiss a woman," she said.

"I know how to kiss you." Sterlin kissed the tip of her nose.

From the sliding glass door, Lois Mae's dog appeared, scanned the scene, and walked back in the house.

"I want to get in the hot tub…naked."

He laughed. "Is there another way? I kinda already seen you naked, baby. You look good enough to eat."

"What? Unless you got X-ray vision, you haven't seen any of this."

"Baby girl, the other night I wanted to rip that red dress off you, when you walked up to the stage. My mind let me see right through everything you had on."

"Oh, you like all these dangerous curves?"

"Ah-huh. For sure we get in this hot tub, a rubber ain't gonna survive." They laughed and nodded at each other. "Let's go get tested, so we can—" Sterlin finished what he had to say in a whisper, and then pushed his tongue into her ear, and moved it around slowly.

"Ooh, you so nasteeeee." She laughed, then rubbed and held the back of his head, keeping his tongue right where it was.

"You like that?" he asked.

"You just don't know."

Sterlin rose and stood in front of her.

He pulled off his shirt, his chest shining in the night. He released his belt buckle, and slowly unzipped his jeans. He waited to see if Lois Mae would follow his lead.

She stood and dropped her skirt. She was in her bra and panties before he was out of his pants. She turned away a moment and removed her bra, then faced him with her nipples looking candy-sized, chocolate-flavored Dots. He was amazed that such large breasts held up so firm.

Lois felt a bit embarrassed that her panties were beyond damp. She did not want to leave them on the bench soaked in her juices. She left them on as she stepped down into the hot tub.

"Ooh hot, but nice." She walked around in the water, then spun around and faced the stairs. Sterlin towered over her. Her eyes blinked once from the sweat and blinked again at the visual. At six-four, he was a physical specimen with the athletic build of a Zulu warrior. He had a strong, firm, wide, and long erection. Her heart was pumping fast. *I don't think I have ever seen anything like that, not even in a video.* She stared at what she wanted and smiled. She wanted him to slide inside her glory. The head of his manhood was well above his navel. He comically mocked Superman with his fists on his hips. "Oh, besides scaring a girl, you gonna show off the goods? You're too much, and maybe too much for me. I think I understand about breaking off rubbers, whoa!"

Sterlin lowered himself into the hot tub. She was sitting deep in the water, and he walked in between her legs. She leaned in, and with her lips moved his hardness to the side and kissed his navel. His hardness pushed back. While rubbing the small of his back with one hand, her other held his mushroomed erection. It was smooth, and she wished she could feel him slide inside her soft hot wetness. He was pulsating as her thumb massaged the head. He grunted and groaned from deep within his diaphragm.

She moved her hand from the small of his back, and she palmed his ass, caressing his smooth round behind that curved into rock-hard thighs. She fisted the head of his manhood and stroked. Her nails dug lightly into his rear flesh.

She began exploring the shaft of his long manhood with her lips and tongue. She heard him loud and clear as a hiss escaped from his mouth when she put more pressure from her nails into his ass, his flesh pushed back. She stroked the head faster and squeezed tighter, her skillful hands making him submit. He put his hands on top of her head as she rubbed his hardness all over her face. She enjoyed the smooth texture, imagining what it would feel like inside of her.

His dick is so damn pretty. Damn, I want him to…shit, do anything to me. The hot tub bubbled, and the skyline watched them boil.

Sterlin's hands ran through her braided hair. He stood her up and kissed; juice ran from their mouths. She sat down and panted for air and water.

His eyes were lost in space, and he groaned with pleasure from her nails softly imprinting the flesh of his ass.

He reached for the bottled water, tilted his head back, and dripped water into his mouth. With a mouthful of water, he stooped down and laid his lips just above her breast. Slowly, he parted his lips and let the chilled water cool her flesh. He stood and teased her nipples with the wet tip of his hardness while Lois Mae's fingers were underwater sending circling jolts of pleasure to her clit.

The music from the house switched to the blues version of Prince's "Purple Rain." Sterlin looked down into Lois Mae's eyes and saw her pleading for more. She had a fetish; she had a thing for his ass. She made him turn around, and he felt her lips kissing his back and working their way down, dancing at the crease of his ass, making him spread his legs wider. He felt her hands push into the middle of his back, forcing him to bend over. Her face and tongue planted pleasure. His hardness throbbed, and he could not help but stroke his manhood, while her tongue kissed him where the sun don't shine. His body shuddered as he backed up into the rare ecstasy.

When Lois Mae released her tongue from everything she could touch, he turned and pushed her back. He lifted her legs out of the water and placed her feet on his chest. Lois Mae's feet held up her five-eleven frame, they were not the feet of a small woman. However, men loved to look at and touch her pretty feet. Against his broad chest, her feet were pretty and dainty. She massaged his skin until he took one foot in his mouth.

"Baby, that looks so sexy sucking my toes. I like that." She laid her head back, her eyes rolling to the sky as he licked each toe. Sterlin licked the bottom of her foot, then switched to the other foot and did it all over again. All she could do was groan, moan, and lose control of her breathing.

After Sterlin's tongue bathed her feet, he slid down to his knees. Her breast nipples floated on the surface, and he sucked each one—her nipples becoming long and almost chewable. He stopped, looked at Lois Mae, and said, "If I haven't told you, let me say now: you are so damn sexy." He took a big breath, and went under the water. She felt his tongue sliding into her inner hot spring. Her lips did a drumroll, and her breathing became sporadic. His tongue was on a deep-sea, treasure hunt until he found her black pearl of sensitivity. His tongue circled and licked the precious jewel. She was amazed at how long he was *going down* while under. Before he came up for air, he tasted a rush of her sweetness from her hot spring as her thighs shuddered.

With his head above the water, he heard Lois on the edge of screaming. Sterlin put his arms around her and held her tight. The intensity of her orgasm had made her hold onto him as if she was scared, but she felt safe in his arms.

She said in a faint voice, "Honey, I know we have to hold back," she blew out a disappointed breath, "from you going inside me, but I want to get you off. Tell me, tell me what I can do. I'll do anything to please you." His eyes and a slight nod of the head told her to exit the hot tub. She smiled, knowing he had something in mind.

They kissed as they dried each other off, then he turned her in the direction he wanted her to go. He followed her curves with his hardness pointing at her behind. In his bedroom, they kissed and tangoed all over the bed. His fingers found her clit, and he made her cum again.

She did not get a chance to catch her breath this time. Sterlin turned her over onto her stomach, and slapped on her ass. She promptly popped her ass up. He enjoyed the visual of her spread as he rubbed some oil on her behind. He mounted her and slid his manhood back and forth between her ass cheeks. She felt his hardness massaging between her cheeks. The force of his weight on her, along with his hardness, was making heated friction.

"Ooh baby, ride me. Let me feel you squirt that cum all over my ass," she ordered. He was grunting and thrusting, letting her firm behind be her insides for him.

He worked harder and faster, making no effort to hold back his grunts as he grabbed her hair. She pushed her ass up higher as she felt him slowing, then hold still. His deep voice bellowed, "Fahhhhhhhhhhh!" A warm flow of thick liquid landed between her shoulder blades and trailed down her spine to the small of her back. His body shook, and she thought, *Maybe I don't want him to cum in me. That was hot.* She smiled and had an inner laugh as he rolled over.

Five minutes passed. Sterlin was still breathing heavy. Lois Mae reached over and touched his face. "Hey, you, you gonna leave a sista hanging. There's a flood on my back. I don't want it to drip all over the place."

He lifted his relaxed body and left the room, returning with tissue and a warm, wet towel. He washed her up, then spanked her butt one time to let her know he was done. He left the room again and returned with water. They lay next to each other, talking until the morning light, before falling asleep tangled, but comfortable.

38
Looking Glass

Larentzo walked into the den and plopped down on the couch. "You're up early," Ayman said as he paused a game video.

"Yes, sir, I was hoping you could give me a ride to school. I want to lift some weights and put in some extra shooting." Whenever Larentzo spoke, he always looked the person in the eye. However, this time, his eyes seemed to be pulling nails from the floor.

"Are you tired?" Ayman asked. "If you need some more sleep, go back to bed."

"I'm not tired." Larentzo's eyes closed and reopened with a blank stare.

Ayman slowly pushed himself out of his chair, "Come on in the kitchen and let me put something in your stomach. I haven't eaten anything but this coffee myself. I don't think my doctor would like me calling this food. I have a meeting a little later on, so I can drop you off at the gym on my way."

One of the things Ayman had established when Larentzo moved in was they would not talk about basketball at home. "You might as well kill the last drop of OJ that you left in there."

"Oh ah, I'm sorry, I meant to."

"Goldlyn did the same thing when he lived with me. I've been guilty too. My ex-wife would give me a glare that could freeze hell over." Ayman laughed. "Sometimes we men do things a woman thinks is cute for a minute, then they grow tired of our mess."

"Young man, you seem a little down. There can only be one thing a young man could be down about." Ayman chuckled and shook his head. "Grits is like the perfect love."

"How is that?" Larentzo asked.

"You want cheese in your omelet?"

"Yes, sir."

Ayman continued his talk about grits. "How we desire love, well, grits can be just like that." Ayman laughed while he shared what his grandfather had shared with him. Larentzo sat on a barstool, looking perplexed. "Most women will cook your grits just like you want them. For sure she'll try. Whether she loves you or not, she will boil and stir a pot of grits for her man in the fashions he likes, as a sign of wanting to please her man as he wants to be pleased. There are plenty of things a woman is going to do her way, and there is nothing you can do about it. And, many times her way, ends up being the best way, but if she's pissed off, and she's cooking your grits, heed my warning."

Ayman picked up a clear glass pot and held it up for Larentzo to look at. "You might want to avoid them being mad at you if they're boiling a pot of grits." Ayman laughed and thought about Al Green. He walked over to the kitchen iPod docking station. He found some Al Green and turned it up.

Larentzo said, "In St. Lucia, it is said you don't want hot oil from fried plantains poured on you. Is that the same thing?"

"That sounds about right," Ayman said.

Ayman started pouring grits into the boiling water as he spoke. "Everybody likes their grits a certain way. Some folks like 'em thick, some watery, or buttery, or creamy, or maybe with salt and pepper. I compare them to a woman. A woman can be sweet, or salty, peppery, spicy, thick, or thin, and creamy or stiff." Ayman laughed harder than he intended and snorted as he poured well-beaten eggs into a skillet. He handed a big spoon to Larentzo to stir the grits. "We as men have a lot to do with how a woman will be. It all depends on how we stir the pot."

"Coach, are you talking abou…" Larentzo stopped, not really sure what he wanted to say.

Ayman cleared his throat. "If you think I'm talking about sex, young man, that would be a part of it but not the whole of it. But you ain't having sex, right?"

"Coach—"

"I'm just messing with you, so please don't answer that question, but you better be using protection. Anyway, a woman wants to feel you are caressing her mind and heart, not just for the moment, but forever from the first moment they know they like you."

Larentzo dished up a big bowl of grits for himself. He was adding pepper and butter when Ayman put a huge omelet on his plate.

"Coach."

"Yeah."

"Tyreene told me she wants to slow down, and maybe not see each other as much. I don't understand."

"Woman's prerogative. It's another one of those things that's been around since Adam and Eve."

"I told her I loved her. I thought that's what she wanted to hear."

Ayman kept silent for the moment. He fixed his grits just the way he liked his with sugar, butter, and cream. He slid his omelet onto his plate and put ketchup on his plate before he spoke. "Son, let me tell you one thing. For sure, I'm no love doctor. My house is not a home anymore, ever since I lost the one I loved. I lost the one I loved in your freshman year. I've tried love again, but…" Ayman went silent. Only the forks and spoons scraping a bowl or plate made any sound. He thought about how short-lived his love affair with Vanita had been.

Larentzo broke the silence. "I remember your wife. She was so nice to me. The day I got here from the island, she hugged me and let me know I was in a good place. She said I was her son now, as well as all the boys who played for you. She asked me to tell her my life story. I did, and she cried. I felt bad, but she said I had nothing to worry about anymore."

"Yeah, she's a good woman." Ayman's eyes seemed to lose vision as he stared into gray sky filtering through the windows. "She supported most of what I was about." He walked over to the patio door, watching a grazing deer in the backyard. As if he was talking to the deer, he said, "Even the best of couples have problems. We had ours, and it finally took its toll. Since she's been gone, I've tried love again, and I picked someone who couldn't cook grits, but she could throw the hot water." The deer looked up as if it was listening, but then went back to foraging. Ayman walked away, fixed a new cup of coffee, and forked some more food.

"Coach, I think I understand what you mean about grits. But I don't know why Tyreene wants space from me."

"Most likely it's not about space; it's about fear."

"I don't see why she would be scared."

"Larentzo, the same things that make you a good basketball player and a good person, present a certain type of uncertainty to a woman. Your focus is on being the best you can be in basketball. However, that can cloud others' perception of what is important to you. You're a rising star in many people's eyes. She sees people pulling at you, because you are a good person who sometimes doesn't know how to say no. It could be she doesn't know where she fits in.

"This is hard on a woman. I'm sure she wonders if you'll be here next year. You could be across the country with some other pretty girl being your biggest fan. That goes along with all the fans competing for your attention. For her to feel that sometimes she's just one of the many in your world, it might be hurting her heart. Her pulling back might be her way of supporting you by giving you space, and maybe the freedom she thinks you need."

"Freedom." Larentzo's eyes squeezed, and then they opened.

Ayman reached across the counter, and put his hand on Larentzo's shoulder and said, "She's unsure there's a place for her in your future."

Ayman already knew of the dating couple's dilemma days before. Tylowe had called and spoken to Ayman to warn him of the pending situation. Tylowe thought the upset might affect Larentzo's focus on the court. Ayman knew Larentzo was just like him. When trouble arose, often Ayman threw all of his attention into basketball as an escape. Larentzo, as of this morning, wanted to go to the gym when most kids wanted a day off.

"But I told her I loved her."

"Words," Ayman said, staring like he was peering through the young man. His thoughts wandered back to when he and Vanessa were young. "They're just words. Do you love her, or are you in love with her? A woman hears what you really mean. Did you say it as if you were shooting free throws?" Larentzo's silence was his answer.

"The confidence you have in yourself can come across as arrogant in the love game. In some ways, a woman wants to feel you are weak for her. Confidence is charming in the sports world, but it's not always good in the love game." Larentzo scraped his plate clean. It was a nervous cleaning. He had worries on his mind about losing his girl.

The only part that felt good was hearing Ayman telling him things he needed to hear as a man of moral authority, mentoring and counseling. Ayman continued, "She is trying, I suppose, to find where she fits in your life. A woman will wonder from time to time. It's not about the money you bring home. It's not about the awards you win, or how others admire you, but those things can be a trigger. I'm telling you I know." Ayman's voice trailed off.

"I don't know what I can do to make her believe," Larentzo said.

"A woman needs to take some responsibility in a relationship to be able to tell you what she needs. In a nonemotional way, they need to be able to tell you. It's not okay to say, 'I don't know what I want.' This leads to breakdown and ultimately failure in staying together.

"I'm sure she's being honest, and not trying to see what you will do. I don't see Tyreene as that kind of woman. Men and women often think they have no option in how they go about finding out about their mate's feelings." Ayman stood up to leave the kitchen and said, "Hey, I cooked, you clean the kitchen and start the dishwasher. I'll get ready to go. Pre-wash the pot I cooked the grits in. Grits tend to stick just as soon as they dry, no matter how you cook them."

Letdowns

The morning after, Sterlin prepared to leave for a meeting.

Lois Mae asked from her smiling face nestled in his pillow, "Are we okay?"

He chuckled. "I know this is the morning after. Yeah baby, we're okay. We're better than okay. You can call me your boyfriend, or man." He smiled. "I'm happy."

"Would you go to church with me?" she asked.

"I haven't done a lot of church lately, but I'll go with you. I went to church with Ayman and Vanessa when they were married, but not as often now. Remember, your auntie had me in Sunday school."

"That's right, you owe me, for giving my auntie a bad time." They both laughed.

Tylowe sat at the Golden Spoon restaurant talking to his friend, Suzy Q, as she preferred people to know her. They were all the way in the back with her back facing the door when Sterlin and Ayman walked in. Tylowe arose from his seat, and she leaned back in her chair.

She sat with her legs gymnastically wide apart. Sterlin and Ayman stared at each other and then at Tylowe. Her feet were on each chair to the side of her. You could not see her face. Her eyes peered from deep in a dark-colored sweatshirt hood. She looked as if she was trying to stay warm, or hide. The cutoff sleeves exposed pale arms, but she was a small woman with arms that had buffed biceps. Long dragon tattoos highlighted her forearms.

Tylowe laughed. "Suzy, stop making my friends think you're crazy."

"Well, I am crazy, mate, eh." She chuckled. "I want yer friends there to sit across from me. I want to look in their eyes. Plus, three hot Black chaps sitting across from me, I'm in jungle-fever heaven, despite the fact I don't like men. Damn, damn, damn!" She removed her hood, revealing a resemblance to Drew Barrymore. Her speech was heavy with British jargon.

Sterlin and Ayman both did a double-take as Tylowe laughed and said, "She's harmless, guys; it's her strange humor. You can trust my friend Suzy Q like you trust me."

"True that, mate," she said, "but I do like to look at fine Black guys. Say, do you think you two could change your names to Wendy and Lisa?"

Ayman picked up on her humor and her preferred lifestyle. "So would you be Prince, and we're the Revolution?" He reflected on what Tylowe had told him about their old college buddy, Elliot, and how Suzy Q had helped Tylowe when he had to deal with a tough situation. Sterlin shrugged his shoulders; he did not get the musical jest.

The three sat down as Suzy wanted them to. "I'll make this quick, mates. Tylowe here gave me the preliminaries. I can help, but when I ask a question, give me a complete answer, eh? If you need to ask me why, it's a waste of yer time and mine. I will not ask unless I need to know. Are we good, eh?"

Ayman responded, "I need your help. I need protection from the weird elements out here. I'm too much in the public eye." Suzy Q nodded her head, a smirk.

A waitress came to the table to take orders. When she walked away, Suzy Q did nothing to hide her stare at the woman's swaying hips. After the woman disappeared around the corner, Suzy Q spoke casually, "You'll rarely know I'm around until you need to see me. I understand yer problem female has stepped back from harassing you."

"It appears so," Ayman said, "but I really don't know for sure. She made some serious threats."

"I'll handle it, mate. And don't worry, I'm not an assassin. I just fix problems when they need to be fixed. I don't hurt people unless they try to hurt me. I protect people."

Ayman nodded. Suzy Q then looked over at Sterlin. "And what about you, big boy?"

Sterlin almost seemed intimidated. His voice was soft; it didn't have its normal deep timbre. "I need your help to see who's causing me some trouble, maybe an ex-female friend."

Suzy Q rolled her eyes and lifted her head to the ceiling. She stared for a long moment at Sterlin and Ayman before she spoke. "Tylowe wants you guys to be safe out here in this crazy world, but one thing: when I bring you information, you may not like it, but remember, I'm just the messenger. Oh, another thing you two grown fellows should know; there's a huge difference in how a female behaves and a woman acts.

"A woman grows past her hurts and mistakes, in so, she doesn't let it affect her relationships. A female is constantly trying to find herself. Take here yer good buddy, Tylowe. He has a woman at home waiting for him, but she also has a life outside her husband that gives her a sense of completeness." Tylowe smiled in knowing.

Suzy Q leaned forward and spoke slowly, "Now, give me your

e-mail addresses, and I will send you some questions. Answer them completely, and I'll get busy. I want you to respond by tomorrow in full detail. Things could be happening right now; you just never know, eh."

The team had to make up a conference game because of a snow-out in Montana a few weeks earlier. That would make them play five games in less than eight days. A team letdown lost at the wrong time could derail East Seattle City University's league standings. Monday's practice was sloppy. The coaches had yelled and scolded the players for lack of intensity.

Finally, a player who rarely made a mistake, made his third one in a row. He let a ball go out of bounds and didn't hustle to save it. Coach Sparks had enough. He called an end to practice and ordered all the players to study hall.

He yelled, "If you're not going to practice hard, I'll be damned if I'll let you go hang out with your girlfriends. Go! All of you, two hours of study hall. And, I'd better not hear about anyone being at a party. If anybody is one second late for the bus in the morning, you'll be running line until Seattle never rains again." He turned to Sterlin and the other coaches. "And for those boys who can't get a girlfriend, no jerking off." He and the other coaches finally had something to laugh about.

Coach Lorrie, the female assistant, joked, "Well, Coach, I think going to Montana, we might want to protect the sheep there from the jerk-offs." They all tried to hide their laughs as the boys left the gym. Coach Lorrie said on a serious note, "Our boys know Montana is not Georgetown, and that has them cocky. Unfortunately, we're going to a strange place, with strange food and strange people, while our boys' heads are up their butts."

"That's when upsets occur," Coach Sparks said.

"You know that's right," Sterlin agreed.

The game was close to the end, but ESCU played poorly. The players thought they could play hard whenever they wanted to, and still win. They lost.

The possibility of a year-end conference tie loomed. A tie could mess up their playoff position within the league and home court advantage.

While Sterlin was on the road, he and Lois Mae wore out their cell phones.

"I have other good news for you. I already have my test back, and I have a clean bill of health. Oh, I can't wait to feel you go inside me," Lois Mae said.

"Hmm, ah yeah, I got mine too. We good to go, baby!" Sterlin hummed into the phone, happy with the vision he was going to feel something he had not felt in years, his flesh sliding into her warm wetness. The thought had him reach and hold what he wanted to put inside her. He felt the blood filling and hardening. Then he thought about the other reason he had always used protection. "Lois Mae, I guess I'm assuming that you're on birth control."

Her breathing could have pushed the phone away from his ear. She said nothing. He waited a moment, wondering if he said something wrong. "Lois, Lois Mae," he said louder.

"I can't have children, Sterlin. I can't." Her voice sounded as if sand was passing through her throat.

"Talk to me."

"My first husband...he, ah...can we talk about this when you get back? I'll meet you at the airport. I don't want to talk about this over the phone."

"Hey, baby, we said we wouldn't hide anything from each other." Sterlin kept his tone even, but he was quickly losing his calm inside.

"Sterlin, please let me tell you what's going on when you come back. I have nothing to hide. I would have told you...in time, but this has been happening all so fast. I had no idea we would have this conversation when we are both in our forties."

"Okay, we haven't touched on the subject of children, yet."

"Ah, you want children?"

"Yes, if I ever found the right woman."

"I can't have children."

"Can't or won't?"

"Let me talk to you, when you get back, please."

The phone might as well have been cut off, with no sound or conversation for about a minute.

Sterlin hung up. He loved her the moment he awoke that morning after she had slept next to his bed while he was sick. He knew he was in love with her now, weeks later. He had wanted to tell her first, but now he thought, maybe she was hiding something.

When Love Comes Home

"Here." Lois Mae handed Sterlin something balled up in her hand. Her eyes flirted as she forced his hand into his pocket with the gift. "Don't let anybody see it." She was so happy to see him, but she was sleepy. His plane had arrived late, and she had fallen asleep waiting in the car in the airport-parking garage.

Ayman walked by. "I would stay and shoot the breeze with you two, but I have to meet someone at my house."

"All right, I'll see you at the gym first thing in the morning," Sterlin said. While waiting for his luggage, Sterlin put his hand in his pocket and realized what the gift was.

It was something silky and slightly damp. He knew they were panties. He cut his eyes over at her. Her presence, like every time in their short time together, she helped take emotionally guarded fences down. He missed her. He loved her. He would listen to what she had to say. He made a commitment, not only to her, but to himself. He would not run.

What was hidden in her closet? Not wanting a child, or unable to? He had told her all about his past life, and he thought she had too. What was her story? He decided he would give her the time to tell him what he needed to know.

Her panties in his coat pocket distracted him. He found the crotch area, and he rubbed his fingers in that spot, then raised his fingers to his nose. His head swam in her pheromones.

They made it to the car with just a few words spoken. She started the car and turned on the heat. Music finished the seduction. Their tongues raced past each other's lips, their heads changing positions every three seconds.

Romantic spoken word mixed with a jazz groove. Sterlin grabbed Lois Mae's hair, and pushed her head tighter to his face. His other hand squeezed her thigh. She led his hand under her dress and she parted her legs wide. His middle finger quickly found uncovered wet flesh, and slid into her wet tightness.

"Oh-oh, baby." Lois Mae's breathing was louder than her words.

"Why are we still here?" he asked.

"Well, if you're gonna kiss a woman like that..." She shook her head and put the car in reverse. "Damn!"

Forty minutes later, Stevie Wonder's greatest love songs were playing. They were in the hot tub, talking. She sat in his lap, telling her story.

"I just couldn't talk about this over the phone. I heard the frustration in your voice, and I felt bad." Sterlin rubbed her back slowly, and he could feel her rapid breathing. Her breasts rose intermittently, and appeared to swell while drops of sweat dripped off her nipples like teardrops. Her eyes were wet as she said, "This is hard on me, to tell you what's going on with me."

He kissed her shoulder and wiped her eyes, then kissed her cheek. "Okay, baby, just tell me." His voice lay soft and low under the rising stream.

"I was foolish. I knew better. I let my first husband come back into my bed one too many times. He mounted every female dog, dead or alive..." She squeezed her eyes tight as if wringing out her past. "He poisoned my body. I wanted children, but I can't have any. I had PID—pelvic inflammatory disease. From my ex giving me an STD, more than one kind," her voice whispered, "I went too long without knowing I was infected. So...I'm sterile." She gulped for air, and lifted her head to the nighttime sky as if a string was pulling her head up. Her lips moved, but no audible words left her mouth. She was talking to God.

Lord, please, he's the man you sent me, right? Please make him understand. Let him know I'm not dirty, and I would bear him children if I could. I'll make it up to him any way you would have me to. Please.

Sterlin let her have her quiet moment.

She turned her head and stared. Her words rushed out in one breath. "I have herpes along with the fact that I can't give you a child."

She felt Sterlin's body tense up. He took a hard swallow.

She took a big breath and slowed down. "In this world many women and men have it and still have healthy sex lives. There is a stigma of misunderstanding and lack of knowledge. People assume the worst, but I rarely have an outbreak. My body gives me a warning when there's a problem.

"Maybe I should have told you when you suggested that we get tested, but when do I tell you? The moment you kissed me, I just didn't know. I'm guilty of wanting to tell but not knowing when. Some men have turned away from me after I told them. Most men won't even talk to me." Her voice was too soft to hear everything she said, but he understood her emotions. She repeated, "Just when do I tell you?

"Sterlin, if you don't think this is something you want to deal with, I'll understand but I still want to be your friend, always." Her eyes focused on him, but she could not read his expression as she could most of the time. She turned her head away. She wanted to leave, and started to ease out of his lap. He stopped her.

"You're not going anywhere." He affectionately patted and squeezed her butt. With his other hand, his fingers turned her head back toward him, their eyes aligned and penetrated.

"I have two things I have to say to you. Well, three. First of all, I love you, I really do. I'm in love with Lois Mae." Her eyes burned from the sweat creeping in at the corners, but she forced them to stay open. "The next thing, I don't care about you having something that a lot of women deal with. You know your body, so if you talk to me about what's going on, we'll be fine.

"Your ex caused you to be in the state you're in, and I can't hold that against you. I would be lying if I said I'm not disappointed that you held back from telling me right away about all these important issues. On the other side of this, we just started, and the talk of children, wow! Maybe I shouldn't have brought it up. I know the way my life has been, the chances of meeting someone who I would want to have a child with were narrowing."

Sterlin slowly rocked his head from side to side. "It says a lot about you and the impact you have already made in my life already. I can be happy with just you and you alone." She spread her lips wide on his bald head, as if she was devouring or sucking in all of him.

He cupped some water, let it run over her breasts, and spoke close to her ear. "We're in our early forties, not the age when most people are planning on having children, but some people do."

"Well, yes, most people are almost finished raising their kids by their mid-forties."

His voice was hesitant but he had to ask, "Lois Mae, can we do that egg implant thing? You know, how they take my sperm and mix your eggs, then put them in you."

She spoke slowly, "Baby, my body cannot carry a child. I had a hysterectomy to stop heavy periods. I thought it was the thing to do after I found out I couldn't have a child." Her voice perked up, trying to change the mood by telling him, "One good thing for us, I stay horny. I hope that will keep you happy. I hope you can keep up."

He looked at her as if she had lost her mind and slapped her butt a little harder.

"Oh, daddy." She squirmed in his lap, and they kissed until she let him crawl out of the hot tub for something to drink.

He returned with cranberry juice. The stereo played Stevie Wonder's "Knock Me Off My Feet." Sterlin took her hand and led her out of the hot tub. He put his arms around her naked body and he pressed himself tight to her full breasts. He led her in a slow dance, the two brown bodies blending with the black sky while city lights sparkled around them.

Steam swirled around and between the lovers. They danced slowly, slower than the music. He spun her around and started to grind on the spread of her rear. She felt his hardness and pushed back as if he were inside her, riding her.

Her body was everything he wanted in a physical feminine body. Her sexy, full figure with its curves and height fit his large frame. He reached between her thighs and found her wet, not hot-tub wet, but an aroused female slippery wet. She spread her legs and rotated her hips, inviting his finger inside. Her swollen lips were open wide, and his finger slid deep inside her tightness. She bellowed air and groaned.

"I want to feel you inside, baby. Baby, give it to me," she pleaded. "Give it to me," she demanded. She reached back through her legs trying to find him, to lead him into her hot flesh.

He had her weak and spoke knowing he was in control.

"Yeah, okay, if you think you can handle this." His voice was strong and confident, knowing his manhood was about to spread her and touch her deep. He put his hands on her waist and spread his legs, angling his body, finding her heated wet opening.

"Oooh, slow, baby."

He grinned while looking at the back of her head. He reached for her hair and pulled lightly with a firm grip.

She felt the head of his manhood making a path inside her heat. Her body tensed, and she said, "Baby, it's been awhile. Just hold it right there for a second."

"Okay, but you feel good. You got the good stuff."

"Do it feel good, baby?"

"I want to hump all over this ass." He let the head of his manhood go in and out, right at her opening, but going in a little deeper each time, while her body started to relax. Lois Mae started to work her hips, putting rhythm into riding Sterlin's hardness while he held her hair. He slapped her rear.

"Aaah, that's right, daddy; spank that ass."

"Boogie On Reggae Woman" jammed through the speakers. "Fuck this!" Sterlin said. He pulled her out of her wet heat, and climbed out of the hot tub pulling her along as if he was a caveman and she was Bertha Butt, the cavewoman. They made it to his bed and she climbed up on all fours. Her ass spread and became bigger and rounder. He admired the view as she did a rump-shaking motion. He placed his lips on her ass and kissed her all over and finally let his lips and tongue dance from the small of her back and down through the crease of her ass. She trembled in pleasure. He made it all the way under her to her clit with one long dragging of his tongue. He turned onto his back and she sat on his face. Now her whole body shuddered, and her toes clamped. His tongue and finger did a duet, making her crazy.

He had her juices all over his nose as he sniffed her scent. Sterlin could feel his manhood stiffening harder than a coil spring, and she was coming and let it be heard. After resting for a short moment, he pulled from under her and stood. Standing at the edge of his bed, she backed her ass up as he angled his body to slide back inside her hot, tight wetness. He pumped and humped, riding her stand-up doggie-style. With the tip of her two fingers, Lois Mae polished her own clit, circling fast, keeping up with Sterlin's driving pace. He was ramming her like he wanted to drill her through the bed. She felt pleasure and sweet pain.

She screamed out in erotic breathing, "Ah, ah…ah…ah…ah… give it to me. Come on, baby, ah…ah…ah…ride me, baby."

With his hands on her waist, he pushed her down, driving her breasts into the bed. He let his manhood come all the way out of her, then all the way back inside and kept humping, but harder.

She cursed and turned her head into the pillow to drown out her orgasmic screams. He slowed just a little. Her toes curled with another orgasm, her foot cramped, and her left leg was shaking. She reached back and grabbed her leg, trying to stop it from shaking. Sterlin kept humping, but slowly.

He was grunting and breathing like he was sprinting from wild dogs. Hot wet friction from Lois Mae's pubic hair, her skin and her juices had him about to cum.

No longer steam from the hot tub but sweat from his face dripped on her back. He was about to cum, and he commanded her, "Don't move. Ugh, ugh, ugh…yeah." He held still, holding his upper body up as his hips pressed tight to her rear. She felt him fill her with a warm liquid explosion.

Their bodies relaxed with Sterlin still inside Lois Mae. They turned on their sides and curled into each other. Sleep and dreams bonded their bodies, and love was finally home.

41

The Folks Sitting in the Pews

Suzy Q met Ayman at his front door. He was tired and wanted to schedule the meet for the morning, but Suzy Q had information to give to him on her time.

"I'm sorry, but you push harder than some of my players wanting playing time. With our flight delayed by almost two hours, and for the fact that we didn't play well, and I had to go by the gym first, I wasn't eager to see anyone right away."

She ignored Ayman and walked past him as he carted in his bags.

"Nice place, Coach. Got a beer?"

"I have some dark beer on tap in a mini keg, plenty cold. Come on in the kitchen."

"This here's a kitchen, eh!"

"The ex, she remodeled it." They sat at the center island. "We need to keep our voices down. I have a young man from the team who stays with me. He's asleep I assume, but—"

"I understand. Okay, this is what I know. Let me start by saying, you Americans are a strange bunch when it comes to yer churches."

"Huh?" Ayman watched Suzy Q take a big swallow of beer from a mug he had poured for her. He smiled thinking he couldn't chug his beer down like that, even on a 100-degree day.

"I was able to find out a lot about yer female friend, Vanita, through one of her fellow church members. It seems gossip is a staple for yer church people, eh. I mean no offense, mate, but blather and scandal in yer Black church seems to happen as much as yer prayers." She laughed.

Ayman chuckled. "No offense taken when you tell the truth, and that one there is the truth."

"Anyway…" She took a big gulp of beer to finish the mug, and Ayman poured her another from the tap. "I think you may be clear of any more problems from yer ex-girlfriend. There is a history of Vanita going on and off her meds. Each time another man falls into her web of confusion. A few men have taken advantage of her confused soul, though. And I have to admit, she is a looker."

"Yeah, she is beautiful, and it's sad. I thought I was headed toward a great love."

"Airball," Suzy said and caught Ayman's attention.

"What do you mean?"

"When you shoot over or under, airball, eh?" Suzy Q's Canadian slang amused Ayman.

"Yeah, I shot over the hoop with her."

"She's back on her meds, according to my information. They also had a deaconess hold some kind of prayer service for her."

"Just like the Black church to pray and send in someone with no expertise." Ayman shook his head and smirked.

"What do you mean?"

"The Black church has a long history of not helping its people in real need of help. Even in a small Black population in this region, the churches are full of women and some men who need more than prayer. In Vanita's case, she needs professional counseling, yet a deaconess holds her hand and tells her it will be all right. Just leave it to a higher power." Ayman's head shook in disgust.

"Are you not a God-fearing, church-going kind of guy?"

"Yes I am. I owe everything to God. I have not done anything good without God, but what I mean is this. Most preachers lack expertise in any field of knowledge other than the pulpit of saving spiritual souls. That doesn't help people in need of mental help, drug addictions, or lack of financial understanding. Those three things plague the people who sit in the pews. Preachers, all they do is focus on building bigger buildings and filling the seats. The people sitting in the seats receive prayer, which is the spiritual help they need but little else is offered to help change their lives.

"If Sister So-and-So needs bunions removed from her feet, she'll ask the preacher and the church to pray for her. They will pray that the good doctor will have the smarts to do his job. The good preacher needs to lead his people to mental counseling and professional therapy when it's needed. The people need help to find financial assistance besides check cashing centers and payday-loan offices, the legal loansharking business. The church needs to help find pros in the areas of need for its people.

"If these preachers want more money in the collection plate, help teach their flock how to avoid money woes. It's a church's responsibility to educate the people sitting in the pews. Selling fried chicken dinners and peach cobblers is the equivalent of mom-and-pop grocery store management. Those skills can't run a major department store. That backcountry, sharecropping, just-get-by attitude…" Ayman almost snorted when he laughed at his assessment.

He kept his sermon going, and Suzy Q listened. "If I have a drug addiction, what good can an eighty-year-old deacon with no expertise do? He can pray for me, and yes, I need prayer, but I also need the help that God put here on this Earth.

"You'll hardly ever see an AA or NA meeting in the basement of a Black church. Them church folks think one of them AA or NA people might steal the canned chicken from the church pantry. The truth is, there is very little social network help available in

Black churches. Preachers will ask for the last dime to go in the offering plate from a single parent. When the single parent can't keep the lights on, that single parent will go ask the church to pray for them.

"As a coach, I have had players with drinking or drug problems. I pray right and pray often, hoping I can help find the right help for the individual. Then I go seek the professional that can help. It only makes sense.

"Some of my players' families have financial problems. The rule for me as a college coach is, I can't offer any financial help. There is no rule that says I can't guide the family to financial experts to help set up budgets and job counseling, and I have done this numerous times. These same kids I've recruited, their churches had done nothing. Oh, they prayed for the kid not to get hurt and make it to the NBA."

"Wow, Coach, I didn't know much about your Black church. Are there any good ones?"

"I'm on my soapbox being judgmental which can be just as bad as the people I'm talking about, but I'm a doer; at least that's more than can be said about some of these churches. Yes, there are, and I don't mean to throw all Black churches under the bus for their problems, and, I'm sure white and purple churches have some of the same problems.

"With such overwhelming problems, preachers need to use all the tools God gave them to lead their churches." Ayman's shoulders dropped. He was done with his sermon.

Suzy Q changed the subject. "Well, as far as Vanita is concerned, I think you can stand back and let it go. I will keep you updated."

"Suzy, did some Black woman from Vanita's church just open up to you and tell her business?"

"Well, the truth is, I have a woman friend...ah, she...ah, well, she used to visit me in Vancouver. We dated some years back. She's Black."

"Hey, Suzy, I'm not tripping over what you do or whom you do. I have a female on my staff who leads an alternative lifestyle. As far as I'm concerned, she's a person who can help me at what I need to do, and that's all that matters."

Suzy smiled. "I know, Coach, who's on your staff. She's pretty. Anyway, this woman I used to date, she's involved in yer city government, and is a church socialite. I asked her if she knew anyone at the church Vanita attended. My friend knew the gay choir leader who gossips like a pigeon pecks."

"Gay choir leader?"

"Yep. He's not what yer people call on the low-down or down-low. He is flaming, hellish, red-hot poker gay. I don't know about all the other stuff you spoke about in the Black church, but this I do know: you have a lot of church folks living in the closet, and some out of the closet. Besides finding out about yer lady friend, I found out other stuff. I might have to join a Black church. I for sure should tell all my gay guy friends about what's going on up in them church hymns and pews." Suzy Q laughed.

Ayman shook his head. *That was the last thing a Black church would admit to.*

"So anyway, you think I'm in the clear?"

Suzy nodded. "I will stay on top of this and keep you updated." They headed to the doorway. "I take it you don't know your ex comes to town and visits with friends."

"No, nobody has said anything. Which friends?"

"Remember, I find out things, and you're a smart man. You shouldn't ask questions when you have the answers."

She opened the door and flashed the peace sign without looking back.

42
Rolling Through The Rushes

Even though Sterlin had the longer night, he was in the coach's office before Ayman the next day when the head coach walked in with coffee and bagels.

"I got some grub. You want some?"

Sterlin smiled and bopped his head to some Johnny Guitar Watson music. "Nah, man, but are you busy tonight? Come on by my place around seven for dinner."

Their desks faced each other. Ayman stood at his desk looking down at his friend. "What, you cooking?" Ayman raised his eyebrows.

Sterlin shook his head. "Come on, man, don't make this hard on me. All the years I ate at your place with you, well, my woman—"

"Wow, listen to you, *my woman*." Ayman laughed.

"Okay, okay, don't give me a hard time. You're the one who said I needed a woman I could be proud of."

He was happy to see his best friend with one woman, but sad for himself. In a perfect world best friends would have the loves of their lives at the same time.

He had two separate visions. In one vision, he saw he and Vanessa, his ex-wife, walking through Sterlin's door. In the other vision, he saw Vanita and Joshua walking through Sterlin's door with him.

"Are you coming or not?"

Ayman laughed. "Oh, boy, check you out."

"You don't think I'm committed to this, do you?" His voice was not agitated, but monotone.

"You're wrong, but the only thing that's relevant is what you think and how you feel. I'll be over for dinner. Okay, all right?" Ayman threw a small, palm-sized foam basketball, missing Sterlin's head on purpose. "And don't be getting an attitude with me over a woman."

"Whatever, just be on time for dinner."

Ayman smirked, then laughed out loud. "Well, I know she can cook with all that butter churning on her backside."

"Oh, man, what's up with looking at my woman's butt?" Sterlin was laughing too.

"Payback!" Ayman stared at his friend and dared him to respond. Sterlin had no comeback and just shook his head, smiling. He tossed over some game stats, which Ayman scanned. "Can you go watch a game over at Franklin High School? We need those twins over there to know we're already watching them as sophomores. I'm going to watch a kid at Rainier Beach High."

"I got it covered. Hey, have you heard from Tylowe's friend, Suzy?"

"Yep, I have. She's good. She belongs on her own TV show, *The Canadian Girlfriend, P.I.* She found out my situation with Vanita seems to be cool now."

"I wonder when I'm going to hear from her. After giving her all my life's history, wow, I need to know what's up. I even gave her information on Lois Mae. She had me e-mail her names of all the women I could remember dealing with for the last two years."

Ayman laughed. "Yeah, well, I bet that e-mail about crashed your hard drive and took forever to download."

"Forget you, man." Sterlin threw the foam basketball back at Ayman and he caught it.

"You need to know if your ass is safe, and your new woman don't have to deal with one of your crazy-ass freaks from the past," Ayman said.

"You're right; I can't get over how sick some folks can be. The red paint crap. Lois Mae thinks it may be a guy she drop-kicked in the middle of a date. You know, I'd like to mess him up."

"Well, whatever-whoever, let Suzy Q do her thing. That's what she's for, to keep us clear of the bullshit." Ayman stared hard, seeking response from Sterlin.

"I'm good, I'll wait, but I still wanna F somebody up." Sterlin pulled out his cell phone. "Hey, baby-gurl, he's coming. Okaaaay, I'll ask." Sterlin's eyes slowly scanned Ayman's face, and he rolled his tongue around his mouth.

"What?" Ayman saw a question hanging on the tip of Sterlin's tongue.

"Ah, she has...ah, lady friends she could ask to come over for dinner that you might wanna meet."

Ayman rolled his eyes. "Oh hell no! And I mean no!"

Lois Mae was laughing because she heard Ayman.

"I guess you heard. I'll call you later." He hung up.

Sterlin was going to make a smart-ass remark, but Ayman's glare said don't go there.

Lois Mae leaned her head on Sterlin's shoulder and rubbed his chest. The following morning, they were relaxing with the early morning dew, sitting on a park bench overlooking Alki Beach.

They had slept all over each other throughout the night as if they were one person. Sleeping next to each other was just as sweet without sex. With the cold air and waves rolling in, they cuddled under a blanket watching the dark sky separate from the dawning light of day. Lois Mae's dog sat at their feet.

"Do you think he enjoyed my cooking?"

"Yeah, baby, he left stuffed. Those shrimp enchiladas with mole sauce and the seafood caldo de pollo soup was off the hook. I didn't know you had it like that. What are you trying to do to a brotha?"

"I'm trying to do what a woman should do for a man. The man you are, who did wake me up this morning and not tell me where he was taking me. I want to do for the kind of man who has me sitting here before the sun comes up." Lois Mae reached up and kissed Sterlin's cheek.

"Do you know you and Ayman ate a whole lemon meringue pie? Plus, you ate the last of the enchiladas. Dang, honey, where does it all go?"

Sterlin moved her hand down to his thigh and edged her close to his crotch.

She slapped his thigh. "You don't need anything else going down there. If that thing gets any bigger, I'm gonna have some of it cut off." She put her hand in front of his face and moved her fingers like scissors. "Snip, snip."

"Well, let me get up and go run with the dog before you do something you'll regret."

"Ah baby, it won't hurt if I take a little off, will it?"

"No more coffee for you. It's making you delirious." Sterlin handed over his keys, wallet, and cell phone. He and Selena walked down to the sand and started to jog along the edge of the water.

The powerful brown and black dog and her chocolate man were fine art in Lois Mae's eyes. With the Puget Sound waters in the background and the ferry in the distance, Sterlin's movements mesmerized her. She was finding Sterlin to be a masterpiece of a man. His physical size was minor compared to his softness. She could see how he could be hurt in such a way he would hide within himself. Yet he was as manly as any man could be.

His cell phone vibrated in her hand and startled her from her daze. Instinctively, she thought to answer, but caught herself. A moment later it vibrated, showing he had a message. *Who's calling my man this early in the morning?* She laughed but did wonder. For a moment, she wanted to look at the names in his phone. She told herself, *I'm not a young, immature, insecure woman. She threw her head back and smiled. If he's going to do me wrong, there is nothing I can do to stop him.* She hoped for the best.

Sterlin and Selena returned. She handed him his phone and other possessions, and she did not mention that his phone had a message. She was proud of herself. Ten years ago, she would have questioned him. Sterlin trusted her to let her come into his life; she would do the same for him.

He sat down, and she stood up with the blanket and sat back down in his lap. She looked around. It might have been too early or too cold for others to be around yet. She draped the blanket wide to cover both of them. It looks as if they were trying to just stay warm. She knew all the condos and apartment windows behind her could expose anyone's imagination to what she was about to do. She reached for his hand and guided him to reach into her sweatpants. She spread her legs. Sterlin reached her wet daybreak; his middle finger massaged her clit. Her mouth opened wide breathing in the ocean air. Her deep sigh met the sound of waves rolling through the rushes.

43

What Happens in the Dark

Vanita read everything in print about the East Seattle City Sharks. Every quote by Coach Ayman Sparks read twice. She could hear his voice, sometimes in her dreams. She missed the man. He was mellow, calm, and under control. He was a sweet lover in and out of the bed. He loved and cared for her son, and Joshua missed Ayman.

It was not her bipolar mind that controlled her thoughts about him now. She was back on her meds and back in counseling, committed to staying mentally healthy again. The part of her soul that could love, and did love, loved Ayman Sparks. She missed him. Vanita felt a hurt that pills could not fix.

Her Sunday morning ritual before going to church consisted of reading her Bible. Her Bible sat unopened. The Sunday sports section had won out. Morning sun filtered between early apple blossoms in her backyard, and another sign of new things to come, a missed period. Vanita felt her insides stirring with strange cravings. She yearned for oysters, peanut butter, and butter pecan ice cream, just like nine years earlier when Joshua was conceived. A test strip she peed on said a new life was in her.

Outside of her control now, there was a man she had chased away with her evil twin, AKA manic depression. Ayman Sparks was gone, but she had a part of him. What to do? She took her birth control pills...pretty regularly.

She made her way over to the gas fireplace and pushed the button for some extra morning warmth. Tea in hand, she sat on the couch and propped her feet up. Her cozy robe and the fire warmed her body, and she reminisced of late nights with Ayman on the couch.

She dreamed of how it was when Ayman came over one night. Instead of staying home, he had brought over the laptop he used to prepare his basketball operations. She leaned on him and read a book while he did his prepping for the next game. She loved being next to him even though his mind was busy.

Now she was alone, reliving a moment. She often broke his concentration by caressing his cheek or any other part of his body. They usually went up to her bed after making out on the couch like teenagers.

One night, while wearing a long sheer nightgown, she danced in front of the fireplace, absorbing all his attention. She stared at him as the firelight was dancing with her and on her body. Her dance became a lapdance.

As she lay there on her couch this Sunday morning, she was remembering the hot, steamy moments she had shared with Ayman. His touch from the past crept into her cerebral stream. She felt a tingling and a wetness creeping between her thighs. She squeezed her thighs tight.

Her thoughts engulfed her with scintillating visions of the time she had spent with Ayman that were passionate and scorching; can't-get-enough-of-his-touch memories. Her mind went into fantasies of the lovemaking were right there on her couch where she lay now, wanting. She closed her eyes and felt him in a hallucination, an illusion feeling him methodically moving inside her with a sexy, slow rhythm. He was deep in her, filling her carnal appetite.

Vanita untied her robe and let one leg fall to the side, reaching in to touch her wetness. Her thighs shuddered, imagining his tongue circling her clit, but it was her fingers reaching, sliding, and guiding her to fulfill her desires.

She remembered he had made her feel a powerful orgasm from his hands squeezing her breasts, while licking her clit. After he made her cum, he stood above her while she watched and felt his hardness drip a long, slow, clear stream of life onto her nipple. The slippery jiz went sliding onto the dark spot of her breast. Her finger massaged her nipple into hard firmness.

She kept her eyes closed tight, visualizing his manhood pointing up as she reached to cup his balls, but as she lay there alone now, she cupped her hand over her pussy and flicked her middle finger in and out of her wetness. It drove her to grind her hips into the couch cushions. Her juices were running and making a wet spot on her robe under her. Vanita was so wet it was seeping through her robe and dampening the couch.

That night on her couch with Ayman had left a wet spot. After he had stroked himself while standing over her, he slowly lay between her legs and almost in one motion, he entered her. The couch was narrow. She had put one leg over the back of the couch, as it was right now. Her foot trembled against the wall; it was making a light knocking sound.

He grabbed the end of the couch, holding tight, helping him to push deep into her lushness. He rubbed his thick moist lips and hot tongue wildly behind her ears and over her collarbone. Humping and driving his pelvis, the plump pillows on the couch sank with no resistance. He reached under her and squeezed her behind, helping her meet his thrusts. Vanita's toes curled now in her daydream, she could have pulled paint off the wall with her toes while she masturbated. Ayman long-stroked her tightness that night. She pushed her hips up to meet him, and their hips hammered each other.

Finally, he forcefully flipped her over. She loved for him to manhandle her, controlling her. She raised her rear up. He put his hands tightly on her waist, holding her in place. Firmly humping, his grunts were animal-like.

"Harder, harder," she implored him, consumed with adrenaline then and now. Alone with her lusting desires, she made her fingers work hard circling her clit. Her face was tight anticipating the oncoming orgasm. She relived Ayman pulsating inside her when he released his warm life inside her. She knew his final grunt. She missed it now as her own orgasm arrived, her legs clamped together, and her fingers came to a sudden stop. Sounds deep within her sounded like she was taking hard, short, fast inhales of breath.

She opened her eyes and came back to reality. Her mouth was dry. She wondered if she'd woken her son. Trees in the window moved like strangers passing by. It was lighter outside now.

She closed her eyes to go back into the dark. She felt a cramp in her stomach. Was it just her imagination? The pain in her soul made her cry aloud. The thought of Ayman's fluids erupting in her and the warm feeling of his cum shooting in and then seeping back out, made her wail now; she slapped each side of her head in anger. Why hadn't she taken her birth control pills regularly, instead of every once in awhile and then swallowing two or three, playing catch-up? He had asked her several times about birth control and he was willing to use condoms, but she had reassured him they were okay because she was on birth control.

Every day and eight or less months from now, she would know the pain and the pleasure. Vanita's eyes flickered with tears and darkness. She knew what happened in the dark always came to light. She closed her eyes again and after the pain subsided, she fell into a light sleep and relived last Saturday.

She was sitting in the Golden Spoon almost incognito, looking over at Ayman. He didn't see her in a corner booth as she kept her big hat titled downward. She watched his fork go toward his mouth. His tongue met the golden hot slice of pancake. Her mind went there, to when his tongue used to meet her golden hotness. She squirmed in her seat, just like she used to when she felt his touch all over her body. She turned her head and watched cars going up and down Rainier Avenue. She needed distraction. She stirred her grits...again. She looked in his direction for the tenth time or more because she couldn't help herself. This time her eyes froze in place. Like the ice in her glass, her soul cracked. Her ears no longer heard the O'Jays singing "You Got Your Hooks in Me" over the restaurant sound system, and all the conversation going on disappeared into silence. A woman had taken a seat across from him. Vanita picked up her steak knife...then she realized it was one of Ayman's best friends she had seen twice and met once, her name was Sonya. She was with him that night they'd first met, and later she brought by some paperwork for Ayman while she was at his house. Her crazy feeling deflated knowing Sonya wasn't his type, and she was his just his friend. Vanita looked away and saw the knife in her hand; it was held in the stabbing position.

Now a week later after church, Vanita suggested to Alicia they should go to brunch at the Golden Spoon. Inside, Ayman Sparks was sitting in the back with some of his players. She spotted him, as did Alicia. His back was to them, and, Alicia steered Vanita quickly into a booth and facing away from him.

"Did you know he comes here? Is this the reason we damn near drove across town to the Rainier Valley, when we could have eaten in Renton?" Alicia asked with spitting fire shooting out of her eyes.

Vanita stared out of the window.

"Well, whatever you do, don't you say a word to him. You know he doesn't want to talk to you." Alicia's anger tightened her eyes, and she glared at Vanita.

"I know, and I won't say a word. I just had to—"

"No, you don't need to see him! Let him go! Even pictures of him, throw them away. You will have to learn to love him from a distance. No more contact. It's over! There will come a time the right man will be there, and you'll be right for that time, but not right now."

Vanita reached across the table and spoke as if she were out of breath. "I will never find a man to love me like Ayman could have. If only I had stayed on my meds and told him."

"There will be a man who will accept you as you are. If only you tell him up front what you're dealing with. Ayman might have been the one, but it's been ruined, so let him go!"

"I will always have a part of him, no matter what." Vanita's voice drifted to her lap.

"You're being a bit melodramatic." Alicia shook her head and stared back toward Ayman. and then back to Vanita and shook her head no at Vanita.

Vanita ordered warm apple juice. She had no appetite. Her stomach was uneasy. She was queasy with a part of Ayman growing inside.

45
It's Raining Hard

It was early morning, and Sterlin's back was curled into Lois Mae's body. She was holding him, as much as she could hold onto his six-four body. The phone rang, not his cell phone. The dog sleeping next to the bed arose, stretched, and shook.

"Hello. Hey, Suzy Q," Sterlin said. "Yeah, I was sleep, but I've been waiting for you to call. Ah, yeah, come on by. Yes, she's with me. It's okay."

He turned to Lois Mae. "Hey, babe, the woman who's checking into who has been harassing us?"

"Should I be here, or do you want to talk to her in private?"

"I want you here. We don't know who's been trippin', so you might need to hear what she has to say."

"Okay. Damn baby, you hear that rain? It's pouring hard."

"I know, but it ain't like that Texas rain where everything floods, and those freaking snakes come out of the ground."

"Yuck, I don't miss that. I'll take our Seattle rain anytime. I'll cook breakfast." Lois Mae had pancakes on the table forty minutes later, and Sterlin was killing a tall stack when the doorbell rang.

Suzy Q eyed both Sterlin and Lois Mae as she sat across from them. *This is not going to be easy.* She played hard but Suzy Q wasn't in the inside. "I don't know who did the red paint thing yet, but I am pursuing some leads."

"What things do you know?" Sterlin asked.

Suzy Q hesitated before she said, "Roberta, eh?"

"Roberta Who?"

Suzy Q looked at Lois Mae and said, "You know a Roberta Martin, don't you? She also goes by Bobbie...Bobbie Martin."

Before Lois Mae could answer, Sterlin repeated, "Bobbie Martin?" Hearing the name of Bobbie Martin, Sterlin thought of the redhead psycho who had knocked over his motorcycle. Bobbie Martin was on the long list of women he gave Suzy Q who had come and gone in his life.

"You think she's the one who's been doing the red paint crazy-ass shit?" Before Suzy Q could answer, Lois Mae spoke, gradually letting each word take its time coming out. "I know a Roberta, and I think her last name is Martin. She's a friend of a friend."

Suzy asked Lois Mae, "Is yer friend's name Velvet Williams?"

"Yes."

"Are we talking about the same person?" Sterlin asked.

Suzy nodded and then said, "Yep, Roberta and Bobbie are the same person."

Sterlin looked at Lois Mae and said, "It's the woman I told you about who knocked over my motorcycle and tried to run me over right before Christmas." He looked back at Suzy. "So, she's the one who's been messing with us, not the guy Lois Mae went out with? Maybe she's the one calling my cell phone and hanging up."

"No, I don't think she's the one, but she might be calling your phone. I'll have to look into that."

Sterlin was huffing and puffing, and could blow a house down.

Lois Mae leaned back on the couch and thought she knew what

was coming. Her worst nightmare was seeping into her reality just like straight shots of 100-proof corn liquor. She felt drunk. She thought back to the day Skillet had brought Roberta over, and who was also pregnant. She examined Suzy Q's face.

Suzy Q may have been a woman who dated only women, but that didn't change her understanding of what a straight woman would feel or understand. The two women read each other's female awareness of *knowing*. Suzy Q nodded her head. The man sitting in the room was clueless.

Lois Mae said to Sterlin, "I know you told me a lot about your past. Yeah, you did tell me about Roberta or Bobbie, or whatever she goes by, but you left something out."

"What?" He sounded accused and defensive.

Before Lois Mae said anymore, Suzy Q interrupted her. "He's totally blind about how. He don't know, honey."

"Know what? And I only know her by the name of Bobbie."

"She's pregnant with your child," Suzy Q said, point blank.

Sterlin's face looked like she had to be talking to someone else besides him.

"And you know this how?" He tried to look out of the corner of his eye at his lover's face. She was behind him, and his huge shoulder blocked what he so desperately needed to see.

"I always used protection. Why didn't she say anything? It has to be somebody else's." He stood and looked down and saw Lois Mae's face. She looked lost. He sat and calmed down to listen.

Suzy Q went into the uncomfortable details. "When you let me know you and Bobbie had a casual relationship, and you had problems with her, I investigated her. I was able to befriend her ex-roommate who is bisexual. You did know that her ex-roommate was bi, eh?" Sterlin nodded, hoping that detail would not have to be discussed. "I was able to find out Bobbie Martin has a bun in the oven and is about to give birth. She really wanted you to herself, so much so that she did something to your condoms. She poked holes, or after you two had sex, she may have transferred yer fluids and put them where you didn't want them to go. Well, she told her ex-roommate she did something for you to get her pregnant."

Sterlin sounded as if he had indigestion. Lois Mae's eyes squeezed tight, so tight they hurt. She raised her arm up as if she was in church about to testify. She felt dizzy, got up, and left the room quickly. Sterlin stood to go after her. Suzy Q stopped him.

"Eh, hey, mate, let her have some time alone. Whatever happens is going to happen to you two. I have other news for her."

"What, there's more?" He sat down and let his head fall back. He noticed dust on the ceiling fan and remembered how cool it was that Bobbie kept his house spotless. The current paid house-cleaning service fell short. He chuckled at how ironic life could be. He wanted his mind to be anywhere but where it was.

"Yes, there's more. But we'll let her come back before I tell her something about her friend Velvet."

"Skillet?"

"Is that what Lois Mae calls her?"

"Yeah, or she used to. So, she knows Bobbie. I thought I knew her from somewhere when I met her."

Suzy Q shook her head and said, "Small world we live in. You just never know."

"How did this happen to me, now in my life? To have a child with someone I would never want to have a child with is horrible."

"Eh, not to be judgmental, but you have been partying hard for a long time, mate. Throw the dice and..."

Sterlin felt as if he had motion sickness.

Lois Mae returned and sat down. She held a glass of water with both hands, squeezing the glass so tight it was on the edge of shattering. Her head was up but her eyes seemed to focus on the tip of her nose. After a deep breath, she said, "What is before me, prodigious birth?"

"My only love sprung from my only hate!
Too early seen unknown, and known too late!
Prodigious birth of love it is to me
That I must love a loathèd enemy"

The three sat silent, Lois Mae accepting her plight for loving a man, accepting what was before her, and accepting what tomorrow would bring for accepting it all.

Sterlin sat humbled by life, accepting his sins and acknowledging whatever he must do next.

Suzy Q said, "You quote Shakespeare, Juliet accepting her fate. I say you are an honorable woman."

Lois Mae moved into within an inch of Sterlin's face. "I am hurt, as I should be, but you did not sit in judgment of me for my inability to give you a child. I know you love me, I will love you through whatever all this may bring." She laid her head on his shoulder with her face turned away.

"I need you two to focus on a few other things right now," Suzy Q said. "You need to make decisions about the extent of the involvement you want in this child's life. Roberta is putting the child up for adoption."

Lois Mae gasped, put her hand over her mouth, and said, "I remember, she is...that's what she's doing. Do you want your child?"

Sterlin slowly but assuredly nodded his head.

She smiled a tight-lipped smile and said, "Right answer." Her facial expression went back to one of hurt feelings. "Whether you and I are together, I want to be there for you. Another woman may not stand for this, but you made a mistake before you knew me."

Suzy interjected, "Well, you'll need to get into legal mode rather quickly in order to stop the ball from rolling, eh. I understand you do have rights. If she is giving up the child, the father has rights."

"I know the law professor at the school," Lois Mae said. "He handled my legal affair when my second husband was murdered. I'll call him, and get you going on the right path."

"Yer second husband was murdered, eh?"

"Yes, my second husband was killed in a robbery."

All Sterlin could do was stare at the woman he loved. Now he was causing her another major pain in her life. For a moment, when she left the room, he thought she was leaving him. To call her a good woman was an insult to how great a woman she was being to him. He wrapped his mind around that feeling, staring at her and sitting speechless.

Suzy Q had one more piece of news. "Velvet or Skillet, your friend, who you know is pregnant, might be pregnant by your ex-husband, Vance."

"What?" Lois Mae shouted. "Tell me she is not seeing him after all that has happened."

"I don't think she is still seeing him, but...I don't want to give away my investigative techniques, but I had to check out the people closest to all of you. People shouldn't use public computers. The servers can be hacked pretty easily. Yer friend communicates with her pregnancy counselor on her work computer. She isn't sure if it's some African guy or Vance, the guy I know as your first husband. He may have raped her."

"Damn, is there nothing you don't know or find out?" Sterlin was amazed.

"The more I know, eh, the safer you'll be. This is what I do. That is why Tylowe hired me."

Lois Mae's face had lost the pained expression, and anger reddened her brown skin. Hearing about Skillet made her skin itch. She and Sterlin sat deflated, empty, and needing. Suzy Q talked about a few things more and said she was sorry about the information she'd brought them.

"I'm still hot on the trail of the red paint, and I'll update you when I know more."

After she left and Sterlin closed the door, Lois Mae said, "Can we go and sit in the hot tub, and pray or meditate, or just sit still and be quiet? I know it's raining, but I want to feel as though some of what is happening will wash away, even if it just washes away for the moment. Then we have a lot to talk about."

After practice, Sterlin sat down with Ayman and told him what had transpired.

"This is not going to be easy," Ayman said. "I can't be sad for you, because you have to be positive in your approach to how your future is changing, fast. Uhm, I'm going to be an uncle, huh?"

"Yeah, you are. I don't know what all this means as far as time is concerned, but—"

"I'll be fine," Ayman said to assure Sterlin. "Take all the time that is warranted. This is the kind of experience in life when you wish you were a year ahead in time. Preparing with so little time, knowing what's coming, you'll need complete focus. You see, you're not having a child by a woman you will ever be with, so frustrations and anger could be around the corner with each step you take. Question, can your child's mother stop you from taking custody?"

Sterlin put his feet up on the desk. "The adoption thing is a tangle of legalities. Lois Mae made a call on my behalf and got some basic info."

"Are you wanting to be a single parent? Before you answer that, remember, this is going to be a newborn."

"I need to step in and step up."

"Right answer!"

Sterlin's eyes widened. "I'm not going to have a child out there in this world and act as if I don't care."

"If you don't step up, I'll fire you." Ayman meant what he said with a smile. "You know the kid, Shawl King, that we had here the first year, the second boy I recruited."

"Yeah, he was going to be good, except he was better at making babies."

"Yep, he was good with every young girl around town too. I had three women come to me pregnant in just one year. They came complaining because he told them he would take care of them when he signed with the NBA."

"NBA." Sterlin laughed. "He wasn't that good."

"You know I had to boot him, since he wouldn't do the right thing."

"You don't have to tell me to do the right thing, but as an uncle you're on the short list of babysitters." They both chuckled a bit.

A few kids were still in the locker room hanging out. Ayman closed the office door. He started writing game information on the white board while starting in on another conversation with his back turned to Sterlin.

"On the serious side, you know I tell these boys they need to consider who they have a child by. No matter what, a child is half of someone else's DNA, from what the child will look like: skinny, big-boned, emotions, and brains.

"You know even if the other side is disconnected from your child, the soul of the other half runs in the veins. I was raised by neither my mom or dad, but I know they are inside me, for good or bad."

Sterlin clicked on e-mails and typed as he spoke, "I hear what you're saying. I've been told by Dad I'm just like Mom in many ways. Depending when he said it, I hated hearing that. I know there were times my dad and I didn't get along because he saw my mom in me. Now I'm having a child with a woman I cared nothing for, and for that, it's my bad."

A player knocked on the door, and Ayman opened the door to listen to something the kid had to say; he addressed the kid issue and then dismissed him. Ayman closed the door and resumed their conversation. "Not to focus on the negative, but be aware, on her side of the family, there could be addictions or mental illnesses, health concerns. You saw what I went through with a woman's deep, manic, emotional problems.

"There is something else to think about. Hear me out on this now. Your child is half-Black, but in this world, he'll be all Black." Sterlin closed his laptop down and focused on Ayman, staring him in the face.

Ayman took a big breath. "Take a look around us. Seattle and its fake sense of liberalism will slapped us back into the reality of redneck-ism. You know the line, 'I don't see color; I just see people.' The ultimate insult too…" Ayman stopped speaking for a moment. He blew out a long breath before more of his personal feelings spewed. "Yeah, we are equal all right, just as long as we don't act too 'Black'! In other words, don't call 'em on their bullshit."

Sterlin slowly nodded, listening to what his friend had to say.

"You and I are accepted because we win, but even then we are held to a higher standard. Bottom line, I hope you raise your child to know they are not some kind of rainbow child." Ayman sat down and waited for a response.

Sterlin reached into the bottom drawer. He pulled out something that he and Ayman would do only if all the kids were gone. It was a fifth of Evan Williams bourbon whiskey. He poured a double shot. Ayman and Sterlin referred to the reach into the bottom drawer as *Tryin' Times*. They kept a bottle in a brown paper bag, and one of them had written the nickname, *Tryin' Times*.

Sterlin swirled the mix around in his glass. "I know what time it is. Shit, I was born in Texas. I know it bothered you that I slept with so many white women. Maybe you think I let a part of my Blackness escape my reality. I know live in a world that is not color-blind despite what I did in the dark." Sterlin took a big gulp of his drink. "Seattle, or any city, I know what time it is. I have always known where I could not go as a Black man with a white woman on my arm. You'd think the most hell I would have paid for dating white women came from Black women. Yes, I have had sistas slice me in half with their comments. But it don't compare to the condescending wicked-witch shit I received from other white men and women. White women don't care for me dating other white women when they don't have courage to do what their pussies want them to do. And of course some white men...they come at me with that short-dick, jealous, hating crap."

It was silent in the office for awhile until Ayman spoke. "Look, man, you know where I'm coming from on this. You and I recruit young Black men in homes that are in mostly white environments. Often that kid is blind to racism. The courts put Black kids in jail and send white boys home for the same crime; they don't know that yet.

"For sure, in Seattle and all around here, there are a lot of racially mixed kids. We see mixed kids try to hide their race because of racism. Same shit from decades ago when some Black people tried to pass as white if they could." Sterlin nodded and kept listening.

"For some Black parents their suburban lifestyle has given them a false sense of reality. Racism is harder on that Black person when the racist cop, boss, co-worker, or legal system screws him; that's when he'll go postal. His feelings are hurt because his perfect world is a lie. Those naïve people thought racism is back in the day and not relevant anymore. It's not too farfetched to some of these kids to think Martin Luther King freed the slaves."

"My child will be prepared for it all," Sterlin said quietly.

Ayman reached for the brown bag, and poured a drink. "And, let's clear the air here. I have never cared about who you dated— white, Black, brown, or blue. I only wanted you to find one love, whoever she might be."

"Well, I have found one love…and one child now." Sterlin lifted his glass. Ayman did the same, and they toasted, *To Tryin' Times*.

The phone rang. Ayman answered, and three seconds later, he bolted from his chair, telling Sterlin to come with him.

The parking lot had blue lights flashing. Somebody had dumped red paint on both of their cars—Ayman's classic 1966 Jaguar and Sterlin's Dodge Magnum.

47

On the Curb

All Ayman could do was sit on the curb and stare. Sterlin spoke to the campus police and the Bellevue City Police. He gave them Suzy Q's phone number to contact for references to the problems he had already experienced.

Tow trucks loaded the vandalized vehicles. Ayman simply could not talk; he waved off any conversation. The man who normally was cool under pressure sat deflated. It had taken five years to restore the Jaguar to show quality and a functional daily driver. He watched his baby roll up the ramp of the tow truck. The shiny chrome dripping red paint was starting to dry like tear stains.

Insurance would repair and restore, but the assault against his pride and joy was like scalding hot water hitting his soul. He reminisced about the day he had finished restoring his classic. It was while he had love and was in love with Vanessa. She had bought the car for him as a project to keep him home instead of living in the gym.

He and Vanessa had gone for a long ride that day. When they came back and pulled into the garage, he and Vanessa ripped their clothes off and they made love on the backseat christening his pride and joy. He smiled inside at the pain he felt now, remembering.

That was then and this was now. What was happening? Could it be he was the intended target of harassment? He was the figurehead of a high-profile basketball team. Fanatics and haters of all types could be on the attack. This incident would make the news and thirty seconds of the late TV news, but that was the least of Ayman's and Sterlin's concerns.

Sterlin felt his life had crossed over to hurt his best friend. Sterlin's car was as simple as going down and buying another one, and his personal taste as easy as adding a few details. Ayman's car was beyond press and fit, or paint by the numbers. The Jaguar was a work of art.

As the police were leaving, Lois Mae drove into the parking lot just in time to pass the damaged cars. She got out of her car with her hand over her mouth.

"Baby, are you all right?" she asked Sterlin.

He gave her a glare for a moment. "I don't have paint on me; it's on my car."

Her head slowly shifted to the side, and her mouth shaped into an "O." They stared at each other for a moment before she said, "I'm just concerned about you. I may have asked a dumb question, but really, what would someone say? Let me know and I'll try to be perfect next time. Do you want to chop off my head? This has been a trying day already. This is where we stand by each other, right?"

Sterlin's shoulders drooped. His inner conversation yelled at him, *FUCK, what the fuck is wrong with me? This is a good woman; don't blow it.* His misdirected attitude turned tail and backed up. He took a huge breath. "I...I didn't mean that, and I know you know I'm out of balance right now." His voice soaked into the ground he was speaking toward.

"Let me take you home, baby. It's going to be okay, and—"

Sterlin put his finger across her lips. "Let's just go."

"Does Ayman need a ride?"

"No, he keeps one of his motorcycles here in the back of the gym. He wants to be alone. When things go bad, he goes it alone."

Lois Mae walked over to her car while Sterlin walked over to Ayman sitting on the curb. He reached his hand down, and Ayman pulled himself up. The two men hugged and held much longer than men who were insecure with their own masculinity. Lois Mae watched, tears trickling down her face.

She approached the two men and took their hands. She held Ayman's hand firmly and squeezed Sterlin's hand tight. "Will you guys let me say a little prayer?" She didn't wait for an answer. *"Heavenly Father, we come to you and ask that this shall pass. We find ourselves in your grace to erase these hurtful moments. We ask that you guide the evil in the ones who have transgressed against us to find a place of solace to correct their evil ways. We ask that you forgive us for what we might do if given the chance to even the score. Amen."*

Ayman smiled and shook his head, thinking about what he might do if given a chance to stomp the sole of his shoe into the soul of the vandalizing ass. He leaned over and kissed Lois Mae on the cheek, then turned and walked away.

Sterlin and Lois Mae went to the car. "I can't believe you asked the Lord to forgive us for what we might do. Pray for forgiveness after we get even?"

"It doesn't hurt to ask in advance."

"Well, prepare to ask again, because if we get the chance, we're gonna mess somebody up."

"That would not be wise. Remember, you're soon to be a daddy."

Sterlin stopped and froze. "Yeah…yeah."

48

The Payoffs and the Playoffs

League championship kept Coach Sparks focused on the prize. Two weeks after the cars were vandalized, the regular season ended. The playoffs started with the hope of another run at *March Madness*. The Jaguar was being repaired by the best, as Ayman's insurance company did not cut corners. It worked out that Coach Sparks would film a commercial in the future to highlight that fact.

Ayman told Sterlin how much money they were paying him. "One of the perks of being in the public view, corporate America will find a way to use you. The insurance company is going the extra mile with my Jaguar just so they can brag about their good service. Of course, the guy down the street will get his rates raised."

The team felt his hurt, and they might have been madder than he was that someone had violated their coach. Most of the kids, at one time or another, had ridden in his car. Some even had a chance to drive the car if he was in it. Coach Sparks had picked up most of the recruited kids from out of state on their first trip to Seattle.

The team's record of 23-7 would get them invited into the

NCAA tournament, but if they won their conference, it would seat them high in the NCAA tournament bracket.

Sterlin was days away from being a father. The birthmother, Roberta/Bobbie, had signed the papers to give up her child for adoption, but the law favored Sterlin, because he had no knowledge of the child before she signed adoption papers. With quick legal work by some high-powered lawyers, Sterlin would soon be changing diapers. He had a good woman by his side to help. She pledged to him whatever he needed.

One week after Sterlin had his Dodge Magnum repaired, he traded it in. Splattered red paint thoughts on his hot-rod chariot did not sit well in his mind. Unlike most parents with a newborn on the way, he bought a new Ford Mustang GT. The new hot rod with its retro styling had every option available, and then some. He ordered a custom babyseat with two-tone racing stripes.

Ayman saw the new car in the parking lot where there were still red spots on the ground. All he could do was shake his head, but smiled in knowing his friend. Lois Mae had ordered a baby seat too. She was committed.

Red-paint blues had Suzy Q shadowing both coaches and Lois Mae. Nothing made sense. Why the red paint? Maybe somebody got a great deal on sale. All she could do was keep everyone alerted and advised on how to stay safe.

During the playoffs, the team was hot. Great defense led to fast-break baskets and dunks, and Larentzo's scoring average went up. NBA pundits said the kid was showing signs of being a sure high, first-round draft choice.

ESCU won the conference championship in a tight game. Next, *March Madness*, the NCAA championship, started in a week. The only problem was not knowing what bracket the team would be seeded in. If they ended up in the West bracket, they could possibly play UCLA, USC, or Gonzaga in an early round. The team had some experience, with a good mix of seniors and underclassmen. Larentzo and Hafeez Rasheed were playing like two of the best guards in the country. Shervey, Nomo, Reiser, and Foley, the other main players, played tough and together.

Coach Sparks felt the team could compete with any team after their tough season schedule. They had beaten Georgetown, and they had beaten the University of Washington.

ESCU ended up in the Midwest bracket, with their first-round game against Duke. It promised to be a war. Duke had eliminated East Seattle City University last year. The motivation could not have been better. The Midwest bracket first-round games were in Albuquerque, New Mexico. Ayman and Sterlin were headed to their alma mater's city. Coach Sparks and the team flew down that night after finding out where they would play. He wanted the team practicing in the high altitude for an added advantage.

Sterlin flew in the next day after attending to some legal matters. The two best friends had first met and played basketball at the University of New Mexico. With the birth of Sterlin's child, and the team playing well, life was going good with some strange twists.

49

Strange Twists

A new baby girl arrived with Sterlin out of town with the team. In advance Sterlin and the lawyers had arranged temporary foster care rights for Lois Mae if he was out of town. She was mothering Sterlin's child. *Strange twists*, she thought as she prepared baby formula. *I wanted a child of my own. I can't have a child of my own, but the man I love has given me a child to care for.*

She cried often, feeling how good God had been to her as she watched the baby girl, who still did not have a name. For now, her name was Baby Girl, and she rested in a crib. Lois Mae was tired, but sleeping was not an option. She was exhausted from so much, so quick, so deep into another life. Her mind would not shut down.

Baby Girl made facial contortions as babies do when they sleep. Lois Mae felt some sadness that she did not have a chance to go shopping for the baby. Online shopping, rush delivery and setup took the place of the joy of picking out just the right crib.

Maternal instincts, Lois Mae thought. *What are they? Do I have them? Is there something I'm feeling, or not feeling? Am I adopting feelings?*

She knew fairy tales did come true in the books she read, and she knew every woman wanted the perfect man. Her perfect man came with a baby. Was she Sterlin's dream come true in a woman? Would he grow indifferent to her at some point? Her emotions spread wide and deep. Talk of marriage in the future had crossed their lips, in more of what if. They had only been in love less than two full moons. Her support for Sterlin, she promised, no matter their future together.

Baby Girl opened and closed her hands and Lois Mae reached into the crib to hold the little hand. Her pale skin took Lois Mae's mind to other thoughts. *As Baby Girl ages, people will ask if she's mine. Maybe if she's with me, people might ask if her father is white.* She laughed quietly to herself.

Her first sexual lover had been white. She laughed with just a twinge of anger. *A child never asks to come into this world. Half the children in Seattle seem to be mixed race. Hell, a lot of white couples have adopted a Black child. I know they would've taken a white child in if a white not addicted to Meth was available.* She laughed too loud. *What white couple goes in and asks for a Black child as their first choice? I guess they marked the box; it don't matter.*

Baby Girl stirred in her crib. Both her hands and feet went up in the air, and she relaxed. *She must be still dreaming as if she was still in the womb, but she's here with me. I despised her mother from what I knew of her, but I don't see her mother in her. I see Sterlin; I feel Sterlin in her. Strange twists and turns I'm taking. Somehow my steps seem guided.*

Sleep overtook Lois Mae for a short while until Baby Girl awoke, wet and wanting to be fed and held.

Skillet called often, but Lois Mae avoided her. After Suzy Q had reported what she knew about Skillet's baby, Lois Mae could not handle that situation now. With her ex-husband being the possible sperm donor, the thought turned her stomach. *How could she, if she willing did.* She cringed.

With one arm holding Baby Girl, she shook bottle formula onto her skin. The temperature was just right. Carrying a bundle of new life in her arms, Lois Mae wept because it felt right, and for what felt uncertain. Her tears baptized Baby Girl's forehead.

Vanita opened the SUV door for Joshua, who wore an East Seattle City University jacket Ayman had given him. Vanita's ex-husband had agreed to spend Sunday afternoon with their son. Some things never change. The ex would not come by her place, so they agreed to meet at her parents' home.

Vanita and her ex arranged for Joshua to spend the night, even though it was a school night. She had an early morning doctor's appointment. She had made a decision. Her mouth went dry with each thought of her choice.

After seeing Ayman in the restaurant, she understood it was truly over. He had a life, and keeping a part of him growing inside her had become less attractive. She watched her son unbuckle his seat belt. His dad opened the door for him. The smile on Joshua's face, that joy, was the only joy she had.

Her decision went against her morals and her spirituality. Within that, her courage levels erratically fluctuated. As she waved good-bye to her son, Vanita drove away with a child inside her. It was hard to swallow, knowing she would return a different woman. The side effects of her meds made her mouth dry, but she was experiencing another kind of dryness.

The next morning Vanita waited for a cab. A pre-spring sideways blowing rain did not help the blues of the oncoming day. It was cold outside, and she kept her coat on while waiting.

The cab ride seemed too short, when it pulled up to a small two-story office building. A sign read, *The Bothell Lagoon Health Clinic.* She handed the cab driver his fare but did not exit the cab until the driver asked if she needed help.

She pushed a doorbell while looking up into a security camera, then entered the building after a short buzz and click released the door. Once inside, pleasant but avoidant of any personal conversation by the office, help guided Vanita through the paperwork. No windows, no clocks, and nauseating smooth jazz made her want to move through one of the two doors in the room—the one door that led to the back, or the other she had just come through, the entrance.

"We take checks, or credit card, or cash," the woman said, faking a smile, not too big, not too small, with no teeth showing. She accepted Vanita's credit card with a professional office demeanor. Ten minutes later, a woman in a green hospital smock entered the room with her version of a smile—not too big, not too small, also with no teeth showing.

"Come with me, please, Ms. Irving."

In a back office a short conversation took place, with questions of "have you talked this over with your partner, priest, or friend?" Then the conversation turned to information about what would happen, and what to do afterward. The woman escorted Vanita to a small, medically equipped room. There was the table...the table with the stirrups. The woman handed her a gown.

After her vitals were monitored, she got a shot in the arm to calm her nerves, and then the wait for the doctor. Five minutes passed. Vanita changed her mind. She grabbed her clothes and dressed quickly. The nurse happened to come back in to let her know the doctor was almost ready for her.

"I can't do it," Vanita said, not really talking to the nurse as she reached for her purse. The nurse moved calmly out of the way and waved her hand in the direction Vanita needed to go—a sign it was a common experience for the nurse.

"I'll call you a cab," the nurse said in her professional demeanor with that smile—not too big, not too small, with no teeth showing.

Two cabs from the same company showed up at the same time. Vanita left when another woman was getting out of a third cab. The woman looked sad and despondent. That woman had a man with her. He appeared nonchalant. The drizzle had turned to pounding rain that sounded as if it were attacking the world and wanted inside the cab. An hour later, Vanita was home with the covers over her head.

50

These Curious & Pathetic Facts of Life

Round one, game one, and one down, ESCU put a whipping on Duke University. Some thought it was an upset. The great Duke team never lost a first-round game. ESPN sportscasters were amazed at ESCU racecar speed.

A rich supporter flew Sterlin back to Seattle on his private jet. Everybody wants to be a part of a winner, and the supporter offered a return flight before Game Two.

Suzy Q picked up Sterlin at the airport and took him home to see his newborn daughter. She hired extra security to help protect Sterlin and Lois Mae, and Ayman's dwellings. She let Sterlin know she thought she had a lead on what could be going on, but she chose not to release any information until she was totally sure.

Sterlin opened the door to his home, and heard Lois Mae yell out, "Go wash your hands and come hold your child." With Baby Girl in her arms, they passed in the hallway. Sterlin kissed Lois Mae on the forehead, then on the lips. He went to wash up, and they met in the bedroom. She lifted his daughter to Sterlin. He hesitated, unsure of how to hold a child that size. Lois Mae said, "Come on, you can do it. She's yours to hold and behold." She quoted for him:

"This curious and pathetic fact of life:
that when parents are old and their children grown-up,
the grown-up children are not the persons they formerly were;
that their former selves have wandered away, never to return
again."

"Okay, who are you quoting now, and what does that mean?"

"Mark Twain," she said and explained the quote. "Each moment from now on your child is changing, never to return to what she has changed from. So, hold your baby, as she will be changing even as you hold her."

"Let me sit down," he said.

She teased him, "Chicken, scaredy-cat. She's your child; hold her."

As she had seen in him, he was tender, and he started to cry like a baby, sobbing. He took his daughter in his arms and rocked. Lois Mae put her hand on his huge bicep. Sterlin's daughter had a massive protector, physically and spiritually. Lois Mae took so many pictures she had to stop and download them to make room for more.

Game Two, versus BYU. Sterlin was back on the bench with a picture of his baby girl in his inside coat pocket. Stella Mae was the name he'd chosen for his baby girl. Stella Mae Baylor's picture was near his heart.

BYU did all they could to slow down the ESCU team. They kept the game slow, and they had taller players. BYU went after their missed shots with aggressive fervor to keep ESCU from fast-breaking. For three quarters their plan worked. Coach turned up the defense with full court pressure, and BYU cracked. ESCU won by fifteen.

The team stayed in Albuquerque while Sterlin went home to be with his daughter and his lover for a couple of days. It felt good walking into his home with a family waiting for him.

To Lois Mae's credit, she made sure he kept his focus on basketball and made him leave in two days. They hired a nanny to help, so she could teach for a few hours a day, get some exercise, and get some sleep.

She and Sterlin took some time to go shopping, and he noticed she seemed somewhat distant. He asked her several times if she was okay, and her answer was always "yeah." They made love that night. The sex was good, but quiet laughter, trying not to wake a sleeping Stella Mae. Afterward, Lois Mae went into the distant mode again. He had to fly back in the morning and wanted to know what was on her mind. While he was giving his baby a bottle at 2 a.m., he sat on the edge of the bed next to her.

"Talk to me. Forget avoiding whatever it is. It doesn't look good on you, baby. You know you want me to know that there is a problem, but I can't read your mind yet." She smiled, looking up at him. "I'm sitting here holding my daughter, feeding her a bottle as I'm asking you to tell me what's bothering you. I've heard you always be honest in front of children." His eyebrows lifted, he stared, and smiled at Lois Mae. "I care about what's on your mind. Talk to me."

She sat up and looked him in the face. "As you fly back, as you walk day by day, I'm in a strange position. As Stella Mae grows, I'm left out in the cold if something happens to you. My heart beats strong for you and her, and at this moment we three share breathing on God's earth...but she is yours. Stella Mae is all yours. I understand that, but..."

Lois Mae got out of the bed, walked to the bathroom, and came back with tissue. She sat next to Sterlin and Stella Mae and wept with her words, "If God takes you from me, somebody will take Stella Mae. I have no rights, just my heart on the line for you and her.

"This is a major undertaking to involve myself in your life as it stands now. I thought I could just stand by your side, no matter what. Don't get me wrong, I'm here for you. Yet this feeling I could be pushed aside, it's driving me crazy. I know right now you don't need any more drama, but this is how I feel, Sterlin. Maybe I'm living my dream of having a child through you and Stella Mae. A therapist might say I'm crazy. I know a lot of other women might think I'm weak and needy. I might be all those things. What I do know is I love being here. I love you. I love that child in your arms." She leaned her head in and under Sterlin's arm and stared down into Stella Mae's tiny face sucking on her bottle. Stella Mae opened her eyes and stared back.

Sterlin let out a deep sigh. "Baby, I know what this means to you, and I hear what you're saying. I know I can't do this alone. I need you. I know the impact of making a bad decision about whom I let in my life. You and Stella Mae are the best things to come into my life. I understand your fear."

Lois Mae had done a lot of crying for joy and pain in the past two weeks. Now she sat sobbing out of control. Sterlin held his lover under one arm and held his love in the other. "Honey, give me a minute to figure all this out," he said. "You make a lot of sense. I want my daughter to have you in her life, no matter what."

He put his baby girl back in her crib and slid back into bed, holding Lois Mae tight. He told her one more time in the morning before he walked out of the door, "I'll make sure everything will be all right. I love you."

51

Pirates and Booty Busters

It was March Madness, the NCAA National Basketball Championship. East Seattle City University had won through all the rounds, and now was headed to the Final Four. The team came home for the week before heading to see if they could make history.

The team's plane landed to waving banners celebrating the team successes. The team buses drove to the Seattle Center and parked under the Space Needle. There was a stage to receive congratulations, and the school band played. It was a madhouse of excitement. It was more than Coach Sparks wanted; crazed people cheered as if they had won the whole thing.

A Seattle tradition, the Seattle Seafair Pirates, were men masquerading as pirates, shooting fake guns in the air. People cheered and shouted wearing big foam shark heads. It was one huge civic party. All Ayman could think was, *we haven't won what we want to win yet.*

After the team captains and others spoke at the microphone, Coach Sparks said a few words of praise for his team. Then he asked everyone to help keep the players focused. "We can have the biggest party ever if we win it all." The big crowd roared.

The team proceeded into elevators heading to the Space Needle for a few publicity pictures, then the buses would take them home. Lois Mae called Sterlin on his cell to find out how long would it be before she and Stella Mae could have him all to themselves. He said hopefully in less than an hour.

After the photo shoot, the team went down to ground level and started to board the buses. The last elevator down, the coaches got off and walked toward the buses. Ayman and Sterlin were last in line.

A loud clapping noise rang out and sounded like more pirate gunshot boom, but all the Seafair Pirates looked to be gone. People jerked and looked around.

A woman's voice in the distance shouted, "Stop."

With all the noise at the Seattle Center, people ignored the commotion. The coaches started to enter the bus. Ayman fell to the ground. He had been shot, and when he tried to sit up, his body went limp. His eyes stared straight up at the crown of the Space Needle, blood pooling under him. Panic set in, eyes widened, and shouts and screams erupted. The bus rocked to one side as the boys looked out of the windows.

Sterlin dropped to his knees and hollered louder than the gunshot, "Ayman!" Kids started piling out of the bus. The team trainer dropped to the ground to check if Ayman was breathing. He was. Sterlin shouted to the other coaches to get the kids back on the bus, get out of the windows, and stay low. Having grown up in Texas, he knew to stay low if a gun was in play.

Larentzo was having none of it staying on the bus. He was on the ground with Sterlin and the trainer. In the distance more gunshots sounded. People were screaming and running away from the noises.

A doctor who happened to be at the event came to Ayman's aid. Ayman was slowly closing his eyes, then opening them like he was trying to stay awake. The doctor turned him onto his side, found the wound, and applied pressure. He called on his cell phone for emergency aid. It was wrenching for Sterlin as he listened to the doctor give the details over the phone. Ayman's vitals were not good. He was in life-threatening danger. Police and Seattle Center Police cordoned off the area.

Sterlin thought about how cool Ayman could be in a tough situation, and he tried to do the same. He got on the phone and called Tylowe to meet them at the hospital, and he had Meeah go over to his house. Sterlin thought about Lois Mae's fears, and here it was, in his face as wailing sirens approached.

Behind a van in the parking garage southwest of the Seattle Center stood Suzy Q, out of breath from running and dodging bullets, but she was mostly pissed off. She pulled out a white-tipped cigar. She didn't smoke, but she had been trailing a man who did smoke that type of cigar. She thought it looked cool, not on him but on her. Suzy Q stared at the man she had just shot.

She pulled out a small writing pad and pen with one hand, and tossed it on the ground. In her other hand she had a 9mm handgun pointed at the man cowering on the ground in pain. "Eh, old chap, yer going to write me a little story, and I think you should hurry. You see, that there bullet in yer rump could be near a main artery. It would be a shame if you bled to death out yer ass."

The man looked at his own gun a few feet away near his feet. When he started to reach, Suzy Q fired a bullet into his foot. It went through his flesh and blistered the cement. The man screamed and whimpered.

"Damn, I missed yer big toe." She chuckled. "I'm sorry, sir, but you ain't thinking straight, eh."

The man in agonizing pain was Lois Mae's ex-husband. Suzy Q had eliminated everyone who could possibly be responsible for all the misdeeds and started following Vance, Lois Mae's first husband.

Suzy Q produced a digital voice recorder. "Sir, I was going to have you write, but you seem to be a bit uncomfortable. So, old boy, answer me a few questions. Right now, before I add to your pain, eh. Yer either going to live in a cemetery or a penitentiary. You got choices."

He responded, panting, and groaning, "What do you...want?"

"Why did you shoot at the coach? I think you may have hit him, you asshole."

"I was trying to shoot that guy, Sterlin. He's the one screwing my ex." Vance was in severe pain and winced with each word.

"Did you have something to do with the death of dear old Lois Mae's second husband?" She raised her gun and aimed at his face.

"Yeah, yeah...I did. I broke into their house to get the jewelry back I had given her. She...should have given it all back to me. That bitch...also had tapes of me jacking off that I let her have when we were married."

"Bitch, huh?" Suzy Q's voice dared him to say bitch again.

Vance softened his belligerent tone. "She claimed she threw them away, but I didn't trust her. I never did find them tapes, and then her husband...he came home and caught me. I had to off him."

Suzy Q watched the man suffer before she asked another question. "You raped Lois Mae's friend, Velvet, didn't ya?" Suzy moved in closer with her gun and recorder. She wanted the right answer, not necessarily the truth.

Vance told the truth. "Yeah, I drugged her ass and took the funky pussy." The man almost smiled in the middle of immense pain.

Suzy Q cut the recorder off and jumped on the foot she had shot. He screamed and howled like a coyote caught in a trap.

Suzy Q's voice went deeper than hell. "You sorry piece of fish gut. Since you think you like calling women bitches and hurting women, I want you to scream like a female dog-bitch. Come on, mate." She jumped again, landing like she was sticking a landing from a gymnastic vault. She smiled and said, "A man may be dead or dying because you got a jealous little weenie."

The man pleaded, squealing, "Please take me to a hospital. The pain, the pain!" Vance started crying.

"One more question," she said and put her finger to her lips to hush him. She turned on the recorder again. "Tell me, why the red paint?"

Vance was trying hard between breaths to talk. "I...wanted to... to send a message...a warning, blood was going to spill. Lois Mae always wore red lipstick. She only wore it to entice other men. I hated her red lipstick."

Suzy Q cut the recorder off and stared at him while moving the white cigar tip around in her mouth. She pushed her 9mm into the flesh of Vance's ass near the wound. He gurgled in a high-pitched yelp.

"Shut the hell up, you freaking lily-livered puke. You sound like a toy poodle getting it up the ass from a Great Dane."

People were coming. She moved his gun near his hand and told him, "Yer going to be a cripple with half yer foot shot off. You got a bullet near yer asshole. Yer not going to fare too well in prison, old boy. Get ready to be passed around as a penitentiary bitch. The booty busters in prison, once they find out you shot the coach of the team, it's going to be your ass bent over on the regular." She said the last words slowly, looking him in the eyes. "I think you know what you should do. You can finally act like a man and save everybody the hassle and save yourself a lifetime of hell. You killed a man. You may have killed two men. You raped a woman and impregnated her. I'm sure there's more yer sorry ass has done. You have caused too much grief. Like I said, I think you know what you need to do."

With his gun near his hand, she backed up, keeping an eye on him. She reached for her private investigator badge and held it up high for the approaching police.

She had her gun still pointed at Vance, when a female police officer came up alongside her. She asked Suzy Q to lower her gun as she trained her own on Vance. Vance had his gun in his mouth.

Boom!

52

Tomorrow is Not Promised

At Harbor View Hospital, the experts on gunshot trauma, a surgeon explained Ayman was stable but in serious condition. Ayman had a collapsed lung from the shooting, and the loss of blood added some complications. The bullet was not in a critical place, but had to be removed. Sterlin had power of attorney for Ayman and gave the okay for the surgery.

He paced the maze-like halls. He felt trapped until he saw Lois Mae running his way. Her hug could have collapsed Sterlin's lungs. Tylowe contacted family and friends. Sterlin would not let the team come up to the hospital. He did let Larentzo come since he lived with Ayman.

After three hours, they wheeled Ayman out of surgery. "He's stable and he'll be fine; he should have a smooth recovery," the doctor said. Sterlin explained moments later to everyone in the waiting room. People held hands, hugged, and said more prayers. Sterlin told Larentzo to call his teammates.

"Tell them Coach is fine and recovering, and practice is tomorrow as Coach would want it to be. Remind them, although this is distracting, we are in the Final Four. One more thing, tell them to give thanks to their higher power, as Coach would do for them, for tomorrow, is not promised to anyone."

The police gave statements that the perpetrator who had randomly shot Coach Sparks, later took his own life. Outside the hospital, news trucks and satellite dishes pointed to the sky. ESPN analyzed. There was talk that Ayman might never coach again. Sterlin only cared that his best friend and brother in spirit had almost lost his life.

Vanita walked out of the bedroom, stunned at the breaking news of Ayman's peril, constantly repeating the horror. She had just wakened from intermittently napping through days of feeling hopeless. She held the rail at the top of her stairs, groggy and upset. Her life decisions plagued her mind. She felt queasy. She opened and closed her eyes and succumbed to the dizziness, tumbling end over end like a rag doll, her body hitting every other step on the way down. The first collision knocked her out, and each one after that did damage to her elsewhere.

Hours later, she came to. She had to crawl to the phone; her entire body felt bruised, and even the touch of the phone against her skin hurt. Vanita called Alicia, who called 9-1-1 and started making her way over. While sitting on the floor, she saw blood coming from under her gown and passed out again. Another emergency went through the doors of Harbor View Hospital, but this time it was too late to save a life.

56

You Were Lucky

Ayman opened his eyes to the sunrise on the late March morning. He had awakened earlier around 3:00 a.m., when the nurse told him of his injury. He had her turn on ESPN, and he heard the repeating story of the shooting. He called Sterlin at home, and they spoke for about fifteen minutes. He had drifted back to sleep by 3:30.

High up on the tenth floor, the Eastern sun woke him later. A woman sat sleeping in a chair with her head in her hands, leaning on her arm. Her hands were pretty, and her face was gorgeous. Ayman stared in disbelief. His chest felt tight. He could see on the monitor, his heart rate easing up, along with his blood pressure.

He sat up, slowly testing for pain. It felt weird, but he did not hurt too badly. His movements awoke her.

"Well, hello," she said.

"Hi, long time, no see." Ayman looked at his ex-wife, Vanessa. Two years had passed, and she had changed. Her face had filled out, and her body was rounder, but she was still beautiful. She might have even been more attractive than before.

"I knew I would see you at some time or another," she said,

"but this is not what I had hoped for." Vanessa stood and stretched.

"How long have you been here?"

"I flew in a little before midnight, just as soon as I could. It looks like you were lucky. How do you feel?"

"Ah, I'm a bit tight in my upper body. I have no clue what it should feel like to have a bullet in my back and then have it removed. My breathing feels all right. I just don't feel like I can take a deep breath."

She moved closer to his bedside. "Sterlin called me and I was coming soon, anyway, now that I'm an auntie."

"Yeah, that is the real story of the day, week, and year. The boy has a child. He's a single parent."

Ayman's regular doctor, Dr. Ron, and a female doctor entered the room. "Ayman, you're sitting up. Good. It's hard to keep a good man down," Dr. Ron said, and looked over at Vanessa. "It's Vanessa, right?"

"Yes, I remember you, Dr. Ron. Nice to see you again, but I wish it was under better circumstances." Vanessa moved away from Ayman to make room for the doctors to look at his wound.

"Mr. Sparks, I'm your surgeon, Dr. Franklin. Tell me how you're feeling." They examined him as they spoke.

"I feel tight. My breathing feels weird, but I guess I'm doing okay." The doctors and Ayman discussed his medical prognosis. Ayman asked Vanessa to stay while the doctors were there.

"Well, aren't you the superhero?" Vanessa said after the doctors left. "They said you can go home in a couple of days."

"Superheroes can dodge bullets or at least bounce them off." He stared at her and turned his head away. "I called you, and I left you a message. You never returned my call."

"I'm here now. Fear has been our foe. I dialed but couldn't hit 'send.' Then a bullet hits you to chase away my fear. I'm here now is the best I can say." They didn't speak for twenty minutes but they held hands. She broke the silence. "So tell me, was it some crazy jealous husband who shot you?" she teased.

Ayman opened his mouth but before he could say anything, she stopped him. "Honey, I'm just kidding."

She had used a term of endearment, and it felt better than the painkiller in his IV. "Sterlin filled me in on a few things," she told him. They kept talking for an hour before he felt sleepy. She went back to sleep in the chair waiting for him to wake again.

Vanita drank warm apple juice through a straw. She was in a room on the fifth floor of Harbor View Hospital. Her face did not show much swelling, but it felt puffy. Alicia flipped channels away from any news concerning Ayman or the East Seattle City University Sharks.

Vanita had lost the baby, and the doctors performed a D&C on her. The doctors decided to watch her for twenty-four hours.

"Does my son know?"

"Hell no!" Alicia's voice hit like another tumble down the stairs. "Don't you tell your son that you were pregnant, never. It's bad enough you left him over at his father's house all this school week. He thinks you fell and that he'll see you back at home soon. In my opinion, you may want to keep this to yourself. I can't believe you chose not to tell me."

"Would your reaction be any different now?"

Alicia didn't answer but moved to another subject. "You were lucky in a strange way. It sounds like some crazy man was after him or somebody on the team. You and Joshua could have been mixed up in that mess."

"Please, Alicia, I've been through a lot this week."

"What other stuff went on this week? What went on that you chose to leave your son over at his father's place, anyway?"

"Nothing happened."

"Vanita, nothing will change in your life until you are able to be up front and honest at all costs. No matter who it is or what it is, you're gonna have to tell the truth about what you are and who you are. The right man will be there for you when you learn to be honest with yourself. Sure, a lot of men will run if they hear you are sometimes emotionally off-balance."

"You mean to say bipolar," Vanita clarified.

"Okay, but you can't hide who you are no more than Oprah can hide her money. You have a son who loves you as you are. At his age, he already understands his mom has some bad days. I put up with your butt. Your mom and dad understand to a point. You have to trust God that He will run away the men who can't handle you being bipolar. The ones who see the real you will do what it takes to support you." Alicia walked over with a warm face towel and gently wiped her friend's face. Vanita wanted to sleep and wake up at leaving time. When she did fall asleep, it was nightmare time.

She was well aware that Ayman was in the same hospital. The news service all reported that Coach Sparks was doing fine, and quick recovery was the prognosis. After all that had happened, she did not want to be near him. Her healing from the hurt in her body and her soul could not happen if she was close to Ayman. She begged her doctor to let her go home that day, but he wanted her to wait a day. He gave her a shot to calm her, the second time that week she had been injected to help relax her. It did not help the first time, and by midnight, she was still awake, unreleased from her compelling thoughts.

54

Skeletons & Ghosts

Sterlin walked in and found Vanessa and Ayman smiling. The two of them used to be the only family he was close to. He avoided any heavy personal conversation. They spoke about practice.

"You have to totally act as if you are in charge, because you are. If the kids see you waffling, they'll only play with the confidence you display," Ayman said.

After Sterlin left, Ayman and Vanessa sat quietly until she said, "I should get going. I'm staying with Tylowe and Meeah. I'll come see you tomorrow if you want."

"Yes, please come back. You know there's plenty of room at the house. I do have a young man from the team staying with me. His name is Larentzo. You might remember him. He's a great kid, and he's dating Tyreene."

"Meeah told me about them," Vanessa said as she took a deep breath.

"What's wrong?" he asked.

"Meeah and Tylowe, I know have room, and get to see the girls." He smiled. She did not. "Ayman, the boy is your son!"

He stared with a pained look.

"Did you hear what I said? He is your son!"

"What in the hell are you talking about?"

Vanessa pulled out an old envelope from her purse and placed it on his lap. "Read." She started to leave the room.

"No! Don't leave, please stay." They stared at each other for a long moment before she sat back down. Ayman pulled out a letter dated from four years ago. It was written in poor English and handwriting.

The letter read:

"Sir Ayman, i write you in hope. i don't do well here in St. Lucia. i pray you know this is Tina, the one you call your tall kandy. i see you have good luck in yer life and you come back to St. Lucia many times. but i never see you since wer young. my life bad. wen you play for your baskitball team and i play for my soccer team we had fun kissing and lovin on the beach at night. then you no come here for long time i don't know what to do i have child from you from nights on beach wit you. i do best I can do but life no luck i fall to drink. i use white powder. i put Larentzo in orphan home. yer boy he play baskitball all the time. he best here on St. Lucia many school team from states come to watch him play. he only want to play for you."

The letter rambled on haunting like skeletons and a ghost. Ayman's vitals fluctuated with every heartbeat and short breath he took. He looked away from Vanessa. He understood she had known for a long time. He understood the last year of their life they had lived a lie about what he had done twenty-three years ago as a young man, and it pierced deeper than a bullet now. He finally got the courage to look at Vanessa.

She spoke to him, but her eyes darted to other places in the room. "Do you remember when I used to tell you, you got things going on? Well, now you know. I know I disappointed you when I did not give you a child, and later had my tubes tied.

"Then, we became older, and you had kids around you all the time, from the big kids down to the little ones at your basketball camps. It ate at me. I know I became bitter, and I know I failed to support you as a wife, then the letter came.

"For the record, I did not open it. It came just as you saw it. I tried to cope. From the day Larentzo arrived, I hugged him and let him know he was in a good place. I told him he was my son now. I said that to all your boys, but I meant it much deeper with Larentzo.

"I had him tell me his life story. He had it bad growing up. I felt so bad that you were not there in his life to help raise him with more than he had."

A nurse came in to check on Ayman and to change his bandage. The room was eerily silent as the nurse went about her business.

When she was done, Ayman said, "Where does it begin and where does it end? I'm always trying to do the right thing. I would have stepped in and raised him. I would have told you I fathered a child. I would have brought him to the States long ago."

"I have no doubt that you would have," she said. "It just became too much for me."

Ayman cut her off, "We both did our fair share in letting something good get away. I was too controlling with the demands of my career."

"Yes, Ayman, at times you were." They sat quiet for a moment.

"You don't know how much I miss fighting with you, and then making up with you. I used to think you started fights just so we could make up," he said.

She chuckled. "I did it sometimes, and other times I wanted your attention. Ayman, I need to go. I need to get away for a few hours, but I'll come back later. Now that this is out, I feel a weight has been lifted off me. Plus, I think you should meet with your son as your son."

Ayman nodded. He wanted to sleep, and he wanted his mind to slow down. Vanessa stood and bent over him, moving as slow as a second hand on a clock. She kissed him, turned and walked away. He smiled at the fact that she used to have a little round petite behind. He always wished her butt were bigger. Now it was much bigger, and it switched hard with each step she took. He smiled, but he saw much more. He felt his heart want what he already had, and spiritually he had never let go of.

She still cared enough to be at his bedside. Vanessa had come to see him despite the pain of knowing Larentzo was his son.

My son...Larentzo.

His son. Why didn't he know? He saw Larentzo one day at the house staring at a picture of Ayman in his early twenties. Later he himself, walked by the picture, and gazed at how much the boy kind of resembled him at the same age, and he laughed. One day after practice, Larentzo walked by the office returning from the shower half-naked, and Sterlin remarked, "Damn, that boy is built like Dr. J. and walks like him too. You know they used to say the same thing about you when you were in college."

Should I have known?

Goldlyn Mayfield, Ayman's adopted son, walked through the door. He looked lost, and tears rolled down his cheeks. At six-six, and twenty-six years old, he was a beautiful crying Black boy.

Vanessa walked back in behind him and said, "Look what I found. He was sitting out there not wanting to disturb us. I had a chance to see him last week when his team played Golden State. He stayed with me overnight, and we talked all night."

"Pops, you're okay, right?" Goldlyn sounded like Isaac Hayes, even with his thick tongue. Ayman knew he read lips better than hearing, so he motioned for him to come closer. "Son, I'm fine. I'm too stubborn to let a bullet keep me down."

Goldlyn reached over and squeezed Ayman's hand. Vanessa put her arm around Goldlyn's waist and leaned on him. She started to cry.

"I thought you were leaving. I can't have all these tears in my room flooding the tenth floor," Ayman teased.

"I am. It's just we...all of us...together. Well, okay, I'm leaving, but I'll be back later." She turned and left. Ayman watched his ex-wife leave the room again. Goldlyn scanned Ayman's eyes. His deafness sharpened his skills in other areas, and reading a person's eyes was easier for him.

"Pops!" Goldlyn exclaimed, "You're in a hospital bed after being shot."

Ayman smiled. "I didn't get shot in the eyes."

"I can't stay. I only have a pass from the team to fly through. We have a game tonight."

"All right, you guys are winning your division, right?"

"That's why I have to get back."

"Okay, but I have some other news I want to share with you soon as you have time."

Goldlyn leaned over and kissed his adopted dad on the forehead. He left, and Ayman drifted off to sleep. He awoke with game strategies. He reached for the phone to call Sterlin, held the phone, and told himself, *No.*

He called the nurse in and told her he felt some discomfort and could not sleep. After a brief up and down, taking a birdbath, and clean sheets, he lay back down. The nurse gave him some pills and he went back to sleep.

Dreams of Vanessa and dreams of basketball at first controlled the movie behind his eyelids. Then came pictures of being on a beach years ago with a beautiful St. Lucian woman. He rested well with the increase of the IV painkiller and sleeping pills, but his dreams were all over the place. At 11 p.m. the nurse increased his IV painkiller and gave him some more sleeping pills.

More dreams came in living color that felt real. He had the vision of the hall lights in the hospital dimming with the door to his room closing. When the lights were gone, he could hear someone talking in his dream state, *"I miss you."* Her voice was soft, angel-like as her hand caressed his face. He smiled, floating in his dreams. The vision of her beauty next to him made him groan. He felt her lips on the side of his face.

"I will always love you, Ayman. I thought I could keep a part of you, but it was not to be. I'm glad God did not let the evil world take you. I think about how you made love to me, touching me all over and in me. You made me do things I will never do again. Well, I messed that up, but I still touch myself thinking about you. I loved you watching me touch myself."

The monitor above his head showed his heart rate and blood pressure rising.

Her voice kept swirling in his dream. *"You are a good man. I will pray for you, and I hope you see me in your dreams as I see you in my wants and wishes. Good-bye, my love."*

In the dark, his eyes met light, when the door to his room opened. The light in the room woke him up, and he felt groggy, and uncertain. He had a hard-on. Feeling it, he laughed knowing he had been in bed way too long. He was horny. *Wow*, he thought, and spoke aloud to himself, "I'm having all kinds of dreams, damn."

He waited for his hard-on to go away and then pushed the call button. When the nurse came, he went to the restroom. The nurse changed his sheets again and told him he really sweat a lot. "I don't normally," he said. "Maybe it's all this medicine that's giving me these powerful dreams."

While the nurse changed his bandage, she joked with him, "You need to wash your face to remove that lipstick smudge. If my husband came home with that telltale sign, he'd be in big trouble." She pointed to his cheek, and smiled. "Nice shade of red."

Ayman rubbed his face. There was some kind of smudge. He shrugged it off, took some more sleeping pills, and went back to sleep to let more dreams touch him.

55

The Lifting of Heavy Loads

Practice started slow because the boys had been on an emotional weathering of joy and pain-winning and losing. The media hounded them; there was no rest for tired young minds. The stupid repeated question was, "What do you guys think your chances are?"

One of the seniors, Shervey, overheard one of the freshmen make a comment at practice, and it set him off: "Well, it was a nice season while it lasted." Shervey already had a way of putting fear in freshmen; he was hard on teammates who didn't hustle.

"You stupid-ass fssh...get the hell out of here if you don't think we can win." He walked in an aggressive manner toward the underclassman. Sterlin let Shervey get close before he blew the whistle.

He called everyone over, and reminded them that Coach wasn't dead and was doing very well. "He is in your head if you let him speak. We will win if it's in our will."

Larentzo spoke up, "I challenge each of you to be as focused as I am."

The rest of practice the boys sweated enough to cool hell. The task at hand: East Seattle City University versus the number one team in the nation. The University of North Carolina team was bigger, almost as fast, and had tradition behind them.

Everyone had picked North Carolina to win even before what happened to Coach Sparks. The ESCU team would head to Cincinnati for a Saturday afternoon game. One of the sports jocks on KJ-Stupid radio said the team was headed to a massacre.

While Sterlin was at home, he would not let his daughter out of his sight. Suzy Q had sat them both Sterlin and Lois Mae down and played the recording of Vance's confession.

Lois Mae felt mixed joy and pain. How could she ever have been married to such an evil man? Him being dead, taking his own life, felt horrible. What felt worse, the truth about her second husband made her weep. Sterlin held her throughout the revelation. She was sick, almost losing her stomach while hearing how Vance took advantage of Velvet. He had been date-raping women by drugging them. She would call her friend soon and offer to help anyway she could.

Vanessa came by later that evening to see Sterlin's baby girl, and the two ladies fawned over Stella Mae. The two had crossed paths back years before, they recalled, at a social function, and they remembered each other. Vanessa told them both that if Lois Mae wanted to go to Cincinnati with Sterlin, she would stay with Stella Mae.

Sterlin was torn. He would have loved to have his woman there with him on his biggest day as a coach. He thought of Stella Mae being away from the only person that had been there from day one, and he decided not yet.

Oddly, Vanita walked out of Harbor View Hospital the next day at 9 a.m. as Vanessa walked in. They were just feet away from each other in the revolving door. In passing, the two ladies breathed the same air. They had cooked in the same kitchen and had showered in the same shower. They had slept in the same bedroom. They had shared much more, but passed each other without knowing who the other was. It was a new day for both. Their eyes briefly met and their facial expressions sent acknowledgments of, "Hello, have a good day."

The doctors released Vanita earlier in the day than she expected, so Alicia could not make it to pick her up at discharge time. She wanted to go, so a cab would have to do. She felt soreness all throughout her body and a strange newness of a fresh start. Her life was far from perfect, and she would have to work to stay sane in her crazy world. Last night she had kissed away the last of the world she had lost.

At the cabstand she had her leather shoulder bag of hospital stay accessories and the weight was evident. Laying it at her feet, she heard someone say, "Looks as if you need someone to carry your heavy load." Vanita turned, smiled, and turned back. As always, most men saw her beauty and had to say something.

A mixed-race Black man stood behind Vanita. His eyes were deep black, contrasting with his complexion. His facial features suggested he might be Asian. His shoulders were at the same level as Vanita's. He was not tall, but no one would call him short.

"If you're going any distance, don't take any of the old cabs. Wait for one of the new hybrid cabs. They put the more honest drivers in those."

She turned and said thank you, curious why and how he knew this. "And you know this how?"

"I work for the city as an inspector for public transportation quality services."

"That is some title."

"Yeah, I know." He laughed a warm laugh. It made her smile for the first time in awhile. A moment of awkward silence ensued. She had not turned away from him, so she broke the silent stalemate.

"I too work for the city, as a court reporter."

"Really? Well, if you are taking any of the public transportation systems, I hope you are finding courteous providers."

"I don't find myself on the public trans system often. I just needed a ride home today." Vanita needed a pleasant conversation. Everything had been so serious in her life lately.

"My name is Jabin."

"I'm Vanita. I don't think I've heard that name before. Nice name."

"Thank you. Not that I'm Hebrew, but in the Hebrew language my name means perceptive one."

"Perceptive one, huh? Are you perceptive enough to know you should not be talking to me?" Vanita smiled but felt defeat inside. *He's another man that if he knew anything about me…If he had any sense at all, he'd holler for help.*

Jabin seemed to read her mind. "I'm perceptive enough not to judge you as you are judging yourself." His smile disarmed. His response opened a door, and she decided to walk through and give her testimony. If he walked away, she would trust that God was working on her behalf.

"I don't know you, but I'm going to tell you why I'm here. I'm going to tell you…" She took a deep breath and blurted, "I'm a woman who has to be on medication to control much of my life." She smiled and chuckled at what she was about to say. "I can sometimes be emotionally off-balance." Jabin stood unfazed, wearing an expression that said, *I'm listening.*

"For me, today is a new day," Vanita said. "I have to do things in a new way. Maybe I'm talking to you, a stranger, because I'm tired of not talking. I'm tired of hiding inside myself. What does your perception tell you?"

Jabin's body language and demeanor made her feel safe. "My perception...my life experiences have taught me to be up front, too. I can appreciate anyone who does the same."

While they talked, several taxis came and went. The world kept turning. They moved from the taxi stand to a little coffee stand with tables. They sat at a table with a big umbrella left unopened. The spring sun had healing powers in the middle of a busy world. They had some tea while Vanita shared and poured out her soul, her life. She thought he would tell her, "Have a good day," and leave. But he never flinched, and he made it easy for her to open up.

"Here is my city official badge. I am authorized to take citizens home if need be. Would you like a ride? Would you accept a ride home from a man who has been clean and sober for two years by the grace of God? Would you like a ride home from a man who goes to church more than once a week? Would you travel with a man who lost his wife and almost lost his child to a drunk driver? That same night I was too drunk to take my daughter and my wife to my daughter's school play. My wife, God bless her soul, she hated to drive at night. As it was, another drunk took her life. Or maybe it was me in a way, because I sat home sobering up, feeling sorry for letting them down again.

"Now, I raise my daughter on my own as a single parent. Would you like a ride home from a man, who will not judge you? My judgment comes from somewhere else, and not from any man or woman. Would you like a ride home?"

Vanita picked up her heavy bag and looked in the direction he wanted to head. Jabin took her bag. "Let me carry your heavy load."

Ayman was sitting up, puzzled because he had found several long black hairs on his pajama top. Vanessa was near him yesterday, but she had reddish-brown hair. All the nurses had sandy-blonde or brunette hair. He sat clueless but enjoyed seeing Vanessa's smile walk through the door. She had wanted to talk to her ex-husband for a long time to clear the air.

She had a letter for Ayman. She thought it fitting he should read another life-changing letter. She put the letter in his hand and said she would come back tomorrow. He wanted her to stay, but she insisted he read the letter, and she would see him tomorrow. The letter read:

Ayman, I love you and I have always loved you. Yes, our marriage was far from perfect, but what is? I wanted to blame you for my lack of happiness. I just did not have the confidence in myself to be happy. I know I was hell on you, and you in return, you kept your distance from me. That was hell on me.

At this time, I want you to think it's possible for me to have grown. I understand me better and I believe I can be the wife you wanted and needed.

Yes, Wife.

Would you like to be married to me again? That's a lot to think about with all that's been going on. Yet, seeing you, I know what I want. I want us as one again.

I promise not to run if we stumble with small problems. We can both be headstrong. I'm going to do all the things you need to see. I hope you can do the same.

I miss the things we did together, like cooking. You always sat in the kitchen, and we talked while I cooked and watching game film., I really miss going to church with you, having your arm around me as we walked into church. I felt the Lord wrap his arm around us. I miss us walking in the morning and a lot of evenings, us walking around

Green Lake or Seward Park. I miss driving down to Tacoma in OUR Jaguar, and walking on the waterfront down there. As you can see by the size of my butt that I miss walking with you and your long strides made me work. I know you miss the scent of my sweaty behind. Don't act as if you don't.

I saw you looking at my butt. Yes, it has spread, but I want you to be the man I work all this butter for. I wasn't bad. remember? I know you do!!!!!

I miss us growing older. We are here on this earth to help each other as we go day by day. Your grandfather repeated that to me often, and right before he passed away, he told me again.

With that in mind, this one time, sweetheart, I wanna be your wife again.

Vanessa Sparks

I still carry your name, and you know this.

59
Perfect Circle

"The team is ready, and I believe they will play hard. Practice for the last two days has been great, at times maybe too intense." Sterlin reported to Ayman on his last visit before heading to the airport.

The team buses sat outside with banners that read, "Coach Sparks is with us every step of the way." Music played outside the hospital: Bobbie Brown's "Every Little Step You Take." The cheerleaders danced and crowds cheered for a show of support for Coach Sparks. He waved out the window and did a couple of interviews. The whole team crowded around his bedside. He gave a low-key speech, letting them know he was proud of them, and expected them to win.

At the airport, Lois Mae had Stella Mae wrapped in a blanket, and Sterlin kissed them both good-bye. Before he turned away, he handed her a large envelope. "Open it, please, when you get home." He kissed her again.

At home, Lois Mae put Stella Mae down for a nap and poured herself a glass of wine. She laughed to herself. *If I had birthed this child, I would be breastfeeding. Instead, I'm having a glass of Merlot.*

She had another thought. *My breasts have been tender, and that is something I rarely have experienced. Hmph.*

She opened the large envelope and read. It was Sterlin's will, living will, and life insurances in the amount of a $500,000 each for Lois Mae and Stella Mae. It made her blink five times. Lois Mae was named as sole caregiver to Stella Mae if anything should happen to Sterlin. Other documents were inside the envelope to support and protect her and Stella.

If anything were to happen to both Sterlin and her at the same time, Ayman and/or Vanessa would be next in line to care for Stella Mae and next in line, Tylowe and Meeah would become Stella Mae's guardians.

Sterlin had taken notice that Lois Mae was always quoting from classical writers. He thought to give her a quote to help her move on from the past.

Finish each day and be done with it. You have done what you could. Some blunders and absurdities no doubt crept in; forget them as soon as you can. Tomorrow is a new day; begin it well and serenely and with too high a spirit to be encumbered with your old nonsense.

Ralph Waldo Emerson

He finished the note by writing:

Now you have Stella Mae Baylor and me, Sterlin Emerson Baylor, and we have you, Lois Mae. When you're ready, you'll be Mrs. Baylor.

With the team flying away to a game he had worked hard to achieve an opportunity to coach, Ayman felt cold and alone. He had one good thing to rely on; he could feel Vanessa holding his hand. She wanted him, and he had her back after two years of separation and divorce. No one could take her place. He had felt other love-love, but there was only one when it was all said and done. They had come full circle. He replied in a short return that yes, he would marry her again.

The doctors were going to release him the next day, and Ayman asked Vanessa to help him do something important. She hesitated but agreed with certain stipulations.

The doctor said he could fly if the plane's takeoff, altitude climb, and descent were slow. In a private plane, and no coaching whatsoever as Vanessa's stipulation, he would fly to Cincinnati. With her beside him, he would sit in the locker room. No one was to know except a select few. He would be near his life's work and the woman he needed.

60

You Could Never Let Me Down

Game time, and as much as the East Seattle City University Sharks prepared for the pressure, even if they had Coach Sparks, the game was a bomb waiting to go off. The explosion could send them home brokenhearted or into basketball immortality.

Seconds away from tipoff, Sterlin checked to make sure his cell phone worked. He decided to connect with Ayman if he felt he needed to. Ayman did not want Sterlin to look to him, but Sterlin told him, "If I'm to be a good coach, I need to use all my resources."

Two rows behind the bench sat Tylowe, Meeah, and their daughters. A nod from Tylowe let Sterlin know Ayman was in the locker room. They decided not to let the players know until halftime that Coach was there supporting them.

Vanessa made sure there was a comfortable chair in the locker room, and a doctor checked on Ayman when they first arrived. A beautiful female doctor, a lung specialist, Dr. Monie, examined Ayman. It made Vanessa smile, knowing no sexy, big-leg woman doctor feeling all over her man was going to take her man, ever.

The bomb went off early in the game. North Carolina was fast and strong. They played as if ESCU was still warming up, and North Carolina was trying to end the game. Ten minutes into the game, ESCU was down by ten points, 16-6. They guarded Larentzo in a double-team defense, but he still had scored all six of his team's points. He scored on a three-point basket and was three for three from the free throw line.

Coach Baylor made frequent substitutions to keep his players fresh, and it made a difference within the next ten minutes. ESCU was still down six but playing better, and North Carolina could not pull away.

Coach Baylor used a Coach Sparks tactic spotting the weaker ref, the one that should have made foul calls but didn't, perhaps intimidated by the big game. During a time-out, he yelled, "Don't be scared to call some fouls." That ploy might have backfired, but Coach Baylor yelled at the ref right in front of the media table.

In the next four minutes, North Carolina committed five fouls to East Seattle City University's one. The Sharks pulled within three points right before the half.

Halftime score, North Carolina, 44, East Seattle City University, 41. Larentzo had scored twenty-four points while making all ten of his free throws.

In the locker room, Ayman moved to an area where the players could not see him. A TV crew was allowed to film parts of the halftime dialog to air in Seattle right after the team went back onto the floor.

Coach Baylor went over game adjustments on the board, and the other assistants had their say before Coach Baylor asked the team, "What would Coach Sparks say right now?"

The room was silent, but from around a corner they heard, "It is halftime. We have not won or lost, and the game is not over, so it must be zero to zero." Coach Sparks walked around the corner.

The camera crew caught the roar of the players and the joy on their faces. Sterlin stood in front of Ayman to keep the players from mobbing him. He raised his hand for quiet; he was not physically able to talk very loud.

"Play for the successes of your team. Not for me, not for you. Play for the joy of the people you play with. Your effort is the real trophy that no one can ever take from you. It has been a tough season, yet look where we are. Through our hard work and focus, we have come this far. I love everyone in this room."

Ayman stopped speaking and took time to scan every face in the room. "The road trips, all the practices, the injuries, and the minor setbacks, are a part of the reason we are here today. No mistake has been too much. No one win has been more important than any other. You should recognize your true worth in the effort you give today." Coach Sparks signaled the TV camera to turn off before he continued.

"The other team, the nation loves them. But right now you'll have the world eating out of your hands if you give your best effort." He went silent. He was out of breath and took a moment to gather himself before he said, "I want to shake each one of your hands as you run for your life onto the court."

Each player did just that. Larentzo was last in line, and Ayman said to him, "Son, and I do mean, my son, do yourself proud. You could never let me down. I already know what kind of man you are. In time, I hope you will know what kind of man I want to be for you. Know this, I love you."

Larentzo put his arms around him lightly to not hurt his father. Ayman lifted his arm slowly and put his hand on Larentzo's head. It indicated he wanted his taller son to lean down. He did, and Ayman kissed his son on the forehead. Vanessa then hugged Larentzo. He turned and ran out of the locker room.

The second half started with a bomb. East Seattle City University went on a ten-point run without North Carolina scoring a basket. The stadium was rocking. The sportscasters said they could not believe what was happening. Larentzo drove the lane and dunked so hard, the ball bounced off a North Carolina player's face. He dunked again two plays later, and North Carolina called time-out. Their players looked stunned.

The rest of the game went back and forth. Each team went ahead by a few points, then the other team would come to take back the lead. North Carolina had more players to rely on in a tough game, and it started to show with six minutes left. It looked like ESCU had all its fingers in the dam, but it was still leaking. The team had foul problems. Coach Baylor called timeout and he had one of the assistants talk to Ayman in the locker room. Ayman told him he knew what to do.

Sterlin told the team during the timeout, "Go to our X-zone defense and trap passes three and four. Make sure we block out for the rebound and fast break every time. This is how we play ball, and we are not going to change. Larentzo, make sure you stop before the three-point line if you don't have the ball every time."

The defense worked, and the game was tied with forty-five seconds left. North Carolina went ahead by two and Coach Baylor called his last time-out with twenty-four seconds left.

There was time to talk on the phone because a TV commercial extended the time-out time. The TV sportscasters debated whether ECSU should go for two points and tie the game, or try to win with a three-pointer.

This time, Ayman answered with direct information. Sterlin insisted that he be a part of what he had built. It was not about whether he thought Sterlin could make a decision. It was about so many times before when they made a joint decision at the end of the game.

Coach Baylor took pride in telling the team that coach Sparks had a part in the play he was calling. The players nodded and shouted, "Yeah, let's go!"

Coach Baylor gave the instructions, "Okay, guys, this is how we do this. They will be looking for Larentzo to take the last shot. Nomo and Reiser, stay on right-weak side. Nomo, you are the third option for a three. We are going to put the ball in your hand early, Larentzo, on the left strong side. Dribble to the corner. They will come with a trap just as soon as you head that way. Pass out of the trap early to Hafeez at the top of the key. We would have fooled them into thinking you gave the ball up. Make a strong V-cut as if you are going for an alley-oop. Shervey and Foley, set a picket-fence screen. Larentzo, come off the screen and pop out to the three-point line. Hafeez, Larentzo should be open. If not, drive to the basket or pass to Nomo."

At twenty seconds, the ball came into Larentzo. He dribbled away some time off the clock, acting as if he were looking for a shot. At twelve seconds, he dribbled to the corner. The trap came fast, and he passed out of the trap on cue. At eight seconds, he V-cut, and came off a perfect screen. Hafeez passed the ball to Larentzo, who was open. His body lifted into the air with perfect shot style. The crowd was deafening. Cameras flashed. The ball left his fingers with two seconds on the clock. All eyes widened; a defender hit Larentzo at the same time, and a foul was called, the shot missed, and time ran out with the score, North Carolina, 81; East Seattle City University, 79.

Since he was shooting a three-pointer, Larentzo had three free throws coming. Two would tie the game, three to win. Larentzo was fourteen for fourteen from the free throw line, and he had a total of forty-four points.

The pressure. He made the first one. The second bounced around the rim and went through. The game was tied, 81–81.

The stadium roared and as the floor shook like an earthquake. No matter what, the game was going into overtime unless Larentzo made the next shot for the win. He studied the rim. He bounced the ball, and went into his shooting motion. The ball left his fingers. It rotated in the air. Lights flashed. People gulped air. Players from both teams covered their eyes. The ball hit the rim and bounced—bounced, and—

Epilogue

The start of another season. Coach Sparks yelled, "Get back on defense!" The freshmen made mistakes, and Coach Sparks was whipping them into mental shape.

On the other side of the court, Coach Baylor was praising the players who ran the floor hard. Another year, and the lives of the two coaches, the two best friends, showed in how they worked together.

Their lives had changed in many ways:

Ayman and Vanessa remarried over the summer. Their life was working. Ayman officially elevated Sterlin from assistant coach to co-head coach. They shared duties which allowed Ayman to spend more time with the woman he loved and had missed more than anything in his life. He learned to spread the work among all his assistant coaches.

Vanessa felt the love he had for her, and she cherished all he did. In return, she gave him space and encouraged him to do what he loved. They still fought and made up with mad crazy love-making.

He bought her a classic 1967 Mercedes-Benz convertible, and

he worked in the garage, restoring it for her in his free time. They could not wait for the day when they could christen the two-seat convertible...somehow.

Vanita and Jabin were in couples' pre-marriage counseling. She felt for the first time in a relationship with a man, that she could be valuable. She had found a man who was tolerant, forgiving, and accepting. He had a woman who believed in him and did not judge his past failures and upsets. Vanita was consistent in taking her meds, mainly because Jabin made her feel she was enough woman just as she was. Her fear that she was not enough in the past had driven her to misstep. The insecure feelings happened less, and she was handling them better. Vanita was a happy woman. Her son would soon have a sister. Jabin's daughter benefited from Vanita making sure she had everything a young girl needed emotionally.

Velvet Williams had her baby, and a blood test showed the African was the father, not Lois Mae's ex. The African had hit the lotto and had to pay $2,500 a month in child support.

Stella Mae and Lois Mae bonded as if blood ran between them. At eight months, Stella Mae was tall and beautiful and walking already. Lois Mae rejoiced when people said Stella Mae resembled her. She was shopping for a wedding dress. The wedding was going to be on Thanksgiving morning. She and Sterlin had made plans to adopt a child the first part of the New Year, so Stella Mae could have a brother.

Of all the places to be playing, Larentzo was on the same team as Goldlyn in the NBA. It did not matter whether he made that last free throw or not. His father, Ayman Sparks, had told him, "Son, you could never let me down." The ball went in, and ESCU did win the game.

Larentzo and Tyreene were engaged to be married after her upcoming senior year. Tyreene's father. Tylowe wrote a poem in his journal about all that had happened.

All lived on a canvas bleeding through a life of uncertainty

Waiting for brush strokes to complete them into masterpieces

Good souls with lost passions stood as wallflowers on the round stages of life

Broken hearts each searched for dancing partners

For they were not to dance alone

At center stage of pain and sorrows were rending souls

Divine guidance, cleared pathways, leading to meditations, prayers, leading to choreographing a return of faith

Love from above descended onto the stage

Changing from old-ways was their way of giving thanks for those blessings

Then they bowed to the world

Now they dance as completed works of art

ABOUT THE AUTHOR

Alvin Lloyd Alexander Horn has lived and breathed the North-west air and floated in all the nearby rivers and streams leading to the Pacific Ocean. As in the writings of Hemingway, and poetry of Langston Hughes, and novels of Walter Mosley, their writings are all the byproduct of their youthful environments and travels. Alvin's African-American experiences in his Emerald City background shine through in his poetry, short stories and novels.

Growing up in the "liberal on the surface" Seattle lifestyle, Alvin experienced seeing Black people with jobs, who could go most places, and had no stereotypical ghettos. He feels his writing was triggered by his mother sending him to the library when she placed him *"on restriction, often for daydreaming in school."* He also credits the "little gray-haired white lady, the librarian" for intro-ducing him to the likes of Richard Wright and Zora Neale Hurston. Upon reading the work of Nikki Giovanni, Alvin knew he wanted to be a writer of love stories and poetry.

"Some of my erotic writing imagination came from my dad leaving *Playboy* magazines in a not-so-secret place. My friends fixated the pictures, but me, I just read the stories, most of the time." Alvin also had a storied athletic career as an athlete and coach and as a musician; the knowledge and talent from those backgrounds shows in his writings.

Alvin played sports at the University of New Mexico in the mid-'70s, and had a short sports career after college. Before launching his writing career, there was a fifteen-year stint in the aerospace industry. For the last fifteen years, he has worked in the field of education, teaching life-skills, poetry and creative writing, while working with at-risk kids. Alvin is a highly acclaimed spoken word artist which has allowed him to travel and promote his art of words. He has balanced his writing career alongside doing voice-overs for radio and TV, music, video, and movie productions, and acting. His writings have appeared in many periodicals ranging from fiction to erotica.

Alvin is all over the Northwest reciting poetry and playing stand-up bass at different venues, but does love Houston, Hot-lanta, Vegas, Vancouver, B.C., and most parts of California, and New York. Most of all he loves being on the back deck of his houseboat writing love poetry and stories.

Alvin is the author of *Brush Strokes*. You may visit the author at www.alvinhorn.com or https://www.facebook.com/pages/Alvin-LA-Horn

UnWritten Love Letters

I write in my daydreams
Unwritten love letters
I can make love to her with my mind and body
But
Not with paper and pen
I have plenty to say
In a love letter to her
I could make her fall in love...in love...in love
But I can't write a love letter for her
It's not that I don't want to
Complicated nerves
My fingers revolt
My fingers work just fine if I brush stroke my passions onto
   her skin
Finger paint her hot
She'd feel my fingers in slow motion from her neckline...to
   past her behind
But she wants a love letter
Yet I can't make my heart force my hand to write to her
I want to

Paper waits for me to come

My hands want to orgasm on paper

I want to lay hard lead down

I want to leave wet ink ... imbedded

My hands when I touch her, they work just fine...touching her

My hands can make her do things

But can't I write to her what's in my head and heart

Cruel unintentions

I just want to put my words on paper written for her to read
how I feel

I recite verses to the sky

Hoping they will float to her ears

Yet I know she wants a card, a letter, a note on the
refrigerator, under her pillow, attached to flowers, that I
wrote that reads, "I love you"

A pen between my fingers seems to be out of ink

I let music speak for my fingers

I serenade lyrics in place of my #2 pencil

I spin vinyl with pops and clicks

Terence Trent D'Arby

Sings

Sign My Name

As I think about her the needle is stuck and repeating for hours

"Sign your name

Across my heart

I want you to be my baby

Sign your name

Across my heart

I want you to be my lady"

I can't make a pen or pencil write, no matter what I do, but
she wants to read "I miss you"

I can't take my pencil, and compose, "I want you"

It's not fear

I could erase any proof if I really didn't care

I want to provide written evidence of my feelings

Just my fingers can't print what my heart is doing

Bleeding my soul

I ride down the road in my 1969 Pontiac

My foot is on the gas as if I can't get to her soon enough to at
    least tell her…I love her

I turn the volume up of the 8-track player that has no bass
    and is just loud enough to hear with the windows rolled-up

I hear blue-eyed soul

Fire & Rain

The song adds to my frustration

I can't write a song down for her

James Taylor whines

I walked out this morning and I wrote down this song

I just can't remember who to send it to

I've seen fire and I've seen rain

Thank God, she's my friend and she takes me as I am

Yet her eyes say she wishes, I could write a love letter to her

Maybe I can ask Bewitched if she would wiggle her nose

She could make ink flow from my mind and appear on paper

If my oral ways could make a pencil stand up and write on its
    own

I could be rich but I would never sell my secret…it would only
    be for her to see my love on paper

I could sing a letter

I could ask someone else to write down my dictation

I could type my feeling

I could step back in time and use Windows 95 or DOS

But

I know she wants my hands to write my love for her on paper

I didn't know what to do until I turned on the TV and saw a
video from before a time I was born
A simpler time
Black & White, and rabbit ears
A time when typewriters were the way of the time
I see Ella Fitzgerald singing the right song to help me get
across my feelings
Ella sings,
"Love letters straight from my heart
Keep us so near while we're apart
You're not alone in the night
When you have all the love I could write
Love letters straight from my heart"
I'm gonna write her a letter... she may not be able to read it,
but she'll know it's just for her

Footnote, my style:

This poem, "Unwritten Love Letters," came about because of my past. I have very limited ability to hand-write with a pen or pencil. Plain and simple, I cannot take a pencil and write more than a few sentences without writing them backward or writing letters backward, yet it looks correct to me. Why, I have a learning disorder; my brain waves get confused and it comes out through my writing hand, yet I could read and comprehend at a high level in school. Teachers and school counselors would marvel at my test scores.

The name for my disability, Dysgraphia. Dysgraphia, damn, I hate that name (it sounds like some psycho s#*+). Anyway it involves me having difficulty with my fine motor skills and motor memory. I know what I want to write, but by the time the signal reaches my fingers holding a pencil, it's a mess.

Back in school, in the sixties and seventies before special education, if you were a nice kid they just passed you along in many cases. Who cares if he can't seem to spell? He can sing, dance, play instruments, and recite poetry. I played the lead roles in all the plays, and by the time I was in high school, I was a stud on the sports field, so I was passed along. Now, of all the people in the world, for years I worked in education, go figure.

Back in the day, I would trade writing services. People would write my assignments out for me and in return I'd let them copy from my imagination whatever they needed in different situations. One thing I did, I used to recite love letters for my friends to give to girls or boys. True fact, some girls gave up their virginity to my love letters to my friends. I won't say if it worked for me. (Sometimes I laugh so hard, tears roll.) Finally, as I really wanted to write all these poems, short stories and novels you have been reading, I got over my embarrassment and sought help by first getting a correct diagnosis. In my late thirties, I learned a system of calm, limiting stress, sometimes a white noise or music playing, and as long as I use a keyboard, I do all right. I'm like many people whose mind types faster than their fingers; with me, often my mind will type pages before my fingers catch up. I've learned to laugh at myself from my heart, instead of my mind beating up on me for what I can't do, and I celebrate what I can do.

My disabilities in many ways have created my style of writing, much like in the way a blind person sees life another way, certain sense reroute, thus, creating a style. Like listening to Stevie Wonder play drums. He hits the drums on the right beat, but he hits different drums on those beats much different from other drummers. His drumming sounds unique, but still correct. I hope you keep enjoying my gift, and my style.

For our children's sake:

Often our children may seem to be slow learners or have issues in school. It's easy to blame the system or the teachers. Well, look at them too, but also look a little deeper and wider. A parent's pride or embarrassment should never stand in the way of helping a child achieve. The blame game does nothing down the road. Like most children, I learned to mask or distract from most of my learning disability. I recited most of my English/Language Arts school work to classmates and they wrote my work down for me; in return they got to copy from my imagination or mental retention for their own assignments. My conversational skills on multiple subjects with adults often blinded them to my other shortcomings. Often children with high IQ's mask the most problems.

If your child is disengaged in the learning, the class clown, picks on other kids for their shortcomings, has to be forced to read, and many other tell-tale signs that something is not right, look deeper and be vigilant. Don't ever say *I've done all I could.* Maybe your child may need glasses, or has hearing problems, or even has bad teeth that may keep a child from wanting to talk in front of the class. Minor things to you, may be major to your child. Any number of reasons can slow a child's progress, and they tend to act out in many different ways in masking their problems, and most of all, they don't know what their problems are. It is up to you, and if you do, you might have a child that will achieve great things or simply have a good education, and we all want that.

—Alvin L.A. Horn

I Want to Write for You

I'm scribing about you and I

Going places with you and my pen

I'll write splendid rhymes and majestic verses as we are revered by
the world's reading eyes

My pen will be our badge, and crest of honor of written chronicles in
royal museums

I'll write our story to be

I'll compose a beautiful storybook of a first-class passage through life
with thee

Our journey of life, I will publish in hardcovers and magazine
subscriptions

I'll write scripts of non-fictions of our love going to secret places

Making love in dangerous places that's in chapters one and chapter
infinity

I'll protect you by writing poems so hard, and so wickedly on point,
thugs will run for cover in libraries

I'll write tour guides to get lost in the most legendry romantic places

I'll write poems of what we see, and feel, and what we know

I'll write fables of adventures of lost lovers disappearing but we are
known to be alive

I'll pen sagas of the great moments in time that we made love on private islands and in air balloons, and castles, and in outer space, and in dreams we are yet to have

I'll write our diary in the sand, but 20,000 Leagues under the Sea

I'll write poems on the bottom of your feet and on your backside, and on the dark side of the moon

Let us dig the earth and bury our tales alongside Adam and Eve

In the center of the earth, I'll write journals in the gold we pass by

As we come out the other end of the earth we'll autograph the bestseller I wrote to honor our love

Sail with my desires to pen every sunrise and nightfall

I'll write poems from ink drained from the stars

I'll write parables from the blood of lovers past

I'll write narratives from the account of kings who wished they could have loved their queens forever

I'll write about the love I have for you with no plot, as I only conspire to live another day to write for you

I'll write volumes of novellas of poems of our love into a historical literary masterpiece

The title: My Never Ending Love Letter to You and Me

Signed, your author of love

Trembling

I felt her trembling
As her heart was tumbling
I would throw my heart in her direction and catch her heart from
   falling
If only I knew in what direction her heart was headed

Collapsing in my arm leaning against my heart
I feel her tumbling
I understand
We all have fallen at some time or another

Tears, I taste off her lips
I see her eyes holding fear
The uncertainty of what had been in the past seeped in the way of
   the present
I'm holding her dear
I want her near
I want to stand guard from the spears of those pains of yesteryears
Love ghosts, I will fight with my do right soul

Castles had been made of sand in my own journeys
I understand, of what was
Love shadows can loom
We all wish our eyelids could squeeze away nightmares
I would chase away all her fear if I knew what her fears were
I'll stand like a knight in front of her heart is all I can do

Trembling
I heard stumbling words
As she searched for what to say
I touch her lips with my lips to calm her and tell her all she needs to know
I feel you
I see you
I hear you
I know you
Tremble no more my dear

Click-Clack

"Shoes off," he said.
She strutted by
She kept strolling by as if she was doing something
She was messing with his mind
Click-clack
She put a little extra in her swing-set
It was slight erotic torture
She was being a project engineer, building a steam engine in his
  desires
Out of the corner of his eye he admired her high-heeled twist of her hips
Click-clack
"Shoes off," he said again. "You know I'm trying to script a
  masterpiece."
She just smiled and left the room knowing nothing could script what
  she was doing to him
Just as he started to write a new chapter, here she came again
All of a sudden he couldn't even spell kitty-cat, but it was on his mind
Click-clack
Smelling good from a distance, and always looking very beautiful

Her stroll across the room had meaning
Brick house with a view
Breaking him down
Click-clack
Heels and toes
Skin barely covered
His eyes fore-played
As that's what she was doing to him without even touching him
  from across the room
She went into the kitchen
Click-clack
She came back with a chocolate strawberry
Now it was her heels and her working her lips
He was frozen and hot
She was melting him
She left the room again with her click-clack seductive music
Now he wanted her to come back
She did, only now, nothing else remained but her heels
She started to remove them
He said, "Wait. I'll do that for you."

I've Got the Romantic Blues When I Think of You

Sitting here by a mental fire…alone

Happy you're mine

So sad, I'm not yours

Time has changed us, to be apart

I've got the romantic blues when I think of you

I pour myself a glass of wine

And I think back to our time…together

I'm left smiling, living in the past

Seeing red and blue flames tangling, as we used to do on the bed, as
   we used to do on the floor, and as we used to do in the shower, and
   outdoors, and as we used to do where I sit now alone

Living in the past

I've got the romantic blues when I think of you

I keep my mind away from missing you

I keep my heart from hurting

By rewinding to the good times

To those sweet sexy times, I throw up a toast to you

I talk to you, and hear you laughing

A doctor might call me crazy, but baby, I'm just crazy for you

I haven't aged a day, since you've been away, because I'm stuck in time, reliving our last times

I think about the last time I pinned you to the wall and kissed you so hard, you almost lost your breath

I find myself back under your dress while you're pinned to that wall

You see my arm rising up and you feel my hand squeezing your nipples

You feel my lips parting your thighs as my tongue caresses you all the way up

And when I arrived I found your round marble of sweet throbbing sensation

I remember for sure, because you lost your breath

As I rise up from my squat I share your juices from my lips with kisses of your honey taste

Oh Damn!

I've got the romantic blues when I think of you

I'm alone spending time romancing memories of sweet sexy times with you

How is it I can feel your tongue from my shoulders down my spine and you're kissing my ass in the dawn

Your body heat is grinding, you're wanting, you're waking me up to your earlier morning dew

I feel you being too tight or me being almost too big as you ease down on my flag pole

That look on your face is priceless

Every moment I have spent with you is priceless

Now that you are gone physically, you are still here with me emotionally

I'm sitting here by a mental fire…alone

Happy you're mine

So sad, I'm not yours

I've got the romantic blues when I think of you